THE
EMPATHY
PROBLEM

GAVIN EXTENCE

HODDER &
STOUGHTON

First published in Great Britain in 2016
by Hodder & Stoughton
An Hachette UK company

1

Copyright © Gavin Extence 2016

The right of Gavin Extence to be identified as the Author
of the Work has been asserted by him in accordance with the
Copyright, Designs and Patents Act 1988.

A CIP catalogue record for this title is available from the British Library

Hardback ISBN 978 1 473 60521 3
Trade Paperback ISBN 978 1 473 60522 0
eBook ISBN 978 1 473 60523 7

Typeset in Guardi 10/16 pt by Palimpsest Book Production Limited,
Falkirk, Stirlingshire

Printed and bound by Clays Ltd, St Ives plc

Hodder & Stoughton policy is to use papers that are natural,
renewable and recyclable products and made from wood grown in
sustainable forests. The logging and manufacturing processes are
expected to conform to the environmental regulations of the
country of origin.

Hodder & Stoughton Ltd
Carmelite House
50 Victoria Embankment
London EC4Y 0DZ

www.hodder.co.uk

THE
EMPATHY
PROBLEM

Also by Gavin Extence

The Universe versus Alex Woods
The Mirror World of Melody Black

For my parents, who taught me:

1. There are many things more important than money.
2. It's OK for boys to cry.

PART 1

The Tumour

Malignant

It was the size of a golf ball and lodged deep in something called his anterior insular cortex. And now everything should have fallen into perspective; that was the platitude. Minor inconveniences, trivial delays, the petty irritations of day-to-day life – none of these things should have mattered any more. Traffic jams should not have mattered any more. But the reality of having a malignant brain tumour, Gabriel found, was not nearly so edifying.

Petty irritations were more irritating than ever before, and being stuck in a traffic jam was a luxury he could ill afford.

Under normal circumstances – circumstances before the tumour – he would have utilised this time productively. He would have checked the overnight news on his iPad, looking for anything that might affect the markets when they opened in ninety minutes' time. This was the way he had started every working day for the past ten years. Now, instead, he found himself calculating how much of his remaining life had been wasted in this line of unmoving cars.

The answer was one seventeen-thousandth. According to his consultant at the clinic on Harley Street – Armstrong or Anderton, or whatever the hell his name was – Gabriel Vaughn could reasonably expect to live for six more months. And this morning he had spent an unacceptable proportion of that stuck in stationary traffic.

He hadn't planned to move. In fact, he didn't know he *was* moving until his index finger made contact with his chauffeur's left shoulder – and once it had, it was difficult to tell who was the more surprised. In the last three years, ever since Gabriel had been given a chauffeur, the journey to work had followed an unwavering regimen of absolute silence. Every morning at six o'clock precisely, the car – a Mercedes-Benz S-Class in gunmetal grey – would be waiting outside Gabriel's apartment block. The chauffeur would open the door and utter a polite 'Good morning, sir,' and, if he was lucky, Vaughn would reciprocate with a curt nod. There had never once been physical contact. Now, it caused both men to jolt, as if by a mild electric shock.

Gabriel was the first to recover. He settled back in his seat and glared at the anxious, disembodied eyes in the rear-view mirror. 'Let me out,' he said.

'Sir?'

'I want to get out.'

'Um . . . here?' The chauffeur gestured at the surrounding traffic, an uncertain, wobbly gesture, such as might be made by a man treading water in the middle of a vast lake. 'There's not really anywhere I can—'

'Never mind that. Just let me out.'

The chauffeur hesitated, looked around briefly, then tightened his hands on the steering wheel. They were just outside Deutsche Bank, penned into the inside lane of the dual carriageway by a taxi, two BMWs and a Bentley. 'You want me to . . . open the door?'

In all honesty, it hadn't occurred to Gabriel that there was any viable alternative to this. He hadn't considered the possibility that he might cut out the middleman and simply open the door for himself. After all, he had never had to do this before; and, on reflection, he had no intention of starting now. Given the circumstances, he saw no sensible way of retracting his demand. He wasn't going to show weakness in front of the chauffeur.

'I'm going to walk,' Gabriel said. 'It will be quicker.' He managed to intone the latter as a rebuke rather than an explanation, as if his driver were personally responsible for the state of the roads that morning.

There was only a flicker of hesitation. The next moment, the handbrake had been applied and blind obedience took over. To a chorus of blaring horns, the chauffeur got out and opened the rear passenger door.

'Have a good day, sir.'

Gabriel didn't answer. He didn't nod either. He grabbed his briefcase from the back seat, then disappeared through a momentary gap in the traffic.

2

The Camp

Gabriel did not blame his chauffeur, not really. He blamed the camp. Because there was no good reason for the City to be this busy first thing on a Monday morning. Granted, the financial sector did go to work two or three hours before everyone else, so it was a given that there would be *some* traffic. And it was at least plausible that something else had caused this gridlock: a major pile-up or a breakdown in a bottleneck or a suicide on the Central Line. But in his gut, Gabriel knew this was far too much to hope for. This was purposeful disruption; he would have bet his chauffeur's life on it.

It was only a ten-minute walk to St Paul's, but this was ten minutes more than he would have chosen to spend power-walking on a public pavement. It wasn't that he was averse to exercise; he spent a minimum of forty minutes in the gym every day, in the pool or on the weights or rowing machine. Naked, in front of the mirror, his muscles could fairly be described as 'sculpted', even though he seldom used them for any practical purpose. They were essentially cosmetic.

Nevertheless, the minimal effort required to propel his body half a mile through central London should not have been a problem; except that he hated to exert himself outside of a controlled climate. The sensation of sweating under a shirt and long autumn coat was deeply unpleasant. When Gabriel Vaughn sweated, he liked to know that he would be washing the sweat away within the hour.

Compounding his physical discomfort was the mental distress that came with being late for work. Gabriel was a man who thrived on routine, not because of some innate psychological predisposition but rather because he needed a vice-tight schedule in order to optimise his day. Thus he should have been behind his desk twenty minutes ago, no later than twenty past six; and ten minutes ago, he should have been walking into Mason's office for the first meeting of the day (the pre-meeting meeting). Of course, it was entirely possible that Mason had also been held up, depending on the level of chaos these protesters had managed to engineer. But that was not the point. Gabriel wasn't paid 3.4 million a year to roll into the office whenever he felt like it.

By the time he reached Cheapside, he had regained most of his composure. There was no sign, yet, of anything out of the ordinary, no early morning marches or assemblies, no barricades in the streets. But this did nothing to dispel his certainty regarding the cause of this morning's traffic jam. Simultaneously, as Gabriel approached the west side of the cathedral, he was able to bolster his conviction that most of the protesters were far too lazy to be up and organised this early in the day. Under normal circumstances, this apparent contradiction might have been problematic. But when it came to the camp, Gabriel was willing to lower his usual standards of logic and rationality by a considerable margin.

They had arrived ten days ago, one bright and seemingly unremarkable Saturday morning, armed to the teeth with banners and tents and tarpaulins. The first he'd heard of it was via a text from Mason.

Turn on the fucking news.

Nothing else. Gabriel hadn't received a message like this since Lehman Brothers went belly-up in 2008.

What confronted him, this time, was a roiling sea of people on the steps of St Paul's. They had beards and tattoos and piercings and megaphones. They had placards bearing slogans such as **WE ARE THE 99%** and **WHY SHOULD WE PAY FOR THEIR CRISIS?** According to the BBC, there were several thousand of them. They had been planning to occupy Paternoster Square, home to the London Stock Exchange, but had been thwarted by a last-minute court order and a police blockade. Like much of central London, Paternoster Square appeared to be public land but was actually private property.

It belonged to the Mitsubishi Corporation.

Gabriel had never been so relieved to discover that half an acre of his native soil had been acquired by a Japanese conglomerate. The only downside was that all those people had to end up somewhere. And they had ended up just round the corner, right on his doorstep.

So for six consecutive working days, Gabriel had had to walk through their midst just to get into the office. It was unavoidable. Mason Wallace Capital Management was based in Stanton House, the entrance to which faced directly on to St Paul's

8

Churchyard. Directly on to the camp. And since the whole area was pedestrianised, this was one of the few situations in which having a personal chauffeur conferred no real advantage. Traffic jam or no, for the last fifty metres of his commute, Gabriel was on his own.

Assets and Liabilities

Today, he was able to slip round the periphery of the camp without major incident. He was snarled at by a woman with a face like a hunting accident – all metal and misaligned teeth – but he'd grown used to this over the past week. Even when he wasn't stepping out of his chauffeur-driven Mercedes, it was impossible to mistake Gabriel Vaughn for anything less than what he was. A man who had made more money in the past six months than anybody in that camp would earn in a lifetime.

To make matters worse, he was also relatively young – thirty-two – and extremely handsome, though it was only in the last week that Gabriel had appreciated how his wealth and youth and looks could be a liability as well as an asset. But what could he do? He only owned expensive suits, and even if he'd had the wardrobe or inclination to dress down, that still wouldn't have solved the problem of his exceptional face. Gabriel had been born beautiful, and, short of wearing a balaclava, there was no way to remedy this. He just had to accept the resentment his features sometimes provoked.

As always, there were two security guards posted in the foyer of Stanton House, and Gabriel managed a cheery wave as he passed them on his way to the lift. Not easy, but well worth the effort, given the situation outside. Gabriel habitually divided the rest of humanity into two distinct categories: people who were useful and people who were irrelevant. Needless to say, the second group was a thousand times larger than the first, and it was almost impossible to transition from one to the other. But over the past ten days, the security guys had done just that. With the barbarians hammering at the gates, you wanted to make damn sure the men guarding the gates felt appreciated.

4

Steel and Glass

From the outside, Stanton House was fairly nondescript. It looked much like any other office block – high-end, but nothing spectacular, not by London standards. On the inside, however, it was exquisite. There was a central atrium that flooded the interior with natural light. The offices were panelled with polished wood, and leased by an international cartel of lawyers, accountants and money managers. The Internet connection was so fast you could download a terabyte of porn in less than seventeen minutes. It was a twenty-first-century temple.

Mason Wallace Capital Management was situated on the top and most expensive floor, having moved up from the third floor, the one below, after the previous occupant had imploded during the 2008 crash. There were some who had questioned the cost-benefit ratio of moving the entire office up one flight of stairs, especially when it would necessitate a full refit to bring the 'new premises' up to spec. But Mason had been swift to dismiss their lack of vision.

'For God's sake, people!' he'd admonished.

Mason's managers were all men; but in this instance, rhetoric was far more important than accuracy.

'Vaughn!' Mason's arm swung in a wide arc over the board table, like a compass needle seeking magnetic north. 'Help me out here. Why should we move? Please explain this to Sherman *et al.*'

Gabriel fixed Sherman with a shark-eyed stare. 'Image.'

'Image! Vaughn, you've just added another ten K to your bonus.' Mason leaned back in his chair and cracked his knuckles theatrically. 'Sherman, let me clarify this for you. Imagine, just for one second, you're a client looking to invest twenty-five million. There are two funds you need to decide between – both with great records, annual returns north of fifteen per cent. But one's on the third floor and the other's in the penthouse. Which do you pick?'

A deep silence hung in the boardroom. No one chose that moment to point out that the fund in the penthouse had recently gone bust. That was why the space was now available.

'Image, people! We're looking to grow our assets by forty per cent *minimum* in the next three years. And this,' he pointed both index fingers at the ceiling, 'is just the start.'

His words had been prophetic. In the next three years, Mason had grown the fund faster than anyone would have believed possible, and today, assets under management stood at just below four billion pounds – a figure higher than the GDP of a number of African nations. But even Gabriel found it difficult to attribute too much of this growth to the change of office. Most of it had come from betting on the collapse of the Greek economy.

Mason

Today he was standing in front of the window, his back to the door. As with most of the executive offices on the fourth floor, Mason's overlooked St Paul's Churchyard. Until ten days ago, this had been a good thing.

'Look at them,' Mason spat. 'Just look at them!'

Gabriel didn't know if this request was rhetorical or not, but he wasn't going to spend the next fifteen minutes talking to Mason's back. He closed the door behind him, then joined the other man by the window.

'I've been thinking.' Mason jabbed his finger against the triple glazing. 'We need to hire a hitman. Just one Russian with an AK-47, that's all it would take.' He stepped back and, squinting through an imaginary sight, performed the universal mime for death by machine gun. 'What do you think? Have a quick whip-round after the morning meeting?'

Gabriel pretended to weigh this proposition. 'How much would we need?'

Mason shrugged. 'Going rate's a quarter of a million per victim,

14

but I'm sure we could negotiate a discount for buying in bulk. How many of them are there?'

'A few hundred.'

'Fuck it. We'll ask the investors to chip in too.'

'Or we could just move to Mayfair.'

'Ha!' It was Mason's standard laugh, a single explosive guffaw. 'Vaughn, we're going nowhere. It'll be winter soon. Then we'll see how much those cocksuckers like their tents.'

He spun and slapped Gabriel on the shoulder, gesturing with his other hand to the black leather sofa, perpendicular to his desk. It was where the most important clients – those with the highest net worth – sat when they visited the office, and it was where Gabriel sat for fifteen minutes every day during the pre-meeting meeting. Mason seemed too agitated to sit this morning. He paced for a while and then half-perched on the corner of his desk. He could do this because his desk was always kept entirely free of clutter. The only things on it were a couple of computer screens, a phone and a small engraved sign, which read:

THE BUCK $TOPS HERE.

Mason had stolen the idea from President Truman, who had kept a similar sign on his desk in the Oval Office.

'OK, Vaughn. To business. What's going on this morning? Where the fuck is everyone?'

'The City's gridlocked. I had to get out at Deutsche Bank and walk. Something to do with our friends down there, I'd imagine.' Gabriel gestured at the window. Mason nodded grimly. 'You might want to push the meeting back. Kilner and Shipman have made it in, but it looks like anyone coming by road from the east is basically fucked.'

'Fine. We'll give the rest until twenty past. After that, no excuses. Anything major from the weekend?'

Brain tumour.

'The Euro summit went pretty much as expected. Lots of strong statements, no real action. Certainly nothing to bolster the markets. Spanish and Italian bonds are still in freefall.'

'Awesome. What's this I'm hearing about an earthquake in Turkey? CNN says the death toll's a hundred and rising.'

'Eastern Turkey. Bunch of goat herders. Doesn't affect us.'

'What about Syria?'

'Getting more interesting by the day. The whole region is ready to blow. Arms are a potential goldmine. As is oil.'

Mason grinned, showing all his teeth. 'So what's new? High risk, though.'

'It's just a matter of timing. Get that right and we'll make a fucking fortune.'

'Get it wrong and we're liable to get our balls blown off.'

Gabriel shrugged. 'That's why we'll get it right. I'm very fond of my balls.'

'Ha!' Mason slapped his leg. 'Vaughn, you're a man after my own heart. Anything else I need to know?'

The tumour: it's grade four. That means it's large and extremely aggressive. Also, it's inoperable. Conventional surgery would likely do more harm than good. And it's stuck in a part of my brain that's involved in 'emotional processing', which is one of the reasons my moods have been so fucking weird lately. Don't worry, though. I'm not going to let it affect my work.

'Nope. That's everything.'

16

6

One Month Ago

He was crying on the Tube. That was the moment the balance tipped, when suspicion became certainty. Something was terribly wrong.

At first, he'd tried to convince himself that there must be a simple, non-life-threatening reason for his tears. The mere fact that he was on the Tube might even be explanation enough. After all, Gabriel had not used the Tube since 2005. That he was doing so now was the result of a series of awful misjudgements.

It had all started the previous evening, when he'd phoned Chelsea Courtesans to try to make an appointment with Melissa.

Gabriel had been using escorts, on and off, for the past decade, and during this period the experience had generally got better and better. As with so many service industries, prostitution had come on in leaps and bounds with the development of online shopping. By the late noughties, it wasn't that different from going on Amazon. You could flick through galleries, check profiles and even read user reviews. But, unfortunately, no one had managed to eradicate the problem of direct human interaction entirely. All of the online agencies still insisted on some minimal vetting to check you weren't a psychopath, and this meant talking to you on the phone. Usually, these conversations were brief and straightforward, but every so often, you encountered an operator who made matters more complicated than they should have been.

This was the case that Saturday.

Admittedly, it was short notice, but Gabriel had made it clear that he was willing to pay significantly more than the going rate.

'Three thousand pounds,' he told the operator.

'Sir, she really isn't available. If you—'

'Five thousand.'

This was Gabriel's solution whenever he encountered a seemingly intractable problem. He threw money at it.

'Just do your job and pass the offer on,' he said.

The operator ignored this demand and tried to redirect him to some newbie called Nikita. Twenty years old, probably fresh off the plane that morning. But Gabriel was not in the mood for something new. He wanted the comfort of familiarity. Even odder, he wanted a woman who might be able to hold down a conversation for more than two minutes. And with these eastern Europeans, that was by no means a given.

He should have cut his losses at this point. Instead, he ended up going out for 'drinks' with Ainsley and Shipman. They met in a bar in Fitzrovia. Shipman was dating a model, and she had brought along one of her friends, also a model. The whole evening was excruciating.

It wasn't that Gabriel felt awkward being the 'third wheel'. The problem was that Ainsley's date – the other model – made it clear from the outset that she was more interested in Gabriel than in Ainsley. This was understandable since Gabriel *was* far more interesting than Ainsley. Plus Ainsley really didn't know how to talk to these women. It was embarrassing to watch. Here was a man on a seven-figure salary, but put him next to a beautiful woman and he was completely out of his depth. Gabriel, in contrast, had never had the slightest problem talking to models. Why would he? In a different life, he could have been a model himself.

'So, Gabe. You seeing anyone at the moment?'

She had to shout it across the table to make herself audible over the music. This was after two hours of being politely brushed aside. She'd just been to the bathroom to powder her nose, apparently in preparation for this last dignity-destroying gambit. Unfortunately, Ainsley had likewise spent half the evening icing his beak. Now he was sweating like a fat man in a sauna, while imagining he was James fucking Bond.

'Ha! *Gabe* doesn't really do relationships, do you, Gabe? Just prostitutes.'

Gabriel smiled thinly. He had half a mind to take the model home with him, just to teach Ainsley a lesson. Not that there was anything inaccurate about what the other man had said. Gabriel didn't do relationships – not since the Catherine debacle. Still, he wasn't going to tolerate being undermined like this.

He went to the bar, ordered a Scotch that cost more than a plane ticket to Scotland, then sought out the most attractive *non*-prostitute he could find. She was an actress, apparently, and seemed to find it hysterical that Gabriel had heard of neither her nor her TV show.

'I'm in finance,' Gabriel told her.

19

She found this hysterical too. In fact, she seemed to find everything Gabriel said hysterical, and she had a laugh like a penguin being murdered. But that was neither here nor there.

'Are you, like, one of those evil bankers who make a million pounds in bonuses every year?' She licked her lips while jabbing him repeatedly in the chest with her index finger. 'You *look* like one of those evil bankers.'

'No, not at all like that. I co-run a hedge fund. And my bonus is dependent on how I perform. Last year it was two and a half million.'

At this point she spilled most of her drink over the bar.

'Let me get you another.'

Three drinks later, she asked him if he wanted to come back to her apartment.

'I have toys,' she added.

7

Toys

Nowhere near as much fun as it sounded. Gabriel spent twenty minutes trying to operate a device made of fluorescent pink rubber while she writhed and moaned in a manner that did nothing to boost her acting credentials. After that she told him that she *needed* him inside her. So he obliged, and there was plenty more writhing and fake moaning – on both sides – before a climax that could only be described as mediocre.

Shortly afterwards, she passed out – which would have been a blessing, had she not passed out with her head on Gabriel's chest. When he tried to move her, she made a strange sort of whimpering sound and locked her arm even more tightly round his waist. It wasn't until eight the next morning that he was safely able to ease her back to the other side of the bed and start collecting his clothes.

He managed to get out of her apartment without waking her, and then briefly considered flagging down a cab before dismissing the idea as lunacy. Gabriel had a policy of never getting into a London taxi on his own. The problem was that London cabbies – every London cabbie he'd ever met – wanted to talk, and Gabriel did not like talking to taxi drivers. He'd once tried to pay one *not* to talk him – he'd offered twenty pounds – but the driver had been so incensed that he'd actually stopped the cab and demanded that Gabriel either apologise or get out.

Gabriel had got out.

Could he call his chauffeur just after eight on a Sunday morning? He could, but how long would he have to wait for the car to arrive?

The only other option was the Tube. Probably the quickest choice, and at least it would be quiet at this hour. And unless Tube etiquette had changed drastically in the last year, he certainly wouldn't have to talk to anyone. Or even suffer eye contact.

Best of a bad bunch, Gabriel decided.

He took out his phone and used the GPS to find out where he was – somewhere just off Gloucester Road – and then walked the few hundred metres to the Tube station.

Ten minutes later, the tears had started.

Crying on the Tube

For several minutes, he thought he was going to vomit. He had no idea what else the sensation could be. He was shaking. He had his face in his hands. There was a knot in his stomach that seemed to be simultaneously tightening and unravelling.

Vomit, it turned out, would have been far more innocuous.

Gabriel Vaughn had not cried since he was seven years old, but now it was as if he were picking up exactly where he'd left off. These were just the tears a seven-year-old boy might cry, a series of ragged escalating sobs, rising in both volume and pitch. There was no hope of containing them.

'Hey, man. You all right?'

Gabriel didn't know who had asked this question, because his face was still buried in his hands, but the possibilities were narrow. There hadn't been many people in the carriage when he got on: two or three adolescents who looked as if they must work in shops or fast food outlets; a woman with a suitcase, and another reading a paperback; two young, dark-skinned men with beards. Gabriel had sat as far away from the Beards as possible.

He understood statistics, of course – that was a large part of his job – so he knew how idiotic this was. He had more chance of being killed by falling masonry than by Islamic extremists – considerably more. Yet still he couldn't help himself. He spent too much of his time watching the news.

'You all right, bro?'

Gabriel tried to nod that he was fine, while still crying and holding his face, a manoeuvre that resulted in him rocking back and forth in his seat. He could sense that at least some of the carriage's other occupants were starting to shuffle away. Then someone came and sat next to him and placed a hand on his back. One of the women; he was able to deduce this from her scent – sweet and slightly spicy. Gabriel, in contrast, smelled of alcohol and sex. And he could not stop crying.

It was the worst five minutes of his life.

In a fortnight's time, his doctor would go through the results of the MRI scan with him in a soft, solemn voice. Shortly after that, the biopsy would deliver more dire news. And on both occasions, Gabriel could find only one thought to console himself: at least he wasn't back on that Tube train.

Time seemed to ooze like treacle, and Gabriel sat and rocked and wept. Anguish – that was the word he used to describe the incident to the first doctor, the one who referred him for further tests. It sounded absurd, after the fact, but it was the only word that came close to explaining what had happened that morning.

And then it had stopped. One minute he couldn't think for emotion, and the next it had simply vanished. He was aware that the hand was still resting on his back, applying a consistent, gentle pressure.

Gabriel felt mortified. He kept his face buried, because he had no better option. What do you say to the woman – the absolute stranger – who has just patted your back through five minutes of unbroken crying?

He waited for the doors to hiss open at the next station, then sprang for the exit. Unfortunately, he mistimed it and found himself lurching straight towards another passenger who was trying to board the train. He had to spin mid-stride to avoid her, and as he did so, he caught a glimpse of the woman who had comforted him. Except it wasn't a woman. It was one of the terrorists.

Gabriel didn't stop moving. He more or less fell out of the train, then ran for the nearest escalator.

9

Hang the Bankers?

Gabriel stood in his office – pretty much identical to Mason's but thirty per cent smaller – and surveyed the vista below. It was ten thirty and the camp was starting to get lively. It wasn't just the Occupiers anymore. Broadcasters were setting up wherever they could find space. Camera crews were looking for angles. Journalists were hunting out subjects to interview. The only good news, so far as Gabriel could see, was that numbers were certainly down from last week, when it had been an all-out media circus. The bad news was that the twenty-four/seven coverage of the site had transformed it into a major tourist attraction. By the end of the previous week – the first week of the occupation – people had been flocking to the steps of St Paul's, and the trend looked set to continue. Already, Gabriel could see the predictable lines of Chinese tourists queuing for photographs against the backdrop of the tarpaulins, or just staring transfixed by the spectacle of British 'democracy' in action.

Inevitably, this ongoing scrutiny did not encourage the protesters to rein in their act. Instead, the camp seemed to become more theatrical in direct proportion to the number of onlookers. The megaphones came out, the guitars, the bongos. Thankfully this was just a dumbshow from Gabriel's vantage point. No one had yet invented a bongo that could penetrate the xenon-filled triple glazing of Stanton House.

The banners, however, were another matter. Even though it was theoretically possible not to look at them, this was only true in the sense that it's possible not to look at a car crash. New ones were appearing all the time, and they were getting more creative. Today, Gabriel found his eyes fixated on a double bed sheet that had been unfurled on one side of the food tent. The following design had been daubed on it in thick black paint:

HANG THE
_ANKERS

The attacks, Gabriel felt, were getting more and more personal.

He understood the root of the problem, of course. The basic gripe was that he had money and they did not. Yet he assumed many of these people had done humanities degrees. This was the choice they had made; no one had held a gun to their collective head. Gabriel had half a mind to make his own banner and put it in his window: NEWSFLASH: THERE'S MONEY IN FINANCE; SOCIOLOGY DOES NOT PAY.

But Gabriel thought that banners were extremely immature. More importantly, he had no intention of entering into a dialogue with these people.

Good Priest, Bad Priest

At the beginning of the occupation, Mason had made a prediction. He had said – with a confidence bordering on fanaticism – that it would all be over within the week. His contacts in the City of London Corporation had informed him that the wheels were already turning. There was a sea of police officers, which looked poised to surge at any moment. They had full riot gear: shields and truncheons and visored helmets; and hopefully a few tasers thrown into the mix as well. The eviction would be clean and swift.

And then, at an alarming speed, things started to change. The media free-for-all was just the beginning.

Two days into the demonstrations, the canon chancellor of St Paul's emerged from the gloom of the cathedral and asked *the police* to leave the premises. He said that the Church had no objection to peaceful protest, especially when it was in a righteous cause. Then, borrowing a megaphone from one of the demonstrators, he began to quote the Bible. In fact, he quoted St Paul himself – the first epistle to Timothy.

'For lo!' shouted the canon. '"We brought nothing into this world, and it is certain we can carry nothing out. And having food and clothing let us therewith be content. But they that will be rich fall into temptation and a snare, and into many foolish and hurtful lusts, which drown men in destruction and perdition. For the love of money is the root of all evil: which while some coveted after, they have erred from the faith, and pierced themselves through with many sorrows."'

'That son of a bitch!' bellowed Mason in the next day's morning meeting. He had a copy of the *Evening Standard*, which he now flung across the board table, narrowly missing Ainsley's head; the canon's impromptu sermon had also been reprinted in the *Guardian* and the *Independent* and every other left-leaning rag in London.

A few days later, the dean of St Paul's – the canon chancellor's boss – would issue a statement making it clear that the words of the canon (not to mention St Paul) did not necessarily reflect the Church's official stance on the occupation. He asked that the protesters leave peacefully, saying that until they did, the cathedral would have to remain closed – due to health and safety concerns. Gabriel didn't know from precisely where this change in direction originated; but he did know that the Church of England derived a significant proportion of its income from its five-billion-pound investment portfolio, which was part-managed by some of the largest hedge funds in London.

The canon chancellor resigned soon afterwards, citing irreconcilable disagreements regarding the Cathedral's handling of the demonstrators. Shortly after that, the dean resigned too, with everyone else citing his appalling mismanagement of the situation.

It had started as a PR disaster for the financial sector, and evolved into an even greater PR disaster for the Church; and all the time, the camp became more and more entrenched, both physically and in the public's consciousness. The day after the canon chancellor's initial speech, the police presence was already starting to wane. A senior officer made a statement saying that as long as the protest remained peaceful and law-abiding, they were hoping to keep policing to a minimum, leaving just a small contingent at the site to ensure crowd safety. Two days after that, a block of Portaloos was delivered, and Mason became apoplectic.

'Granted, they're a bit of an eyesore,' Sherman ventured, 'but if it stops people pissing in the street—'

'Sherman, get with the fucking programme!' Mason raged. 'This isn't about pissing. It's about symbolism!'

But Gabriel knew how to read between the lines. This wasn't about pissing *or* symbolism – not really. It was about Mason's initial prediction.

Mason could not stand being wrong.

Ring Ring

Gabriel's reverie was interrupted by the phone. It was Nicola, his PA. She wanted to run though his schedule for the afternoon. Along with fielding his calls and fetching him coffee and pastries from Starbucks, keeping on top of Gabriel's schedule was one of Nicola's key duties. Her job was a degrading one – Gabriel realised this – but it was also well-remunerated (as long as one judged this matter according to PA standards, as opposed to hedge fund standards in general). Mason Wallace Capital Management paid her thirty-three thousand pounds a year. Experience had shown that this was the minimum salary at which any competent PA would *stay* working for Mason Wallace Capital Management.

Nicola was extremely competent. She was also fairly old, for a PA. Gabriel didn't know how old, exactly, because he made a point of taking no interest whatsoever in her personal circumstances. Nor had he played any part in her recruitment. After the Catherine debacle, Gabriel had effectively been barred from hiring his own staff. Everyone in HR agreed that this was for the best.

Until the day she started working for him, Gabriel had never even set eyes on Nicola. Consequently, she was a huge success. She had now been Gabriel's PA for over a year. She had fetched him more than a thousand cups of coffee from Starbucks. She had deflected hundreds of unwanted phone calls. They had never had sex against the filing cabinet. Gabriel was getting more done – making more money – than ever before. Or this *had* been the case, until very recently.

'Nicola, I'm flat out at the moment,' Gabriel told her. 'The schedule will have to wait.'

'But—'

'Listen, Nicola. I genuinely don't have time for this. We'll talk in half an hour. Bring coffee. And a muffin. Blueberry.'

He hung up before she could respond, then went back to his window.

The Cycle

It was a time of slogans. It had been for at least the past three years; and this was another thing for which the media, in Gabriel's opinion, was largely to blame.

It began with the bursting of the sub-prime bubble, which resulted in the credit crisis, which then mutated into the even pithier credit *crunch*. That was the one that every paper, pundit and broadcaster leaped upon, and afterwards, all journalistic restraint went out of the window. Over the subsequent months, and then years, it had seemed that they were all competing to see who could come up with the most elaborate metaphor to explain what was happening – and, more importantly, to damn those responsible.

Financial engineering, predatory lending, toxic assets, the fiscal cliff, financial weapons of mass destruction, global economic meltdown – the list went on and on, with the terms becoming ever more alarmist. Gabriel had even seen the headline **ASTOCKALYPSE** used at one point – on the day the markets suffered their biggest plunge since 9/11. But, thankfully, that was one term that had not caught on.

Within the hedge fund community, the language was subtler, and far more realistic. No one talked in terms of crisis or failure. Even the phrase 'boom and bust' was widely derided for its whiff of histrionics. In hedge funds, they simply talked about the *cycle*. After all, there was nothing fundamentally new about the 2008 downturn. Granted, it had been bigger and more dramatic than usual, but aside from that it was nothing special. The cycle was a cycle because it could do nothing but keep on turning.

For Gabriel's part, he didn't really care whether the general economy was expanding or contracting. He could make money at any point in the cycle. This was what he did. It was what every professional trader did – or at least tried to do. Though this was something the general public did not seem to grasp.

Casino banking – that was the slogan increasingly used to characterise his line of work. Gabriel had seen those words on more than one placard recently. But this was a phrase that left him feeling conflicted. On the one hand, he quite liked the air of glamour it invoked. On the other, he understood that the phrase was not intended as a compliment.

The problem was that the sloganists understood nothing about the world of finance. They had the ridiculous notion that everyone was getting paid vast amounts of money while doing no real work. They had no idea what a hedge fund actually did.

What a Hedge Fund Actually Does

If Gabriel had been called upon to explain his role within the supposed City casino, this is what he would have said: he was the guy who spent his days on the blackjack tables, counting the cards.

What this meant, in reality, was that he crunched data – a mountain of data. He trawled through companies' quarterly statements. He read thousands of pages of stock reports, or, more often, the reports on stock reports – prepared for him by a small team of junior analysts. He spent hundreds of hours dissecting the news from America and Europe; from China, Africa, the Middle East. He knew more about what was going on in Iraq and Russia and Saudi Arabia than did many members of the Foreign Office. These were the things he *had* to know if he was to make effective bets. And more often than not, it took months. Months and months of painstaking research and complex mathematical modelling.

Aside from the vast amounts of money involved – and the

cars and clothes and property and women that the money could buy – there really wasn't much that was glamorous about Gabriel's job. It had little to do with risk, and a great deal to do with risk management. Which was why people invested. They knew that in the long run, the odds were stacked firmly in their favour.

Of course, this wasn't to say that hedge funds never failed. Plenty of funds had folded during the last crash – those that hadn't seen the storm coming. And ten years before this, at the end of the previous cycle, there had been some truly spectacular implosions. The most famous was Long-Term Capital Management – ironically named, in hindsight – which had lost a small fortune during the collapse of the Russian bonds market. Then there was Amaranth, which in 2006 had managed to lose six billion dollars in a matter of weeks, with a series of badly timed bets on natural gas. Because no investment strategy was risk-free; and, however skilled and talented, fund managers were still fallible human beings. Gabriel wasn't thinking of himself so much at this point, but rather of some of the other fund managers he knew.

But, really, the failure of the few was a minor issue in the industry as a whole; and the investors were sophisticated enough to understand and contextualise the overall risk. These were large institutional investors and high-net-worth individuals, people with plenty of capital to play with. From time to time, the odd pension fund got wiped out too, when something went badly wrong, but this wasn't an issue at Mason Wallace. As a rule, Mason preferred not to deal with pension funds, because they represented too broad a spectrum of interests, and the investors tended to be overly concerned about how and where their money was being spent.

Capital Gains

Within the wider industry, Mason Wallace defined itself as an aggressive global macroeconomic investment vehicle – though Mason preferred the term 'juggernaut' to 'vehicle', and only had it removed from the firm's website upon the insistence of the marketing department. It was likewise a marketing decision that saw the firm renamed. In the beginning, it was simply Mason Capital Management, until Mason was informed that investors tended to trust two surnames more than one. One name could suggest autocracy and narrow vision, but two implied balance, stability and shared interests. However ridiculous this sounded, Mason wasn't one to dispute the established wisdom of market research. He immediately renamed his company Mason Wallace Capital Management. Wallace was Mason's middle name.

Whereas many hedge funds had highly specialised strategies – they traded only in metals, or distressed securities, or any number of specific financial instruments – Mason Wallace's policy was simply to chase the money. They invested in all manner of stocks, bonds, currencies, commodities and derivatives, adapting strategy to situation. This was seen as a riskier approach by many financial analysts, but Gabriel knew that personnel mattered far more than philosophy. A complex or variable strategy, in the hands of the capable, was infinitely safer than a simple strategy run by a second-rate team. And, anyway, at the most basic level, the industry was structured to provide plenty of additional assurances to investors.

As far as the sloganists were concerned, the last three years had proven that within finance, in general, there was no punishment for failure. If a large retail bank crashed, the taxpayer would be forced to bail it out, and the bank managers would still get to walk away with their bonuses and six-figure pensions intact. But in hedge funds, this was absolutely not the case. In a hedge fund, it was private capital that was at stake, and if the ship went down, the management went with it. Furthermore, as with all senior hedge fund personnel, most of Gabriel's remuneration was legally tied to the fund's performance. His basic salary, taken out of the fixed management fee, was just a few hundred thousand per annum. It was the performance fee that paid his bonus, and that only kicked in if the fund was in profit.

Of course, many of the less informed commentators would argue that this was yet another incentive for rash speculation – since everyone was under continual pressure to maximise profits. But this was ignoring the failsafe that every fund had built into the system. At Gabriel's level – the level where the decisions were implemented – everyone was contractually obliged to have half their bonus reinvested into the fund. Between them, the management team had over one hundred million pounds staked on their own strategy, so recklessness was in no one's interest.

To Gabriel's knowledge, everyone at Mason Wallace was more than happy with this set-up. The reality was that no one needed any cajoling to keep the vast bulk of their remuneration holed up in the Cayman Islands, where the fund was domiciled. For his part, Gabriel was already being clobbered with a six-figure tax bill every April, most of which would be squandered on benefits and bureaucracy, or public services he had no intention of ever using. So he felt no qualms at the notion that the lion's share of his income was not *technically* income, and should not be taxed as such.

Gabriel had never been to the Cayman Islands because Mason Wallace didn't have an office there – just a bank account and a postbox. But had someone been required to front operations abroad, he would have been the first to step forward. He imagined a sea view – palm trees and near-naked women – with not a sign or slogan or Portaloo in sight.

A Muffin, Blueberry

When Nicola knocked on the door, exactly thirty minutes after their brief exchange on the phone, Gabriel was still standing at his window. He had no idea where the time had gone. Before telling her to come in, he sat down behind his desk, ruffled some papers and awoke his computer from its deep slumber. Not that Nicola would be able to see the screen from the other side of the desk, and not that it mattered, one way or the other. Gabriel wasn't obliged to look busy just for the benefit of his PA, any more than he was obliged to tell her that he'd spent most of the morning staring out of his window, mentally justifying his existence to the Occupy tribunal.

Nicola was having some difficulty negotiating the door while carrying two cappuccino grandes and a blueberry muffin, but Gabriel did not get up to help her. He had his eyes fixed on the latest figures from Bloomberg, as if he were terribly preoccupied and could not afford a single second away from his desk. Eventually, she managed to jostle the door open with one hip, and then slid inside before it closed on her. At this point, Gabriel pretended to notice her for the first time. He gave a tiny nod of acknowledgement as she set down the coffee and muffin, then gestured that she should take a seat.

'Nicola, let's make this as quick as possible. What have you got for me?'

'Two calls you need to return. One from UBS, regarding the option on BAE. The other is from someone called Cannock, regarding a stock pitch. He says he emailed you last week. Several times.'

Gabriel sipped his cappuccino, then leaned back in his chair, interlacing his fingers. 'UBS I'll deal with. Cannock can wait. If he calls again, I'm in a meeting. Or I'm out. Alternate the two.'

Nicola tutted. 'Gabriel, how long have I been doing this job? Please leave the excuses to me. I have a compendium of them.'

Nicola was one of the few people at Mason Wallace who called Gabriel by his first name. They had trialled 'Mr Vaughn' when she started, but since she was at least a decade older than him, it had felt too ludicrous to continue with – even by Gabriel's standards. Plus it sounded more like a reprimand in her mouth. Very matriarchal. That was probably one of the reasons HR had hired her.

'Fine. Just keep him dangling until I tell you otherwise. What else? Lunch?'

'Nothing today. But you do have an early one tomorrow. Another potential investor. German. Midday at the Savoy.'

'OK. Remind me again tomorrow morning.'

'Of course.'

'What about this afternoon? How's that looking?'

'One fifteen: meeting with Ian and Iain to collate research on the EnCore Oil takeover.'

'Nope. I'll need an extra half hour to prep. Reschedule for two o'clock.'

'You're supposed to be seeing Karen at two thirty. She needs to go through last quarter's performance figures for the investors' newsletter.'

'Push that back to three thirty. Do I have anything at three thirty?'

'No, not specifically. But you do have to talk to Compliance at some point today. New EU legislation. It's important.'

'Fuck.'

Compliance's role was the legal side of the business. It was their job to ensure that the letter of the law was upheld, and its spirit as seldom as possible. Dealing with them was tedious beyond belief.

'Reschedule.'

'You've already rescheduled. You were meant to talk to them by the end of last week at the latest.'

'I've not had a good morning. There's no way I can timetable it before seven. No, make that seven thirty.'

'Seven thirty? You want me to call Compliance and ask them to cancel any plans they might have for this evening?'

'Yes, I want you to ask them that. And when they kick up a fuss, suggest something tomorrow instead. Then it's them rescheduling, not me.'

Nicola exhaled audibly. 'What time tomorrow?'

'Around lunch.'

'You're having lunch at the Savoy.'

'Right.'

'Gabriel, can I speak frankly?'

'No.'

'Is there anything the matter? I mean, I'm used to a certain amount of awkwardness when it comes to your timetable, but this is taking things to a whole new level. For someone who's supposedly busy, you don't seem very focussed.'

'Focussed?' Gabriel creased his forehead, as if considering this suggestion carefully. 'Nicola, I'm fine. Tell Compliance I'll talk to them tomorrow morning. Ten thirty on the dot. OK?'

'Ten thirty.' Nicola nodded. 'Unless, of course, they call your bluff and agree to see you this evening.'

'Nicola, it's no bluff. If they agree to seven thirty, that's what we'll go with.'

Gabriel took a large bite from his muffin, signifying that the matter was settled.

Two Days Ago:
The Biopsy Results

It had been a minimally invasive procedure. Partly, this was due to the position of the growth; partly it was because Gabriel had insisted that his scalp remain intact. He was given a local anaesthetic. His head was clamped into a metal frame. A tiny incision was made, just a couple of millimetres across, and a fine needle was passed through, deep into his grey matter. It was precision-guided using a three-dimensional computer-generated map of Gabriel's brain, though it was still a human being – Armitage, the neuro-oncologist – who was wielding the surgical instruments.

The following Saturday, he was back at the Harley Street clinic, waiting to go through the results.

'It's not good news, I'm afraid,' Armitage told him. 'The biopsy shows that the tumour is malignant. It's what's called a glioblastoma. Glioblastoma multiforme. It's aggressive and in a difficult location, which makes resection problematic. We do have options, but they're limited.'

Gabriel said nothing. He didn't know what he *could* say. Despite being a man with a very high tolerance for jargon, he felt bombarded with polysyllables. Not that the technicalities were important. Gabriel understood the words malignant, aggressive and difficult, and this was enough. The rest was just a shield for the doctor – because in some situations, plain English was not helpful.

It was obvious that Armitage was waiting for him to react. Gabriel suspected that people usually did react at this point. Or their spouses or family reacted. But, of course, Gabriel didn't have anyone else with him.

The silence was getting awkward.

Armitage coughed. 'It's a lot to take in. I understand that. Would you like me to get you a glass of water?'

Gabriel nodded. 'Please. Sparkling.'

Armitage picked up his phone and tapped three digits. 'Frances, could you bring in a water for Mr Vaughn? Sparkling.'

'Can you remove it?' Gabriel asked, after Armitage had hung up.

'Conventional surgery isn't an option I'd recommend in this instance.' Armitage slid a copy of Gabriel's MRI scan across the desk, and pointed with his pen to the area that had been circled in red. 'This is the tumour here. It's located in your right anterior insula, which is in a very deep fissure between your frontal and temporal lobes. Any attempt to remove the tumour would be risky. We'd be cutting three centimetres below the surface of your brain, and the surrounding region is highly complex. There *is* a surgical procedure, but it's usually performed only for low-grade tumours, where the prognosis is better.'

'What do you mean?'

'Mr Vaughn, I have to be honest with you.'

At this point Frances came in with a litre bottle of sparkling water and a tall glass. Armitage waited until she'd left – an excruciating thirty seconds – before continuing.

'The prognosis for this type of tumour is poor. Even with surgery, the average survival time is eleven months from diagnosis. And with your tumour, we'd have to cut through healthy tissue just to access it. We have to weigh the risks against the limited benefits.'

'Oh.' Gabriel considered the full bottle of sparkling water for a few moments. 'So what options *do* I have?'

17

Options

'Our first choice would be radiosurgery. It's similar to conventional radiotherapy, but delivered at a much higher dose, and with much greater accuracy. The aim would be to kill as much of the tumour as possible while leaving the surrounding tissue unharmed.'

'Will I lose my hair?'

'No, Mr Vaughn. The radiation is targeted with sub-millimetre accuracy. The machine we use for the procedure is state-of-the-art. It's called the CyberKnife. It uses real-time 3D imagery and robotics to target only the tumour cells. The procedure is non-invasive and completely painless, and can be performed right here in the clinic. It takes just a few hours, and you'd probably go home the same day.'

'What about work? Would it interfere with work?'

Armitage pursed his lips in a very small frown. 'Well, in theory, you could go back to work as soon as you wanted. There are some side effects from the radiation – usually mild nausea and fatigue – but they tend to pass within twenty-four hours.' He tapped his pen a couple of times against the scan pictures. 'However, we'd also want you to have chemotherapy, starting as soon as possible. For this type of tumour we use a drug called Temodal. You'd take it daily for the next six weeks.'

'At home?'

'Yes, you can take it at home, although we would want to keep a close eye on you at first. The side effects from the chemotherapy tend to be greater, and ongoing for as long as you're taking the drugs. Again, nausea and fatigue are common, as are anxiety and insomnia. There is also the possibility of hair loss or thinning, though this is a relatively rare side effect. It affects fewer than one in ten people. As for the more common side effects, they can be treated if necessary. Anti-emetics if the nausea is bad. We can also try various medications to help with sleep and anxiety levels.'

Gabriel considered this for a few minutes. 'So, again, there's nothing that should stop me from working?'

Armitage's frown deepened. He looked straight into Gabriel's eyes for a few moments; Gabriel looked back without blinking. 'Mr Vaughn. With the radiosurgery and the chemotherapy, we would be aiming to reduce the mass of the tumour by eighty to ninety per cent. This will help to control some of your symptoms. And, hopefully, it will extend your life by several months. Six or seven would be a reasonable expectation. But it is not a cure. I need to be certain you understand that.'

'I understand that.'

'Then forgive me, please. But my advice to you would be *don't* go back to work.'

Gabriel poured himself a glass of water, his hand rock-steady. Not going back to work was unimaginable; he'd known this from the start. But he had no intention of explaining this decision to

Armitage. He wasn't sure he could. 'When can you book me in for the procedure?' he asked.

'We'd want to do it as soon as possible.'

'It will have to be another Saturday.'

Armitage didn't challenge this. 'We'll start you on the Temodal today. You need to take it daily on an empty stomach, one hour before food. And you should continue to take the steroids every six hours. Are you noticing improvements? Fewer headaches?'

'Yes.'

'How about your mood?'

'I had another. . . episode a few days ago. But it wasn't as bad. It happened in the evening when I was at home.'

Armitage nodded. 'The steroids will continue to reduce the inflammation around the tumour and this should help. But some ongoing emotional lability is likely, even after the radiosurgery. It's common with a tumour in this location.'

'Yes.'

Emotional lability. This was the medical term for Gabriel's new propensity for crying like a child – though he understood it could refer to any sudden and inexplicable change in mood. More commonly, it manifested itself in anger. When Armitage had first used the words, a couple of weeks ago, Gabriel had misheard. He had thought the term was emotional *liability*, and still believed this to be a much more apposite phrase.

'If the episodes get worse, contact me. We'll try you on an anticonvulsant. But, for now, I'd rather keep the medication to a minimum. We've talked about driving, haven't we?'

'Yes.'

'Good. It would be safer not to. And there's a chance your insurance will no longer be valid.'

Gabriel nodded, and left shortly afterwards.

His car was parked just round the corner from the clinic. It was a Ferrari 458 Italia, in yellow. It could go zero to sixty in 3.4 seconds and had a top speed of over two hundred miles per hour. This was extremely useful in central London.

18

How Do They Sleep?

On the Monday evening, Gabriel left Stanton House at a little after eight o'clock. He nodded to the two new security guys on his way out, then tried to skirt round the edge of the camp as briskly as possible, without making eye contact with anyone. It didn't work. Halfway to the Mercedes, a man in a tatty cardigan stepped out in front of Gabriel and shoved a flyer in his face. Gabriel took it and placed it in his coat pocket without looking. He was in no mood for a confrontation tonight.

His chauffeur had seen him coming and was ready with the door when Gabriel reached the car. 'Good evening, sir.'

Gabriel nodded and got in.

Once the car was moving, Gabriel took out the flyer and inspected it. There was a question at the top, in bold: **HOW DO THEY SLEEP?** Below this was a list of pension statistics:

'SIR' FRED GOODWIN, RBS: **£342,000** PER ANNUM

LARRY FISH, RBS: **£1.4 MILLION** PER ANNUM

'SIR' JAMES CROSBY. HBOS: **£572,000** PER ANNUM

PETER CUMMINGS, HBOS: £369,000 PER ANNUM
ADAM APPLEGARTH, NORTHERN ROCK: £305,000
PER ANNUM

Gabriel skipped to the end: **These are some of the men who caused the financial crisis. Their broken banks are now owned by the British taxpayer. WE are paying for these pensions, with money that could otherwise be used to fund the salaries of 250 new nurses! Write to your MP and ask why.**

Larry Fish aside, Gabriel wasn't impressed by any of these pensions. He folded the flyer and returned it to his pocket.

The journey home was mercifully swift. Gabriel was back in his apartment well before eight thirty, and as always the interior was spotless. His breakfast bowl had been washed and his super-fruit granola had been returned to the cupboard. The bed was made and the bathroom had been cleaned, with fresh towels placed on the towel rail. The dirty laundry had been collected; and Gabriel didn't have to look in the wardrobe to know that last Friday's clothes would have been washed, ironed and returned.

Every evening it was like magic. Gabriel had never once set eyes upon the cleaning woman. He'd never spoken to her, either, because she was employed via an agency. Gabriel didn't even know for certain that she *was* a woman, but one assumed, obviously.

His apartment was on the fifth floor of a building overlooking St Katharine Docks. From his balcony he had a view of the yachting marina and, beyond this, Tower Bridge. It had two bedrooms and he had paid just under two million pounds for it. But that was a couple of years ago. It was probably worth much more now.

He went to the fridge and poured himself a glass of water, then took his daily Temodal. He'd take his steroid just before bed, around eleven, so that the next one wouldn't be due until his alarm went off at five fifteen. Not that there was much chance of him sleeping through the night. So far the 'fatigue' he'd been warned about had not been forthcoming. Just mild nausea and more insomnia.

He thought about the flyer in his coat pocket, with its ridiculous question: how do they sleep? Gabriel couldn't speak for the now-unemployed ex-directors of RBS and so forth, but he did know that, as a rule, everyone in finance slept extraordinarily well. How could they not? In a hedge fund, the normal working day was twelve hours minimum. In an investment bank, fifteen-hour days were not uncommon. Gabriel had spent the first four years of his career in investment banks – first BarCap then Goldman – and he had never slept better. Out like a light every single night. Of course, it helped, too, that he owned one of the most comfortable mattresses money could buy. His bed had cost more than the average family hatchback. It was very difficult *not* to sleep well in a bed like that.

So a month or two ago, Gabriel would have found the flyer question nothing short of hilarious. But now the humour of the situation was rather spoiled. For the first time in his adult life, Gabriel was not sleeping well, and the drugs were making this worse.

He went down to the ground floor and did twenty minutes in the steam room followed by fifty lengths in the pool. Yesterday, he'd spent an hour in the evening lifting weights, hoping this might tire him out. Unfortunately, though, it had had the opposite effect; afterwards, he'd felt tense and agitated.

Tonight was an improvement. He didn't feel relaxed, but he did feel physically tired. Back in his apartment, he ignored medical advice and poured himself a large glass of 1982 Château Latour. He had bought it at Sotheby's. It wasn't the sort of wine anyone in their right mind would consider drinking alone on a Monday evening, and half an hour after starting it, he began to get emotional. He was overcome by the irrational desire to speak with his father. Instead, he picked up the phone and rang Chelsea Courtesans to book an outcall from Melissa on Friday evening. On Saturday, he had his appointment with the CyberKnife.

After he'd finished his wine, he went to the bathroom, brushed, flossed and applied his pre-sleep anti-ageing moisturiser, knowing, of course, that there was no longer any real point to this. But the alternative – *not* applying his anti-ageing moisturiser – was too bleak to consider. Sometimes, the comfort of routine was purpose enough.

Driven

Gabriel stared at the back of his chauffeur's head, wondering what, if anything, was going on in there. What did the other man think about during these short and silent journeys across central London? Did he resent that this was his lot in life, driving an expensive car he did not own for a man who earned a hundred times what he did? Maybe he enjoyed his job, though, in truth, Gabriel found this almost impossible to believe. When he tried to picture the career path that ended in being a chauffeur, he could only imagine a series of missteps and bad decisions – or, more likely, an absence of decisions. He didn't think that anyone would *plan* to eke out a living as a professional driver.

As far as Gabriel could see, this was the key difference between them. It explained why he had status and economic power and his chauffeur did not. Gabriel had made positive life choices. He'd taken the opportunities that came his way.

Yes, he'd be the first to admit that he'd been born with certain advantages. He'd been born with a brain, for a start; he'd been aware from a very young age that he was far more intelligent

Gabriel knew, of course, that there were people in the world who were simply born into money and power, and he understood the resentment this could provoke. For much of his education – first at a private boarding school, and later as a student of philosophy, politics and economics at Oxford – he'd lived side by side with these people. But he'd always been on the outside looking in. Gabriel's father was not rich – he was a chartered surveyor who'd had to scrimp and save to provide for his son's education, at least until Gabriel's potential was recognised and he was awarded a scholarship to cover the fees. At Oxford, he'd never been invited to join any of the exclusive societies and dining clubs that many of his coursemates were part of. They all understood that he didn't have the right background – which was another way of saying that he didn't have the right bank balance. Gabriel couldn't afford to patronise – and occasionally trash – the finest restaurants in Oxford.

Consequently, he'd never identified with those who'd had their money handed to them on a plate. He identified with the strivers, the people who'd had to beat their own path to economic success. And, as far as he could see, the vast majority of people who worked in the City fitted this profile. No one fell into a career in finance. You had to have drive, a real work ethic.

This is what he would have told anyone who questioned

57

whether he *deserved* his salary, his two-million-pound home, his personal chauffeur. He hadn't been born into a life of privilege. It was something he'd built for himself.

Focus

They pulled up in front of the Savoy a little before a quarter to twelve. A doorman came out and held an umbrella over Gabriel's head for the ten-metre walk from the car to the lobby. Gabriel didn't thank him. He wasn't going to thank someone for doing what he was paid to do. And, anyway, he had more important things to worry about.

The German – Metzger – hadn't arrived at the restaurant yet, which was understandable, given the time. But Gabriel hated having to wait, especially at the moment. He needed to keep his schedule tight, and his mind busy. Unfortunately, he also had to make a good impression. A fifty-million-euro potential investor wasn't huge, not by Mason Wallace standards, but neither was he someone you'd risk being late for. It was the sort of appointment that demanded the utmost professionalism.

Under normal circumstances, this would not have struck Gabriel as a potential problem. He was the most professional man he knew, and his ability to make the right impression – with the people who mattered – was something he'd always taken for granted. But now, as he was escorted to his table, he was conscious of an unfamiliar feeling in his stomach, an . . . uncertainty that he found deeply troubling. He should have felt at home in the Savoy, but he didn't. The 1920s interior felt almost surreal. Everywhere he looked there was lacquered wood and distressed mirrors; there were too many angles and reflections to deal with.

Anxiety. It wasn't like it had been on the Tube, but it felt like a precursor.

He didn't know whether to order a drink. Alcohol might be the obvious thing to settle his nerves, to take the edge off, at the very least, but he also had his suspicions that alcohol was partly to blame for this newest episode. He hadn't been quite right since the Château Latour, and he had no doubt that it had contributed to another bad night's sleep: the dream about his father, waking up with a head full of inexplicable guilt.

He ordered a bottle of water, then changed his mind and ordered a Scotch on the rocks, which he downed the instant the waiter had turned his back. He put the empty glass on the empty table to his left and crunched a couple of breath mints in his mouth. If Metzger wanted wine, then Gabriel would join him, but until then, it was probably best to stick with the water. Stick with the water, and go over the game plan.

Gabriel fixed his eyes on his napkin to avoid looking at the mirrors. What *was* the game plan? Usually, this wouldn't have been a question worth considering. Be charming. Exude confidence. Don't be the sort of man who has to drink whisky before midday just to hold it together.

Go over the figures, discuss the fund's investment strategy, talk about likely returns, settle any doubts.

You've had lunches like this dozens of times before. You can do this stuff in your sleep. You're an extremely impressive man.

'Mr Vaughn?'

Gabriel may have jumped – he didn't know, and he didn't know if it would be noticeable, anyway. Either way, it was worth it for the spike of adrenaline.

'Herr Metzger.' He rose from his seat to shake the German's hand. '*Guten tag.*'

Gabriel took it for granted that any foreign words uttered by an Englishman should be met with an appropriate display of admiration and gratitude, so it was disappointing that Metzger didn't seem all that impressed. Possibly, the clammy handshake had ruined the effect. Gabriel's palms were sweating, which he'd previously assumed was just a figure of speech.

'*Sprechen sie Deutsch*?' Metzger asked.

Gabriel twisted his mouth into a smile. *Deutsch* he knew, and *Sprechen* he could have a confident stab at. 'I'm a bit rusty, I'm afraid. I think we'd do better to stick with English for now. If that's OK?'

Metzger nodded. 'Of course.'

Gabriel found that he had no appetite whatsoever, so he ordered the beluga caviar to start, since it was bound to be tiny, and the fillet steak for his main, since it never hurt to be seen as a fillet steak eater. Metzger had the lobster bisque followed by the pork, veal and pistachio pie. They drank a £350 bottle of Bordeaux, which was sufficient to turn down the volume on Gabriel's anxiety, though it still remained there in the background, a disconcerting hum. Fortunately, there was much about this meeting that was pure routine. Despite his internal discomfort, Gabriel felt that he at least knew the script he was supposed to be following, and soon enough, the conversation had moved to firm and familiar ground. It was the sort of small talk that wasn't really small talk at all. It was a chance for Metzger to find out more about Gabriel's credentials, and it was the type of interview at which Gabriel had always excelled.

'How long have you worked in finance?' Metzger asked.

'All my adult life,' Gabriel told him. 'I started playing the markets when I was at university. Other people spent their spare time socialising; I spent mine teaching myself everything I needed to know about trading shares. I graduated with several thousand pounds in equity and a job already lined up at a top bank. By the time I was twenty-four, I was in charge of a quarter-million-pound investment portfolio at Goldman Sachs.'

Metzger nodded at this. 'It's an impressive amount for a young man to be entrusted with.'

'It was a stepping-stone, nothing more.' Gabriel made sure he held the other man's eye, hoping that he looked more self-assured than he felt. 'The truth, Herr Metzger, is that I've never seen myself as an *employee*. I'm an entrepreneur, like you. I don't need a monthly salary to feel secure. The rewards are much bigger if you're prepared to put your own money on the line. That's why I got out of investment banking and joined a hedge fund.'

Gabriel understood the value of tailoring your image to your audience. Not that there was anything inaccurate in what he'd said. He'd just selected the details most likely to strike a chord. Metzger had a package-delivery empire that he'd built from scratch, so he was always going to respond well to the self-made man narrative. If Gabriel had been dealing with someone who sat a little higher on the social scale, then he would have talked more about his private schooling. If he'd been dealing with an American, he'd have made at least half a dozen references to being at Oxford, since he'd never met an American who wasn't impressed by this.

It was all about building a rapport – or pretending to build a rapport, which was practically the same thing.

With Metzger, it seemed to be working. The German nodded approvingly, then asked: 'How much of your own money do you have invested in the fund? If you don't mind me asking.'

'Not at all. It's the first question *I'd* ask if I were in your position.' Gabriel took another sip of his Bordeaux, then leaned back in his chair. 'My stake in the fund is just over seven million. Not a huge amount, but it's the bulk of what I've earned at Mason Wallace. Basically, my life savings.' He shrugged, as casually as he could manage. 'So, if you're asking me how much faith *I* have in our strategy, then there's your answer. I'm happy to bet everything I own on it.'

The words had been used many times before, so Gabriel could focus all his attention on the delivery.

It seemed to have paid off. After a moment, Metzger's poker face cracked into the narrowest of smiles. He held up his wine glass. 'It sounds, Mr Vaughn, like you're going to retire as a very wealthy man.'

'Yes. I am.' Gabriel clinked Metzger's glass, then emptied his own. 'If you'd excuse me for a moment?'

In the toilet, it took Gabriel several minutes to stop trembling. He stood at the sink and ran cold water over his wrists until the episode had passed.

The groundwork was laid. All he had to do now was stay on message: *we're alike, our interests are the same, you can trust me with your money.*

Gabriel stared into the mirror for a long time, trying to reassure himself that he at least *looked* the same as he always had. Then he straightened his tie and went back to the restaurant.

The Arrival Hierarchy

It seemed that the mysterious gridlock at the start of the week had been a one-day aberration. The Tuesday and Wednesday commutes had run like a Swiss watch, and by Thursday morning, Gabriel was convinced that everything was back to normal. Or what passed for normal these days. The camp was still there. As was the golf-ball-sized brain tumour. He assumed it was, anyway; his emotions continued to be a liability.

He got his chauffeur to let him out next to the policemen, since this was now the obvious place to be let out.

'Have a good day, sir.'

Gabriel nodded at his chauffeur, then nodded to the policemen, who both nodded back, while at the same time looking thoroughly miserable. This was understandable. Thirteen days in, the occupation was clearly getting tedious for them. It was 6.14 a.m. It was cold. They were at either the start or the end of a long, poorly paid shift. Gabriel could only imagine that they drew lots by now, with the losers being condemned to eight hours of mind-numbing *non*-policing. The protest remained stubbornly, squalidly peaceful.

64

For Gabriel's part, the camp was still an annoyance, but it also continued to exert a perverse fascination. It was like watching footage of a primitive tribe and trying to work out the meaning behind its weird, arcane rituals. Every so often, he'd be looking down from his window and he'd see something new going on down there – a gathering on the steps of St Paul's, speeches, sermonising, raised hands. It looked like they were voting in some sort of sham parliament. He had no idea what they expected to achieve, from this or any of their other ridiculous pantomimes. One day, half of them had been dressed as zombies. Another time, they were all wearing these sinister squinty-eyed masks. Gabriel had had to call Nicola in to ask her if she understood the significance of this. Apparently, it was a reference to some film called *V for Vendetta*, which Gabriel had never heard of. He had a state-of-the-art home cinema system – 64-inch high-definition smart screen, 7.1 surround sound, silver-plated cabling – but he only used it to watch Bloomberg, BBC News, CNN, CNBC and pornography.

In the foyer of Stanton House, he nodded at the two security guards without breaking his stride, then headed up to the top floor. All the lights were on in Mason Wallace as they were programmed to come on at 5 a.m. for the cleaners, who then had an hour to ensure the premises were spotless – floors vacuumed, bins emptied, toilets scrubbed – by the time Mason arrived for his 6 a.m. shit. Mason was always the first in. His company had an informal – but nonetheless rigid – arrival-time hierarchy that correlated with the actual hierarchy, in that the more senior your standing, the earlier you got in to work. It was a form of one-upmanship not uncommon in the world of finance. In an investment bank, it would be lunacy for any employee wanting to progress to be at their desk later than 6.30 a.m., or to leave it before 9 p.m. You didn't necessarily have to be *working* at your desk; you just had to be seen to be there. This was the surest route to promotion. It was like the competition where everyone has to keep a hand on the car and the last man standing gets to drive it away. But played every day of your working life.

At a hedge fund, the hours weren't quite this insane – a twelve-hour office day was perfectly acceptable – but there was still a large element of prestige, and often self-justification, associated with working longer than anyone else. Appearing to be a permanent fixture at the office sent a clear signal that the company couldn't possibly function without you.

Thus Mason was always the first to arrive, at six, followed by Gabriel, no later than 6.20, followed by the rest of the managers, between 6.30 and 6.40. The senior analysts started to arrive from 6.55, just as the managers were going into the morning meeting, followed by the junior analysts from 7.10, and the backroom staff – HR, Marketing, Compliance – from 7.30. The receptionist and PAs got to roll in around 7.45, as the managers were coming out of the morning meeting.

Technically, Gabriel was no more senior than Ainsley or Sherman or Shipman or any of the other portfolio managers. But everyone knew that he was Mason's heir apparent. Three years ago, aged just twenty-nine, Gabriel had made his move and claimed the 6.20 spot as his own. No one had ever challenged his right to it.

The One-Hundred-and-Forty-Third EU Summit

'OK, ladies. Would someone care to explain this to me?'

Mason flung a selection of the morning's papers across the board table. The *Financial Times* had a picture of Angela Merkel locked in tense talks with Nicolas Sarkozy while David Cameron hovered like a spare part in the background. The *Telegraph* had led with the headline **EU LEADERS DITHER OVER RESCUE PLAN**, while *The Times* carried a half-page picture of a punch-up that had broken out in the Italian parliament during a debate on economic reform. This, Gabriel noted, ran alongside a second story declaring **ST PAUL'S TO REOPEN BUT MAY SUE PROTESTERS**. That at least was unequivocal good news. The *Express*, meanwhile, had decided to plump for a three-quarter-page headline proclaiming **GERMANY WARNS OF WAR IN EUROPE**.

'All fucking great,' Mason continued, 'except I'm hearing everything has gone tits-up in the last three hours. Bloomberg says there's been some sort of last-minute deal. Anyone want to fill me in?'

Gabriel felt seven pairs of eyes swing towards him. He didn't want to be the one to answer this question, but, at the same time, he wasn't going to give Ainsley or Sherman the satisfaction of seeing him falter. He looked up from the image he'd been gazing at – one middle-aged Italian with his hands round another middle-aged Italian's throat. 'Merkel did a press briefing at four o'clock this morning. The banks have agreed to accept a fifty per cent write-down on Greek debt.'

'I told you!' Ainsley admonished. 'She was always going to get this pushed through.'

Gabriel shrugged. 'Eventually, yes. It just happened a little quicker than we were expecting.'

'Quicker than *you* were expecting,' Sherman countered. 'You realise what the forecasters are saying? The Asian markets have already rallied, and London's bound to follow suit. It could open up by as much as one and a half per cent.'

'Maybe,' Gabriel conceded. 'But we all know it will be back down by tomorrow. Monday at the latest.' He paused and stared at Sherman, then Ainsley, challenging them to dispute this. 'The truth is there's no real substance to this deal. It doesn't change the fundamentals, and the markets are going to realise that soon enough. What's happening now is just a blip.'

Sherman snorted, looking round the table for backup. 'Yes, Vaughn, it's a blip. That's not the point and you know it. We should have been all over this. Instead, we listened to you and now we've been left with our pants round our ankles.'

'Completely fucking exposed,' Ainsley added.

Gabriel shot him a withering glance. 'Thanks. I think we all got the metaphor. And I'm glad you're feeling so vocal this morning. It's easy to be a genius in hindsight.'

'Oh, come on! This is *not* about hindsight. It's about you taking your eye off the ball.'

Gabriel looked briefly around the table to gauge the mood. Shipman, Kilner, Gould, Hadfield – none of them looked ready to leap to his defence. Even Mason seemed happy to let Gabriel stew in this situation for a while.

Smelling blood, Ainsley pressed on. 'If you'd done your homework yesterday, you'd have seen the way the wind was blowing. Merkel had already secured the trillion-euro bailout – that was no mean feat. And there were plenty of reports that Sarkozy was about to strike a deal with the Chinese. The banks were always going to buckle. It was a bet we should have taken. If we'd gone long on the euro, we'd already be looking at a substantial profit.'

There were a number of supportive murmurs around the table. Mason raised his hand to call for silence. 'Ainsley, I don't want to hear about how much we could have made. Let's keep our minds on the task at hand. What's our exposure, and what do we do about it?'

'We look set to lose a few hundred thousand when London opens,' Ainsley replied, keeping his voice neutral. Gabriel suspected that he was inwardly rejoicing. Ainsley would happily trade a few thousand of his own money to score points over his colleagues. He was that sort of prick. 'In the short term, we should cut our losses on a number of positions – certainly on the forex. Currency is going to be unpredictable over the next few days, at least.'

Mason nodded. 'Agreed. Vaughn, you fucked up. Now let's draw a line under this and move on. What else came out of the summit? Where do things stand on the financial transactions tax?'

'The Germans are still determined to push it through,' said

Gould. 'As are the French. There's a lot of talk about shifting money back to the *real* economy.'

'Fuck the real economy!' said Shipman.

This was met with a chorus of approval from everyone in the boardroom. Everyone except Gabriel. He had shifted his gaze back to the photo of the fighting Italians. He was trying to envisage his hands round Ainsley's neck. But, for some reason, the image refused to crystallise.

Short-Term Plan

Gabriel spent several minutes crying in his office. Four minutes and ten seconds, according to his Rolex. After that, he was able to get straight back to work.

He'd started timing the episodes because Armitage was bound to ask about them on Saturday, and having some solid statistics made the whole thing marginally less excruciating. The real worry, of course, was that sooner or later he was bound to have another public incident – while talking to Nicola or, God forbid, in the morning meeting. His short-term plan, in any such scenario, was to drop everything and run to the nearest toilet, later claiming a mysterious stomach bug. For this reason, he'd stopped using the lift, preferring four flights of stairs to the risk of being locked in a confined space with another human being. If anyone asked, he'd tell them it was part of a new fitness regime. But hopefully, he'd only have to get through two more days of this. Armitage had said that the CyberKnife should alleviate his symptoms with immediate effect, and Gabriel was taking this as gospel. The alternative, like so much of the future, did not bear thinking about.

For now, it was better to keep his focus on work, especially after yesterday's fuck-up.

He spent the next forty minutes dissecting the post-summit analysis.

The euro was continuing to climb.

China was preparing to buy up half of Europe's sovereign debt.

David Cameron had issued a statement: 'Good progress has been made, but further progress is needed.' As oratory went, it wasn't exactly Winston Churchill. But Gabriel was willing to forgive this. If you took away the word 'good', the Prime Minister's soundbite gave a far more accurate picture of what was happening in Europe than the markets did. It might have been pique, but Gabriel was convinced that investors had overreacted. Whatever small deal had been struck, it didn't change the underlying facts. Greece still had a debt it would never repay, and Italy, Spain, Portugal and Ireland were all living on borrowed time. It wouldn't be war that undid Europe, as the *Express* prophesied; it would be a slow but inescapable decline into insignificance – the gradual breaking of the component parts, possibly under the well-heeled boot of a Chinese overlord.

There was something about this thought that troubled Gabriel, but it was difficult to figure out what. It wasn't that he had a strong objection to the Chinese; someone had to rule the world, and rather the Chinese than the Arabs. Nor did he have any sense of patriotism as far as his home continent was concerned. Like any sane individual, he understood that the European 'Union' had always been a car crash waiting to happen. The divide between the efficient northern economies and the lazy southern economies was just too great – and that was before you even entered the financial minefield of *eastern* Europe. As far as Gabriel could see, what was happening across the Mediterranean at the moment was simply economic Darwinism.

But there were much wider implications to consider. It wasn't just that a few hundred million southern Europeans were going to get buried alive under a mountain of debt. The gloomier prospect was that the failure would again be systemic, dragging down weak and strong alike. Or it might have been gloomy, in different circumstances. Given his personal situation, it was no longer something he had to concern himself with. But the truth was that he'd never much cared about the fate of Europe, or even the world. This was just the background that moved the markets. His dislike of Muslims aside, Gabriel did not have opinions as such; just a detailed understanding of financial implications. And even this was starting to slide.

Without thinking about what he was doing, Gabriel abandoned his desk and went to stand at the window. Nothing new out there, of course. The banner on the food tent – GLOBAL DEMOCRACY NOW! – hadn't been changed in the past forty-eight hours. Everything was the same, just shabbier. Thirteen days of pigeon shit and traffic fumes were starting to take their toll. Worst of all, the camp was starting to look like a normal part of the cityscape. After less than a fortnight, it was difficult to remember what the steps of St Paul's ought to look like. In moments like this, Gabriel was almost thankful for the Portaloos, which at least remained stubbornly garish and incongruous – a reminder that this was *not* how things should be.

Casting his eyes across the panorama, Gabriel found his gaze settling on the police officers in their high-vis jackets. It was difficult to tell from this distance, but he thought it was the same two he'd seen earlier that morning. They were standing in the exact same spot, arms folded, postures stiff. Gabriel felt weary just looking at them – though he was willing to concede this may have been the Temodal. After four days, the effects of the chemotherapy were starting to show.

He went to his desk and called Nicola in.

'Coffee?' she guessed.

'Espresso, Nicola. You'd better make it a double. And a pain au chocolat.'

'Right. Anything else?'

'Yes, actually. Could you come to the window a second?'

Gabriel thought he saw Nicola roll her eyes. But she came over, as requested.

'You see those two policemen down there? About ten metres north-east of the Portaloos.'

Nicola looked in the direction he was indicating, then turned back to him, her expression faintly irritated. 'Yes?'

'I'd like you to take them some coffee too.'

Nicola stared at him.

'Two Americanos, and some sachets of milk and sugar.'

'Gabriel, Starbucks don't do sachets of milk. They never have. They add the milk when you order.'

'Oh . . . Well, I guess you'll have to ask for a little jug, then. Or they can put some in a separate disposable cup.'

Nicola looked at him for a few seconds, pouting slightly. 'Can I ask why? I assume this isn't just a random act of human kindness?'

'No! Of course not. It's more that . . . Nicola, those men down there are doing important work. Without them, we'd have anarchy. I want them alert and vigilant.'

'OK. . . And should I take them some pains au chocolat too?'

Gabriel glared at her. 'Don't try to be smart, Nicola. It doesn't suit you. Just take them the coffee. Say it's from Mason Wallace. That's all you need to do.'

Nicola muttered something as she left, but Gabriel only caught the words 'whim' and 'absurd'. Which was more than enough, given the context.

He sat behind his desk and closed his eyes. He didn't want to look at any financial data for the next ten minutes. Although he couldn't articulate why, for the first time since the crying spell he was feeling just a tiny bit better.

Seven Years of Awkward Lunches

That night, Gabriel dreamed about his father again. They were having lunch in a restaurant that was simultaneously jam-packed and eerily quiet. In place of windows, a huge lobster tank ran the length of the room, giving the impression that they were dining at the bottom of the sea. His father was sitting in frosty silence while Gabriel attempted to tell him about the tumour. But every time he opened his mouth, something happened to interrupt him. The waiter appeared several times to tell them about today's specials. Then Gabriel's phone kept going off in his pocket, its ring as shrill as a siren. At one point, Catherine came over and threw a drink in his face.

He woke up an hour before his alarm, sweaty and still exhausted, yet unable to fall back asleep. He got up, poured himself a glass of water and took his steroid.

That the dream had felt horribly real did not surprise him. If he'd had to summarise his relationship with his father over the past decade, then it basically did boil down to a series of awkward lunches. But when he looked back, Gabriel was never sure why this had been the case. Ever since he was a child, their relationship had been conducted mostly at a distance, but he couldn't remember it being such a challenge in the beginning. He used to talk to his father on the phone, as a teenager and at university, and it had never struck him as a particularly daunting task. It was only after he'd graduated and taken his first job in the City that their relationship entered a more difficult phase.

At first, this was mostly a matter of logistics. Gabriel left for work before six every morning, and wouldn't get home until ten in the evening. At the weekends, he had to attend to all the mundane tasks that kept his life ticking over – going to the dry-cleaners, shopping, getting his hair cut – while at the same time trying to catch up on all that missed sleep. So when could he possibly find time to talk on the phone? The trouble was that people who didn't work in the City could not comprehend what life in the City was like. When you told them that you worked an eighty-hour week, minimum, they simply refused to believe it.

This was certainly the impression Gabriel got from his father, and after a while, it did start to grate. Gabriel suspected that there was an element of disappointment, too. He knew his father had always hoped that he'd pursue a career in politics. If Gabriel had been working round the clock in Westminster rather than Canary Wharf, his father might have been prepared to cut him a little more slack.

But Gabriel's new timetable was not up for debate. As a graduate investment banker, on a two-year provisional contract, he could not afford to take any time off – not if he hoped to progress. This was why the occasional weekend lunch was the only realistic option. If his father was down in London on some other business, it was not out of the question that Gabriel might manage to see him for a couple of hours. Yet when he suggested this, in an email, his father seemed to think he was making a joke.

Nevertheless, when the two of them did meet up for the first time in London, Gabriel was hopeful that things would be easier. He saw it as an opportunity to make a real impression – to give his father a better appreciation of how hard he worked, and how successful he was becoming.

With this in mind, he booked a table at a swanky new restaurant in the City. It was on the thirty-eighth floor of one of the steel-and-glass towers on Bishopsgate – sky-high dining with prices to match. Despite the cost, Gabriel resolved to be intensely relaxed about the whole affair, to show that this was just how his life was now and it was no big deal. He also thought that this attitude would help his father, who might otherwise feel a little out of place.

It didn't work. For some reason neither man could relax, and from the outset the conversation felt forced and dissatisfying. Whatever common ground Gabriel and his father had once shared, it was evident that a vast gulf now separated their existences, and the ultra-modern City setting only served to exacerbate this. Even before the main course had been brought out, Gabriel found himself repeatedly checking his watch, and it was a gesture that his father was quick to comment on.

'Is there somewhere else you need to be?' he asked

'Sorry. Force of habit,' Gabriel told him. 'I'm so used to having to micromanage my schedule, sometimes I find it hard to switch off.'

It was completely true, yet, like so much else in that lunch, it struck an artificial note.

But worse was to come when the bill arrived. Naturally, Gabriel had assumed he would pay for everything, but his father seemed deeply uncomfortable with this notion. He kept repeating the absurd idea that he wanted it to be 'his treat'. Gabriel tried to diffuse the situation with a mixture of decisiveness and gentle humour: he slapped his credit card on the table with a hearty laugh and said:

'It's fine, Dad, really. I think I probably earn a tad more than you do these days.'

It was a line that would have gone down well on the trading floor, where that sort of mock-serious one-upmanship was common currency, but Gabriel could tell straight away that his father was offended. It was only later that he understood why this might be the case. His salary wasn't vastly superior to his father's at this point – he'd started at BarCap on sixty thousand basic, with a bonus that was never going to surpass the low five-figure mark, however well he performed. By City standards, he was a low earner, especially when you considered the hours he worked. But he still had a starting salary that was more than his father had achieved in a thirty-year career. Gabriel could see, in hindsight, how this could provoke a certain amount of embarrassment – or even resentment.

Unfortunately, the gap between their pay-packets was never going to get any smaller, and that first lunch pretty much set the theme for every one that was to follow. The restaurants got more and more expensive, as did Gabriel's clothes and haircuts, but the basic atmosphere was always the same. Gabriel had hoped that his father would eventually adapt to his new and improved circumstances, but it never happened; and increasingly Gabriel felt unwilling, and unable, to make any concessions regarding his own behaviour. He wasn't going to slum it in *Pizza Express* just because his father had an aversion to Michelin stars. Why should he?

The truth was that after that first meal, Gabriel struggled to remember the specifics of all the rest. They tended to blur into a messy collage of false smiles and stilted discussions about the economy. The only other lunch he recalled in detail was the last one, which must have happened in 2007 or 2008. That was the occasion when he had decided to take along his then 'girlfriend' – a decision that, before the event, seemed perfectly reasonable.

The woman he was seeing was a personal trainer, and she was awful in almost every way imaginable. Gabriel understood that it probably wasn't normal to have such a low opinion of the woman you were sleeping with, but he found he couldn't help himself. Aside from her body, which was fantastic, there was very little to like.

She was called Zara – even her name was terrible – and she advertised herself as a 'trainer/exercise guru to the rich and famous'. Gabriel had never heard of any of the people she claimed as clients, but she still insisted on talking about them incessantly. She talked too much full stop. After a few weeks together, Gabriel had actually taken to gagging her in bed, under the pretence that it was a long-held fetish; and had he been able to extend this practice beyond the bedroom, their relationship would have been greatly improved.

Despite all this, the logic of taking her to lunch with his father was obvious. She would act as a sort of shield, for a start, protecting him from the ordeal of two more hours alone with his father. And with Zara present, there were unlikely to be any silences. Best of all, it didn't matter if she found the experience as unpleasant and awkward as he generally did. Gabriel couldn't have cared less.

Of course, as it turned out, having Zara there just added a whole new dimension of horror. Halfway through the meal, while she was telling his father an anecdote about a new protein drink she'd discovered, Gabriel resolved that this would be the last of the lunches. Neither he nor his father was getting anything out of the ritual – that much was painfully obvious.

Better just to stop it dead.

Four years down the line, in the 4 a.m. gloom of an apartment his father had never seen, Gabriel had no intention of reviving the mistakes of the past. He was not going to set up another lunch with his father, and he certainly had no intention of telling him about the tumour.

The attempt would be futile. He didn't need a dream to tell him that.

25

A Left-Wing Rant

Gabriel wasn't a man who left the office unless he had a legitimate reason for doing so. He left the office if he had a scheduled lunch meeting. He left the office if it was after 7.30 p.m., or 6.45 on a Friday. He left the office, usually, if the fire alarm went off. He did not leave the office just because he needed some fresh air. Or not before today. He'd worked at Mason Wallace for seven years, but this was certainly new territory.

He'd taken his second steroid of the day, washed down with his second espresso. But, afterwards, he still felt half-asleep. So he went to the toilet to splash some cold water on his face.

It was when he exited the toilet that things began to go awry. He should have taken a right; instead he turned left.

He found himself walking, rather briskly, past cubicles of underlings, past the receptionist, down four flights of stairs and out into St Paul's Churchyard.

It was cold, and Gabriel was wearing neither his suit jacket nor his coat.

At no point did he feel as if he had made the decision to be standing here like this. It was, self-evidently, not the sort of decision he would have made. Which led him to conclude that it must have been the tumour. The tumour had made a bad decision on his behalf, and, for now, it seemed to have no intention of letting him go back up to his desk.

There was some sort of speech happening on the steps of St Paul's. A man with long hair and a thick face of stubble, about Gabriel's age, was bellowing into a megaphone. Gabriel couldn't hear much from this distance, but whatever the man was saying, it seemed to be going down well with the crowd of three hundred or so that had gathered at his feet.

Gabriel – or more likely the tumour – decided to take a closer look.

He was still sufficiently himself to feel a strong sense of paranoia as he threaded his way through the camp and towards the assembled mob. He was painfully conscious of how good he looked, in contrast to everyone else out there. His trousers and shirt had been hand-tailored by Desmond Merrion and were part of a suit that had cost him thirty thousand pounds. Of course, it was unlikely that anyone in the crowd would be capable of recognising a thirty-thousand-pound suit, but still; his clothing was clearly not that of the average office drone. Fortunately, everyone's eyes seemed fixed on the speaker, and Gabriel was able to join the back of the crowd without attracting any attention. Once there, he removed his tie and put it in his trouser pocket, while at the same time trying to work out what the speaker was saying that had got his audience so riled up.

'. . . that's what we've been fed continually for the past year. *We're all in this together*. Well, I'm sorry, Mr Cameron, but that's not the way we see things. It's not the way things are.'

A chorus of jeers and catcalls erupted in the crowd. The speaker waited for them to dissipate before continuing.

'"The price of this financial crisis is being borne by people who absolutely did not cause it." These aren't my words. They're what Mervyn King, Governor of the Bank of England, told the Treasury Select Committee earlier this year. And I don't think anyone could accuse Mr King of being particularly radical in his outlook. You do not have to be a radical to hold these views; the evidence speaks for itself. The men who caused this crisis have held on to their bonuses. They've held on to their six-figure pensions. Meanwhile, it's our public services that are being stripped back, our wages that are plummeting, our taxes that have been stolen!'

There was spontaneous applause at this point – applause in which Gabriel felt obliged to participate. He didn't want to stand out from the crowd; and, anyway, he was a taxpayer too. That he paid as little as he could get away with was a moot point. In absolute terms, he was willing to bet he'd contributed more to the bailout than anyone else in that crowd.

'The plain fact,' the speaker continued, 'is that we are not all in this together. We are paying, they are not. And when you examine the realities of our political system, it's not difficult to see why.

'Let's start with the Conservative party. Over half of its funding comes from the financial sector – bankers, hedge funds and private equity. If the Tories were a corporation, then the City would be the majority shareholder. So we don't have to look very far to see who's really cracking the whip here. Not that I'd imagine they have to crack it very hard.

'Increasingly, we are ruled by a wealthy elite whose interests are *not* the interests of the ninety-nine per cent. Two-thirds of our current Cabinet ministers are millionaires. They own an estimated seventy million between them and, in many cases, this wealth has simply been inherited, passed down from even richer parents. We have a Prime Minister, a Chancellor and a Mayor of London who were all members of the Bullingdon Club. They operate in a different world from the rest of us, a world where the fate of our public health service and state schools are wholly irrelevant. Let me ask you this: when do you think George Osborne last set foot in a public library? How many of *his* friends and family are going to be affected by the spending cuts he's now enacting?

'Our country is in a political mire. But the truth is that this can't be pinned on the decisions of just a few over-privileged and self-serving ministers. The real problems we face are systemic, and they operate right across the party-political divide. If you look at what has happened in Parliament over the past fifteen years, you begin to see how finance and big business has infiltrated almost every area of Westminster. We've had scandal after scandal – cash for honours, cash for questions, cash for access. The lobbying industry – which is often little more than legalised cash for access – is now worth an estimated two billion pounds per year. Meanwhile, the relationship between the City and Whitehall is getting ever cosier, and the revolving door has never spun faster. We have an increasing number of politicians, ex-prime ministers included, walking out of Parliament and straight into million-pound consultancies – at the same banks that ruined our economy and were then allowed to raid our Treasury. We have a small army of civil servants and special advisors moving back and forth between government and the industries they supposedly regulate. We have private accountants who are sent into HMRC to advise on tax policy, then return to their parent companies to advise the multinationals on how to avoid paying tax!'

This last sentence was screamed down the megaphone, prompting a new wave of fury in the audience. Gabriel attempted to look suitably scandalised.

'The point,' the speaker shouted, 'is this: we cannot and should not expect change to come from within this morally bankrupt system.'

There was a roar of general approval.

'One of the questions now being raised – in the City and in Parliament – is whether or not this camp, this occupation, is a *legal* form of demonstration. And there are no prizes for guessing what their conclusion will be. Because at this moment in time, the law is not designed to protect *us*. It is designed to protect the rich and the powerful. If you want to know why the cost of this crisis is not being borne by the people who caused it, this is the simple answer. The law is on their side. It protects their bonuses, their pensions, their privilege. And our politicians have no intention of changing this. *They* are all in this together, and that's something *we* have to change.'

Gabriel didn't know if this was the end or not. But he had heard enough. He was now the only person not clapping, and if he stayed too long, someone was bound to pick up on this fact.

He slipped out from the back of the crowd and went back to his desk.

The Two-Thousand-Pound
Massage

Gabriel had long held the suspicion that sex, at its core, was always a financial transaction. It was something that women sold and men bought, regardless of how you chose to dress it up. If you wanted to reduce matters to their simplest economic terms, there was no mystery why this should be the case; it was just supply and demand. Demand for sex was always greater than supply. There was a finite pool of attractive, fertile women, and a lot of very thirsty men ready to bid for them.

If you weren't paying for sex upfront, then you were paying for it in other ways. You bought drinks or dinner. You sacrificed your time going to the cinema or, worse, the theatre – all for the sake of sex. There was no other reason a heterosexual man would choose to go to the theatre.

Because of these obvious facts, Gabriel found that using prostitutes was a far more honest way of conducting one's sex life. It was actually the market economy working at its brilliant best. For a mutually acceptable fee, Gabriel got sex – delivered to a consistent, professional standard – with no complications or entanglements. And the woman got generously remunerated. Hell, most of these women, working at the high end of the market, had a lifestyle that any girl in her early twenties should be envious of. They earned more per hour than most doctors or lawyers. They were treated to the finest food and wine and clothes that life had to offer. Because often you'd start in a restaurant or bar or casino, and in this respect it wasn't that dissimilar to regular dating. The only major difference was that the preamble was no longer a necessity – it was a choice, a pleasurable bonus for both parties. And, actually, when you got down to it, there was no doubt that the sex was also something that these women *did* enjoy. Or they did with Gabriel; he was under no illusions about that. He treated them with respect and courtesy. He was a handsome man, and a more than competent lover. These were the facts of the matter – plain and indisputable. So, by any standard, these girls were getting a pretty sweet deal.

That night, the night before the CyberKnife, Gabriel would not take Melissa out to a restaurant or casino, even though this had been a vague thought in his original plan. As much as he didn't want to be on his own that evening, he also found the idea of being anywhere busy – anywhere other than his apartment – tiring and confusing. But he'd booked Melissa for five hours, from eight until one, and unfortunately there was no way he could spend all this time fucking. Even in the best of circumstances – fit, healthy and on cocaine – he would have struggled. So the key to this evening, Gabriel had decided, was a very slow build-up – conversation, several glasses of wine, a sensual massage to relax him – followed by half an hour of frantic, obliterating sex. After that, he'd hopefully be too tired to think.

He'd fall asleep with Melissa beside him, then she could let herself out in the middle of the night. As plans went, this seemed a good one.

Gabriel left the office early – 6.42 – and was back home by 7.05. He spent twenty minutes in the gym working on his deltoids, just to get his blood pumping, and then headed back upstairs to shower and change.

Melissa knocked on his door at eight o'clock exactly. She was impeccably dressed in heels and a midnight-blue evening dress. Under this, as per Gabriel's instructions, she would be wearing a black basque with see-through panelling.

Melissa was twenty-four years old – or that was the age she claimed to be. She might well have been in her late twenties, but Gabriel was willing to forgive this small deception – not uncommon in women at the older end of the high-class market. She was a brunette – since Gabriel had sworn off blondes after the Catherine debacle – and her body was sensational. Though, really, that went without saying. You could buy a perfect body for as little as two hundred pounds an hour. It was everything else – the poise, the elegance, the ability to hold an intelligent conversation – that you paid a premium for. Of course, a cynic would have said that you were paying the extra money in order to normalise the transaction, to make it seem something other than what it was. But Gabriel was not a cynic. He knew that when you paid more, you got more. In this sense, premium sex was the same as premium anything. It was the same as buying a really good suit. You didn't pay top dollar for something generic; you paid for something that was made to measure.

Melissa was educated. She read *The Times* and the *Financial Times*. She knew about wine and fashion, travel and current affairs. She had opinions – good opinions – on the EU and corporation tax and government spending. She was extremely easy to talk to on a wide range of subjects, and for the next hour or so, talk was all they did. The lights were dimmed, the vintage champagne was being kept at a constant 9°C in the electric cooler. Melissa sat next to Gabriel on the black leather sofa, her head tilted attentively. Every so often, she flicked her hair from her eyes, or ran her long fingers slowly down the stem of her champagne flute. It was all very calculated, of course, but Gabriel had no objection to that. These little flirtations were essential to the build-up – a continual reminder of the incredible sex they would soon be having.

After her second glass of champagne, she told him she was going to the bathroom to freshen up. Gabriel stripped down to his Armani underwear, then lay on his front on the bed, waiting for Melissa to join him.

Moments later, he felt the gentle weight of her buttocks as she straddled his thighs and started working the well-defined muscles of his upper back and shoulders. She took her time, her fingers exerting a soft, languorous pressure as they made their steady descent down Gabriel's torso.

It was only when she started to nuzzle into his neck that Gabriel realised something was terribly wrong. He felt comfortable and relaxed, but that was *all* he felt. Melissa had started to suck gently on one of his earlobes. He could feel the fabric of her basque and suspenders rubbing against his bare skin. And he was entirely flaccid.

With this insight, Gabriel stopped feeling comfortable and relaxed. Melissa, meanwhile, remained blissfully unaware of the problem. She had wrapped one arm round his stomach; her hand was already reaching below his waistband.

Then she hesitated. It was the briefest hesitation imaginable, just a flicker of a pause, but for Gabriel, that was enough. He knew in that instant the situation was unrecoverable. And after a minute or so of increasingly inventive manipulations, Melissa withdrew her hand and pushed gently against his side. He didn't want to roll over – eye contact was the last thing he wanted – but he didn't see any other option. Melissa took his hand and placed it on her perfect breasts, the undersides of which were visible through the see-through panelling of her basque. She was still smiling, of course, but it was now a smile that hovered in some uncertain territory between seduction and encouragement.

'Um . . .' Gabriel couldn't find any words to mitigate his humiliation.

'Maybe you'd like to watch something?' Melissa purred.

In the circumstances, this was not a helpful suggestion. Gabriel did not want to watch something. The thought of watching other people having sex was, for once, extremely unappealing. 'Actually, I'm not feeling all that . . . great. It's . . .' Gabriel withdrew his hand from Melissa's breasts. 'You see, I've been put on this medication for . . . migraines, and I'm not really supposed to drink at the moment—'

'It's fine. Honestly, it's OK. It happens.'

This was a kind thing to say, but Gabriel would have bet a lot of money that it did not happen very often with Melissa. Possibly, this was a first.

'I'm tired,' he told her. 'I've been working some insane hours recently.'

'Would you like me to go?'

Gabriel didn't say anything.

'Or I can stay, if you prefer?'

'Thank you, Melissa. I know it's a strange request, but would you mind just staying until I'm asleep?'

'I've had stranger requests, believe me.'

'I don't think it will be long. You can let yourself out afterwards.'

Melissa smiled, and somehow it seemed a much warmer smile than before. For a heartbeat, Gabriel considered telling her about the tumour. But if there was a moment when this felt feasible, it passed very swiftly.

They settled under the covers and Melissa curled her body into his. Weirdly, this did not seem such a strange thing to be doing.

Gabriel fell asleep breathing the warm scent of her hair; and knowing that when he awoke, in a few hours' time, he would be alone.

Under the CyberKnife

Gabriel had a dilemma. On the one hand, he really didn't want to tell Armitage about his erectile dysfunction. On the other, there was no one else he *could* tell, and he had no intention of spending his last six months unnecessarily impotent. There was a likelihood, he thought, that this might be yet another side effect, from either the medication or the tumour itself. And if that were the case, then Armitage, as his doctor – his extremely well-paid doctor – had a duty to find and prescribe a remedy. Granted, it had only been the once, but that was once too often as far as Gabriel was concerned. The notion that he might have to repeat yesterday's catastrophe was simply unacceptable.

In the end, he decided that the humiliation of having to discuss this matter was outweighed by the potential humiliation of having to go through it again. And, anyway, Armitage had asked him for an update on his progress. There was never going to be a less awful time to broach the subject.

So Gabriel gave the shortest possible summary of the problem, and then spent considerably longer explaining that this had never, ever happened before. This detail was clearly important, since it provided strong evidence that this was a short-term difficulty, most likely with a simple medical cause. But for some reason, Armitage seemed reluctant to endorse this view.

'I'd think it more likely that there are a range of factors under-lying the, er, problem,' he told Gabriel. 'I mean, it's perfectly understandable, given the circumstances. You're under consid-erable stress, and it's not uncommon for chemotherapy to affect one's mood and energy levels. Really it's—'

'I want you to prescribe something,' Gabriel interrupted. 'I don't find any part of this understandable. It's never happened before and I don't want it to happen again.'

'No, of course not, but . . .' Armitage cleared his throat deli-cately. 'Mr Vaughn, have you spoken to your partner about these concerns?'

'My partner –' Gabriel decided it was easier to go along with Armitage's terminology '– is aware of the problem, obviously.'

'No, I think you misunderstand me. What I meant was, if you talked to your partner then I'm sure he or she would—'

'She! She's a she. She's called Melissa.'

'OK. And I assume that Melissa does . . . she does know about your situation?'

Gabriel felt a hot bubble of irritation rising in his stomach. 'Listen, Armitage, I'm going to level with you. Melissa is a pros-titute. Our relationship is sexual. That's all it is. And I'm not paying you to interrogate me. I just want a simple solution to a simple problem.'

This statement had its intended effect. Armitage almost imme-diately started tapping away at the computer, and a few moments later a prescription had been printed and signed. But before

Armitage handed it over, he also took a small card from his desk drawer. On it was printed a woman's name, telephone number and email.

'Mr Vaughn, my considered opinion is that you really would benefit from talking to someone – preferably a counsellor – about the issues you're facing right now. You're free to ignore this advice, of course, but you should at least think about it. That's all I'm going to say on the matter.'

Gabriel took the card and prescription and put them in his wallet.

Fifteen minutes later, a technician was positioning him on a strange, cantilevered platform under the CyberKnife. Everything was white. The whole room and its equipment looked like part of a science fiction film.

Gabriel lay on his back as the robotic arm started to move, as if of its own accord, until it was positioned a foot or so from his right temple. He could see what looked like the barrel of a gun out of the corner of his eye.

'OK, Mr Vaughn,' the technician said. 'We're ready to start. You don't need to worry about any small movements – the machine will adjust for them. But other than that, you should try to remain as still and relaxed as possible.'

Gabriel kept his eyes wide open, staring at the featureless ceiling. There was a small humming noise, no louder than the hum of a refrigerator. And with that, a highly concentrated beam of radiation was fired into his head.

PART 2

Emotional Liability

Futility

Gabriel felt no better. If anything, he felt worse, and this was despite Armitage's assurance that the procedure had been a success. Gabriel had seen the before and after scan images, had listened to the neuro-oncologist's painstaking explanation of *what* he was seeing: a reduction of the tumour by around eighty-five per cent. He was bone-tired after the radiosurgery, but that was only to be expected. Give it a few days, he was told, and some of the symptoms would likely start to abate.

So he had been back at the office Monday morning, still guarding his 6.20 slot. By the end of the day, he had managed to fill his bin with empty coffee cups. Nicola had been down to Starbucks so many times she was complaining of blisters.

'You should wear more appropriate shoes,' Gabriel told her.

'And you should reacquaint yourself with my job description,' Nicola snapped. 'I'm not your personal waitress. Honestly, Gabriel, I've learned to tolerate a lot working for you, but there are limits.'

In spite of his caffeine intake, Gabriel still fell asleep on three

different occasions. Fortunately, this was always in the privacy
of his own office, but he also came perilously close in a late-
afternoon stock presentation, and knew that without a more
drastic intervention a public embarrassment was all but inevitable.
So, the next day, he started taking cocaine. Not a lot – a line
before meetings, or when he needed to read a long report – just
enough to keep him functioning. To any outside observer, he
was sure he was back to his normal self – decisive, focussed and
confident. And in private, when the drug began to wear off, he
felt increasingly like a zombie.

When the exhaustion did begin to recede, it was replaced only
by a feeling of profound hollowness. Or perhaps futility would
be the more accurate term. Before the CyberKnife, Gabriel had
envisaged his tumour as a sort of parasite living in his head, and
imagined that as this invader was weakened, his native strength
would swell. Of course, he knew that there was no cure for him.
He knew that the 'success' of his surgery would be measured in
months rather than years. The fraction of the tumour that
remained would immediately start to regrow. But, still, shouldn't
there be some temporary respite? If eighty-five per cent of the
problem was gone, why didn't he feel even ten per cent better?

The truth was that Gabriel lacked the emotional vocabulary
to grasp exactly what was happening to him in the aftermath of
the radiosurgery. The closest he could come, at the moment,
was to think about a time in school when he'd scraped all the
skin off his right kneecap during a rugby match. That injury –
the incredible rawness of flayed flesh – could be compared with
how he felt now. It was as if an outer layer of himself had been
peeled back, leaving something too sensitive to touch.

Being at work, while feeling like the emotional equivalent of an open wound, was not easy. But *not* being at work, Gabriel found, was even worse. Now more than ever, the weekends were something to be dreaded. All that staring empty time. Before, he would have found something obliterating to fill it. He would have gone for a fast, purposeless drive in his Ferrari, or phoned Shipman to arrange a round of golf. He would have booked a couple of hours with Melissa. But right now, driving was out of the question, as was swinging a golf club; and even with Armitage's Viagra, Gabriel wasn't sure he'd be able to sustain an erection. He wasn't sure he'd be able to sustain consciousness.

The first Saturday after the CyberKnife, he managed to sleep in until 10 a.m., but that proved to be his limit. He watched CNN for a couple of hours, then drank half a glass of wine, then vomited into his kitchen sink.

After he'd brushed his teeth, he phoned for a taxi to come and remove him from his apartment. He told the woman on the other end of the line that he was booking on behalf of a Russian client who spoke no English, so on no account should the driver attempt to speak to him. When the woman asked where his client wanted to go, Gabriel told her the first place that came into his head: St Paul's Cathedral.

The Light of the World

Gabriel had worked opposite St Paul's for seven years, but he had never been inside. Now seemed a good time to change this.

He had read about the cathedral reopening a week ago, through the fog of post-surgery exhaustion. Church officials feared that visitors – families and parties of schoolchildren in particular – would be kept away by ongoing safety concerns surrounding the Occupy camp. Since Gabriel liked neither families nor school-children, this suited him perfectly.

But when he stepped inside, he was disappointed to see that the media or the Church, or both, had seemingly overstated the issue. Of course, he didn't know how many people would visit St Paul's on an average Saturday at the beginning of November, but to his eyes, there seemed no shortage of attendees. He found himself joining an admissions queue in which he was sandwiched between a large group of French teenagers – the schoolchildren who were meant to be staying away – and an insufferably lower-middle-class couple who were grumbling about the modest entrance fee. Presumably, they thought the state should pay for their sightseeing.

It was then that Gabriel realised this was perhaps the worst time to visit the cathedral. Because the truth was obvious: these people – the middle-class lefties, the French – were exactly the sort who'd have no objection to finding themselves in the midst of an anarchist protest movement. For them, it was a bonus.

But by the time Gabriel had reached this conclusion, he was already at the ticket desk, and he had no intention of turning round. The thought of being here, among people he hated, was still marginally better than being at home, by himself.

Once inside the main part of the cathedral, he took a sharp left to get away from the French school party and found himself walking, rather briskly, towards the rear of the building. There was, Gabriel felt, a lot of contradiction in the interior architecture of St Paul's. Yes, the stonework – the vast columns and statues – was impressive, as were the stained-glass windows, but there was something really quite tacky about the chequerboard tiling of the floor. And the less said about the seating the better. In place of pews, there were rows of cheap stackable chairs. Bare wood on tubular metal frames – chairs so aesthetically unappealing it could only be deliberate, a kind of homage to austerity.

Gabriel had no idea how to sightsee, but he soon became aware that he was trying to do it far too quickly. He was walking at a normal London pace, while everyone else seemed to have slipped into a strange stately glide. On more than one occasion, he was caught off guard when the person ahead of him suddenly stopped without warning to inspect a plaque or engraving. To make matters worse, at least half of the visitors were listening to the audio guide through their headphones, rendering them all but oblivious to the here and now. It was like being repeatedly stuck at the traffic lights behind someone who hadn't noticed they'd turned green. The best course of action, Gabriel soon decided, would be to find the quietest corner of the cathedral and stay there, at least for the time being.

He ended up sitting on a plain wooden bench beside a small altar far to the left of the dome. There was a painting hanging above the altar entitled *The Light of the World*. It depicted a white-robed Jesus carrying a lantern in one hand and knocking at a cottage door, overgrown with weeds, with the other. The inscription below read:

BEHOLD, I STAND AT THE DOOR AND KNOCK; IF ANY MAN HEAR MY VOICE, AND OPEN THE DOOR, I WILL COME IN TO HIM, AND WILL SUP WITH HIM, AND HE WITH ME.

Gabriel stared at the writing for some time, then at the painting again. He was not a fan of art that had to be 'interpreted', so he welcomed the fairly straightforward written exposition of what was going on. Nevertheless, he was still bothered by some of the details of the picture. In particular, he couldn't help but notice that Jesus wasn't carrying any food. So if the householder *did* open the door, he would be the one providing supper.

'It's a remarkable image, isn't it?'

Gabriel turned to see a clergyman – pale, clothed in a floor-length black robe, almost a dress – encroaching on his personal space. Late twenties, at a push, with a Boris Johnson mop of blond hair. Most likely a closeted homosexual – or perhaps not even closeted; it was difficult to keep up with the Church of England's increasingly liberal stance on such things. He had an encouraging smile that Gabriel found as irritating as his unsolicited opinions.

'Actually, it's a very misleading image. Jesus lived in the Middle East – assuming he lived at all.' Gabriel pointed an accusing finger at the ghost-white messiah looming over them. 'He would not have looked anything like this. He would have looked like an Arab.'

Gabriel fixed the young clergyman with the withering stare he usually reserved for the boardroom, expecting this to send him scurrying. But to his annoyance, it seemed to have the opposite effect. The clergyman nodded graciously, his smile never wavering.

'Yes, of course. But every culture paints the divine in its own image. There's African art that depicts Christ as a black man. There's Chinese art that depicts Him as Chinese. It's a question of how we're being asked to relate to what we're shown – of how the artwork speaks to its audience in a specific time and place.'

Gabriel felt outmanoeuvred. More than this, he felt out-bullshitted, which was even worse.

'If you're interested, William Holman Hunt, the artist who painted this piece, is buried in our crypt. There are some beautiful tombs down there.'

'The crypt?' Gabriel narrowed his eyes. 'Where's the crypt?'

The clergyman pointed to the opposite side of the cathedral. 'The stairs are just to the right of the pulpit.'

'Is it quiet in there?' Gabriel demanded.

'Er . . . yes. It's usually quiet. It's . . .' The clergyman laughed, a little nervously. 'Well, it's a crypt.'

Gabriel looked at the clergyman for a few moments with undisguised contempt. Then he got up and walked away.

The Admiral Lord Nelson's Tomb

The crypt was soothingly dark, and as quiet as the gay vicar had promised. But Gabriel had no intention of tracking down William Holman Hunt's tomb. Instead, he headed through the central corridor until he was confronted by two large chambers opening up to the left and right. Signs on the wall informed him that one was the Duke of Wellington's tomb, and the other the Admiral Lord Nelson's. Since it appeared marginally darker, Gabriel opted for the latter. As far as he could see, there was only one other person in the chamber – an old man gazing at the huge sarcophagus that sat on an even huger plinth in the centre of the room. Gabriel moved to the point diametrically opposite to the old man, putting Nelson's final resting place between them, and sat down on some stone steps. Behind him were another tomb and a tall iron fence that separated the Nelson Chamber from the adjoining passageway, the view of which was partially obscured by a line of statues. Gabriel felt pleasantly shut off.

He would continue to feel this way for at least the next three minutes. After that – when the old man came and sat beside him on the steps – he began to wonder if he was inadvertently projecting something, some aura of approachability, of *wanting* to waste his time talking to absolute strangers. Gabriel had a lot of charisma – he knew that – but he could turn it on and off like a light bulb, and he never chose to squander it on people who served no purpose. So why was he now a magnet for lone men with whom he so patently had nothing in common? With the clergyman, Gabriel's physical attractiveness was probably explanation enough. But here a different hypothesis was needed. Judging from the old man's slightly twitchy demeanour, Gabriel's first assumption was that he was mentally ill; and this notion seemed validated the moment he opened his mouth.

'He suffered from seasickness, you know. All his life.'

Apropos of nothing.

Gabriel tilted his head and stared at the old man for several seconds. His face looked as if it had partially melted, with the skin that should have been pulled taut across his cheekbones now hanging like putty from his jaw. He had sunken eyes and liver spots. Gabriel estimated his age to be at least eighty – two and a half times older than Gabriel would ever be. Not that there was much to envy here. The old man might have stepped straight out of a painting entitled *Mortality*. As for his words, either he was suffering from dementia and continuing a conversation that he'd started some time ago in his own head, or he was talking about Nelson. Gabriel decided to give him the benefit of the doubt.

'He also had one arm and one eye,' he replied.

'No, no. That's a small misconception,' the old man rasped.

'He had both his eyes, but he was blinded in the right one in 1794, by shrapnel from an exploding sandbag. He lost his right arm three years later in the battle of Santa Cruz de Tenerife. A musket ball shattered his humerus while his fleet was attempting to take the town. The ship's surgeon had no choice but to amputate, with nothing but brandy for an anaesthetic. Three crewmen held Nelson down, the arm was removed and flung into the Atlantic Ocean, and he was back commanding his troops within half an hour.'

'Oh.' This was not the first word that came to mind, but even Gabriel couldn't bring himself to swear in front of a man who was essentially a walking corpse. Anyway, the story was compelling enough that he wanted to hear the ending. 'So what happened next? Was the town taken?'

'No, unfortunately not. Nelson had an astonishing record in command, but this particular battle was an unqualified disaster. A quarter of his men were lost, the fleet was repelled, and Nelson spent the next six months recuperating in England.'

'Six months?' Gabriel looked back to the huge sarcophagus containing Nelson's remains, minus his arm. 'Didn't he think of calling it a day at that point? I mean, first the eye, then the arm – seems like he was getting some strong signals about where his career was likely to end.'

'Yes, he considered it,' the old man wheezed. 'But for some, the fear of no longer being of any use is far worse than the fear of death. That was certainly true for Nelson. After he lost his arm, his biggest worry was that he would not be deemed fit for service. But his fear of death was greatly diminished. He developed what we'd now call a phantom limb; he still had sensations in his missing arm. He took this as concrete evidence that some part of Man's essence transcended the body: the flesh could die, but the soul lived on.'

Gabriel snorted humourlessly. 'Yes. It's a shame it was just his brain playing tricks on him.'

'You're not a believer?'

'No, I'm not.' Gabriel kept his eyes fixed on the sarcophagus. 'If you look at the way the world is, I don't think there's much room for a benevolent creator. And the soul's just a fiction – a comfort blanket for those who can't handle reality.'

'You're young to have such a cynical outlook.'

'It's not an outlook,' Gabriel told him. 'It's the way things are.'

The old man didn't say anything for a few moments, and when he spoke, he'd apparently decided to ignore this last observation. '"God and my country." Those were Nelson's final words, reputedly.'

Gabriel turned to look at him. 'How did he die?'

'He took a bullet in the spine from a French sharpshooter. When he was brought back to England for burial there were five days of public mourning.' The old man rose ponderously to his feet. 'These days the cathedral hires this room out as a drinks venue. Corporate functions. Can you believe that?'

'Yes,' Gabriel said. 'Very easily.'

The old man gave a small shrug of disapproval, then started to shuffle away. But before he'd reached the sarcophagus, he turned and held Gabriel's eye for a few moments. 'Man can't live without a purpose,' he said.

Gabriel didn't reply. He didn't want to say anything that might deter the old man from leaving.

Exit via the Gift Shop

The exit of the crypt funnelled Gabriel into a brightly lit vault, which, it turned out, housed the café and gift shop. It should have marked a return to a world he understood – a world designed and run according to the all-pervasive profit motive. But, for some reason, the transition felt strange and jarring, like waking up in an unfamiliar bed. After the stillness of the tomb, his senses refused to readjust to the sudden clamour that enveloped him, a jumble of voices, faces and trajectories. Children were being ferried to the toilets by their beleaguered guardians. Coffees and pastries were being served across a narrow counter. An overflow of statues – angels, soldiers, semi-nudes; vaguely hallucinatory – stood like sentinels guarding the rotating postcard display. At the same time, Gabriel had to contend with the competing bustle in his head, which had been infected with a sprawling fungus of Nelson trivia: exploding sandbags, a phantom limb, five days of public mourning. As he threaded his way towards another exit sign, pointing to the stairs at the far end of the room, he couldn't help but wonder how many people would mourn his own passing. His father, he supposed, by default. Mason, from a purely financial perspective. Melissa, ditto. That was the sum total. Since death was death, and the hereafter a childish fantasy, this really should not have mattered.

And yet it did.

Was it just ego, this desire to attach a shared significance to his death? The truth, he knew, was that no one else's life would be very much changed by the ending of his – just as he would have greeted the news of a colleague's sudden demise with little more than idle curiosity. When Gabriel attempted to list the people whose deaths might actually affect him, his mind was almost entirely blank. For some reason, the only person he thought he might miss was Nicola; and he couldn't convince himself that this vaguest of pangs was anything to do with Nicola herself, as opposed to the steady stream of refreshments she provided.

He ascended the stairs alone, exiting St Paul's by the side door that faced out onto Paternoster Square. The echoes from the catacombs faded to nothing, and as he staggered out into the pale November sunshine, a fanfare of soaring strings rose to greet him.

Philip Glass's Violin Concerto, Second Movement

At first, Gabriel was sure he was delusional, that somewhere between the basement and ground level he'd tripped and fallen into the chasm that separates mental distress from all-out mental breakdown. His brain had been on the blink for weeks, and now it had entered a new phase of fucked. This made considerably more sense than the alternative: that the streets outside St Paul's had become mysteriously and classically soundtracked.

But thirty seconds later, the strings were still there, still soaring. The sound was coming from somewhere off to his left. Not from the camp, obviously – they had guitars and bongos aplenty – but, so far as Gabriel knew, no string section.

He hesitated just a moment before going to investigate, feeling very much that he had no choice in the matter, as if he were being pulled along by an invisible thread. Round the corner, there was a small crowd – maybe thirty or forty – gathered at the bottom of the cathedral's steps, and beyond this, on the third or fourth step up, was a woman playing a violin. Just one woman.

Gabriel spent some moments looking for the rest of them, before realising, belatedly, that there was no rest of them. All that sound was coming from a solo electric violin, hooked up to a small amplifier via a row of pedals. Every so often, the woman would tap one of the pedals with the toe of her shoe and another layer of music would be added.

Usually, standing in close proximity to strangers was something Gabriel would only tolerate in a bar queue, but now he stood fixated. He had the sensation of being lifted, of pent-up anxiety diminishing to barely more than a pinprick in some distant corner in his mind. He thought, at first, that it must be the woman herself; except, on further consideration, this made very little sense. Yes, she was young – perhaps a few years younger than he was – and moderately pretty. But certainly nothing to shout about. Her hair was a sort of unremarkable mousey brown. Her skin was too pale, her eyebrows slightly too thick. Minor blemishes, but still. If, on the universal scale of attractiveness, Gabriel was a ten – which he was – then she was no more than a seven; seven and a half at a push.

And yet he could not take his eyes off her. There was something about the music – it had to be the music – that kept him rooted to the spot. Of course, Gabriel couldn't have begun to articulate what the music was doing on a technical level – only on a medical level. Because it felt as if someone had reached into his head, seized the part of his brain responsible for his emotional liability, and started to squeeze.

He had no idea how much time had passed when the last note was played; all he knew was that he wanted more, and it seemed he was not alone. The growing crowd – there were now people behind Gabriel as well as in front of him – had started to applaud loudly. There was also a fair amount of whooping coming from the direction of the camp.

'Thank you.' The violinist flashed a smile, then gave a playful ballet curtsey. 'That was Pachelbel's Canon in D major; the perfect remedy for a cold November day. And next up is the second movement of Philip Glass's Violin Concerto – which I'd like to dedicate to anyone who slept in a tent last night.' This provoked a chorus of cheers off to Gabriel's right. The mousey violinist smiled again, raising her bow like a sabre. 'Solidarity, brothers and sisters.' She said this with a sort of faux-ironic inflection, which made Gabriel feel like he was missing a joke. But he found that he didn't care. He just wanted her to start playing again.

Which she did.

It was as before – starting with just a few looped notes, then building layer by layer until there was a whole ghost orchestra weaving a tapestry of music. Emotionally, however, this piece was very different. Up to this point in his life, Gabriel had never understood why musicians sometimes played with their eyes closed, thinking it some awful artsy affectation. Now, though, he did understand. He didn't know how this was possible, but there were individual notes in Philip Glass's Violin Concerto that actually seemed to *ache*. It wasn't sadness, exactly – more an indescribable sense of longing, of stretching for something a hair's breadth out of reach.

Gabriel didn't start crying, but he thought he was close a couple of times. Despite this, he made no attempt to leave. The violinist's movements were too hypnotic, the music too unnervingly beautiful. For however long it lasted, he was spellbound, and it was only when the last echoes of the violin had dissipated that escape became a plausible option.

Over the next several weeks, there would be plenty of occasions when Gabriel revisited this scene, feeling ever more certain that he should indeed have walked away. But in the moment itself, he found that he could not. There was more applause, more cheering. Several people threw coins into the violin case, which was sitting open on the step below the amplifier. And Gabriel hesitated just long enough for the music to start again. After that, he knew he was going nowhere.

It was another forty minutes before the violinist played her final piece.

'This is my version of Vivaldi's "Winter",' she told the crowd. 'If you like it, then please feel free to contribute to next month's rent.' There were a couple of laughs as she gestured to her violin case with her bow. 'If you really like it, I'll be here same time next weekend, weather permitting. Bring a friend.'

After she'd finished, Gabriel waited until she was busy disconnecting the various pedals, then slipped quickly through the diminishing crowd and dropped a twenty-pound note in the violin case. Then he retreated to the far end of the square.

Ten minutes later, amplifier in one hand, violin case in the other, the woman left the steps of St Paul's and headed down Paternoster Row, the pedestrianised side street that led towards Cheapside.

Gabriel decided to follow her.

Stalking is a very Ugly Word

And this wasn't stalking. Stalking implied repetition, an element of menace and, above all, sinister motives. For Gabriel, this was a one-off. As for his motives, he had no idea – there was obviously no logical reason to be following a violin busker through central London, but that didn't mean he was doing anything particularly immoral.

So why did it feel like he was?

The simplest way to fix this, other than turning round and walking away, would be to catch up with her and start a conversation; walk *with* her rather than behind her. Except, when Gabriel played that scenario in his head, it seemed even creepier – or more visibly creepy, which amounted to the same thing. Plus he didn't think there was anything sensible he could say.

Hi. I'm Gabriel. I don't usually like music, but I have this brain tumour and it's screwed up my emotions, and somehow your open-air violin concert seems to have taken this to a whole new level. Shall we get a coffee and talk about that?

Or he could just offer to carry her amplifier. It didn't look particularly heavy, but it was still cumbersome. The offer would probably appear quite chivalrous. Or it might have done, two minutes ago. Now that they'd walked a couple of hundred metres, the fact that Gabriel had been following her was already implicit, and there were no words or actions to make this seem reasonable.

Consequently, Gabriel thought the safest option was just to continue as he was. As long as he kept his distance, as long as she didn't realise she was being followed, then this was a perfectly victimless crime.

He stayed about twenty metres behind her. This should have been simple, in principle, but it meant that he had to walk at an unnaturally slow pace to avoid closing the gap. The woman wasn't dawdling, but neither did she seem in any particular hurry, and she was encumbered, of course, and at least six inches shorter than him – probably around five foot six. Average height, to go with her not-far-above-average looks. Gabriel's strong preference was for leggy, elegant women – though he supposed this woman's legs could be easily improved with a pair of decent heels, and she had looked very elegant when she'd been playing her violin. But that must have been more to do with the music itself, since he definitely didn't find her attractive outside of this context. If he'd been following her because he found her attractive then that really would have been stalking.

They'd rounded the corner of Paternoster Row and were approaching St Paul's station. Gabriel assumed the woman would be catching the Tube, since this was what average people, with rent worries rather than personal chauffeurs, usually had to do. But she continued past the entrance, so Gabriel continued to follow her, with a strange sense of relief. He hadn't been back on the Tube since the *incident*, and had no intention of doing so now. But it was weirdly enjoyable, following this stranger – Gabriel had to admit that – and it went beyond simple curiosity about who she was and where she was going. More likely, it was the focus this activity required, the reorientation of his attention onto something harmless and trivial. As long as he was following this woman, he didn't have to worry about what he was going to do next.

Gabriel hung back several metres and pretended to check his phone while the woman waited at the pedestrian crossing; then, once they had both made it across the road, he allowed the gap to widen again before he resumed his pursuit. They were heading north along St Martin's Le Grand, and there were fewer tourists here – fewer people to hide among. For this reason, Gabriel made sure that he stayed well back; too far back, it transpired. At the Museum of London roundabout, a bus pulled out in front of him, temporarily blocking both his path and his view of the violinist. It was there for perhaps ten seconds, and when the traffic stated moving again, the woman was gone.

Gabriel crossed the road and kept walking in the direction she'd been heading, but she was nowhere to be seen. But, presumably, if he kept going he might catch her up. She couldn't have gone far.

He walked for another thirty seconds or so before stopping abruptly to take stock of his situation. If he'd been an alcoholic, then this would have been his moment of clarity.

He was standing on a fumy pavement in a fairly unattractive part of central London, trying in vain to locate a woman whom he was following for no good reason, while at the same time causing an obstruction to a large party of American tourists who were now having to bypass him on either side.

Gabriel decided it might be time to phone Armitage's psycho-therapist.

2009 – The Catherine Debacle

She was by far the least qualified and best-looking candidate Gabriel would see that morning; and she wasn't stupid, or not in an academic sense, because she had a 2:1 from UCL. However, that was a 2:1 in some nothing arts subject – English Literature or something like that; Gabriel forgot the details the moment he put her CV down, but he knew it was something of no practical use.

This was completely irrelevant, of course, since he'd decided within five seconds of seeing her that she'd got the job.

Catherine had baby-blue eyes, ash-blond hair, cut just above her shoulders, and a slightly shy smile that nevertheless lit up her face. She looked like Hollywood's absurdly unrepresentative vision of 'the girl next door' – a churchgoing, cookie-baking, be-cardiganed sex bomb whom you couldn't help but mentally undress every moment she was onscreen.

Inevitably, Gabriel was suffering from this same problem as he interviewed her in his office, but he managed to fix his features into an attentive frown as she ran through an elaborate and wholly pointless explanation of how she'd spent the past six months applying for graduate schemes and getting nowhere. The economy was tanking and there were more and more applicants for fewer positions. It was the worst possible time to be trying to start a career, fresh out of university with very little practical experience. Blah blah blah.

Gabriel nodded sympathetically. 'You know, Catherine, I feel for you, I really do. I mean, how old are you? Twenty-one?'

'Twenty-two.'

Gabriel pretended to glance at her CV. 'Right, twenty-two. When I was your age, which wasn't that long ago –' he flashed her a smile that Tom Cruise would have envied '– when I was your age, I was in a very fortunate position. The economy was growing, finance was booming, and I was lucky enough to have the skill set that employers wanted. But things are different these days, I can appreciate that. Actually I feel weirdly responsible for your plight. I mean, it was my sector that caused this mess – or a very irresponsible sub-sector of finance. You should know that here at Mason Wallace we do things very differently.'

'Oh yes, I'm sure.' Catherine nodded earnestly, glancing first at Gabriel, then at Bridget from HR, who had to be present at the interview for some sort of arcane legal reason; Mason had made it clear that she would have minimal involvement in the final hiring decision. 'But I really don't know that much about the financial sector. It's not an area I ever thought I'd be working in.'

Gabriel winked at her. 'You're an intelligent young woman. You'll pick things up in no time.'

Catherine smiled coyly before breaking eye contact. 'In all honesty, I'm not even sure what a hedge fund does.'

'Don't worry. No one is.'

Gabriel risked a quick glance at Bridget, who – no surprises – was scowling. He gave a small shrug, which was in no way intended as an apology. It was a secretarial job, not rocket science. And, anyway, these were stressful times. A face as fresh as Catherine's would be good for office morale.

'I'm not going to lie to you, Catherine. This isn't a very glamorous job. You'll be answering the phone, filing, photocopying. Occasionally, if I'm very busy, I might get you to nip down to Starbucks for me. But the remuneration is very competitive, and there'll be opportunity to progress. If you're ambitious and hardworking, there's no reason this couldn't be the start of a very promising career.'

As soon as Catherine left, Bridget was up in arms. 'Gabriel, this is outrageous. Any one of the previous candidates would be a better choice. You can't hire someone just because you want to sleep with her!'

Gabriel did *not* want to sleep with Catherine; this seemed an unnecessary complication. He just wanted to have sex with her. And had Bridget been one of the guys, he would have felt no qualms about making this important distinction. But as it was, he of course denied her accusation in the strongest possible terms.

'She's not the best person for the job,' Bridget persisted.

Gabriel nodded a few times to show that he was giving Bridget's thoughts on the matter some serious consideration, then completely ignored her.

'Bridget, I think this is one of those issues where we're just going to have to agree to disagree. Thanks for your very valuable input, but I'm making an executive decision. Catherine gets the job. Please get the relevant paperwork sent out ASAP.'

*

It took nine weeks to get Catherine into bed, which seemed painfully slow, but Gabriel was a good judge of character, and he had realised very early on that this was one situation where he'd have no choice but to play the long game. Catherine, unfortunately, was not the sort of girl who was going to have sex with her boss in the first week of a new job – no matter how attractive and charming that boss happened to be. Matters were further complicated when Gabriel discovered that there was a boyfriend lurking somewhere in the wings. Nothing serious, so far as he could tell – they didn't live together – but it was another obstacle that had to be carefully negotiated. Still, he couldn't deny that it made a refreshing change, having to wait for so long. Instant gratification was all well and good, but there was also much to be said for the more measured thrill of the chase.

For weeks, Gabriel kept his flirtations so subtle that it sometimes felt as if he were living in one of those awful costume dramas. After a month, he started dropping the occasional 'Thanks – you're an angel', when she brought him his coffee and pastries; and not long after that, he made a point of touching her – oh-so-casually – on the arm or back whenever he needed her to run an errand.

It soon became apparent that all this groundwork was having its intended effect. Catherine was staying later in the office. Her eyes were lingering on his just that little bit longer. She was continually playing with her hair when they spoke. Then, about seven weeks into the project, she arrived at work one morning looking tired and harassed. When Gabriel asked her if anything was wrong, she revealed that she'd had a 'minor argument' with her boyfriend, who had started to resent the fact that he was seeing less and less of her. Now she was feeling guilty because she thought that he was right; she *was* spending a lot of time at work.

'The hours can be tough here,' Gabriel told her, placing a comforting hand on her shoulder. 'But you certainly shouldn't feel guilty for wanting to do your job well. You're conscientious, and that's a wonderful quality to have. In all honesty, I think your boyfriend's very lucky to have you.'

Catherine blushed the most incredible shade of red, and for the next couple of weeks, the sexual tension in the office was so palpable that Gabriel almost didn't want it to end. But soon after, it was time for the Mason Wallace Christmas party, for which an expensive City wine bar had been hired. Catherine turned up without the boyfriend, and Gabriel kept bringing her glass after glass of champagne, while at the same time imagining how her conversation with the unfortunate other half must have gone. *Oh, it's just a stupid work thing. Honestly, it will be dead boring.*

It was just after midnight when she told him that she thought she'd had 'a little too much to drink'. So Gabriel did the obvious, honourable thing, and suggested that they share a taxi home.

'I'm not sure we're in the same direction,' Catherine slurred.

'No, we're not,' Gabriel agreed. 'But I'm not going to be able to sleep tonight unless I know you're home safely.'

After that she pretty much melted.

They kissed frantically all the way back to Gabriel's apartment, then almost ended up having sex in the lift, before Gabriel realised that there was no emergency stop button in there, which was also true of every other lift he'd ever been in, which made him suspect that the existence of such a button was most likely the figment of some long-forgotten pornographer's imagination.

But this was possibly for the best, because the sex they did have, in Gabriel's emperor-sized bed, was sensational – even if Catherine did start crying very soon afterwards, and wouldn't stop talking about how terrible she knew she was going to feel the next morning.

So Gabriel spent the next ten minutes assuring her that this wasn't her fault; some things were just too strong to fight. Then, when this started to grow tiresome, he gently suggested that if she wanted to leave, he would understand.

But she didn't want to leave, of course – not really.

They had sex three more times before she went home – once more that night, and twice the following morning. And for a while, Gabriel had no doubts that the nine-week pursuit had been worth it.

Catherine split up with her boyfriend not long afterwards, and, for some time, Gabriel couldn't decide if he approved of this or not. Of course, it was difficult to view some anonymous 22-year-old nobody as competition; Gabriel had to assume that he was superior to his 'rival' in every department. Nevertheless, he found that he wasn't completely immune to sexual jealousy, though he wasn't certain if this was a hard-wired response or some subtler aversion to the general premise of sharing. Logic, however, told him that having Catherine disentangled was not altogether good news, since it was bound to make their relationship more complicated than he would have preferred. The boyfriend had, at least, provided something of a safety net.

The truth was that Gabriel could imagine a whole raft of potential pitfalls in continuing to see Catherine; his short-term solution was to ignore these and focus solely on the sex and, for a while, this was extremely easy to do. They were at it like rabbits for the next few months – most evenings, entire weekends and, not infrequently, at work as well. Catherine was young and inexperienced enough that having sex with her boss against a filing cabinet, or sometimes on the desk, must have seemed reckless and passionate rather than sordid. She was also naïve enough to think that no one else in the office knew what was going on. In actual fact, the opposite was true. To Gabriel's knowledge, the only person who *didn't* know was the IT technician, who was possibly autistic.

But Gabriel soon realised that it was in his best interests to play along with Catherine's misapprehension. As long as she was fearful of becoming the subject of office gossip, he had the perfect excuse to suggest that they keep their relationship low-key, at least for now. He even intimated that a workplace liaison such as theirs would likely be frowned upon, if not openly condemned. In truth, it was being quietly applauded – at least among senior management.

If Gabriel had been able to preserve his relationship with Catherine in this state, then there would have been no need to end it. It could have been left to run indefinitely, no harm done. But deep down, he always knew he was living on borrowed time. The biggest surprise should have been that it lasted as long as it did. It was only after several weeks – following a particularly pointed comment from Becky in Compliance – that Catherine started to suspect their relationship wasn't quite the secret she'd supposed it to be. This changed things almost immediately. Once Catherine realised that the gossip had already been and gone, and that no one seemed as bothered as Gabriel had suggested they might be, she saw no reason for them not to 'make it official.'

This, again, would have been a good moment to end things,

except that Gabriel knew how it would look (more or less how it was). So, instead, he decided to hold out for a few more weeks, or possibly a few more months, depending on how quickly the situation deteriorated. His hope was that now the 'relationship' was out in the open, Catherine would stop seeing it as something exciting and illicit and start seeing it as something rather more mundane. He imagined, in his more optimistic moments, a gradual and graceful disengagement, followed possibly by some sort of occasional reengagement as and when the mood took them. Fuck buddies was the term that sprang, rather unrealistically, to mind.

But the longer it went on, the harder it became for Gabriel to persist with this carefully crafted delusion. It was increasingly clear that Catherine did not share his vision of their mutual future – never had and never would. Instead, she began to talk about the possibility of him finally meeting some of her friends. Gabriel could imagine nothing he wanted less – until she also mooted the prospect of meeting her parents, at which point he decided enough was enough.

His new best-case scenario was that she'd handle the break-up with a dignity far beyond her years, realise that there was no way they could go on working together, and clear her desk the very next day.

Unsurprisingly, none of this happened; which left Plan B.

'Vaughn. What can I do you for?'

Gabriel decided to get straight to the point. 'I need you to fire Catherine.'

Mason's expression didn't change, not even a flicker. 'How long has she been with us? Please tell me it's less than a year.'

'Eight months.'

'She's not pregnant, is she?'

'God, I hope not.'

'That's a no?'

'Yes. Yes it's a no.'

'OK. Just making sure. You understand that I have to cover my arse here. I'm not going through a lawsuit just because you can't keep it in your pants.'

'Mason, it's a first-year contract. We both know it's barely worth the paper it's printed on. Anyway, Catherine's not the litigious type.'

'Ha! Hell hath no fury, Vaughn. You'd do well to remember that in the future. Look –' Mason gestured at the chair opposite, '– have a seat a second. You're obviously agitated. Let me get you a drink.' He reached into the small cupboard in his desk, then hesitated before pulling out two crystal tumblers and a bottle of the second-most expensive Scotch. 'OK. You know I'm not one to say *I told you so*, but I do have some conditions. Number one: you don't get to choose your next PA. I'm outsourcing the decision to HR.'

'Agreed.'

'Number two: I'm assuming you'd rather she didn't serve out her month's notice?'

'No, obviously not. I can't imagine anything worse.'

'OK. Then I'm going to have to pay her a month's salary in lieu. And that's coming out of your bonus.'

'Fine. That's, what, a couple of thousand? I'll happily take the hit.'

'Yes, you will. It may be peanuts, but there's a higher principle at stake. I can't have my employees thinking that I'll pay for *their* indiscretions. This is your responsibility, no one else's.'

'Of course.'

'I'm glad you agree. It means you'll have no problem with condition number three.' Mason did nothing to conceal his smirk. 'You also get to break the unhappy news.'

'Oh, Christ. Really? Isn't the two grand punishment enough?'

Mason shrugged. 'You're her manager. You should be the one to do it. I'm not going to risk a mutiny in HR over this.'

Gabriel stared into his whisky for a few moments, searching for an escape route.

'You may as well just down that and get on with it,' Mason told him. 'I'll have another one waiting for you when you're done.'

The Psychotherapist

Armitage's psychotherapist was called Barbara, and she insisted on the first name, even though Gabriel would have preferred a little more professional distance. A lot more. But he supposed he should just feel grateful that she'd been willing to see him at short notice, and on a Saturday.

It was difficult, though. The whole premise was difficult. Gabriel was ill at ease the first moment he met her, and it wasn't just the general absurdity of the situation – the woolly New Ageism of sitting in a dimly lit office in South Kensington and being expected to talk about his feelings. More than this, there was something about Barbara herself that he didn't much like. She had a gaze that was far too direct and penetrating. His suspicion was that she was possibly more intelligent than he was, though only in a narrow, academic sense; not in any sense that mattered. Gabriel didn't feel intimidated by her, because he didn't feel intimidated by anyone, regardless of how many letters they had after their name, or the certificates they chose to paste ostentatiously on their office walls. It was just that he didn't like the way she looked at him, as if she were really looking *through* him. Of course, it probably came with the job, to a certain extent. Yet when he'd imagined this encounter – wondering what the hell he expected to get out of it – the psychotherapist of his fantasy had been not at all like this. She'd been ten, fifteen years younger for a start – the right side of the menopause – with eyes that were soft and understanding, not cold little scalpels. Although it was a situation that seldom arose, Gabriel did not find that talking to post-menopausal women came naturally to him. He felt disadvantaged, as if he were missing a key weapon from his armoury.

But, then, if he was being one hundred per cent honest, he had little interest in talking to any stranger about his problems. What he really wanted was a kind of unquestioning sympathy for hire; and he knew within thirty seconds of meeting Barbara that she wasn't the woman to answer this brief.

The first fifteen minutes were excruciating. She wanted to know about his background, and in particular, his family – which seemed to Gabriel both intrusive and unnecessary. His problems were biological in nature, and since he had already asked for his medical notes to be forwarded, no additional context was required. But when he tried to explain this, Barbara was immovable.

'I'm just trying to get to know you a little,' she insisted, giving a smile that, Gabriel assumed, was meant to be reassuring rather than patronising.

Unfortunately, he could see no way of objecting – not without appearing defensive. The easier option was to outline, in a few swift sentences, that he was an only child, his mother was dead and his father lived in Thetford. None of which seemed to satisfy Barbara.

'When did your mother die?' she asked.

'When I was seven,' Gabriel replied.

'I'm sorry. That must have been awful.'

'I don't really remember it. I was very young.'

Barbara pursed her lips in a small frown, while Gabriel met her gaze without blinking. She could try to make this into an issue – he was fairly sure this was the kind of thing psycho-therapists did – but he had no intention of playing along. And she must have realised this because, after a few moments of silence, she changed tack and started asking about his work. These questions were, initially, much easier to answer. He told her that he loved his job – which until recently had been true – and that since university he'd never wanted to do anything else. But then she asked about how he was managing his illness while working such long hours, and what kind of additional support he'd been offered. So Gabriel tried to evade the question, first attempting a half-joke about how he was now Starbucks' number one customer, then giving a vague and somewhat rambling account of how things had been difficult at first but were slowly improving. Barbara pressed him for specifics, and a barrage of further questions forced him to admit the truth: that he'd told no one; as far as work was concerned, he had no brain tumour.

Predictably, this was met with another small frown.

'You know, Gabriel, I can understand that you want to go on working. If you enjoy your job, if it's something that fulfils you, then you should keep doing it for as long as you can. But you must realise that you can't keep this from people indefinitely. In all honesty, I'm not sure why you'd want to. It seems that you're making things much harder than they need to be.'

'I don't want people to treat me any differently.' This was a response that Gabriel had had plenty of time to rehearse, in the several weeks he'd been seeing Armitage, and it seemed to him more or less unassailable – first, because it was obviously his choice, and second, because it hinted at a quiet strength and dignity in the face of tragedy. He wasn't expecting Barbara to challenge him on this point, as well.

'And why would that be such a bad thing?'

'Excuse me?'

'If people treated you differently. The natural response, I'd think, would be to offer help, sympathy and compassion. What's so terrible about that?'

Gabriel mirrored the psychotherapist's frown for a few seconds, before saying, 'I think you're missing the point. I'd actually prefer to just get on with things.'

'OK.' Barbara was still looking at him in that irritating, knowing way. 'But why is that, do you think?'

'Actually, Barbara, what I think is that none of this is even remotely relevant. I'm not in denial, if that's what you're driving at.'

'Gabriel, I'm not driving at anything. I'm asking some straight-forward questions to help me understand your perspective – and to get *you* to reflect on that perspective. As I've said, I understand completely why you wish to keep working; but I don't understand why you've chosen to hide your illness. You have enough to contend with right now. Why make things even more difficult?'

'It isn't more difficult. It's easier, as I've tried to explain.'

'To my mind, you're spending up to twelve hours a day essentially living a lie. I don't see how that can be anything other than a tremendous strain.'

'Then you'll just have to take my word for it.'

'With respect, Gabriel, that isn't my job. And we're not going to get very far if I'm prohibited from asking certain questions.'

'I didn't say you're prohibited. But I don't see why we have to waste a lot of time on a subject that simply isn't relevant.'

Gabriel stared at Barbara. Barbara stared at Gabriel. 'OK,' she said after a few moments. 'Let's turn this around. Perhaps you could tell me, as simply as possible, why you're here.'

'I'm here because my oncologist recommended you. He told me, perhaps wrongly, that—'

'Gabriel, I'm very sorry to interrupt, but I think you know that's not what I mean. You're obviously an intelligent man, and you don't strike me as someone who'd do something – anything – just because a doctor told you to. You have your own reasons for being here, and I'd like to hear them. If my questions aren't relevant, then tell me what you'd like to talk about. What are you hoping to get out of this therapy?'

He had to think about his for some time, while Barbara waited without saying a word. She *was* clever, he'd give her that, and he had a grudging respect for her refusal to be cowed. Even now, as he was being invited, ostensibly, to take control of their conversation, he had a strong feeling that she was pushing him in a certain direction. He made a point of settling back in his chair and interlacing his fingers, assuming the sort of posture that would come naturally to him in the boardroom.

'I'm here,' he told her, 'because I'm having specific . . . difficulties with my emotions. It's got to the point where they're interfering with my life to a significant extent. I've been told it's a common symptom of a tumour like mine, because of where it is in my brain.'

'Just to clarify, we're talking specifically about the emotional lability? Mood swings?'

'Yes, mood swings. I was led to believe that the radiosurgery might improve matters, but it hasn't. Some of the physical symptoms like the headaches and dizziness have improved, but this emotional thing . . . if anything, it's getting worse.'

'OK. And to be even more specific, what emotions are we talking about? Sadness? Anger?'

'Yes, sadness, but that doesn't really do it justice. When it happens, it's uncontrollable. It's more like . . . grief, I suppose. Grief mixed with dread.'

Barbara nodded. 'Both of which are completely reasonable responses. So that rather complicates matters, doesn't it? I mean, it must be confusing – having to imagine a portion of these emotions as in some sense separate from the rest, as coming from somewhere else.'

'No, not at all! The emotions I'm talking about *are* separate. They're completely separate. They don't belong to me.'

'Is that how they feel? It's just that I find it very hard to imagine how you can experience an emotion and at the same time view it as something separate from yourself. That's the confusion I'm talking about.'

'Yes, obviously they *feel* like they belong to me,' Gabriel conceded, 'at least while they're occurring. But I have no control over them – none at all.'

Barbara thought about this for a few moments, tapping her pen with a forefinger. 'Would I be right in assuming that this is new territory for you – not being in control of your emotions?'

'Yes, absolutely.' Gabriel could have gone further and said that the emotions themselves were new territory, but he didn't want

135

to guess in which direction that would take the conversation. Instead, he decided to keep things simple and explicable. 'It's to do with my job, partly. I have to be in control of my emotions at all times. I have to make clear and rational judgements. If I don't, I'll lose money, plain and simple. That's why I need to figure out how to manage this problem.

'Yes, I understand that, I think. But I'd also question whether it's helpful to assume that your emotions can – or should – be *managed* to this degree. Continually ignoring or suppressing our feelings can make them a whole lot worse.'

Gabriel didn't like this argument at all. He didn't like the terminology of 'suppression', for a start, which seemed to carry the whiff of accusation. But beyond this, he felt that Barbara was again steering the discussion down a blind alley – trying to address a question that was simply not applicable to his circumstances. Because the 'feelings' they were talking about were obviously not *his* feelings. Unfortunately, he could only think of one way of demonstrating this truth – which was to relate the first incidence of his emotional lability, the crying on the Tube, in full. Since this was before he even knew about the tumour, there was no way it could be linked to feelings he was supposedly suppressing.

'It's like my mind's been hijacked,' he concluded. 'That's honestly how it feels.'

Barbara nodded again, before asking, 'And just to be extra clear: there's nothing else that could explain the incident? No context?'

'Correct.' Gabriel thought about the appalling actress and her pink thing, immediately deciding that this, too, was irrelevant – and he had no intention of being cross-examined on the subject. Far easier to omit the information and save himself a verbal mauling. 'There's no explanation for it. Aside from the mere fact of being on the Tube.'

This provoked a small smile from Barbara, which made Gabriel feel strangely grateful. He didn't need her to like him, obviously, but that didn't mean he enjoyed being permanently at logger-heads. If they could at least agree that the Tube was hell, this seemed a step in a better direction.

'Is that how it's been recently, as well?' she asked. 'The same feelings and the same lack of context?'

'No, not exactly,' Gabriel admitted. 'Things have changed a bit in the past couple of weeks. There was another incident . . .' How on earth was he going to explain this? 'Um, you don't happen to know Pachelbel's Canon in D, do you?'

Barbara smiled again, in a way that made Gabriel think he might be missing something. 'Yes, I know it.'

'How about the second movement of Philip Glass's Violin Concerto?'

'You're a classical music fan?'

'No, not at all. But I happened to hear both of these, er . . . pieces?'

Barbara nodded for him to continue.

'Right, well, I heard both by chance quite recently. A busker with a violin and a loop pedal was playing them outside St Paul's Cathedral. That's the context.'

'OK. And what happened?'

'I felt – well, overwhelmed again. Similar to how it was on the Tube.'

'Overwhelmed in what sense? Despairing?'

'No, that's the thing. It was much more complicated than that.

I was moved, I suppose, but it was more, sort of . . . actually, I'm not sure that I can even tell you what it was.'

Barbara thought about this for a few movements, before saying, 'Well, Gabriel, from a certain perspective you might argue that's the whole point of music. It expresses emotions without having to put them into words. Many, many people experience what you're now talking about when listening to music. Your current susceptibility to mood swings might have heightened this effect, but I don't see anything abnormal in the process. It makes sense to me.'

'It felt abnormal,' Gabriel told her. 'It felt like it did on the Tube, like I'd lost control. Except this time I didn't really mind so much. In fact, I didn't really want it to be over.' He affected a small, casual laugh. 'You wouldn't believe it, but I actually ended up following her – the busker – when she left the square. I think I just wanted to, sort of, stretch out the experience a bit.'

Gabriel was aware straight away that his attempt to depict this as an amusing and trivial detail had failed. Barbara was frowning deeply. 'You *followed* her?'

'Not in a stalking way. As I said, it was more . . . Well, it wasn't that I had any sinister motive or anything.'

'Gabriel, stalking is stalking. Your motive doesn't change that.'

'It wasn't stalking.'

'How long did you follow her for?'

'Ten minutes – if that.'

'And would you usually view this as moral behaviour?'

'No, but it's not exactly immoral is it? I wasn't causing her any harm. There wasn't any . . . Christ, there wasn't any weird sexual thing going on here! And I think that's what we usually mean when we talk about stalking. Most people would agree on that.'

'Would they?'

'Yes!'

Barbara stared at him without expression. 'Gabriel, let me ask you this – and I want you to answer honestly. This violinist's music moved you – it overwhelmed you – and that's why you followed her?'

'Yes, that's precisely it.'

'So you also would have followed if she'd been a he?'

Gabriel hesitated.

The hesitation became a long, incriminating silence.

'I think that proves my point, doesn't it?' Barbara put her fingers to her temples and took a deep breath. 'Gabriel. What you're describing is stalking. Please don't do it again.'

An Experiment, of Sorts

Gabriel left Barbara's office feeling mentally battered. It wasn't just the trial of having his thinking challenged at every turn; it was also the sense that he'd lost most of the arguments. He'd certainly lost the ultimate argument, because somehow he had another appointment for next week. This was so unfathomable that Gabriel could only put it down to some psychological *trick* Barbara must have pulled. He felt like a man returning, dumbfounded, to his seat after an encounter with a stage hypnotist.

And yet . . . and yet he didn't actually feel any worse for the appointment. He was tired of reflecting on his emotions, but if he forced himself to be honest, then he'd have to admit that he felt somewhat lighter.

It was a troubling thought. It suggested that talking – just talking! – might have helped. It suggested that he had benefited from something that, an hour ago, he would have placed in the same conceptual drawer as astrology and faith healing. It suggested, most worryingly, that next week's appointment should be kept.

He picked up his car from the multi-storey on Harrington Road and drove it to the multi-storey on Queen Victoria Street, a couple of blocks south of St Paul's. It was a journey of five miles, which, at his Ferrari's theoretical top speed, should have taken ninety seconds. In central London traffic, it took closer to an hour. Usually, Gabriel found that one of the advantages of driving a Ferrari – one of the many advantages – was that most other drivers instinctively gave way to him, as if there were some immutable car caste system to be followed without question. The truth, he suspected, was that many people simply froze, awestruck, at the sight of it, and this provided a continual, exploitable gap in the traffic. But today, the opposite seemed true. There were no gaps, anywhere, and when the traffic did move, it moved at a crawl.

Still, he supposed he could at least forget Armitage's warning against driving in his present condition; if he crashed, he certainly wasn't going to kill anyone. More to the point, he'd rediscovered the simple pleasure of being in a quarter-million-pound supercar, regardless of whether he was getting anywhere. People were looking, as they always did – even in Knightsbridge, it was impossible to ignore a yellow Ferrari 458 – and in their gazes, both admiring and envious, he saw a snapshot of the person he'd always dreamed he'd be. Sunglasses, shirt sleeves rolled back. It was the version of himself that he would have loved to have seen blown up and plastered across a billboard; and for at least a portion of his journey, he was able to maintain this rare state of grace, quite forgetting the time bomb in his head.

Car parked, Gabriel walked to St Paul's Churchyard and did a quick sweep of the cathedral steps. Once he'd satisfied himself that the violinist wasn't yet there, he headed into Starbucks, thinking he would sit in the window and await her arrival. This was clearly preferable to hanging around outside, on the fringes of the camp. As one of modern capitalism's brightest beacons, Starbucks struck Gabriel as an obvious no-go zone for the occupiers, and he felt reassured the moment he stepped inside. The beauty of Starbucks was that you got the same, orderly experience every time: uncluttered décor, clean surfaces, staff who might have been cloned in a laboratory. On the toilet door, someone had pinned a warning that the facilities were FOR CUSTOMER USE ONLY. It was the perfect refuge from the anarchy outside.

Or it would have been. The problem, Gabriel soon found, was that there was no free seat that provided an unobstructed view of the whole square. The frontage of Starbucks was floor-to-ceiling glass, but wherever he sat, Gabriel's line of sight was blocked by too many people and too many tents. The view he needed was the God's-eye view of the Mason Wallace offices – and this, of course, was the obvious solution. The offices in Stanton House were accessible seven days a week, twenty-four hours a day, but they were hardly ever used at the weekends; since the markets were closed, there wasn't much point. The last time Gabriel had used them outside of normal hours had been in 2008, at the height of the collapse. Back then, the whole team had been working round the clock – trying to come up with contingency plans for every plausible economic future.

For this reason, Gabriel thought it extremely unlikely that he'd run into anyone else in the Mason Wallace office. But it wouldn't really matter if he did. He didn't need any excuse for being there on a Saturday.

As it turned out, his suspicion was correct. After he'd signed in to the building – it was something to do with out-of-hours Health and Safety – he headed upstairs and found the entire top floor deserted. He went through to his office, rotated his chair to the window, then sat on one of the arms so that he could properly survey the square below. He was still wearing his sunglasses, and with his coffee in one hand and a bag of pastries in the other, he felt – fleetingly and childishly – like an undercover cop sent on a stakeout.

The truth, of course, was somewhat more questionable. Dr Barbara, Gabriel was sure, would have viewed his present actions as an immediate and unmitigated reneging on his promise not to do any more 'stalking'. She might even have viewed it as an escalation. But Gabriel knew that things were a little more complicated than that. Even though he might have struggled to convince his psychotherapist that his reasons for being here were sound – he wouldn't tell her, obviously – he had no such difficulty convincing himself. He viewed what he was doing, and what he was planning to do, very much as an experiment – as the testing of a hypothesis. He needed to know if it would be the same a second time. That way, he could start to unpick the true cause, effect and meaning of last week's emotional muddle. He could find out who was calling the shots here: him or the tumour.

Escalation

It was the tumour.

Dr Barbara, when he told her the following Saturday, would of course dismiss this suggestion as absurd. He had a choice, and he'd made the wrong choice. It was that simple. Gabriel had no defence, except to say that was not how it felt. He might have put himself in a ridiculous situation, but once he had, the outcome was predetermined.

The problem was, there was a part of Gabriel – a very large part – that disliked this line of argument even more than Barbara did, though probably for different reasons.

For Barbara, Gabriel's version of events was a way of palming off his moral responsibility, and utterly self-serving. For Gabriel, the morality of the situation was a non-issue, and his desire to serve himself was, in this instance, peripheral at best. Far more disturbing was the capitulation of reason to sentiment – a capitulation that he was now reinforcing with a hopelessly circular and subjective argument. So far as Gabriel could see, his rational

144

mind could no longer be trusted. Based on the past fortnight, that was the only conclusion he could draw.

She'd turned up a little after two, as promised, and set up in the same place: on the cathedral steps, a lazy stone's throw from the tents. Gabriel watched her from his office for a few minutes; the perfect insulation meant it was like watching a television switched to mute. She went through what appeared to be a short soundcheck, then spent a while talking to some guy who had wandered over from the camp. Gabriel hadn't actually seen him come from the camp, but he could tell this was the case just from the man's appearance. Even at this distance, he had that air about him – a kind of scruffy, slouching, long-haired, pot-fumed indolence. He looked like a thirty-year-old student, someone who seldom rolled out of his sleeping bag before lunchtime, yet complained non-stop about how he was being brutalised by the iron fist of capitalism. Gabriel waited for him to slope off, then headed downstairs.

He didn't want to miss the beginning, but there wasn't yet any sort of crowd to hide behind, just a handful of passers-by who were curious to see what was happening. Logically, he didn't have any good reason for not wanting to be seen, but the thought nevertheless made him uncomfortable. When a crowd did start to form, he'd join the back of it. Until then, he was much happier watching her from the shadow of Stanton House, his sunglasses masking his unfaltering gaze.

How did Gabriel feel about his actions? At that precise moment, he couldn't have said for sure; but he knew if he'd had to repeat the claim he'd made to Dr Barbara earlier that day – that there was no *weird sexual thing* going on here – he'd have convinced neither one of them. But perhaps that was just the inherent seediness of the situation. It was hard not to feel like a voyeur when you'd spent the last ten minutes watching a stranger from the shadows – a stranger who *was* attractive in some unfathomable and, for Gabriel, extremely unconventional sense. Her skin was still too pale, and her eyebrows too thick, and her breasts at least a cup-size too small. For this reason, he'd have emphasised the weirdness of his feelings far beyond any component that could be called sexual. Nevertheless, his general sense of deviance persisted, at least until she started playing. Then every worry, every question, left him in an instant.

Afterwards, Gabriel did not remember much of the performance. This might have been because of what followed, which was of course the part he would dwell on – the part that *really* worried Barbara. Or it might have been that the edges of that performance blended with the previous week's, to the extent that he couldn't make a clear distinction between the two. The violinist played several of the same pieces again, and their effect on Gabriel was as before. Pachelbel's Canon still lifted him off his feet; the second movement of Philip Glass's Violin Concerto still made him feel as if something inside him was being wrenched. It was beyond words – Barbara had been right about that – and perhaps this, as much as anything, was why the actual details of the performance refused to stick in his memory. He was lost in the music. At one point – and this was the only detail he could firmly recall – he had even closed his eyes. He was still wearing his sunglasses, so no one else would have seen this small humiliation, but *he* knew it had happened, and that was almost as bad. The thinking part of his brain had, at that moment, left the square entirely.

'And when did it come back?' Barbara would ask him, not bothering to water down her sarcasm. 'Did it come back?'

It would have been a stretch to claim that he'd been in such a daze that the next hour, when he followed the violinist for a second time, had also been conducted on autopilot. Gabriel was aware of what he was doing; and he knew that if he'd been well, if he didn't have this golf-ball-sized growth screwing with him, he'd have acted rather differently. So when he followed this time, it was with something like a sense of resigned inevitability. He couldn't imagine going home to his immaculate and empty apartment. Staying put in the square, with the violinist gone, would have been equally pointless. Following was the only option that made sense to him. What else could he have done?

'*Not* follow!' Barbara would counter.

'I suppose it was a bit like being drunk,' Gabriel told her, after weighing this suggestion for a few moments. 'It's not that you're unaware of your actions, or even that you think they're sensible at the time. Stupid behaviour is still stupid behaviour. You just lose the ability to care.'

That was the closest he could come to explaining it: disinhibition on a very large scale.

Two Twenties

It wasn't that difficult, finding a moment when she was again distracted. Gabriel thought she must be overly trusting when it came to her money. Or perhaps it was that there wasn't enough money to worry about – just a couple of fistfuls of loose change. The only notes were the two twenties Gabriel added. He'd pre-folded them around a two-pound coin, and was able to slip them into the violin case as he walked past, as casually as a magician performing a rudimentary card trick. Obviously, he didn't want to draw attention to the sum he was leaving. Most people, he suspected, would have considered forty-two pounds an extravagant donation – though, from his perspective, it meant nothing at all. Based on last year's income, Gabriel earned some-where in the region of eight hundred pounds an hour; his donation to the busker was equivalent to a two-minute toilet break.

She was talking to the guy from the camp again – the thirty-year-old-student type – and even though this had facilitated Gabriel's anonymous donation, he found their proximity inexplicably irritating. The man's appearance was even worse up close, where Gabriel could pick out details like his pierced lip and wigga dreadlocks. Yet the violinist clearly didn't care. There was something in their body language that, if not flirtatious, was certainly warmer than Gabriel would have liked. A negotiation seemed to be ongoing. There were mutual smiles, then, after touching her fleetingly on the arm, the man picked up her amplifier and carried it off to the camp.

The busker started scooping up the money from her violin case, and Gabriel was gratified to see that the two twenties gave her more than a moment's pause. She was smiling when she dropped her afternoon's earnings into a small plastic money bag, which she then deposited in her shoulder bag. A few minutes later, she gave a small wave in the direction of the camp, picked up the violin case and left the square.

They headed in the same direction as before, down Paternoster Row towards Cheapside, but this time Gabriel stayed a little closer. Not scarily close; he estimated he was leaving a good fifteen metres between them, though he was able to reduce this a little as they again approached the Museum of London, where the streets got busier. It was with some dismay that Gabriel realised he was developing more of a knack for this *following* business. It was feeling less difficult, less weird, by the minute.

Of course, it did help that he was able to walk a little faster this time. Without her amplifier, the violinist was walking closer to Gabriel's natural pace. He supposed he had Dreadlocks to thank for this, though he still felt intensely irritated at the mere thought of the man. He wasn't the violinist's boyfriend or anything; that much was clear even from the brief dumb show Gabriel had witnessed. So what was their connection? In truth, the idea that they shared any connection at all bothered Gabriel. This woman didn't look like a left-wing radical (usually, they looked unfortunate), but she was obviously sympathetic to that whole anarchist/communist/feminist viewpoint. Gabriel had seen enough evidence to conclude that he and she lived in very different worlds.

But perhaps this was the point? If he was being absolutely honest with himself, he knew that he'd been unnaturally interested in the Occupy camp from the first day it had arrived on his doorstep – long before the violinist showed up. He must have spent hours just watching it; and why was this, if not for the chance to scrutinise a world that was so utterly unlike his own? He'd have hesitated to say that he wanted to understand that world or its inhabitants, but there was nevertheless something compelling about the small glimpses he'd received. There was the strange sense of peering into the alien lives of others – the same sense he got now, as he continued to follow his violinist.

This was as close as Gabriel would get to justifying his actions. At the very least, he'd proved to his own satisfaction that he was not doing any harm. He was just an impartial observer of the violinist's life, looking in from the outside. Their worlds did not overlap, and he had no intention of doing anything to change this.

It was then that it happened, or almost immediately afterwards – as if the universe were mocking him.

They had just come through the Museum of London underpass, or the violinist had come through. Gabriel was lagging several metres behind, and was still in the underpass. It was likely, he'd later think, that he was quite difficult to see there.

The woman was not difficult to see. She was out in the sunlight, with her violin case in one hand and her bag slung – not very securely – over her opposite shoulder. The kid who snatched the bag was approaching from the other direction, and couldn't have been more than eighteen or nineteen. There wasn't much to him. He was wearing a thick grey hoodie that looked a couple of sizes too big for him. He was probably an opportunist. Probably an addict looking to fund his next fix. That was Gabriel's later assessment of the facts.

Under normal circumstances, it would have been an easy theft. It wouldn't have mattered if there were passers-by, since no one would have had any time to react. In all likelihood, no one would have been watching, and certainly not with the intensity with which Gabriel was watching.

With only one arm free, the violinist couldn't grip her bag tightly enough to put up any real resistance. She was thrown off balance and ended up on the ground, landing heavily on her left hand.

The would-be thief hurtled full pelt into the underpass, giving Gabriel very little time to think. So he acted on pure instinct – though, in retrospect, his instinct was decidedly odd. It might have made sense to stick out a leg or a fist, either of which should have been sufficient to bring this skinny kid down. Even better, he could have grabbed a handful of hoodie, which would have had the same effect but carried less risk to Gabriel's own body. Instead, he simply stepped out in front of the kid, at the last possible moment. He didn't raise his arms or try to brace himself; he just placed himself in the way, like a human sandbag.

The outcome was predictable. The thief was moving very quickly, but he was slight and malnourished, and probably a crack addict. Gabriel had been somewhat weakened by his chemotherapy, but he was still carrying a weight advantage of at least forty pounds. He was six foot tall and had been carefully cultivating his muscles for the past fifteen years. There was no chance he was going to be shouldered aside.

Both men went down.

Gabriel cracked his head against the pavement, felt the air leave his lungs as something bony jabbed into his ribs. After that, there was an indeterminate tangle of limbs. Gabriel managed to roll onto his front and throw his right arm over the shoulder bag. His left hand encircled the thief's ankle – at least until a couple of well-placed kicks dislodged him. He grabbed hold of a Nike trainer, but it was a poor grip, and the kid was thrashing like a feral animal. A moment later, a set of less-than-perfect teeth had sunk into his shoulder, where his coat had been pushed back. Gabriel yelped and rolled away, still clutching the bag. He heard running, and raised his head to see the kid disappearing out of the far end of the underpass.

The whole thing couldn't have taken more than a few seconds.

39

As in the Angel

'Jesus! Are you OK?'

Gabriel didn't know how to answer this question. His predominant feeling, at that moment, was guilt, as if he'd been the one who'd snatched the bag. The violinist was crouching over him, backlit by the exit to the underpass. Gabriel touched his face with his free hand, discovering in the process that his sunglasses had vanished.

'I'm surprisingly fine.'

This was the response he plumped for as he struggled to rise to his feet. The violinist looked far from convinced.

'You're bleeding,' she pointed out. 'There's blood all over your shirt.'

Gabriel glanced down, then brushed at his chest, which of course achieved nothing at all. 'It's just a scratch,' he told her.

'It looks like more than a scratch.'

'The little bastard bit me,' Gabriel admitted. 'His teeth were quite sharp.'

'He *bit* you?'

Gabriel nodded. There wasn't anything else he could add. He handed the bag across.

'Thank you! God, thank you! You're a fucking hero.'

'No, I'm not.' He shook his head in a way that he hoped didn't look self-deprecating. 'Just happened to be in the right place at the right time.'

'No, honestly, that was incredible!'

Gabriel realised that there was no point trying to deny this any further. Whatever objection he raised would only have the perverse effect of making him look even better; not only a hero, but a very modest one, too. His best option was to shift the focus and move on.

'How about you?' he asked. 'Are *you* OK?'

'Yes. No.' She smiled thinly at him. 'Actually, I'm not sure. I guess I'm a bit shaken up.' She held her left hand up and tentatively splayed her fingers, then winced. 'And my wrist's fucked.'

Gabriel had the irrational desire to hold her fucked wrist, which he wisely resisted.

'Are these yours?' She stooped down to pick something up. It was his sunglasses; one of the lenses had cracked almost in two. 'I hope they weren't expensive.'

'Er, no. I mean, they are mine but they weren't expensive. They were cheap. Cheap knock-offs.' Gabriel was usually an accomplished liar, so he knew this story was getting less plausible with every word he added. He decided in this situation the truth might be preferable. 'Don't worry,' he told her, 'they're insured.'

This provoked a small laugh, but it took Gabriel a few seconds to realise that she thought he was joking. He made a mental note: most people did not insure their sunglasses.

The violinist was flexing her fingers again, pouting with concern.

'Perhaps you should get someone to look at that,' Gabriel suggested. 'You might need an X-ray.'

'I don't think I've broken anything. It's probably just bruised, or strained or something.'

Gabriel gave a sympathetic nod. 'Just a little fucked?'

She smiled again. 'Right. But fucked enough. I'm going to have to call work.' She held out the violin case. 'Would you mind holding this for me?'

'No, not at all. You're a musician?'

Stating the obvious, but Gabriel felt it was important to establish this fact verbally, and as soon as possible.

'Yes, violin. I'm meant to be playing in a couple of hours' time.'

'Oh.'

'Exactly. Not going to happen. Would you excuse me a second?'

Gabriel didn't know what to do with himself while she talked on the phone. He stood just outside the exit to the underpass, as if keeping vigil. A small group of people walked past. A couple of them eyed him warily. A couple more made a point of not looking at him at all. Gabriel would have liked a full-length mirror so that he could take a proper inventory of his appearance. In addition to the blood smears on his shirt, his trousers had ripped at both knees. When he touched the back of his head, where it had struck the pavement, he found that his hair was matted with more drying blood. And he felt weird, though he had no idea if this was because of the head injury, the tumour, or something else entirely. When he looked at the violinist, holding her mobile to her ear, bathed in golden sunlight, he felt the same sense of lifting he'd experienced back in St Paul's Churchyard.

He didn't mean to listen in on the phone conversation, but it was difficult not to catch snippets.

'No, I'm fine. Honestly, I am. Some guy rescued me.'

Rescued. Gabriel had never rescued anyone before, and he quite liked the way it sounded – despite his misgivings regarding the context.

After she'd hung up, she returned the phone to her bag and walked back to him.

'I got told I should call the police.'

'You should call the police,' Gabriel agreed.

'I don't think there's much point. The police aren't going to do anything. They'll take a statement and file it. I don't think they're going to spend a lot of time following up on this, do you?'

'No, possibly not,' Gabriel said. 'But – well, you *were* mugged.'

'Yes, I was.' The woman looked away for a few moments, taking a couple of slow breaths. 'How old do you think he was? Sixteen, seventeen?'

Gabriel frowned; the notion that he might have been wrestling a *child* – with limited success – rather diminished his heroics. 'I'd say he was at least eighteen,' he asserted. 'Old enough to be tried as an adult.'

The violinist shrugged. 'Even if that were true, I don't think it would do a lot of good, would it? You saw him. He needs help rather than a sentence.'

In Saudi Arabia they'd chop his hands off.

Gabriel suppressed this thought, and said, 'Maybe just a fine?'

The woman gave a short, hollow laugh. 'I'm not sure how he'd pay it.'

'He'd probably have to steal a couple more bags,' Gabriel conceded.

This made her laugh much louder, and more warmly, and for a few moments, Gabriel was oblivious to the pain in his head

156

and shoulder and knees. He was oblivious to everything else, in a way that would later trouble him.

'Listen, you don't smoke do you?' the woman asked.

Gabriel shook his head. He had never smoked; it yellowed the teeth and led to premature ageing of the skin.

'Right. Me neither. I quit six months ago. This is the first time I've really wanted to smoke in ages.'

'I'm sure there must be a newsagent nearby,' Gabriel told her. 'I don't mind walking with you.'

She was still smiling at him. 'You're supposed to talk me out of it.'

'Don't do it,' Gabriel said. 'You'll regret it tomorrow.'

What he did next was another small escalation – though given everything else that had happened, he didn't think he had any good alternative.

He was still holding the violin case. He transferred it to his left hand and held out his right. 'I'm Gabriel,' he said.

'As in the angel?'

'Yes. As in the angel.'

The woman brushed a strand of hair from her face. It was difficult to tell because the light was starting to fade, but it looked as if she might be blushing a little. 'I'm sorry – you must get that all the time. You're probably sick to death of it.' She took his hand. 'Caitlin.'

'Caitlin. Nice to meet you.'

'Right.'

'Apart from the mugging, obviously.'

Stop flirting with her, you fuckwit.

This was another thought that Gabriel managed to suppress. He was getting quite good at it.

A and E

They agreed that going to a police station would be pointless, but for some time, he persisted in telling Caitlin that she should have a doctor look at her wrist.

'It's your livelihood,' he kept saying.

Gabriel was certain he'd never used the word livelihood before – never in his thirty-two years on the planet. He was more used to thinking of work in terms of performance-contingent bonuses and tax-efficient compensation structures. In comparison, a livelihood sounded to his ears like something an organic farmer might have – something earthy and wholesome. But the evening was doing awkward things to his vocabulary, and once he'd settled on this word, he found himself stuck with it.

He was aware, also, that his ongoing concern over her wrist might seem excessive; she was increasingly insistent that the injury was superficial. But in some sense, Gabriel felt that he was simply going along with the role in which she'd cast him – the role of rescuer, which he was hesitant to relinquish. Added to this, there was a part of him that *did* care excessively about the fate of her wrist. The thought of her not being able to play her violin bothered him; it also bothered him that it bothered him, which introduced a whole new dimension of anxiety. Most worrying of all, though (and perhaps closest to the truth), was the idea that he was simply stalling – looking for some way to prolong their encounter. Gabriel wasn't just suggesting that she see a doctor; he was suggesting that *he* take her to see a doctor.

'I appreciate it, I really do, but you've done enough already. I'm sure you have somewhere you need to be?'

'It's nothing I can't cancel,' Gabriel told her.

Of course, in reality he had nowhere he needed to be. He didn't even have a plausible reason for being where he was. Not that this was likely to present a problem. Gabriel had recovered his wits enough to know that he didn't have to invent some elaborate story to justify his whereabouts. The faintest suggestion that he'd been heading *somewhere* would be sufficient, since no sane person would ever imagine otherwise.

'Look,' Gabriel said. 'I don't think I can leave you alone right now. Not after what's happened. I'd really like to get you to a doctor, just to be certain.'

Caitlin looked at him in a way that told him she was considering it.

'Or is there someone else I can call for you? A friend. A boyfriend?'

'No. Thank you, really, but there's no one you need to call.'

No boyfriend.

Gabriel turned back towards the underpass as if considering further options.

'Jesus, Gabriel – your *head*.'

Evidently, the wound was worse than he'd assumed. Or perhaps

159

it was just an effect of the low sunlight; orange light on congealed blood could not have looked pretty. Either way, the revelation of this other injury instantly changed Caitlin's mind.

'OK, we need to get *you* to a doctor,' she told him. 'Come with me.'

Gabriel didn't resist when she took his hand. Given everything else that was going on with his head, a cracked skull seemed rather trivial, but he wasn't going to explain this, obviously. 'I'll get my head looked at if you get that wrist seen to,' he said.

Caitlin flagged down a taxi on London Wall, while Gabriel was on his phone, trying to locate the nearest emergency room.

'Bloody 'ell, mate,' said the taxi driver, after he'd given Gabriel a once-over in the rear-view mirror.

'You should see the other guy,' Gabriel told him.

The taxi driver didn't laugh, or even smile. Neither did Caitlin. It probably didn't help that she *had* seen the other guy – the emaciated teenager.

'We need to get to an A and E,' she told the taxi driver. 'Wherever's closest.'

'You've got the Royal in Whitechapel or St Thomas's just across the river. Which would you like?'

'Wherever's closest,' Caitlin repeated.

'They're about the same, love.'

'Take us to the Royal,' Gabriel said. He was basing his decision on nothing more than the name, which he hoped would not turn out to be ironic.

The only consolation he could think of, when they arrived, was that perhaps St Thomas's was even worse.

Gabriel hadn't been in an NHS hospital for at least a decade, and he'd never had to visit Accident and Emergency. It was like stepping into some baffling dystopia, and had Caitlin not been with him, he'd probably have stayed in the doorway, gaping in horror. Fortunately, she seemed happy to take the lead; he only had to follow, keeping his face impassive.

There was a reception, of sorts – a long laminate-topped counter that lay below a smeared plastic window. It looked like the same plastic the riot police used for their visors and shields. There was a small grille through which you could talk to one of the receptionists – though Gabriel didn't have to say anything yet. Caitlin gave a quick summary of the injuries they'd sustained, pausing only to check Gabriel's surname, and then they were directed to take seats in the waiting room.

It wasn't like any waiting room Gabriel had been in recently. Those were more like hotel lobbies: leather sofas, potted plants, muted lighting; glass-topped coffee tables offering a selection of the broadsheets. Here, there wasn't even a water cooler. There were vending machines selling crisps and chocolate bars and hot drinks, but Gabriel suspected you were in danger of catching MRSA just by looking at them.

They sat next to each other on plastic seats under harsh fluorescent lighting. Diagonally opposite was a man in a football shirt who seemed to be bleeding out of *all* his facial orifices. Next to him, there was another man who was lying face-down over several seats, either asleep, unconscious or dead. There was a drunk, too – Gabriel could smell the alcohol on him from a distance of five metres. He was slumped against one of the vending machines at the far wall, muttering to himself. He appeared to have lost most of his front teeth – though it was impossible to tell if this loss was recent.

Caitlin was, by default, the only person Gabriel wanted to look at. She had her violin case in her lap and was wearing a sort of resigned smile.

I'm sorry for bringing you to this terrible place, Gabriel wanted to tell her. Instead, he opted for: 'Hopefully we won't be here too long.'

Caitlin raised her eyebrows; they were very expressive, but still too thick for his taste. 'Gabriel, when did you last visit A and E?'

'First time,' he admitted. 'This is me officially losing my A and E virginity.'

'Wow. You *have* led a charmed life.'

'Yes, I suppose I have.'

Gabriel didn't know what else he could say to this. But he didn't have long to dwell on it. Soon afterwards, a nurse came out of a door just to the right of reception and shouted their names.

'Caitlin Beighton and Gabriel Vaughn?'

Gabriel did like the way their names sounded together. It was as if they were being announced at a social occasion. More significantly, it meant that they didn't have to sit in the waiting room any longer. Even though Gabriel had been the one who'd pushed, initially, for this trip to hospital, he could only feel relieved that their stay would be not be protracted.

He followed Caitlin into a small examination room, expecting to be greeted by a doctor. Instead, he was confronted by the cheerless face of the same nurse who'd called for them. Her name badge said that she was the triage nurse, and Gabriel's relief turned instantly to dismay. He'd never been through triage before, but he understood, and disliked, the principle. It meant that patients were seen in order of need. Gabriel was used to preferential treatment based on more reliable factors – your connections or your bank balance. Here, it didn't even matter if you were more *deserving* of prompt treatment than someone else. Gabriel might, in all honesty, have struggled to make this case for himself, but he thought that Caitlin should have been allowed to go ahead of the football fan – not to mention the drunk. He doubted that either one of them was the victim of a crime. More plausibly, their injuries were in some sense self-inflicted – whether through brawling, poisoning or inebriated negligence. Yet by the look of them, both would get to see a doctor long before he or Caitlin did.

The nurse asked them some brief questions and made some notes. It took less than five minutes, after which they were ejected back into the waiting room.

'I take it *you* have been in A and E before?' Gabriel asked Caitlin.

'Yes. Unfortunately, I have.'

'Right. So how long might it take for a doctor to see us? Just so I can prepare myself.'

'Prepare yourself?' She seemed amused by this statement.

'Mentally,' Gabriel clarified.

Caitlin glanced around the waiting room before replying. 'I don't know. I wouldn't be surprised if we're here for a couple of hours.'

'God, really?'

'Really.'

'Two hours? Two *hours*?'

'Yes, Gabriel, two hours. Minimum.' She rolled her eyes at him. 'Is the thought of spending two hours with me that abhorrent? We can sit separately if you'd prefer?'

'Yes, obviously I would prefer that,' Gabriel told her. 'But since half the people in here look like they've been in knife fights, I think we might be safer sitting together. At least for now.'

'Great.' Caitlin nodded back towards their original seats. 'Now that's settled, why don't I get us some coffees?' She handed him her violin case. 'And when I get back, you can tell me all about yourself. Trust me, the time will fly.'

Fuck, fuck, fuck, fuck, fuck.

Running wasn't an option, since he was holding on to her violin. More disturbingly, he didn't want to run. But now he had approximately a minute to come up with a plausible cover story: basic things like where he lived and what he did.

The thought that he might have told her the truth, or at least some of the truth, did not occur to him until much later. But in hindsight, this was the *only* moment in which a confession – that he was a senior portfolio manager at a multi-billion-pound hedge fund – could have worked. At that point, Caitlin thought he was a good person. More than that – she thought he was a hero. Perhaps that would have overridden any dislike she held for the financial sector? In her eyes, Gabriel might then have appeared as an exception – as a decent man who happened to work in a depraved industry.

But at the time, all Gabriel could imagine was a catastrophic loss of whatever rapport he and Caitlin had started to build.

He told her he was a research analyst. He worked for a small consultancy that collated data, crunched statistics and identified market trends for a range of clients across the private and public sector.

Like all good lies, it had some small foundation in reality. He did spend a lot of his time analysing research; it was probably fifty per cent of his working life. If she asked what sort of research he was involved in, he could provide dozens of innocuous examples. The jargon was there to baffle and bore. In a few swift sentences, Gabriel felt confident that he'd constructed an impenetrable wall of tedium around his supposed job. No one in their right mind would want to probe any further, least of all a musician.

Possibly, he'd overdone it. As he talked, he saw that Caitlin was looking at him far too intently. At first he thought it was overcompensation – the look one might give while trying to stave off sleep in a very long meeting. But then he thought he could detect a hint of amusement, too. She looked like someone who was trying to figure out the punchline to a joke.

When he'd finished, she asked, 'So, Gabriel, have you always wanted to be a data cruncher?'

Sarcasm? Obviously, there was only one sensible response. 'Yes, I have,' Gabriel told her. 'It was my childhood dream.'

'I'm sorry, but I don't think I've ever heard anyone describe their work with less enthusiasm. It was like you were reading aloud from your job description!'

Gabriel sipped his coffee, trying not to wince. It was foul. 'Well, we can't all be artists. Some of us make music, others make spreadsheets.'

'Either you live to work or you work to live, right? It's a cliché, but it's more or less true.'

'Right. And you're very lucky to be in the first category.'

'Yes, I know. Believe me, I've done plenty of God-awful menial jobs in my time. I know how it feels to spend day after day doing something you couldn't care less about. Life's too short.'

'Yes, it is.' Gabriel didn't think there was anything else he could say to this. He tried to smile, but the result was clearly unsuccessful. He supposed it was somewhat ironic that his made-up job had led them off on this depressing tangent.

'Hey, cheer up.' Caitlin told him. 'There are good points and bad points about most jobs. If you work for a consultancy, I'm sure you get paid a lot better than I do. And you get evenings and weekends, too. My social life's a disaster – has been for as long as I can remember. Christ, even when I was a teenager, I used to spend all of my spare time practising.'

'Pushy parents?'

'Pushy self.'

Gabriel nodded knowingly, as if he'd been there too, before realising that, as an apathetic research analyst, he *shouldn't* have been there too. He deflected her attention from this slip by asking more about her job – the one she'd been heading to before the mugging. 'You said you were meant to be playing somewhere,' he reminded her. 'Are you in an orchestra?'

'Yes, the East London Sinfonia. You're looking at the sub-principal first violinist.'

'I've no idea what that means,' Gabriel told her. 'Except for the violinist part. I understood that.'

'I take it you're not a classical music fan?'

'Actually, I think I might be. I've been listening to more of it recently. I could be a convert.'

Gabriel didn't know why he said this. It was obviously opening up a whole new can of worms.

'And what's caused this conversion?' Caitlin asked. 'What have you been listening to?'

'Um . . . You know, Mozart and stuff.'

'Right. Any *stuff* in particular?'

'OK, I'll admit it. I'm completely ignorant when it comes to music. Maybe you could recommend something to get me started?'

Caitlin looked at him for a few moments, drumming her fingers on her violin case. 'I'll tell you what. When my wrist's better, you can come and see me play. I'll get you a complimentary ticket. It's the least I can do.'

'It's a date.'

This provoked a short laugh. 'No, it's definitely not a date. We'll be sitting apart and not talking.'

Gabriel shrugged. 'I've been on dates like that before.'

'Me too. And I have no desire to go on another one.'

'Fine. So I guess I'll have to take you for a coffee afterwards. Actual, non-vending-machine coffee. We can talk then.'

'Gabriel, I think you're being extremely presumptuous here.'

'Presumptuous how? You asked me out, I accepted. There's nothing presumptuous there.'

'I did not ask you out! You expressed an interest in hearing some classical music and I said I'd get you a ticket to see me play.'

'Exactly. One ticket, singular. If you weren't asking me out you'd have offered two.'

'Oh, right. I see. Very clever. Let me clarify: if you wish to bring someone, you may bring someone. I can get you two tickets.'

'No, I'd like to stick with the first offer.'

Caitlin rolled her eyes, but didn't say anything.

'OK. Let's make things simple. After I've heard you play, would you like to go out for a drink with me? *I'm* asking. Officially.'

'You realise I've no idea if you're joking or not.'

'If it's a no, I'm joking. If it's a yes, I'm not.'

'I don't think *you* know if you're joking or not.'

This was an accurate conclusion to draw. The whole trajectory of the evening felt like a joke – a very twisted joke – but it was a joke to which Gabriel did not know the ending. He was flying completely blind.

'OK, fine. It's a date,' Caitlin told him.

Gabriel tried not to look too self-satisfied, but probably failed. The man opposite – he with the many facial wounds – was staring into the middle distance as if he wanted to punch something. And who could blame him? Not only was he bleeding from his eyes; those same eyes were now being forced to witness a scene that could fairly be described as nauseating. Gabriel did not care. His own minor injuries had long since been forgotten.

Bribery – It's like Tipping
in Advance

An hour later, Gabriel had started to think that the hospital staff had also forgotten his minor injuries, and Caitlin's too. The bloody football fan had been seen some time ago, and the drunk had wandered off. But the sleeping, unconscious or dead man remained, his state still indeterminable, and several more people had arrived to fill the vacated seats. By Gabriel's estimation, the waiting room had experienced neither a net gain nor a net loss, which gave the overall impression that nothing at all was happening.

Despite this, it felt less terrible now. In part, Gabriel supposed this was nothing more than desensitisation – proof that you could indeed get used to any environment, however unpleasant. But he also realised that his tolerance of the situation was entirely contingent on Caitlin being there. If she'd left, he wouldn't have been able to last even five more minutes in A and E.

They talked for most of that hour, and it was, to begin with, easy and comfortable. Gabriel did not have to lie very often. The flat he conjured was based on the first flat he'd owned when he moved to London – a cramped, one-bedroom affair in Lewisham. He may have exaggerated how cramped it was for dramatic effect, but for the most part, it felt like recounting rather than outright fabrication. When it came to university, he merely changed his degree to Mathematics, since this seemed a more likely route to a career as a research analyst. Caitlin was unsurprised to learn that he'd been to Oxford. She said he had that air about him.

'What air?' Gabriel asked.

'If I was being generous, I'd call it self-confidence,' she said.

'And if you weren't being generous?'

'Overconfidence.'

Caitlin had been to the Royal College of Music. She had graduated with a master's degree in 2004 and immediately embarked on what she described as 'an illustrious waitressing career' with a few internships and part-time orchestral positions on the side. Her big break had come a couple of years ago, when she'd landed a job with the English Chamber Orchestra. It was maternity cover, and only for one season, but it carried enough prestige to guarantee further salaried positions, culminating in her current one with the ELS. Her pay-packet wasn't something that many professionals would envy, but it was just about sufficient. It allowed her to pay the rent on her small basement flat in Barking.

'Why do you live alone?' Gabriel asked.

'Why do *you* live alone?' Caitlin retorted.

'I asked first,' Gabriel pointed out.

'Yeah, but I'm not sure what you're asking me. Are you asking why I don't flat-share or are you asking why I'm single?'

'Both, but mostly the second.'

Caitlin shrugged. 'I was in a long-term relationship that ended six months ago. We had a flat together that I could no longer afford, so I had to move somewhere smaller. I chose to live alone because the alternative – some sort of studenty flatshare – would have felt like a massive step backwards.'

'Why did your relationship end?'

'Work, mostly. All those evenings and weekends I was telling you about. They don't always make for a happy home life. OK, your turn. Why are you single? Assuming you *are* single.'

Gabriel pretended to be hurt. 'Do I look like a man who'd agree to a date if he wasn't available?'

'Yes, frankly. So it's fortunate for you that I try not to judge people on appearances alone.'

'I think you've failed, in this instance.'

'Well, I'm still waiting to be contradicted.'

'Yes, I'm single,' Gabriel told her. 'Have been for a while.'

'A while? Come on, you're going to have to give me more than that. No half answers.'

Gabriel hesitated, wondering how he could negotiate the Catherine minefield – or whether he should avoid it entirely and come up with something else. He sensed that Caitlin wasn't going to put up with any jokes here, and she wasn't going to be fobbed off. He needed to give her something real enough to stand some scrutiny, but distorted to the extent that he didn't come across as an absolute bastard. It was a tough proposition.

Fortunately, Caitlin's expression told him that this lengthy hesitation was not doing him any harm. It probably hinted at a depth of feeling that he otherwise would have struggled to manufacture.

'Well, I suppose I'm in a similar position to you,' he began. 'Fairly long-term relationship that didn't pan out.'

'Why not?'

'Because we wanted different things.'

It was a bit hackneyed, but it at least had the merit of being true. Completely true and completely misleading. But Gabriel could see that he'd delivered the line with enough conviction to persuade Caitlin; he'd delivered it well enough that she didn't even ask what the 'different things' were. She was happy to assume it was some genuine obstacle that was neither party's fault.

Strangely, Gabriel found it difficult to rejoice in his success. He was experiencing a feeling he was quite unfamiliar with – a disconcerting sense of having got away with something.

It was in this frame of mind that he resolved to find out how much longer they would have to wait. Caitlin told him that the attempt would be futile. In A and E, you never got told how long you'd have to wait; there was a good chance that nobody knew. While Gabriel accepted the premise that waiting times were hard to estimate, he also knew that there had to be some sort of provisional running order. Wasn't that the whole point of triage? Someone should at least be able to tell him where he and Caitlin stood on the current waiting list.

Simply knocking on the triage nurse's door would probably be deemed unacceptable, so instead he went back to reception to see if anyone there could help him. He found himself standing in front of the same receptionist who had admitted them, a woman with dull blond hair that was beginning to grey at the roots. She looked to be at least fifty, but Gabriel wouldn't have been surprised if she was actually much younger. He imagined that premature aging was an inevitable side effect of having to work in A and E.

'Great way to be spending your Saturday evening, isn't it?' Gabriel gave her his best smile; the smile he got back was of strained politeness.

'Can I help you?'

'Yes, I'm sure you can. You see, my friend and I have been here quite a while now,' Gabriel explained. 'I was hoping you'd be able to give me a rough idea of when we'll be able to see a doctor.'

He could tell from her expression that this was a common, and apparently unreasonable, request.

'We were mugged,' Gabriel added.

'I'm sorry to hear that.'

She didn't sound sorry.

'Yes, it was quite an ordeal,' Gabriel continued, pointing to his bloodstained shirt. 'So do you think you might be able to check on those waiting times for me?'

'I'm sorry, but the triage nurse prioritises cases based on urgency, so I can't give a specific time.'

'Yes, I understand how triage works. But I'm not asking for specifics. I just want a rough estimate. What's the average waiting time?'

The woman sighed, then turned in her chair to consult briefly with a colleague. 'Two hours,' she told Gabriel. 'The current wait time is about two hours.'

'OK. And presumably that's two hours from arrival?'

'The current wait time is two hours,' the receptionist repeated.

Gabriel took a short breath. 'Yes, but what I'm asking is whether that means two hours from the moment I arrived or two hours from now. I arrived over an hour ago, so it makes a considerable difference. Do you understand what I'm saying?'

'Yes, sir, I understand, but there's nothing else I can tell you. I don't know what the waiting time was when you arrived so I can't give you a better estimate.'

'Great.' Gabriel rubbed his temples while the receptionist gazed blankly through the riot-shield window. 'Look, I can appreciate that this isn't your fault. You don't have the information. So is there any chance I could speak with someone else? Can I see the triage nurse again?'

'Sir, the triage nurse is extremely busy. She can't spare the time to attend to non-urgent enquires. I realise it's frustrating for you, but if you just take a seat, I'm sure that—'

'OK, it's an imposition. I get that.' Gabriel took out his wallet and placed it between them on the counter. 'You're just trying to do your job, and I wouldn't want you to think that I'm ungrateful for your efforts.'

The receptionist frowned at the wallet. Without looking, and using just his left thumb and forefinger, Gabriel had managed to coax out the corner of a twenty. He was ready to double up if necessary, but he couldn't go much higher than that. He had to leave enough to bribe the triage nurse as well.

The receptionist didn't say a word. She looked from the wallet to Gabriel's face, then pointed at something over his right shoulder.

Despite her unpromising expression, Gabriel thought for a moment that he was being directed back through to triage. But when he turned his head, he saw that she was actually pointing to a large notice on the nearest wall. It read:

OUR HOSPITAL HAS A ZERO TOLERANCE POLICY TO
HARASSMENT. ANYBODY DISPLAYING VIOLENT,
THREATENING OR OTHERWISE ABUSIVE BEHAVIOUR
WILL BE ESCORTED FROM THE PREMISES.

'Oh, come on!' Gabriel said. 'How is this harassment? It's the opposite of harassment – it's like tipping for good service!'

'Either you return to your seat now,' the receptionist told him, 'or I call security. It's your choice.'

Gabriel calmly picked up his wallet, put it in his pocket and walked back to Caitlin.

'Any joy?' she asked him. She already knew the answer.

Gabriel shrugged. 'I tried to bribe the receptionist but she wasn't having it.'

'Well, never mind.' Caitlin patted his knee. 'You know, Gabriel, you have that whole deadpan thing down to a fine art. If you ever get tired of being a research analyst, you should think about stand-up comedy.'

42

The City of London

When they'd arrived at A and E, dusk had been falling. When they exited, two hours and fifty-three minutes later, the sky was the colour of an angry bruise – a blanket of night-time cloud infused with the sulphurous yellow of street lighting. Gabriel pulled his coat tighter over his chest. His instinct was to put his arm round Caitlin's shoulders, but he had no idea how this would be received. Historically, he would have taken it for granted that no woman with a pulse could object to being held by him. Now, with Caitlin, he felt weirdly unsure of himself. Despite three hours of on and off flirting, he could make no reliable assessment of her attitude towards him – not when everything she said and did seemed laced with irony.

It was possible, though of course extremely unlikely, that she didn't even find him attractive.

Instead of putting his arm round Caitlin's shoulders, Gabriel reached up and touched the tender area at the back of his head. It was slightly swollen, but hadn't needed stitches. The doctor had tested him for concussion – a minute of questions followed by ten seconds of walking in a straight line and touching his nose – then told him to go home, rest and take some aspirin. If, in the next twenty-four hours, he started to feel confused or nauseous, he should come back to A and E. Gabriel promised that he would, knowing full well that he would not. Given the choice between another three hours in A and E or a one-way trip to the mortuary, he would have happily taken the latter.

Caitlin's injury had proven less straightforward, though the method used to examine it seemed just as crude. It mostly consisted of the doctor bending her wrist in every possible direction and gauging by her winces how much pain it was causing. After a couple of minutes of this, the doctor had concluded that it was probably just a bad sprain, but she had to come back for an X-ray to be certain. In the meantime, she was told not to do anything that could exacerbate the injury. Playing the violin was definitely out.

She was still flexing her wrist now, as they walked out of the hospital onto Whitechapel Road, her lips narrowed in an anxious pout. Looking west, Gabriel could see the high-rises at the edge of the City; as always, the Gherkin was lit up like a Christmas tree. It occurred to him, then, that he was absurdly close to his familiar patch of London. The Square Mile, St Katharine Docks, Canary Wharf – all the places he'd lived and worked in the past decade were no more than a five-minute cab ride away. And yet this area he was in now might as well have been a foreign country. He knew only two things about Whitechapel: it was the second worst spot on the Monopoly board, and it was the historical haunt of Jack the Ripper. Glancing around, Gabriel did not think it could have improved much since then. Opposite the hospital, the street was lined with pawnbrokers, takeaways and bookies.

In the daytime, Gabriel presumed, the locals would hop from one to the other, selling their cheap tat and stolen goods in the pawnshop before spending the windfall on fast food and gambling.

Of course, he'd always known, in an abstract sort of way, that these pockets of squalor still existed in central London, and that geographically they were pressed right up against the part of the city in which billions of pounds were traded daily. But this was the first time it had ever registered on a visceral level. In this instant, the financial district was literally shining in the distance, a beacon of silver and electric blue blazing through the surrounding grime.

'Gabriel?'

'Yes?'

'Are you sure your head's OK? You were miles away.'

'Right. I was, um, looking at the Gherkin.'

'Yeah, it's hard to ignore. I wonder what the view's like from the top of that thing.'

'Astonishing.' Gabriel wasn't speculating. He'd been in the private members' club on the top floor several times, most recently on the previous New Year's Eve.

'I asked if you're getting the Tube,' Caitlin told him.

'No, I think I'll treat myself to another taxi.' Gabriel gestured to his bloodied shirt. 'Avoid all those awkward stares.'

'Right. Understandable.' She brushed a loose strand of hair from her face. 'So I guess this is goodbye, for now. I'm going to brave public transport.'

'No, let me drop you off.'

'Thanks, but I'd rather save a few quid.'

'My treat. I insist.'

'No, really. That's generous of you, but you've done far too much already. Plus we're not even heading in the same direction. I have to get to St Paul's.'

Gabriel pretended he didn't know this. 'You meeting someone?'

'Uh, yeah, kind of. It's a bit of a convoluted story.'

Gabriel waited patiently while she explained about the busking, and how she'd left some of her equipment with a 'friend'. The irony, of course, was that Gabriel also had to get to St Paul's. He had to collect his Ferrari from the multi-storey on Queen Victoria Street. He probably could have told Caitlin this; she would have assumed he was doing his 'deadpan thing'. Instead, he pointed out that St Paul's was far less of a detour than Barking.

'Besides,' he said. 'It would make me much happier if I knew you were OK. I don't want you getting yourself mugged again.'

Caitlin laughed at this. 'Christ, Gabriel! The Tube station is across the street. I don't think you need to worry.'

'You obviously don't know your history,' Gabriel told her. 'We're slap in the middle of Jack the Ripper territory. So I'm afraid I really am going to insist.'

He flagged down the cab that was approaching in the near lane, then held the door open for her.

Caitlin looked at him for a few moments, a thin smile playing on her lips. 'You know, Gabriel, when a guy identifies an area of the city with a particular historical serial killer, I tend to be more worried about the guy than the area.'

'In general, that would be a very good policy. In the future, make sure you don't get into a taxi with any of those guys.' With his free hand he gestured through the open door. 'Shall we?'

43

Another Awful Decision; Possibly the Worst Yet

As they headed west through the City, Gabriel asked lots of questions about the busking. How long had she been doing it? Where did she play? What did she play? What was a loop pedal and how did it work? Partly it was to fill in the gaps; mostly it was because he was losing track of the gaps. The more they talked, the harder it was to remember what he was supposed *not* to know. The simplest solution was to bombard her with so many questions that all angles were covered. That way, there was little chance of him slipping up.

She told him that she'd started busking one summer at university, as a way of topping up her student loan. It turned out to be far more lucrative than bar work.

'OK, you've got to promise not to judge me too harshly,' Caitlin said.

'I'm the least judgemental person I know,' Gabriel told her.

'Right. Well, I was basically riding the tail-end of that brief media obsession with Vanessa Mae. You remember that? I completely ripped off her business model: got myself an electric violin and some extremely short skirts.'

'Sounds very liberating.'

'Yeah, *so* liberating. It makes me cringe when I think about it now, but at the time, that's exactly what I told myself. I'm sure I managed to cook up some elaborate third-wave-feminist justi-fication for what I was doing. You know: by choosing to dress this way I'm actually exploiting the male gaze rather than being exploited by it.'

Gabriel nodded as if he understood what she meant.

'There was probably a large dollop of neo-Marxism thrown in too, because now I didn't have a boss. I wasn't selling my labour for minimum wage. Instead, I was performing – generally to a bunch of yuppie commuters with far more money than sense. Friday evenings I used to make what felt like a small fortune. You'd get all these over-privileged, over-testosteroned City pricks stage-whispering obscenities and haemorrhaging coins. You know the type: six-figure salaries, egos to match.'

'I know *of* the type,' Gabriel confirmed.

'Well, needless to say, it got very tired very quickly.'

'So you changed the business model?'

'Yep. Ditched the short skirts, started playing to tourists in Trafalgar Square and Covent Garden. My income took an immediate hit, but it kept me afloat through university. A couple of years later, I was cohabiting and money was less of an issue. Then, a few months ago, I found myself almost back where I started – hovering on the edge of insolvency. So now I'm busking again. It was a straight choice between that and a payday loan.'

'I think you made the right choice. Apart from the location.

I'm not sure St Paul's current tenants have the funds to patronise the arts.'

'You'd be surprised. St Paul's is a double tourist trap at the moment. I think as many people come to see the Occupy camp as the cathedral.'

'So it was a financial decision rather than a political one?'

'No, it was both. I saw the images on the news a month ago and it just seemed obvious. Go along, show a bit of support for the screwed majority, and perhaps make a few quid on the side.'

Gabriel looked at her for a few moments without saying anything.

Caitlin smiled and shrugged. 'Hey, it's also a pretty spectacular backdrop to play against. Who needs a tiny skirt when you've got a seventeenth-century cathedral framing you?'

'Why limit yourself? You could so easily have both.'

A few minutes later, the taxi was pulling up just behind a police van, not far from where Gabriel's chauffeur typically stopped. Caitlin turned in her seat to look at him.

'Listen, I assume that you still want to get home and nurse those wounds. But if you don't, you're very welcome to come with me.'

'Do you want me to come with you?'

'You shouldn't read too much into it.'

'I think I should pass. I'm not sure the Occupy movement is exactly my scene.'

'Why not?'

Because I co-manage a multi-billion-pound hedge fund.

'I just think they might be a bit too . . . radical for me.'

'Christ, where have you been getting your information, the *Daily Mail*?'

Gabriel shrugged.

'Trust me, they're just normal people like you and me. People who think that a system that enriches the few by shafting the many is probably a system that needs to change. What's radical about that?'

'Well, I suppose it's the method more than the message.'

'The method? Peaceful demonstration?'

Gabriel shrugged again; he didn't think there was much else he could do.

'OK, that settles it. You are coming with me.'

'I'd love to, but—'

'No buts, Gabriel. This time *I'm* insisting. You survived three hours in A and E. Five minutes in the Occupy camp is going to be a cinch.'

'Five minutes?'

'Yes, five minutes for you to realise that you're being an idiot. I can't see it taking any longer.'

Obviously, there were innumerable reasons not to. In five minutes' time, he could be back behind the wheel of his Ferrari. In twenty minutes, he could be home with a large glass of red wine and . . .

What? CNN? The *Financial Times*? Thoughts of his impending death?

Or he could choose to spend a few more minutes with Caitlin, in a distracting if hopelessly inappropriate situation.

Gabriel passed the cab driver the fare and got out.

A Handsome Devil

Under most circumstances, he would have been worried about his clothes, but today Gabriel was dressed as casually as he ever dressed – pale blue twill shirt, dark merino trousers, autumn coat of some obscure Himalayan goat. Additionally, the trousers were of course ripped, and the shirt was bloodstained. The brands he favoured were so exclusive that most people – people who weren't Saudi princes or Russian oligarchs – would never have heard of them; and he at least knew for certain that all of his garments were ethically sourced, having been hand-stitched in London or New York or Milan. Gabriel could say with absolute confidence that none of his clothes, right down to the underwear, had been made by Indian slave children. How many people, even in the Occupy camp, would have been able to make the same claim?

Since Gabriel habitually arrived at work early and left late, he was used to seeing the camp at night. But being here now, he was struck by how much of the site was illuminated by the surrounding street lighting. In addition, the cathedral itself was lit from every side, and much of this light was reflected off its white walls and back into the churchyard. There were pockets of people scattered around the square, the largest groups clustered around the cathedral steps. From somewhere close to the statue of Queen Anne came the inevitable sound of drumming.

He followed Caitlin to one of the large marquees, which stood opposite the entrance of Starbucks, no more than ten metres from the front doors of Stanton House. Inside the marquee, there were perhaps a dozen people sitting on floor cushions, configured in a loose circle as if engaged in some arcane hippy ritual. Given the choice, Gabriel would no more have entered that circle than he would a coliseum full of wild animals. But Caitlin didn't give him a choice. She grabbed his hand and pulled him after her into the tent, which was lit with a couple of rows of LED strip lighting affixed to the roof poles. Several pairs of eyes swung in their direction, with more than one gaze lingering on Gabriel's bloodstains. It was probably for the best that he was given no opportunity to reuse his 'you should've seen the other guy' gag.

'Hey,' Caitlin said. 'I'm looking for Matt. Anyone seen him?'

'Which Matt?' This came from a Middle-Eastern-looking man in a parka. 'I think we have a few.'

Caitlin held her hand a few inches above her head. 'He's about yay high, with dreadlocks. Smokes roll-ups, kind of scruffy.'

'You've just described about half the camp.'

This provoked a chorus of laughter. Gabriel forced his reluctant mouth into the semblance of a smile.

'You're the violinist,' said a studenty woman with black-framed glasses. 'I saw you playing earlier.'

'Right,' Caitlin confirmed. 'I'm the violinist.'

Gabriel held up the violin case, which he'd been carrying for her, in mute corroboration of this fact, and regretted the gesture almost instantly. He probably gave an impression not dissimilar to the Chancellor presenting the Budget briefcase. He was not used to feeling so out of his depth.

'I left some of my equipment with Matt,' Caitlin went on. 'Generic Matt. He said he'd put them somewhere safe for me.'

'I heard him say he was going to get something to drink,' the studenty woman said. 'It wasn't that long ago. You should try the kitchen tent. D'you know where it is?'

'Left of the steps, near the recycling bins?'

'That's the one. Help yourselves to tea and coffee. You look like you could do with it.'

Gabriel thought she was probably addressing him at this point. 'It's been a long day,' he told her.

Caitlin gave a short wave, then nudged him back out of the tent.

The kitchen turned out to be surprisingly well equipped. It was lit, like the other marquee, with LED strips that ran the length of the roof. On a pallet on the ground there was a huge two-ring stove connected to a fifteen-kilogram butane tank, and not far from this was an electric water heater that was plugged into an extension socket, its cable running out the back of the tent. Piles of clean plates and cups and cutlery were stacked on a wooden trestle table, and several feet back from this, a free-standing shelving unit reached almost to the roof. It was laden with catering-sized pots and pans, and enough food to outlast a siege. Tinned fruit and beans, sacks of potatoes, porridge oats and pulses, gallon upon gallon of bottled water. A couple of large plastic crates were overflowing with fresh fruit and vegetables, and on another row of tables there were clear tubs filled with rolls and biscuits and flapjacks. Next to these there was a sign that read: **EVERYTHING IS FREE BUT DONATIONS ARE WELCOME!** And a couple of feet from this, slouched in a plastic chair, was Matt Dreadlocks. He was holding a steaming mug in both hands and talking to a woman with jet-black cropped hair and neck tattoos. Both turned as Gabriel and Caitlin approached, and Matt started grinning broadly.

'Caitlin! Hey, how's it going? Have you met Lucinda?'

The tattooed woman held out her hand for Caitlin to shake. Gabriel thought she was the least likely Lucinda he'd ever seen.

'This is Gabriel,' Caitlin said.

'Hey, Gabriel. Cool name, man.' Matt had put down his mug and stood up, and now held out his clenched fist. It took Gabriel what seemed like several seconds to interpret the gesture, and when he did, he felt there was but one polite response available to him. Reluctantly, he returned the gesture and the two men fist-bumped.

Matt clapped Gabriel across the shoulder, not troubling to remove his hand afterwards. 'Dude, what the fuck happened to you? You look like you've been mauled by a bear.'

'We were mugged,' Caitlin said. 'Well, I was mugged. Some kid snatched my bag. Gabriel happened to be passing and tackled him.'

'He was a full-grown kid,' Gabriel clarified. 'Probably seventeen or eighteen. Not a child.' He was at least grateful that Caitlin had used the word tackled rather than any more accurate alternative; it was possible that she hadn't seen exactly how it happened.

Lucinda was frowning and shaking her head in disbelief. Matt, meanwhile, had more or less thrown his arm round Gabriel's shoulders. 'You're a hero, man. A real-life hero. And people say civic responsibility is dead! You, my friend, are proof that it ain't so.'

Gabriel nodded modestly. What else could he do?

'Caitlin, are you OK? Do you guys need anything? We have a first-aid tent somewhere. It's pretty well stocked.'

'No, we're OK – or relatively OK. We've already been to A and E.'

Caitlin spent the next few minutes going over what had happened in more detail, with Matt interjecting every other sentence to repeat his assertion that Gabriel was a modern-day Good Samaritan, or a real-life Batman, or some other variant on this theme. Lucinda looked less convinced. Several times Gabriel noticed her looking at him through narrowed eyes. In most other people, Gabriel would have gone so far as to call it a glare, but he suspected, in Lucinda's case, this was merely her default expression. She looked like someone who'd been born with a glare on her face.

'Tea – you definitely need a cup of tea after an ordeal like that,' Matt insisted. 'When did you last eat? You've missed dinner by about two hours, but I think there's some leftovers some-where.'

'I'm starving,' Caitlin told him. 'But Gabriel hasn't decided if he's staying yet. He only agreed to pop in for five minutes so I could prove to him that you're not all foaming-at-the-mouth radicals.'

Lucinda snorted at this. 'Define radical.'

Sleeping in a churchyard for a month, Gabriel wanted to reply. *Neck tattoos that lock you out of mainstream employment.* Instead, he scowled at Caitlin and said, 'I don't recall saying that anyone was foaming at the mouth.'

Caitlin smiled sweetly.

Matt planted his hand on Gabriel's shoulder again. 'Leave him to me. I'll take him over to the re-education tent.' The pressure on Gabriel's shoulder increased. 'Ha! I'm just fucking with you, man. Don't look so worried. What would you like to know?'

Caitlin got up from her plastic chair at this point. 'Actually, I am going to leave you guys, just for a few minutes.' She picked up her violin case from the ground. 'I'd like to put this with the rest of my gear, if that's OK? Away from passing feet.'

'No problem,' Matt said. 'It's all in the tech tent, next door to the generator. Head outside and follow the smell of petrol.'

A minute later, Matt was busying himself making four mugs of tea, and Gabriel had been left sitting with Lucinda.

'You know, you look very familiar,' she told him. 'It might sound weird, but we haven't met before, have we?'

Gabriel felt a small surge of panic, which he quickly squashed. Up to this point, the possibility that anyone in the camp might recognise him had seemed so remote that he'd given it almost no thought. Despite working next door, he'd never interacted with his neighbours in any meaningful way; most of the time, he'd taken pains to avoid them. He was just one among the thousands of people who must pass by every day. And even now, it was clear that Lucinda hadn't managed to place him. She just had a feeling, easily dismissed.

'I think I just have one of those faces,' Gabriel told her with a smile. It was a line, and a smile, that would have worked better if she hadn't so obviously been a lesbian. She still looked unconvinced.

189

Fortunately, Matt seemed keen to back him up. 'Yeah, you're a handsome devil,' he said, stirring soya milk into the mugs. 'Handsome *and* heroic. I think our Caitlin might have a bit of a thing for you.'

Gabriel didn't know if the other man was testing the water here, but his instinct was to stake his claim up front. 'I might have a bit of a thing for her,' he said.

'How sweet,' said Lucinda, her expression dour. 'Love at first sight.'

'Ignore her,' Matt told him. 'She's a cynic.'

'I'm a realist,' Lucinda said.

'How does that sit with being a radical?' Gabriel asked. It probably wasn't wise to antagonise her, but he was struggling to keep his irritation in check.

Lucinda just shrugged.

Matt handed them both mugs of tea before rejoining them on the plastic chairs. 'Listen, Gabe, we're a pretty broad church here. Some of us would identify ourselves as radicals, some as Marxists or anti-capitalists, and some as socialists. But just as many would refuse any of these labels. There are plenty of people here who consider themselves nothing more than freethinkers. There are several who would describe themselves as unashamedly middle-class. This is a movement that doesn't divide people along artificial boundaries. You've seen the banners, right, we are the ninety-nine per cent?'

Gabriel nodded that he had. He saw them every working day.

'Well, it's not just a slogan. It's a genuine philosophy. This is a movement that incorporates pensioners as well as students. Many of us are also holding down full-time jobs. We have a barrister camping here. We have social workers and teachers and artists and graphic designers. We have one guy who served in Iraq and Afghanistan. The point is, we're a wide section of society, with a wide range of beliefs and backgrounds. But the thing we agree on is that the current system has failed. It's failed the majority it's meant to serve. Sometimes, I think that's the *only* thing we agree on.'

Gabriel wasn't sure how to take this statement. He was surprised by it, but that was mostly to do with the number of professionals Matt claimed as part of the camp. Gabriel had assumed that everyone involved was either a student or unemployed and living off state handouts.

'How do you get anything done?' Gabriel asked. 'I mean, if you all disagree over – I don't know, your basic ideology, I guess. If there's that level of disagreement, how can you make any decisions about what you want to achieve?'

'We run a democracy,' Lucinda said, stretching out every syllable. 'A genuine, participatory democracy. We debate, we argue and we vote.'

'Right. Which is also how the rest of the country's run, last time I checked.'

Lucinda laughed as if this was the most naïve claim she'd ever heard. 'Remind me, what sort of debate did we have about the banking bailout? I don't recall *any* serious debate. What I remember is being told that there is no alternative. We have to prop up this corrupt and failed system – or else!'

'Or else the economy would have collapsed,' Gabriel told her, very patiently. It was frustrating to be lectured on a subject in which he obviously had far more expertise than she did, but he had to rein himself in. 'It was presented as a fact because there was a broad consensus among experts that it *was* a fact. No money to pay wages, food and fuel shortages, general chaos. *That* was the alternative.'

It was possible he hadn't reined himself in enough. Lucinda's glare was becoming a snarl.

'I'm not saying it was fair,' Gabriel added. 'I'm just saying that at the time it really was the least bad option.'

Matt nodded. 'Yeah, and that's the tagline capitalism has been running on for well over a century now. The least bad option. It's stirring stuff.'

'And shows a complete failure of the imagination,' Lucinda added. 'Listen, even if what you're saying is true – just for the sake of argument – even if we were on the verge of economic meltdown, that doesn't come close to justifying the decisions the ruling elite have made on our behalf. If there were no viable alternatives to the bailout, there were plenty of alternatives when it came to funding it. Here's a *radical* example: we could have made the rich pay for it rather than the poor. We could have levied the City and collected unpaid corporation tax rather than taking money from charities and libraries and the disabled. If we now own a majority share in RBS and HBOS, we could stop paying the six-figure pensions of the same fucking directors who caused the crash!'

Gabriel held his hands up. 'OK, so rewarding financial incompetence is immoral and idiotic. I'd be the last person to object to that statement. But I suspect that's a legal issue more than anything. I'm sure there are plenty of politicians who'd love to strip Fred Goodwin of his pension. It would be a sure-fire vote-winner. But all that would happen is they'd find themselves fighting and losing a very expensive court case. Like it or not, those men had legally enforceable contracts.'

'Brilliant! That's the best argument I've ever heard, *Gabriel*. If our politicians, our supposed representatives, are powerless to change a law that nine out of ten people despise, what does that tell you about our democracy? Why do we have a legal system that protects wealth and property over the rights of the vulnerable?'

These questions had, of course, been phrased in a way that precluded any reasonable answer, but Matt intervened before Gabriel could point this out.

'Listen, man. No one's trying to tell you what to think here. Most of us wouldn't claim to have all the answers.' Gabriel suspected that Lucinda was excluded from this 'most', but he chose to let it slide. 'But a good starting point is to ask the right questions – the ones that *aren't* being asked in Parliament or the mainstream media. In a way, that's the whole purpose of this camp. We've created a public space where people can talk about the things our elected representatives don't want to address in any meaningful sense. Actually, it goes deeper than that. What we have here is a community based on cooperation and generosity rather than individualism and greed. Everyone here is valued. Everyone has a voice and everyone contributes. It doesn't matter if you're a barrister or unemployed and homeless. The point is, if anyone wants to claim there is no viable alternative to the current system, if anyone wants to say that human beings are defined by the profit motive, then this camp is living, breathing proof to the contrary. It's like Gandhi said, you have to be the change you want to see.'

Under normal circumstances, Gabriel would have told him to leave Gandhi out of this. It didn't matter what Gandhi said; an argument had to stand or fall on its own merits, and Gabriel remained unconvinced that the change anyone wanted to see was tented communes springing up all over the capital. But there was also a part of him that felt strangely ambivalent about at least some of the ideas expressed. Previously, he'd have said that the people who complained the loudest about unfairness – perceived unfairness – were the people who lacked the drive to do anything about it. People who refused to take responsibility for their own life choices, who thought that the state owed them an existence. After all, it wasn't as if Gabriel had been born into a life of special privilege; everything he owned, everything he'd achieved, he'd had to work for, and the same opportunity was there for anyone with half a brain and a willingness to use it. And yet, in some respects, these people were not *that* dissimilar to him. They weren't idle. They weren't content to sit back and wait for someone else to solve all their problems for them. And despite every appearance to the contrary, some of them were in possession of fully functioning brains.

This may have been the thing that surprised him the most. He was genuinely impressed that someone who looked like Matt could sustain a detailed, coherent and even fluent line of argument – regardless of whether that argument had any true merit.

Lentils

Gabriel was saved from having to tar himself with the anti-Gandhi brush. At that moment, Caitlin reappeared, minus her violin case.

'How are you guys getting on?' she asked. 'You all look very intense.'

Matt's hand hovered for a couple of seconds on the edge of Gabriel's personal airspace before moving in to alight once more on his shoulder. 'Minor disagreements about the basic nature of democracy, but nothing irresolvable.'

Caitlin shrugged. 'Well, there's nothing more democratic than everyone disagreeing with each other, right?'

'You got it,' Matt said.

'Absolutely,' agreed Gabriel.

Lucinda gave a short sharp laugh; more of a bark, really.

'So, you two should definitely stay for some food,' Matt told them.

'I definitely am staying for some food,' Caitlin pointed out. 'It's Gabriel who has to make up his mind.'

Two minutes ago, he would have eagerly left. Now he didn't want to. There was no doubt that Caitlin had a calming effect on him. The simple fact of her presence was like popping a Valium or drinking a large glass of wine. Everything was suddenly more tolerable. Even Lucinda seemed, for the moment, less of a pain. 'I could probably manage some food,' Gabriel said.

The leftovers Matt had spoken of turned out to be vegetarian moussaka, which he served to them cold on plastic plates. That it was weirdly delicious was probably a testament to how hungry Gabriel was; given that it contained literally no meat, he could think of no other explanation. The last thing Gabriel had eaten was a chocolate bar in A and E.

'God, this is good,' Caitlin said between mouthfuls.

'Thank you,' said Matt. 'Our chef's . . . well, he's a chef. He usually does catering at festivals. He supplied most of the basic kit for the kitchen.'

'You'll have to pass on my compliments,' Caitlin told him. 'I didn't know that lentils could be made to taste this good.'

'I didn't know that lentils could be made to taste of *anything*,' Gabriel noted.

He thought it was a fairly innocuous comment, but it was enough to make Caitlin laugh. Her hand shot to her mouth in an attempt, only partially successful, to stop a piece of aubergine on its way back out. Gabriel had no idea why this didn't bother him, but it didn't.

Caitlin was shaking, and her face had started to go very red.

'If you're blushing,' Gabriel told her, 'hold up one finger. If you're choking, hold up two fingers.'

She held up her middle finger, her eyes watering.

Matt handed her a paper napkin.

196

Lucinda said that she was going for a smoke and left.

'Gabriel, for fuck's sake!' Caitlin admonished. 'You don't draw attention to someone else's faux pas. Now I've offended Lucinda.'

'I think *I* probably offended Lucinda when I disparaged the humble lentil,' Gabriel said.

'Lucinda is pretty hardcore about her veganism,' Matt confirmed.

'Great.' Caitlin wiped her mouth and set her napkin down on her plate. 'So much for challenging your stereotypes.'

Gabriel shrugged. 'The lentils were tasty, and that's a phrase I never anticipated using. I'd say one stereotype has been successfully challenged.'

The Tea and Empathy Tent

Caitlin was rubbing her arms, and it was this that first alerted Gabriel to the fact that the temperature must have dropped several degrees since they left the hospital. He hadn't noticed that it was cold because his coat, needless to say, was extremely well insulated; when you spent top dollar on Himalayan goat wool, you weren't just paying for the novelty of it.

If Gabriel had been oblivious to the cold, the rising wind was much harder to overlook. Matt told them that it was a common problem around St Paul's, with the cathedral and the surrounding offices creating a wind tunnel that frequently wreaked havoc in the camp. Of course, Gabriel already knew what conditions could be like in the cathedral square, but his experience was mostly limited to the thirty seconds he spent each day getting from a climate-controlled Mercedes to a climate-controlled office. He hadn't really appreciated what camping in this location might entail. Matt pointed out a lot of details – obvious details – that Gabriel had missed. Since they had set up camp on bare cobblestones, tent pegs were not an option. The kitchen marquee had to be anchored by tying its steel frame to whatever ballast was available – the spare butane tanks, sacks of potatoes, three-gallon bottles of drinking water. Many of the smaller tents were weighted down with tins of baked beans, and some had been tied or gaffer taped to the wooden pallets on which they sat. The pallets were even less comfortable than the bare ground, but they were also less cold. They opened up the possibility of sleeping in one-hour stretches. It was difficult to stay asleep for any longer than this because of the cathedral bells, which sounded on the hour throughout the night.

Because of its height, the kitchen tent had been set up in one of the more sheltered areas of the camp, close to the north face of the cathedral. Nevertheless, when the gas stoves weren't running, it wasn't much warmer than being outside in the open. The front was exposed to the elements, at least until midnight, when the kitchen was closed up, and any trapped heat was swiftly lost. Consequently, Matt suggested that they should move to the Tea and Empathy tent, which served up hot drinks – and empathy – twenty-four hours a day, free of charge to anyone who asked. The way he spoke about it, you'd have thought it was the pinnacle of human civilisation. He seemed to believe that tea and empathy were the panacea for all the world's social and economic ills. If a problem seemed intractable, you hadn't thrown enough tea and empathy at it.

Personally, Gabriel would have killed for a Starbucks. He may have been able to change his mind about lentils, but weak tea with soya milk was another matter. He didn't even consider braving the instant coffee. Instead, he sat next to Caitlin and opposite Matt on some fold-out canvas chairs and watched the two of them warming their hands around steaming plastic mugs.

The other occupant of the tent was a doughy New Age type with silver hair down to her backside. Matt introduced her as Cressida, or something similarly obscure. Gabriel assumed she was the on-duty empathiser. Tacked to the tent behind her was a note reading **THIS IS A DRUG AND ALCOHOL FREE ZONE**, which Gabriel found genuinely surprising – though not as surprising as the piano, which sat at the entrance to the tent, slightly to her right. According to Matt, someone had donated it to the camp.

'Strange thing to donate,' Gabriel observed.

'Gabriel, you're an idiot,' Caitlin told him. 'It's the perfect thing to donate, especially to an empathy tent. If I wasn't under strict medical instructions, I'd prove that to you right now. I'd play something that would make you *weep*.'

Gabriel wasn't sure how he felt about this proposition, but he didn't doubt her claim. He was about to formulate this sentiment into something wittier, and less sentimental, when Matt interrupted his train of thought, possibly on purpose.

'You know, Gabriel, just about everything that keeps us running has been donated, from the food to the furniture. You might be surprised at how much support there is for this camp. I think many of us have been surprised by it, but that's the way it's been from day one: people bringing tents and clothes and sleeping bags. And we're not talking about activists here. These are just normal people living normal lives. There's far greater backing for this movement than certain parts of the media would have you believe.'

Gabriel would have liked to find this statement patronising, but if he was being honest with himself, he had to accept that it might be true. He was more than a little familiar with the parts of the media Matt was referring to, and their message had been pretty consistent. The Occupiers were a few hundred left-wing lunatics whom all ordinary, hard-working Londoners considered a nuisance and an eyesore. Boris Johnson had referred to them as 'crusties' and 'boils'.

'It's not just supplies,' Cressida, or whatever her name was, chipped in. 'I believe donations in money are up to around a thousand pounds a day now.'

'A thousand pounds?' Caitlin gasped. 'Every day?'

Gabriel found it both uncomfortable and weirdly affecting that she considered this amount worthy of a gasp. He earned a thousand pounds for every seventy-two minutes he worked.

'It's something like that,' Cressida said, nodding, 'on average. You'd have to ask someone from the finance team for an up-to-date figure.'

Gabriel forced a laugh before discerning, from everyone else's faces, that this was not a joke. 'Really? You have a finance team? How . . . corporate.'

Matt slouched back in his canvas chair, his legs stretched so far in front of him that his boots were just centimetres from Gabriel's merino trousers. 'Organised, man. We're just organised. There are no hierarchies here, no chains of command, but that doesn't mean there's no planning or structure. We have around fifteen separate work groups running different aspects of the camp. The tech team runs the website and keeps the lights on, Legal fights the eviction case; then there's Press, Outreach, Welfare – you name it. Everyone contributes according to their means and abilities. Like I said before, we're not just squatting here. We're demonstrating that there are ways of running a society that don't generate vast disparities in wealth and power.'

'Amen,' said Caitlin.

Gabriel nodded as if he were happy to go along with this. He suppressed the urge to point out that wealth had to be created before you could even think about how to distribute it; it didn't just fall from the sky.

'So, um, what about the thousand pounds a day?' Gabriel asked, after a respectful pause. 'Where does that go?'

'Gabriel!' Caitlin scolded.

'It's a legitimate question,' Gabriel pointed out. 'I'm not suggesting anyone's on the make.'

'It is a legitimate question,' Matt agreed. 'And every penny gets accounted for. Petty cash gets distributed by Finance. Larger amounts have to be approved by the general assembly. Everything's completely transparent.'

'I'm sure it is,' Gabriel said. 'I'm just interested to know how you spend a thousand pounds a day. I can't imagine your over-heads being that high.'

'You'd be surprised,' Cressida told him. 'We are feeding several hundred people a day here. And it's not just the protesters. There are a lot of homeless people too. We provide food, clothing and shelter to anyone who needs it.'

Matt nodded. 'Right. And then there's the court case, and the education programme, the leafleting. Any money that's left over will be used to fund future direct action and on improvements to the camp. I think we're currently looking to buy some solar panels to replace the generator.'

'In November?' Gabriel kept his voice as neutral as he could. 'I'm not sure you'll keep the water heaters going.'

Cressida shrugged off this objection. 'If we have to use less, we'll use less. Most of us agree that the petrol generator is detracting from our wider message about sustainability. We have to lead by example.'

Gabriel wondered if everyone would still be in agreement when winter started to bite, but he kept this thought to himself.

'You know, man,' Matt said, 'you ask some really good questions. What are our objectives and how are we going to achieve them? How are we managing our resources?'

Gabriel wasn't sure that he *had* asked these exact questions, but he nodded anyway.

'You have an eye for logistics,' Matt went on. 'I can tell. What do you do in the outside world?' He shot Caitlin a smile. 'When you're not rescuing damsels in distress.'

'I'm a research analyst,' Gabriel told him, no hesitation. 'I crunch data.'

'Research analyst? Yeah, I'm not surprised. You have that sort of mind. Very sharp.'

'Thank you.'

Matt leaned back even further in his chair, something Gabriel would not have thought possible. 'Hey, if you ever have any time on your hands, you should think about lending us some of that brainpower. Come along to one of our weekend assemblies. We're always looking for good strategists.'

'I'll certainly consider it,' Gabriel lied.

Caitlin patted him on his leg. 'There might be hope for you yet.'

Cressida started to say something about generators hooked up to exercise bikes – keep warm, keep fit, keep the juice flowing – but Gabriel wasn't paying much attention any more.

Caitlin's hand was still resting on his leg, a small warm weight just above the tear on his left knee. Neither of them made any move to change this.

Stealth

As if his life hadn't been hard enough already, Gabriel had now put himself in a position where simply getting in and out of the office was fraught with problems. On Monday morning, he had to get his driver to drop him off round the corner from St Paul's Churchyard, fifty metres back from his usual drop-off point. As he got out of the car, he gave terse instructions that he should be picked up from the exact same spot that evening. Fortunately, the driver was well trained enough not to ask why. Gabriel didn't know what he could have told him. They had been following the same unwavering routine for three years, and this sudden alteration was not an improvement. It was quantifiably worse – by fifty metres.

And the morning was the easy part. Gabriel got into work at least an hour before anyone in the camp started to stir, and now that it was getting colder, it seemed less and less likely that people would be rushing out of their tents at six twenty to greet the new day. The chance of being seen by Matt or Cressida or – God forbid – Lucinda was close to zero.

The evenings were a different matter, though. Gabriel took to lurking in the foyer of Stanton House until he had established to his satisfaction that his path was clear. Then, with his coat collar pulled up and his head down, like a private eye from some cheap TV show, he'd exit the building at double speed and not look up until he was back behind the tinted windows of the Mercedes.

He thought very seriously about buying a hat.

Almost Happy

It was stressful and ridiculous in equal measure, but it was also a very small part of his day. The dash past the camp amounted to no more than sixty tense seconds morning and evening – thirty, at his swiftest power-walk. The rest of the time, he was almost happy, or as close as he had come at any point in the past six weeks.

The downside was that his productivity continued to slide. Watching the camp had always been a temptation, but now it was irresistible. In all honesty, Gabriel knew he was checking the camp far more often than he was checking the markets. He was looking at it with new eyes, too. Whereas before he had seen only disorder and squalor, now he was noticing structure and routine; unfamiliar details. He saw the mini-exodus of workers leaving between eight and nine in the morning – some already in office wear, some in casual clothes but carrying gym bags, presumably planning to get washed and changed en route. The regularity, the same faces leaving at the same time each morning, corroborated what Matt had told him: many of these dissidents were holding down respectable full-time jobs.

Shortly, after the workers had left, a new wave of day activists started to appear. A significant proportion of these protesters were women with children; there actually seemed to be some sort of rudimentary crèche that would pop up every so often near the steps of St Paul's – an area where mats would be laid and soon filled with crawling and waddling infants.

Group meetings, involving up to a few hundred people, occurred twice a day at 1 and 7 p.m. Needless to say, Gabriel had already known that the demonstrators held plenty of these assemblies, but he hadn't realised just how punctual and orderly they were. They happened every day at the same times, and were conducted, it seemed, using an elaborate system of hand gestures to signify the assent or otherwise of the many participants. It was difficult to see from this distance – as were lots of the finer details of what was going on in the camp – so Gabriel soon ordered himself a small telescopic sight off the Internet. It offered five times magnification but was no larger than a marker pen, fitting inconspicuously in his inside jacket pocket. It was designed to sit on top of an astronomical telescope as a star-finder, not on a gun barrel, and this made Gabriel feel marginally less like a psychopath when he started using it.

He spotted Matt and Cressida down there most days, their hair making them easy targets. Lucinda was less distinctive from a distance, but she was a regular attendee at the daily meetings, always scowling and seemingly very vocal, which did not surprise Gabriel in the slightest.

Of course, he was really looking for Caitlin, though he knew there was no chance she'd be down there busking. She'd sent him a text message the Monday after A and E to tell him that the X-ray had shown no breaks or fractures, but she'd essentially been signed off work for the next week. No performing, no practising. *A week of gradual brain-death by daytime TV* – that was what she'd written.

Given these circumstances, Gabriel thought it reasonable to suppose that she might make her way over to St Paul's sooner or later, but it wasn't until the Friday that he spotted her. It was a little after midday, and she was lingering not far from the Tea and Empathy tent, outside which a man who looked like a Buddhist monk was dispensing head massages to tourists. Telescopic sight raised to his eye, Gabriel had been staring at this spectacle for several minutes, somewhat dumbfounded. It was pure chance that Caitlin had wandered into his field of view.

Did his heart skip a beat? Gabriel had never given the phrase any credence – he was certain it had no basis in biological science – and yet in that instant, something along those improbable lines really did occur. It was a shock that seemed to occur everywhere and all at once, like that first jolt of cocaine hitting the bloodstream.

If Gabriel hadn't known already that he was in trouble, this would have confirmed it.

He decided to text her.

I was thinking it's cruel to leave you wallowing in your flat. Perhaps we could get a coffee this weekend? (Together.)

Poetry it was not, but that wasn't the point. Really, he just wanted to see how she'd react when she read the message.

She smiled.

Who said anything about wallowing? I'm out now, it so happens.
I'm thinking about getting a head massage.

Having seen her expression through his telescopic sight, Gabriel
felt himself to be at a distinct advantage in this dialogue, which
was pretty much how he liked it.

Interesting, but it's very rude to leave a question unanswered.
Starbucks this weekend?

Starbucks – really? Not sure I agree with their attitude to corporation tax . . .

Yeah, but they make such great coffee it's difficult to care.

This made her laugh; Gabriel felt like some deranged puppeteer.
Deranged but contented.

We could go to the Ritz if you'd prefer? he typed, thinking that
he was getting better and better at his 'deadpan thing'.

Ha ha. I think I'd rather stay home and stick pins in my legs.

Terrible idea. You'll ruin your Vanessa Mae tribute act.

The conversation went on in that vein for several more minutes.
    Eventually, they would arrange to go to an independent café
and patisserie somewhere in Piccadilly. Gabriel would have loved
to have been able to take Caitlin to the Ritz.

A Woman Pushed to
Her Limits

Halfway through the session – their third – Dr Barbara removed her glasses and placed her head in her hands. Gabriel was unfamiliar with the normal working practices of psychotherapists, but he doubted this was the sort of thing that happened often. There was probably some sort of professional code that discouraged such a blatant sign that composure was being stretched.

'You know, Gabriel, usually I have this whole spiel I do with my clients quite early on because I find it helps with the process. Essentially, I say that this office is safe space. You should feel free to say whatever's on your mind without any fear of censure. My job is to listen, remain impartial and offer advice, not to judge. But you make this so, so hard.'

The last sentence, Gabriel deduced, was not part of the spiel.

'If it helps at all,' he said, 'I don't expect you not to judge me. You can express your disapproval of me and my actions in whichever way you see fit.'

Barbara *hmmphed*. 'I suspect that's because my disapproval means nothing to you.'

'No, that's not true. I mean, I realise I haven't known you for very long, but you're one of the few women – the few people – whose opinion I'd genuinely like to know.'

'Wonderful. I'm flattered that you regard me as a person as well as a woman. And I'm glad that you at least want to hear my opinion before disregarding it.'

Gabriel held up his hands in what he hoped was a gesture of placation. 'I think the most important thing, as far as I'm concerned, is that I just try to give you all the facts as honestly as possible.'

'Bravo, Gabriel. Under any normal circumstance, I'd regard that as a wonderful and astonishingly early breakthrough. But I'm not going to let you twist this therapy into something I don't want it to be. This isn't confession. You don't get to dump your sins in this office once a week and then carry on precisely as you were. I can't condone what you're doing.'

'I'm not asking you to condone it. I think I've made that clear.'

'You're asking me to tolerate it, and I'm not sure I can do that either. This isn't some abstract ethical discussion we're having. You're doing very serious damage to another human being, and it has to stop.'

'Barbara, I think you're being a little melodramatic here. I can understand that the deceit bothers you, but the last thing I want to do is damage this woman. I think I actually make her quite happy.'

'Which will make it even worse when everything comes crashing down. Seriously, Gabriel, how long do you think you can sustain this? As things stand, you have no possible future with this woman.'

'Well, no. But I don't have much of a future in any scenario.'

'Oh, please! You can't possibly use your condition to justify this. Or are you seeing it as some sort of twisted solution to this mess? Do you think you can pursue this relationship – this fantasy – in the hope that you won't be around to deal with the fallout?'

'No, of course not. I'm hoping to manage it in such a way that there won't be any fallout.'

'For heaven's sake, Gabriel! I've heard some wishful thinking in my time, but that's in a different stratosphere. What planet are you living on?'

Dr Barbara placed her fingers at her temples and scrunched her eyes closed, emitting a noise somewhere between a sigh and a groan.

'OK. Let's try to come at this from a different angle, since you seem so unwilling to think about the future. Let's talk about the here and now. Does it not make you uncomfortable to carry on like this? The lies, the pretence, the manipulation. It makes *me* feel uncomfortable just hearing about it.'

Gabriel had to think quite carefully before answering this.

'It has made me uncomfortable at times. It's not that I enjoy the lying, but then there's much more to it than that. The fact is, apart from the details, it doesn't feel like a pretence, and certainly not manipulative – or not in the sense that you mean it. It feels more like I'm . . . well, trying out an alternate version of myself, someone I could have been in different circumstances. You can call it fantasy if you want, but when I'm with her, it feels more real than any . . . relationship I've had before. It feels genuine.'

Barbara shook her head vociferously. 'You think *this* is genuine? If that's true, Gabriel, then God help you.'

'I'll admit it reflects badly on my past.'

'No, it reflects badly right now.'

Gabriel shrugged. 'I don't know. Listen, Barbara, can I ask you something?'

'You can ask. I can't promise that I'll answer.'

'Do you think that I'm fundamentally a bad person? I mean, I understand that you haven't known me for very long, but still, you must have an opinion, based on what you've seen.'

Barbara took some time to respond. From her expression, Gabriel didn't think that she was searching for a way to be tactful. She was going to give him an honest answer.

A Discourse on the Nature of Good and Evil

'Gabriel, I think some of the things you're doing are very bad indeed, as I've made perfectly clear. But I also have a problem with this notion of fundamental evil. The truth is that almost every human being alive has the potential to be good or bad. Aside from a few genuine psychopaths, most people don't do bad things because of some simplistic "badness" inside them. Believe me, this is backed up by a mountain of research across numerous academic disciplines. The idea that people can be labelled *fundamentally* bad is in most cases absurd.'

'OK. Except when they fly planes into buildings, for example. I think we can agree that those people *are* just evil.'

'No, Gabriel, we can't. In fact, that's one of the worst examples you could come up with. That sort of evil is cultivated. It relies on a very complex web of social circumstances, ideology and indoctrination. The men you're talking about probably started life as fairly average human beings. It's just that most people find it unpalatable to believe that normal humans, as opposed to monsters, are capable of such atrocious acts. Well, the fact is that there's a lot of data that runs contrary to this assumption. Have you heard of the Stanford Prison Experiment, for example?'

Gabriel shook his head.

'Well, in a nutshell, it was a psychological experiment carried out in the 1970s. A group of perfectly average college students were divided randomly into two groups – prisoners and guards – and put into a mock prison environment. Within a matter of days, it had basically descended into Abu Ghraib – routine humiliation of the prisoners, sadism, cruel and unusual punishments. The experiment had to be brought to a premature end, but for the short time it ran, the results were unequivocal. If you encourage normal human beings to behave badly, they will. They don't even need any great incentive; just being authorised to do so is enough.'

Gabriel thought about this without saying anything. He could have told Barbara that you probably didn't have to go to a 1970s college campus or Abu Ghraib to demonstrate this idea; you could just hop in a taxi to Canary Wharf.

'The broader point,' Barbara continued, 'is that good and evil are not fixed attributes. Lots of psychologists since the Stanford experiment have looked at the issue in terms of our evolutionary heritage. As a social species, we're capable of cooperation and altruism and empathy and so on, but only up to a point. We're also good at switching off these impulses in certain situations. When it suits our ends, we're equally capable of deceit and greed, and hostility – particularly to those seen as belonging to a different tribe. This is all of us. Do you understand what I'm trying to tell you?'

'Are you telling me that it's not my fault if I behave badly?' Gabriel asked, rather optimistically. 'It's in my genes?'

'No, Gabriel, I'm not telling you that. I'm saying there are situations that nourish the better part of our nature and there are those that do the opposite.' Barbara gave him the look one might give to a wilfully disobedient child. 'As you point out, I don't know you very well, but I suspect very strongly that you've been putting yourself in these latter situations all your life. Based on what I know about your work and lifestyle, I'd say you've been pursuing self-interest with little or no regard for the effect this might have on other people. It's what you're still doing.'

'Yes, you're absolutely right. I'm not going to dispute any of that. But my point is that maybe I can change this. Maybe it's something that's already changing regardless of my intentions. I mean, a couple of months ago, the question of whether I'm a bad person or not wouldn't even have entered my mind. I wouldn't have thought it worth considering. But now . . . now I really don't know what I think. I don't even know if I'm the same person I was before. How much of this is me and how much is the tumour?'

'Gabriel, that's so far outside my area that I don't think I can give you any sort of answer. You'd have to ask a neurologist, or a philosopher, and even then I doubt you'd get a satisfactory explanation. But I also happen to think it's not that relevant to the discussion we're having. It's not enough to say that you feel like a different person, or even a better person. It's your actions that matter, and if you're unwilling to address this, then, frankly, I don't see how I can continue to see you. I don't see why I should.'

'Because I'm dying?'

'Yes, you're dying, and you have my full sympathy. It's a horrible position to be in. But that's not a reason for me to compromise *my* ethical standards.'

'Well, in a way you're compromising them whatever you choose to do. I don't see how I can address these issues on my own. I need your help.'

'Gabriel, do not try to manipulate me. You're not doing yourself any favours here. Besides, I'm not even certain that I *can* help you, not if you refuse to listen. That's half the point.'

'I am listening. I'm listening now.'

'Are you? Then I want you to think about this, Gabriel. Really think about it. If you care for this woman, if you respect her at all, then you either have to stop seeing her or tell her the truth.'

Gabriel hesitated before responding, mostly to show that he was taking these ideas on board. 'The problem, Barbara, is that I'm almost certain I can't stop seeing her. I'm not saying this to be manipulative, but she's the only meaning my life has at the moment. As for telling her the truth, well that just seems like a crueller path to the same outcome. We both know that if I tell her the truth – even a fraction of the truth – she'll never want to see me again.'

'Yes, we probably do know that. But I think it's the option you have to allow her. You need to try putting someone else's feelings ahead of your own.'

Gabriel swallowed. 'I think that's something I can certainly work towards. I just need a little more time.'

'Time is going to make things harder, not easier. The longer you allow this to go on the worse it's going to be.'

'OK, you're right. I know you're right. But you're asking me to change a lifetime's behaviour here. How can that happen overnight?'

Barbara put her fingers to her temples again, and Gabriel took this as a sign she was almost willing to concede the point.

'Gabriel, this is as close I've ever come to throwing a client out of my office. I need to know that you understand that.'

'Yes, I understand.'

'Good. Because from now on, I need you to work with me. You cannot expect things to continue unchanged.'

'I don't expect that. I want things to change, I really do.'

'You'd better be serious about this. No more chances.'

'No more chances.'

Barbara nodded, finally removing her fingers from her temples. 'Then we'll talk again next week. Right now, I feel like I need to get you out of here before I change my mind. If you have anything more to say to me, say it quickly. If not then go away and get some rest. You look like you could use it.'

'Thank you, Barbara.'

Gabriel got up and put on his coat, feeling the now familiar weight of the telescopic sight in his inside pocket. This was one detail he'd neglected to mention. Given the circumstances, it was probably for the best.

Gucci Gym Clothes

Gabriel had taken it for granted all his adult life that he knew how best to dress for any situation. Having said this, the range of situations in which he found himself was limited. Thus he knew how to dress to impress a board of directors or the CEO of a FTSE 100 company. He knew how to dress to set the mind of a billionaire investor at ease. He knew the value of a perfectly tailored shirt, and trousers so smooth they looked as if they'd been ironed by the hand of God. He knew by heart half a dozen different tie knots, and how to match them with any conceivable collar variation. He knew how to impress the women he typically wanted to impress.

With Caitlin, he faced an unfamiliar challenge. On the couple of occasions they'd met up for coffee, he'd tried to dress down, as far as this was possible; but short of leaving an extra shirt button undone, he was struggling for ideas. A big part of the problem was that Gabriel possessed a body that was seemingly made to hang expensive clothes on. Whatever he did to downplay the sophistication of his wardrobe, whatever sabotage he attempted, he always ended up looking as if he'd stepped out of the pages of a high-end catalogue.

Caitlin, in contrast, seemed to have perfected the art of dressing well while looking as if she'd made no particular effort. Gabriel was envious of this; it was the exact look he was failing to attain for himself.

In theory, attending a classical concert should have presented fewer difficulties. Gabriel was fairly sure that formal dress was standard, but how formal was too formal? In the end, he had to phone Caitlin to ask.

'There isn't a dress code,' she told him. 'I mean, normally I'd advise smart casual, leaning towards the smarter end of the spectrum, since the hall's in Chelsea. But in your case, you can just turn up in what you usually wear.'

'What's wrong with what I usually wear?'

'Nothing. That's the point. You always look immaculate.'

'You think I'm vain?'

'Well, you don't strike me as a man who owns an extensive T-shirt collection. Put it that way.'

'I own three T-shirts – two black, one white. They're by Gucci. I wear them to the gym.'

Caitlin laughed. 'Yeah, I can almost believe it.'

'You know, I'm thinking I might just go all out to impress. I look pretty devastating in a tuxedo.'

'I'm sure you do, Mr Bond. But unless you want to get mistaken for the conductor, I'd advise against it. You'll have to devastate the patrons of Cadogan Hall some other time.'

'I was thinking more of the violin section.'

'The violin section will be fully absorbed in playing their violins. You'll be lucky if you receive a passing glance.'

Gabriel decided to change tack. 'What will you be wearing?'

'Black, obviously. I'll be wearing a black dress.'

'I think you should consider blue. Or maybe even red. Red would suit you.'

'Gabriel, you can't have individual members of the orchestra wearing whatever the hell they like. Can you imagine how distracting that would be? Only the soloist gets to wear a different colour.'

'Why aren't you the soloist?'

'Well, the clue's in at least some of the title – the bit about it being a piano concerto. The piano player is the soloist. He's some German wunderkind, and I doubt he'll be wearing red, either. But I can probably get hold of his number if you want to phone him up and ask him.'

'I'm just trying to educate myself,' Gabriel said. 'This is an unfamiliar situation for me.'

'Gabriel, it's a concert, not a situation. There isn't going to be a written exam at the end. Wear something you feel comfortable in – not a tuxedo – and you'll be fine. Trust me, this is not something to worry about.'

She was wrong, of course. Gabriel's big fear was that he'd start bawling mid-performance, though he understood, on some level, that crying at a concert was not the same as crying on the Tube. Some people would even deem it socially acceptable. But for him, the possibility remained strange and terrifying, like an alien craft poised to invade.

Yet he'd felt somewhat reassured when Caitlin had given him the details of what he'd be listening to. It involved two pieces by someone called Rachmaninov: the Second Piano Concerto and Rhapsody on a Theme of Paganini. To Gabriel's mind,

Rachmaninov wasn't a name that suggested emotional excess. Rachmaninov sounded more like a man who might once have held a senior position in the KGB. As for this Paganini, Gabriel was almost certain that Paganini's was the name of a very good Italian restaurant in Mayfair. He'd eaten there several times, and his memories of the place were entirely positive. Which left only the 'rhapsody' part to fret over. Admittedly, this *was* a word with heavy emotional connotations, but as far as Gabriel could work out, it was just a pretentious artistic way of saying that you had enjoyed yourself. So probably not too much to worry about there, either.

According to Caitlin, both pieces were extremely accessible – even for someone like Gabriel. When Gabriel asked her what she meant by this, she told him that they were melodic and relatively short.

Gabriel had thought that all music was melodic – that this was part of the definition – but he decided to let the point slide on the assumption he was probably being teased. Likewise, he wasn't going to fall into the trap of asking what 'relatively' short meant. The subtext was already clear enough: not only was he vain, he also had a lousy attention span.

This was something else he should perhaps try to work on.

Cadogan Hall

Cadogan Hall was near Sloane Square. It was a part of Chelsea Gabriel was familiar with, but he'd never noticed the building before. Tucked down a side street and encircled by designer shoe shops, it was not the sort of building he *would* notice: a converted church, fairly modern, as churches went, with a bell tower rising from one corner and a series of arched alcoves at street level. The façade was illuminated in pale blue light, which made it more striking than it presumably was in the daytime, when it would have been just one more piece in London's mismatched architectural jigsaw. Inside, it resembled a posh cinema. Not that Gabriel had been to the cinema for years, but this was his only point of comparison.

He'd arrived half an hour early, by taxi, and spent the time before the performance in the bar next to the box office. He drank sparkling water and played on his phone. He was avoiding alcohol because of his emotional liability.

Gabriel waited until several people had left the bar before joining the short queue that was being funnelled into the auditorium. So far, it was about half full; he estimated a capacity of around a thousand. The main part of the hall followed a shallow slope down to the stage, and there was a wide U-shaped balcony that ran the full length of the rear and side walls. In terms of demographic, the crowd tended unsurprisingly towards middle age, but there was more than a scattering of arty twenty-somethings and chic thirty-somethings too. The artists aside, most had the reassuring look and bearing of people at the higher end of the pay scale – though not in the same sense that Gabriel was at the higher end of the pay scale, obviously. Gabriel hovered an order of magnitude above the pay scale; his was the kind of income that statisticians couldn't easily plot on the national graph, so they just wrote it off as an anomaly. In contrast, the majority in Cadogan Hall were just normal well-to-do professionals. If there had been a medical emergency, if someone had shouted *is there a doctor in the house?*, it was probable that half the auditorium would have leaped out of their seats.

Couples: that was the other thing Gabriel couldn't fail to notice. It was to be expected, he supposed. Normal people did not go to Saturday night concerts alone. Still, it bothered him more than he would have anticipated, and not just because it made him feel even more out of place. Until recently, Gabriel had never craved a normal life. Family, a semi-detached house in suburbia, a Volkswagen Golf, a mountain of debt – he didn't see why anyone would opt for that kind of life, not when they had any alternative. For Gabriel, the opposite of normal wasn't abnormal. It was exceptional.

But now, as he walked down to his seat, passing couples in every conceivable stage of coupledom, from first dates to those fast approaching their dotage, he couldn't quite suppress the strange sense of envy that had started to bubble in his stomach. He blamed Dr Barbara for this. *You have no possible future with this woman*. Blunt and accurate, like a baseball bat to the solar plexus.

The problem wasn't that he wanted to sleep with Caitlin. It was that he wanted to wake up with her, every day until he drew his last breath.

Admittedly, this was a more modest ambition in Gabriel's case than it would have been for most. He wasn't asking to grow old with her. But the situation was still impossible, whichever way you looked at it.

What was he going to do? Rent a flat in Lewisham? Furnish his imaginary life with décor by IKEA? Throw some underpants on the floor to make it looked lived in? He had considered it. For a few thousand pounds, he could probably hire an agent to do all the work for him, underpants included. But even then, he couldn't imagine it being a particularly robust disguise. It would be more like a film set – fine from a distance and predetermined angle, but not when someone had the freedom to wander around inside.

More to the point, Gabriel didn't have much taste for it. To his surprise, he was finding that there were levels of deception that just felt wrong.

So nothing had happened, and nothing *could* happen.

For the next ten minutes, Gabriel tried not to think about this. He watched the hall filling up around him. He counted the empty seats on the stage. Seventy, eighty, ninety – arranged in concentric semicircles around the piano. He wondered which one was Caitlin's. He wondered if he was the only person in the auditorium conducting a chair count. It was absurd, but it helped to keep him calm and occupied, this simple practical exercise.

Then the lights in the hall went down, and the buzz of hundreds of conversations faded quickly to nothing. It felt to Gabriel as if the room itself was holding its breath.

Catharsis

It started well enough. Gabriel was in the seventh row back, comfortably beyond the reach of the stage lights – not quite invisible, but much reassured by the darkness that enfolded him. If the worst came to the worst, if he did suffer some kind of catastrophic emotional breakdown mid-performance, he would not be sharing his trauma with the whole hall. Just his unfortunate neighbours.

The orchestra arrived on stage section by section, filling up from the back. It seemed almost ritualised to Gabriel, with each group of musicians pausing to bow to the audience before taking their seats. Equally, it might just have been a practical necessity, this staggered entrance, since there were so many people to cram into such a small space. Either way, it was extremely methodical – as orderly as the changing of the guard at Buckingham Palace. Gabriel approved.

Caitlin was one of the last on stage. The violins were at the front, immediately to the left of the piano and conductor's podium. She was directly in front of Gabriel, though he had no idea if this was by accident or design. His ticket had been fairly last-minute, so it had probably been a case of fitting him into a convenient gap. When she sat, she was in three-quarter profile to him, with her hair curled over her right shoulder and a smile straight out of a toothpaste ad. He had never seen anyone so happy to be back at work.

Once the rest of the orchestra were seated, the conductor came out, followed, a couple of steps later, by the German wunderkind pianist. The conductor was indeed wearing a tuxedo, and it was not as nice as Gabriel's tuxedo – the one he'd had to leave at home. The German wunderkind wasn't quite a child; he looked to be a few years older than the adolescent mugger whom Gabriel had fought in the underpass – very early twenties. He was wearing a crisp white shirt with no tie and an extremely shiny waistcoat. The volume of the applause rose and fell, there was more bowing and, finally, everyone barring the conductor was seated.

After all this pageantry, Gabriel was caught off guard by how quickly the music started. There seemed barely a breath between the conductor turning to the orchestra and the flood of sound that filled the hall.

A fleeting shock; Gabriel felt his muscles tense and relax, then a trickle of relief. Yes, the music was stirring – intense even – but it wasn't what he'd feared. It occupied a point on the emotional spectrum that he was reasonably at ease with. After a few minutes, he felt comfortable enough to make some mental notes on the performance. Even if there wasn't going to be a written test, he thought he should try to have something intelligent to say after the show.

His first observation was that the pianist was very good. Even with Gabriel's limited appreciation and experience of music, that was plain to see. It was obvious from the speed at which he was playing, if nothing else. Gabriel found it hard to estimate how many notes per second the wunderkind must have been hitting in the fastest and most twiddly sections of Rachmaninov's Rhapsody, but it was possibly in the region of fifteen to twenty. If he ever tired of being a concert pianist, he would make an outstanding touch-typist.

Gabriel's second observation was that he liked Paganini's theme; it was very catchy. It sort of bounced back and forth like a good tennis rally. *Vibrant* – that was probably a better word than catchy if he wanted to impress.

Third observation: he didn't really care how fast the German boy could move his fingers. Caitlin was much more interesting to watch. No doubt she would have identified this observation as further proof of Gabriel's poor attention span, but as far as he could see, it was evidence to the contrary. His attention may have been selective, but once it had located its proper target, it was going nowhere. Gabriel honestly believed that he could have watched her playing her violin until Cadogan Hall started to crumble around him – if he'd had that sort of time. And he was equally happy in those moments when she wasn't playing, when she was just sitting still and contented, waiting for her next cue. It made him feel peaceful in a way that he hadn't felt for many, many months.

He was only dimly aware that the texture of the music had started to change. There were slower passages creeping in, less intricate but somehow richer and more affecting. Still, Gabriel didn't realise he was in any danger. It was like carbon monoxide poisoning, he would later think – you didn't know it was happening until it was too late.

Somewhere towards the end of Rachmaninov's Rhapsody on a Theme by Paganini, Gabriel started crying.

He cried on and off for the next half an hour, and through the entirety of the slow movement of the piano concerto. But this time it was nothing like the Tube. There was no horror, there was no despair. It was a quiet sort of crying – one that seemed to have little to do with sadness and a lot to do with beauty. Gabriel didn't know how this was possible. He didn't know if it was normal or pathological. And, given that no one around him seemed to have noticed, he didn't know if he wanted it to stop.

He thought subsequently that this would have been a good moment at which to die, listening to those astonishing melodies and watching Caitlin through gently blurring vision; before he'd had the chance to ruin her life.

Pinot Noir

Once Gabriel had washed his face and made sure that he looked normal in the toilet mirror, he went to the bar to wait for Caitlin. He didn't know whether to buy a drink – or drinks – because he didn't know how long she'd be or if they'd be staying. She hadn't specified, and he'd been too preoccupied to ask. Ordinarily, he'd have been able to suggest at least a dozen outstanding bars and restaurants they might go to, all within a half-mile radius of Sloane Square. None of which were suitable for Caitlin. They were too outstanding for her, and this struck Gabriel as a cruel and painful irony. The safest option was to stay put.

Which still left the problem of *what* to drink. After interrogating the bar staff for several minutes, to the evident dismay of the people behind him, Gabriel decided to risk a mid-range bottle of Pinot Noir. Despite being from New Zealand, it was actually very good. He'd ceased to worry about alcohol screwing with his emotions, since his emotions were pretty much screwed to begin with. If anything, a drink might take the edge off. Over the past few weeks, Gabriel had almost grown used to the elaborate emotional cocktail that swirled continually inside him; certainly, he was becoming more adept at identifying its key ingredients. Elation, frustration, anxiety, despair. But in the last half hour, the whole thing had been given a vigorous shake, and a new flavour – guilt – was starting to dominate. Gabriel was not used to feeling guilty. He wasn't sure it was a feeling anyone *could* get used to. That was perhaps its essence. It was the bitter aftertaste that lingered after every other flavour had subsided.

When Caitlin arrived, five minutes later, Gabriel had already polished off one glass of wine and started a second. She smiled as she approached, and he smiled back and gave a small wave, even though she was, at this point, only metres away. For once, Gabriel didn't know quite what to say. It fell to her to break the silence.

'No tuxedo?'

'I was told not to.'

'Well, never mind. You still scrub up very nicely.'

'Yes, I know.'

She laughed at this. 'Right. And I know you know. Gabriel Vaughn: ten out of ten for dress sense, zero for modesty.'

'It masks a deep insecurity about my physique.'

'You're an idiot.'

'And you're the most beautiful woman in this room.'

'Ha! I bet you say that to all the girls.'

'Yes, but this time I mean it.'

He did mean it. 'Glowing' was not a word that frequented Gabriel's vocabulary; usually, he'd have preferred to hack that kind of vague poeticism apart and look for the specific signs – dilated pupils, reddened cheeks, moistened lips – that suggested a woman was up for it. But in this instance, he couldn't really think of a better term. Maybe it was the music or the setting. Maybe it was the Pinot interacting with the chemotherapy medication. In any case, he couldn't take his eyes off her. This must have been fairly obvious.

'Jesus, Gabriel. Don't do that.'

'Do what?'

'I feel like I'm in a staring contest.'

'I'm trying to be sincere.'

'I'm not sure it suits you. I think I might prefer you facetious.'

'You should learn to take a compliment.'

'Well, I would, but unfortunately I'm English, and sober.'

Gabriel took this as an invitation to pour her a glass of wine.

'So . . .' Caitlin took a small sip, nodding her approval. 'What did you make of Rachmaninov? Are you a convert?'

'I liked it.'

'Well, that's a good start. Any other impressions?'

'Um . . .' Gabriel fumbled through his list of mental notes, most of which had been forgotten during the sustained period of crying in the second half. 'The pianist was very good. Quick fingers. I don't think I've ever heard anyone play a piano that quickly before, or use so many of the keys.'

Caitlin nodded intently for a couple of seconds, before collapsing into a fit of giggles. 'Brilliant! That's possibly the greatest analysis of a piece of classical music I've ever heard.'

'Thank you. I try my best.'

'I'm sorry, Gabriel, I don't mean to be a snob. I'm not laughing at you – well, no, I *am* laughing at you, but it's refreshing, really. I mean, most men would try to say something clever or profound.'

'Not me.'

'No, not you.'

'I did find it . . . well, moving, though. If you can believe that.'

'Yes, I can. Completely.'

'I cried several times.'

'Right. I bet you did.'

'And I thought *you* were superb. I should have said that straight away.'

'Thank you, Gabriel. That's very sweet.' Caitlin took another sip of her wine. 'Complete bullshit, but still very sweet. There's no way on earth you could have picked my part out from the rest of the violins, not unless I was out of time or hit a wrong note. Basically, if you heard me, I deserve to be fired.'

'OK, so I couldn't hear you. You were perfectly unremarkable.'

'That's better.'

Gabriel thought for a few moments, taking the opportunity to top up their wine glasses.

'Doesn't it bother you?' he asked. 'Just being . . . I don't know, a cog in the machine.'

'Not usually, no. I mean, we can't all be centre stage all the time, can we?'

'No, but you're obviously very talented. You spend however many hours every day practising, the pay's lousy, and the ultimate goal is not to be noticed. Seems a little perverse, that's all.'

Caitlin shrugged. 'The life of a professional violinist. If I want to indulge my inner prima donna, I always have my one-woman busking show.'

'I'd definitely like to see that.'

'To be honest with you, it's not as rewarding as being part of an orchestra. You get to enjoy the music more. Anyway, sometimes it's nice to be a cog in a machine. I mean, don't get me wrong, you do get some pretty big egos among musicians, but in general, it's . . . well, harmonious, if you'll forgive the pun. I suppose it's like most organisations. You play your individual part, but really everyone's focussed on the end result. That's what's important.'

'Not in my workplace,' Gabriel told her. 'We're all out for ourselves. It just happens that our interests are aligned most of the time.'

'Really?' Caitlin raised her eyebrows. 'The cut-throat world of data analysts. Who knew?'

'Research analysts,' Gabriel corrected. He thought it was important to keep the details of his fake job consistent.

'Right.' Caitlin nodded and took another big sip from her glass. 'God, this wine is delicious. What is it?'

'I'm not sure,' Gabriel lied. 'I just asked the barman to recommend something good, and this is what he gave me.'

'It's *really* good.' Caitlin started to scrutinise the label, then the wine list, her eyes widening. 'Gabriel! This wine costs forty pounds a bottle! Are you insane?'

'Um . . . yes, possibly.' There was an awkward pause while Gabriel struggled to think of a way to rectify this blunder. Blame the barman again? Plead ignorance, as if he'd failed to notice how much he was paying? That was unlikely to make him look good, either. Flattery seemed a better option. 'Well, I figured, it's a special occasion,' he told her. 'At least it is for me. I don't know if it is for you. I wouldn't want to put words into your mouth.'

Between shaking her head in disbelief and covering her eyes with her hands, Caitlin seemed to miss the point of this. Gabriel had never seen any woman so mortified to discover that her glass of wine was better than expected. 'Oh, God, and you've had to sit here and watch me drink it like it's water!'

The desire to make this stop was overwhelming. Acting on instinct, Gabriel reached across their table and peeled Caitlin's hands from her face, keeping hold of them afterwards. 'If you like that wine, it's the best forty pounds I've ever spent. Drink it however you see fit. I'm going to get us another bottle.'

He didn't quite make it to the bar. He'd barely made it out of his chair before Caitlin grabbed his arm and pulled him back. A moment later, they were kissing, hands in each other's hair.

She pulled away before he did; left to his own volition, Gabriel would never have pulled away.

'I think we'd better get that wine to go,' Caitlin said.

Imperfect Buttocks

It was five thirty when he awoke, thinking, momentarily, that he needed to get up for work, that his chauffeur would soon be waiting downstairs. But the bedside clock was not his bedside clock; it was analogue, the hands barely visible in the surrounding darkness. What registered next was the weight of Caitlin's head on his chest, the scent of her hair. His left arm was dead beneath her curled body, with only his fingertips still sentient; they were pressed against her perfect buttocks. Objectively, it was not the most comfortable position to have fallen asleep in. Nor were her buttocks objectively perfect (not even top five, in terms of the many women Gabriel had slept with). There was a dull corner of his mind that understood these facts, and it was being mercilessly shouted down by every other fibre of his body.

He stayed motionless, feeling the gentle rise and fall of her sleeping breath.

Right then, Gabriel would not have traded positions with anybody.

Domesticity

The next time he woke, it had gone eight o'clock. Caitlin was still fast asleep beside him, but at some point she'd rolled onto her back. With some reluctance, Gabriel got out of bed and located his boxer shorts among a heap of discarded clothes. He tucked the duvet back around Caitlin's shoulders before he left the room.

Wandering through to the bathroom, Gabriel found that there was little to add to the passing glimpse of a flat he'd seen the night before. It was small and cluttered, and in terrible need of a refurb. Worn carpets, cracked paintwork, mismatched kitchen units. The lounge was dominated by a two-seater sofa, an upright piano and shelves piled high with CDs. There was a television, but it was not the sort of television Gabriel had seen since the 1990s. It sat on a corner unit next to a narrow window that rattled with the passing traffic. Single glazing! Gabriel was genuinely shocked to discover such a thing still existed, though it did go a long way to explaining how cold the property was. Granted, it was late November, and the sun had only been up for an hour or so, but still. At home, temperature was not something Gabriel ever had to consider. His thermostat was set to a perfect twenty-two point five degrees, day and night, and regardless of whether he was in or out. In winter, the underfloor heating came on, and in summer the air conditioning, and if he chose to walk around the apartment in his boxer shorts, he could – for as long as he wanted. Until now, he'd never even thought about this fact. It seemed such a basic human right.

Gabriel stood shivering on the cold and chipped bathroom tiles as he flossed his teeth and gargled some mouthwash. From his stationary position in front of the sink, he could stretch out his arms and touch all four walls. He urinated, washed his hands under a hot tap that failed to get hot, then went back through to the galley kitchen.

Domestically, Gabriel realised, his capabilities were limited. It wasn't that he was incompetent, exactly; it was more that the basic competence he possessed had not been called upon very often in the past decade. If you were the sort of person who could earn a thousand pounds an hour, then any time spent cooking or tidying was essentially money down the drain; it was fiscally irresponsible not to rely on restaurants and cleaners. But Gabriel did know how to butter a bagel, and he could operate a coffee machine. He found mugs and plates in one cupboard, a wooden tray at the back of another, assembled his meagre but well-intentioned offering and took it back through to the bedroom. He knocked on the inside of the door, causing Caitlin to stir, smile and push herself into a sitting position. With one arm, she held the duvet in place so that it covered her breasts – a gesture that Gabriel couldn't help but regard as touchingly pointless.

'Morning.'

'Morning.' With her free hand, she brushed her hair from her face, then smiled again. 'I don't recall ordering room service.'

'It's part of the package.'

'Wonderful. But for future reference, on a Sunday I like my coffee closer to nine than eight.'

'Future reference? Now that *is* presumptuous. I'd really hoped this was just a one-night stand . . .'

'No problem. But you should know that my one-night stands don't carry over to the morning after. It was fun while it lasted, though.'

'I wish I had a witty comeback, but I don't. If you don't let me back into that bed within the next thirty seconds, I'm going to walk out of this flat and throw myself under the next available train.'

'Well, you're lucky.' Caitlin patted the other side of the mattress. 'I've never been able to resist a man who threatens to kill himself if he can't have me.'

Gabriel set the tray down at the side of the bed and got back in. He kissed both of her breasts, quite reverentially, he thought, before she broke away, giggling.

'I'm sorry, but I think I'd better go and pee first. Not sexy, I know, but neither is a full bladder. Can you wait two minutes?'

'I'm confident I can wait up to five. Beyond that, no guarantees.'

'I'll be as quick as physiologically possible.'

'You'd better be.'

She was back with him three and a half minutes later, shivering slightly. 'Sorry. In hindsight, a dressing gown would have been wise.'

Gabriel enfolded her in his arms. 'Caitlin, this won't do. You're in desperate need of a man to take control of your thermostat.'

'Right. And will said man also be paying the gas bill?'

'Of course. Unless he happens to have blown this month's fuel budget on expensive red wine.'

'In that case, the heating can wait until we're up.'

'Good. So, essentially, you're telling me that the longer we stay in bed the more money you'll save? Very devious.'

'What can I say? I'm a fan of thrift.'

Gabriel ran his index finger across her thigh. 'You know, it's probably for the best. I can't take you anywhere, not wearing yesterday's clothes. I'm far too vain.'

'Well, we could pop over to your place.'

'We could, obviously. But that seems like a lot of unnecessary travelling. I think I'd rather stay right where I am for the rest of the day. The simple plans are always the best.'

'Gabriel, would it be too much of a cliché to say shut up and kiss me?'

'No. In fact, I think I'll lose a lot of respect for you if you *don't* say that.'

'Then shut up and kiss me.'

Lies upon Lies

Gabriel could not remember the last time he had taken a sick day, but that week he took two, Monday and Tuesday. He left answerphone messages with Mason and HR, claiming food poisoning. As far as bunking off work went, food poisoning had to be the ultimate cover story: debilitating, sudden and over just as quickly, with no sign that it had ever happened. No doctor's visit to conjure, no details to divulge. Who in their right mind would want to know?

Thus on Monday at 6 a.m., having just cancelled his chauffeur, Gabriel found himself on the Internet, searching for flats to let in Lewisham. From an initial pool of forty or so, fully furnished, he made a long list of twelve that looked suitable. Then, at eight thirty, he started calling estate agents to find out which of those twelve would be ready to move into immediately – by which he meant today. Waiting for bank transfers to clear would not be an issue, since he planned to pay the deposit and first month's rent in cash.

At ten he was in a taxi, on his way to visit the first of five properties he'd arranged to see.

What had happened to all the guilt? The discomfort? The lines that should not be crossed? In part, Gabriel had simply acknowledged that there was no other option. This was the one and only way he could have a future with Caitlin, however short that future might be. Of course, this didn't solve the problem of his guilt, nor the worry that it was a façade too complex to pull off. But he soon realised that these things had a common solution. Gabriel abandoned the idea of pretending to live somewhere else; he now planned to *actually* live somewhere else, at least at weekends, and probably for the next few days as well. It was the best way he could see to make a property look lived in – to live there. It was a mode of performance he believed was called 'method acting'.

But added to this was a deeper rationale, one that was at first hard to acknowledge, but ultimately liberating. He no longer wanted the life he'd been living for the past decade. His luxury apartment, his creature comforts, even his Ferrari – none of this seemed important any more. And he'd given up caring whether this was a genuine change of perspective or just the tumour fucking with him. He'd realised that it didn't matter; the end result was the same.

Work, however, was a separate issue. Did he still want to go back to work? Was there any point to it? Probably not, but for now, there was no clear alternative. He couldn't see Caitlin during office hours. He couldn't tell her that he'd decided, for no particular reason, to quit his job and live off his savings for a while. Normal people did not have that option. Normal people could not rent a flat in London without a continuous stream of income – they'd be bankrupt in a matter of months. Gabriel, in contrast, could have afforded to rent a flat in Lewisham for approximately two hundred years – and that was based only on his liquid assets. The difference between him and the average Joe was so ridiculous he wanted to howl.

So if he wanted to quit his job, that, too, would have to remain a secret. He still had a straight choice between continuing with work or being at home alone, with only his thoughts to occupy him. At present, this was inconceivable.

Fortunately, Gabriel had told Caitlin little about his supposed flat, apart from the fact that it was cramped – and even a cursory sweep of the Internet had been enough to confirm that this was true of almost every one-bed flat in London. As a consequence, he had some freedom when sourcing his new residence, although he'd realised almost as soon as he started looking that there were a number of practical matters to be considered.

First, the flat would have to be modern and minimalist. Anything else – excessive shelving, old wooden bookcases – would draw attention to how little he owned, and how new it all was. However well-furnished the property was, he'd still have to buy some odds and ends to make it work, and in a very truncated timeframe. But as long as he kept things simple, this didn't seem too big a problem. Whichever version of himself he was being, he was clearly not a man who tolerated a lot of clutter. Caitlin would not be expecting wall-to-wall bric-a-brac.

Second, it had to be within a reasonably large apartment block, where it would be much easier to be anonymous. The sort of place where one could quite easily live for a couple of years and remain a total stranger to the neighbours. A high-rise would be ideal.

Third, the flat couldn't be *too* new. Even from the vantage point of his taxi, Gabriel could see that Lewisham had changed considerably since the last time he'd been there – back when he'd first moved to London and had been commuting to Canary Wharf each day. Like the rest of the city, it had been gentrified, and new apartment blocks had shot up left, right and centre. Gabriel had to be certain that wherever he rented had existed for at least a couple of years, which was how long he'd supposedly been living there.

Fourth, it should be close to the Tube station. Convenient for Caitlin to get to, and easy for him to get out of. It was not beyond the realm of possibility that he might actually have to use the Tube at some point. At the very least, he should probably re-familiarise himself with the commute and the station, in case his knowledge of either was put to the test.

With these criteria in place, it took less than an hour to find his new flat. He was able to dismiss the first one he saw very quickly, because it was too high-spec. The finish was close to flawless. The second he rejected the moment he stepped through the door – to the dismay and bafflement of his estate agent – because it smelled of new paint. But the third ticked every box. On the fourth floor of a 2007 development, it was new, but not too new, nice but not too nice. It clearly hadn't been maintained as well as it could have been. There were blemishes here and there: scuff marks on the laminate flooring, a crack on the shower guard that Gabriel was delighted to discover. At less than forty square metres, it was suitably pokey, too. The double bedroom was pretty much all bed. There was a balcony off the open-plan living area, but it was tiny, and the view could not have been drabber. Certainly nothing to worry about.

Gabriel didn't need to see properties four and five. He got

back into his waiting taxi and went to the estate agents via the bank. He signed a contract, handed over a sizeable wad of twenty-pound notes and received two sets of keys.

By one o'clock, he was sitting at his new dining table with a steak sandwich he'd bought from Marks & Spencer. He'd already had the phone and broadband connected, paid the council tax and sorted out utility providers. He set his thermostat to twenty-two point five, phoned for another cab, took his medication, then headed to the local shopping centre.

58

The Shopping List

1. Clothes, including shoes
2. Duvet, pillows, etc
3. TV (approximately 40 inches)
4. Stereo/radio
5. Phone
6. Lamps — 1 bedside, 1 floor
7. Clocks — 1 bedside, 2 wall
8. Fridge and cupboard basics
9. Cheap wine (keep it below £10 per bottle!)
10. Toiletries
11. Towels
12. Laptop
13. Cutlery, crockery, pans and utensils
14. Cafetière, kettle, toaster
15. Coffee bean grinder

16. Dishcloths, tea towels and washing-up liquid
17. Bins (1 per room)
18. A fruit bowl
19. A plant
20. Fridge magnets?

Budget: ~~£5,000~~ £3,000

How the Other Ninety-Nine
Per Cent Live

Gabriel was a man used to working twelve-hour days, and when he had a budget to spend, it was commonly measured in the millions or tens of millions, not the low thousands. He was methodical and goal-driven, decisive and efficient. In short, filling a one-bed flat with an artificial lifetime of possessions posed no great challenge, even on a two-day turnaround.

By the time he got to the shopping centre, his list of purchases had already fallen into a natural hierarchy of priorities. Since he was planning to stay in the flat that night, there were certain things he needed straight away, like bedding and coffee. Bulkier items – the TV and floor lamp – would be home-delivered and installed. Gabriel had paid his taxi driver to wait in the car park, but there was a limit to how many pots and pans could be crammed into the boot of a saloon.

He spent from two until five buying homewares and clothing – shirts, underwear, jeans and trainers. Nothing he planned to wear; he wasn't sure that some of it would even fit him. It was just stuff to hang in the wardrobe, to pad out the suitcase of clothes he planned to transfer from his actual wardrobe. The materials were cheap, needless to say, but Gabriel took care to keep his style consistent. He couldn't have any obvious incongruity between his real and fake clothes.

He was back at his new flat at five thirty, ate another sandwich, and then started to order groceries on his new laptop. After that, he made his bed, then set about using the handle of a tin opener to try to chip the rim of his coffee cup. It was surprisingly hard to do.

The hours of seven to nine were a flurry of activity. At one point, there were three delivery men crammed into his meagre living area – one installing the TV, another unpacking the floor lamp and another loading food into the bare cupboards. Afterwards, Gabriel paid the TV guy to take away all the empty boxes he'd accumulated during the afternoon.

He fell asleep on top of his new bedcovers around ten, and awoke the next morning to a day that was generally less frantic. It was more about finishing touches. He hung his wall clocks and put up some coat hooks. He went back to the shopping centre and bought himself a fruit bowl and a plant. The latter he was especially pleased with; he found a place for it on the bedroom windowsill, where it stood as incontrovertible evidence that this was a lived-in property.

That evening, Gabriel sat out on his balcony, tired but contented with what he'd achieved. Before he went to bed, he phoned his chauffeur with instructions to pick him up at the new address the following morning. No questions were asked.

Coup d'état

Gabriel knew something was wrong the moment he stepped into the office. Except, how could he have known? The feeling made no sense, so he tried to dismiss it as paranoia, or just the unfamiliarity of having not been there for a couple of days. It didn't help that he was also running late. It was closer to six thirty than six twenty; for some reason, he hadn't factored in the extra journey time from Lewisham.

He didn't hang about when he'd reached his desk. He put his briefcase down, laid his coat over the chair and went to see Mason.

Mason and Shipman, it turned out. That was what was wrong.

'Vaughn, you skiving son of a bitch!' Mason swung his arm towards the door, his middle and index fingers outstretched like the barrel of a handgun. He made a shooting noise, more sinister than childlike, and for want of any other response, Gabriel clutched his chest and flinched. 'You'd better have a sick note for HR or there'll be hell to pay.'

Gabriel shrugged. 'My dog ate it.' He threw a glance at Shipman, who was lounging in the guest chair. 'Shipman.'

'Vaughn.'

'Shipman's been debriefing me,' Mason told him. 'The Asian markets are way down. You know about that?'

Gabriel nodded, keeping his face perfectly neutral. He had not checked the markets since Friday.

'Good, we'll talk about it more in thirty, when everyone else is here.'

A reprieve. Gabriel thought that thirty minutes would give him plenty of time to go online and get up to speed. He knew it was irrational, but his competitive instinct was surging. He glanced again at Shipman, who smiled thinly, like a hyena baring its teeth. He was the kind of man who could detect a sign of weakness a mile off, and at Mason Wallace sick leave was most certainly a sign of weakness.

'How's the stomach, Vaughn?'

'Never better. What doesn't kill you makes you stronger, right?'

'Ha!' Mason slapped the table. 'I think we should sue whoever's responsible for loss of revenue. Name the restaurant and I'll phone the lawyers.'

Gabriel shrugged again. 'I think it might have been Paganini's.'

'Jesus, Paganini's? In Mayfair? Who'd've thought . . . Listen, since you're not dead, Shipman suggested golf on Sunday. Ten o'clock. You in?'

'Sorry. I have plans.'

'You have plans?'

'Yep.'

'On a Sunday morning?' Mason turned to look at Shipman. 'Oh my good God all-fucking-mighty. It's a woman! Only explanation. Am I right?'

Shipman nodded grimly. Gabriel said nothing. He didn't see

any point in denying it – he didn't have any other excuse for missing golf – but at the same time, he would have preferred to have kept Caitlin, the whole concept of Caitlin, as far from work as possible.

'So who is this mystery woman?' Mason persisted. 'You're at least going to tell us her name.'

'Caitlin.'

'Caitlin! I like it. I'm imagining a Celt, flaming red hair, top and bottom. As filthy as they come.'

The effort of smiling at this was physically painful, and made worse by the hearty backslapping that followed.

'OK, Vaughn – you're excused, you're excused. Just don't make a habit of it. And keep it out of the office. While you're here, your soul is mine.' Mason jabbed his index finger into the centre of Gabriel's forehead. 'I need your mind on the job.'

Gabriel continued to smile, feeling nothing but contempt.

The Elephant Man

That evening he planned to catch up on the news. Instead, he found himself watching a film. *The Elephant Man*.

It was a mistake, of course. He'd hit the wrong button on the remote, and should have rectified this at once. Gabriel had no interest in films, especially not *this* film. The red flags could not have been clearer:

1. It was shot in black and white, even though the information display showed that the film had been made in 1980. This meant that someone had actually *chosen* to shoot in black and white, for reasons that could only be arty and pretentious.
2. It was a historical film, obviously. The Elephant Man was a Victorian, so there would be no car chases or explosions.
3. It also seemed unlikely that there would be any sex. There wouldn't even be any attractive Hollywood stars to look at. There would be Victorian women in dresses that covered them from neck to ankle, and The Elephant Man.

And yet, within thirty seconds of starting to watch, Gabriel found it impossible to look away.

The Elephant Man's most prominent tumour covered his entire forehead, though, unlike Gabriel's, it wasn't malign – just extremely hideous. Because of this, he'd been abandoned by his parents and consigned to a circus freak show. But Gabriel had to extrapolate this backstory as he'd switched on twenty minutes into the film, at the point when The Elephant Man had been rescued by a kindly doctor and was being cared for on an isolation ward in a London hospital.

The Elephant Man didn't say much at first, so everyone in the hospital assumed he was an imbecile. Then they found that he could recite the Bible and had exquisite manners – even by Victorian standards. He had a photograph of his beautiful mother that he carried around in his pocket, and whenever he showed it to anyone, they immediately started crying. Later, The Elephant Man was abused by the hospital's night porter, who charged people admission to his room so that they could point and laugh. Inexplicably, this made Gabriel very angry. For some reason, he hated seeing this long-dead historical figure being tormented by the fictional people in the film.

The last scene showed The Elephant Man lying down in bed to sleep, even though he knew it was going to kill him; his medical condition meant that he had to sleep sitting up or risk asphyxiation.

Gabriel wept. Aside from watching Caitlin play the violin, it was far and away the most moving thing he'd ever seen, and it continued to trouble him long after the end credits had rolled. It wasn't just the sadness of it. Gabriel couldn't claim to be comfortable with his newfound emotions, but he was at least starting to get used to their presence. Yet there was something about the film's premise that was deeply unsettling, something he was unable to pin down.

When he fell asleep that night, flat on his back, he found himself imagining that he *was* The Elephant Man. He felt the weight of the tumour, and wondered which night would be his last.

Double Life

Over the next week, Gabriel split his free time evenly between his real home, his fake home and Caitlin's, and soon enough it stopped feeling strange. In particular, having two properties to manage felt like no great stretch. Gabriel knew plenty of people who owned multiple houses in London, many of which remained permanently empty. They were just investments, no different to gold bullion, and would be held for as long as the property bubble lasted. Of course, Gabriel didn't own his second home, but he at least lived there a couple of days a week. It wasn't just an empty asset.

More importantly, Caitlin accepted the flat in Lewisham as genuine. But why wouldn't she? Yes, there was a fair amount of teasing when she first came over, the Friday after he'd signed the contract – numerous jokes at his expense. How many times a day did he clean? (Zero, but right now there was this girl he was trying to impress.) Did he own anything extraneous? (He pointed to the pot plant.) But on the whole, he'd gauged things correctly. She wasn't at all surprised that he had 'OCD tendencies', that he kept his surroundings as neat and unencumbered as a show home. In terms of believability, the flat was the least of his worries.

Far more problematic was his general timetable. It was difficult to make Caitlin understand how his job could be as demanding and time-consuming as it apparently was. What sort of research analyst had to leave for work at six o'clock every morning? Gabriel explained that he didn't have to be in until eight, but he always went to the gym for an hour before hitting the office.

'Honestly, Gabriel! *Every* day? Are you not getting enough of a workout with me here?'

'No. Not unless you can figure out a position that's going to tone my triceps.'

This joke did not go down quite as well as he'd hoped it would. Gabriel had to concoct all sorts of additional excuses. The commute to Charing Cross – where he supposedly worked – was so much easier if he avoided the rush hour, and a spell in the gym really set him up for the whole day. It got the endorphins flowing. It allowed him to face the drudgery of office life with a Zen-like tranquillity.

'I had no idea you were such a fitness freak.'

He affected a sheepish grin. 'Well, we all have our vices. I think mine's relatively harmless.'

Caitlin eventually conceded this point. He was helped by the fact that her timetable was equally awkward at the other end of the day. There were evening performances, late rehearsals, hours at the weekend – it wasn't as if he was unwilling to accommodate all these difficulties. He just accepted them as an immutable part of her routine.

The truth – one truth he could freely admit to – was that

Gabriel would have preferred to spend every spare minute with Caitlin. He felt happy when they were together, and he didn't when they were apart. He really did believe that she made him a better person, and he would have reiterated this belief to Dr Barbara, had he not cancelled their last appointment.

Gabriel did not think he could see Dr Barbara again – and certainly not on his own terms. But this no longer seemed such a pressing point. He felt happier than he had in months, and he felt physically healthier, too. He would have dismissed this as nothing more than a change in perspective, but the next time he went to see Armitage, the oncologist was similarly positive about the state of Gabriel's brain – or as positive as he could be. The latest MRI showed no 'significant' tumour growth since the radiosurgery. It was still there, and it was still incurable; but for the moment, at least, it had been halted in its tracks. If Gabriel was feeling almost normal (the new normal), this was entirely consistent with the medical data. As far as Armitage was concerned, the best-case scenario seemed to be playing out.

What did this mean in terms of how many extra months he might have with Caitlin? Gabriel didn't know, and as far as he could see, this was for the best. It made far more sense to live in the moment, to accept whatever crumb of contentment the universe had chosen to throw him.

63

Dodging the Bullet

Once they'd got past the problem of Gabriel's working hours, and his apparent exercise addiction, they began to establish the rudiments of a shared routine. Gabriel stopped thinking of his double life as merely 'not strange'; soon it felt quite ordinary. But this was a different kind of ordinary, new and exquisite. There were evenings when he would go over to Caitlin's, late, after work, and others when she would come over to Lewisham, even later. There were whole weekends spent together – walks in local parks, drinks in cheap cafés and pubs, countless shared meals. She cooked them dinner a couple of times; he developed an extensive repertoire of 11 p.m. sandwiches. Gabriel was sleeping less, but he was also sleeping better. Much better – though this was not to say his life had become entirely guilt-free. The weekday mornings when he'd stayed over at Caitlin's always felt like a hideous pantomime. He'd be out of her door at five minutes to six, gym bag in hand, and would head off in the direction of the Tube station – with his chauffeur parked just round the corner. It was a precaution that never stopped feeling necessary.

There were other problems too, cracks and strains that began to appear as they spent more time together. These were the issues that Gabriel hadn't really anticipated, and over which he could exercise only limited control.

Friends and family – that was the big one. Gabriel met up with Caitlin after a couple of her concerts, he went to see her busking, and, inevitably, he got to know some of the people she knew: colleagues from the orchestra, friends from university. None of this was planned or imposed. It was something that was bound to happen. And the more it did, the more one-sided it felt. Even at this very early stage, the mysterious void in Gabriel's life – the apparent lack of anyone else – was becoming ever more conspicuous.

His family circumstances were not that hard to explain. Caitlin knew that he was an only child, and that his mother had died when he was young. That he didn't have much of a relationship with his father was abundantly clear, and Gabriel decided to strengthen the sense that this was a thorny issue by implying that he did not get on with his stepmother. Gabriel did *have* a stepmother; his father had remarried ten years ago. She was called Susan, and Gabriel was completely indifferent to her.

The absence of friends – or even acquaintances – was harder to shrug off. What about the people he worked with? Did they never go out for drinks? Very occasionally, Gabriel said; but on the average day, this was the last thing he wanted to contemplate – not when he'd been up since five thirty. And anyway, wasn't it better when it was just the two of them? Right now, she was everything he wanted and needed. No one else mattered.

It was a line sweet enough – and genuine enough – to buy him some time. But Gabriel knew this was all he'd done; and short of hiring some actors to play his 'work buddies', there was little he could do to improve the situation.

But for the time being, none of this felt like an immediate concern. There was only one instance when the elaborate cover story Gabriel had contrived felt genuinely under threat.

It happened one evening quite early on, when Caitlin came over to his following a rehearsal. She appeared at his door looking decidedly perplexed.

'I've just had the weirdest conversation with one of your neighbours,' she told him.

Gabriel suppressed the throb of panic in his stomach and tried to look intrigued. 'Go on.'

'She seemed to think I'd just moved in – wanted to know how I was finding the place.'

Gabriel frowned. 'Which neighbour was it?' It was a question designed to stall until he had something better to say, but he hoped it also gave the impression that there were certain of his neighbours he *would* recognise.

'About our age, tall, strawberry blond.'

Gabriel squinted slightly, then shrugged. 'Well, I suppose it's not that odd a mistake. She's obviously seen you coming and going a couple of times, a new face, and drawn the wrong conclusion.'

'Right, that's what I thought. But she didn't know who you were, either. Drew a complete blank when I mentioned you.'

'Oh . . . OK, that *is* weird.'

What else could he say? He was suffering a complete brain freeze, which he hoped translated into nothing more than a semblance of bafflement.

It seemed like an age until Caitlin broke the tension by rolling her eyes and mock-punching him on the arm. 'Gabriel, how well do you know your neighbours? *Do* you know them?'

'It varies. Some of them I know to nod to in the corridor, others I could possibly pick out of a line-up. A small line-up.' He smiled – his disarming smile – and gestured back towards the anonymous hallway, with its dozen identical doors. 'Well, you've seen what this place is like. It's the essence of modern urban living. People move in and move out all the time. I often think it resembles a hotel more than a block of flats.'

'Yes, it does. You should do something to change that. Start by introducing yourself to the woman who lives two doors down.'

'I'll make sure I give her a knock on my way to work tomorrow.'

'Right. A six o'clock wake up call. Always a good way to break the ice.'

Gabriel cupped his hands at the back of Caitlin's neck and kissed her lightly on the lips. 'You know, I think you may have found the only person in this building who has ever started a conversation in the corridor. Congratulations. You obviously have some special aura of approachability.'

Caitlin leaned into him, and he felt the slight note of tension ease from her body. 'I have a knack for attracting weirdos,' she told him.

'Yes, clearly.'

On the whole, he felt that he'd handled the situation as well as he could.

64

Unfinished Business

'Gabriel? I've got someone called Barbara on the phone for you.'

'Barbara?'

Shit.

'She said you'd know who she was. She's – well, she's pretty insistent.'

'Right . . .' His impulse was to hide, but rationality told him he needed to deal with this. Barbara was sending him a clear message by phoning him at work: she wasn't going to go away. 'OK, Nicola, put her through.'

He tried to sound decisive rather than resigned, and immediately felt he'd failed. He also felt irritated at himself. He should have stalled and got Nicola to say he'd call back. Then he'd at least have had some time to prepare what he was going to say. As it was, he had little choice but to go on the offensive.

'Barbara, there's a reason I didn't give you my work number. You know full well what the situation is here. This feels like a breach of—'

'Save it, Gabriel. You're not in a position to lecture anyone on breaches of trust.'

Gabriel could find no comeback to this, since it was so patently true.

'I've left three messages on your answerphone,' Barbara continued. 'Please don't insult my intelligence by pretending you haven't picked them up.'

'No, I got them. It's just that I've been extremely busy.'

Barbara exhaled nosily. 'Gabriel, are you telling me that you've not had five spare minutes in which to return a phone call? Is that what you're asking me to believe?'

Again, there was no obvious retort. After a tense, guilt-ridden silence, Gabriel decided to apologise. For once, this felt like the only acceptable course of action.

'I'm not going to accept your apology until you agree to come and see me,' Barbara told him. 'I think it's important, don't you?' Gabriel nodded dumbly down the phone.

He went over to her office after work the next day; he finished early and she agreed to finish late. Gabriel wasn't sure why. The last time they'd met, she'd more or less threatened to throw him out. Now, she was going out of her way – giving up her own time – to accommodate him. Gabriel had the sense that he'd become a *project,* a challenge to be conquered. But when he suggested this to her, she was quick to set him straight.

'Gabriel, you're not a project. You're a human being who needs help, no different to any of my other patients.'

'But I *am* a challenge, aren't I?'

'Not in the sense that you mean. This isn't a contest, and it isn't helpful for you to think in those terms. You do it far too much.'

'What do you mean?'

'I mean you have a tendency to approach life as if it's a competition.'

'Well, I work in a competitive industry.'

'Yes, I know. But I don't. Please try to keep that in mind.'

Gabriel nodded slowly. He still felt slightly harangued, but that was his default impression whenever he sat in Dr Barbara's office. He was willing to concede that this might be more to do with his attitude than hers.

'Listen,' she said after a short pause. 'I wanted to see you again for both our sakes. I don't like it when my patients just disappear on me. It makes me worry. Can you understand that?'

Gabriel nodded again. A couple of months ago, he wouldn't have understood it, but now he thought he did. Barbara was the sort of person who believed in a duty of care. She felt she had responsibilities that went beyond the hours she was paid for.

'I'm sorry, Barbara,' Gabriel said. 'I should have called you, I know. But calling felt . . . well, difficult.'

She looked at him for a few moments without saying anything, her lips pursed in a tight frown. 'Gabriel, am I right to be worried?'

'Yes.' There was no point trying to deceive her, even if he'd had the inclination.

'Caitlin?'

'It's complicated.'

'Complicated how? Please tell me you're not sleeping with her.'

Gabriel stayed silent.

Barbara placed her fingers on her cheeks and shook her head. She didn't look angry, or even disapproving. If anything, Gabriel thought she looked sad. 'Well, you know what I'm going to tell you, don't you?'

'Yes, I know. That I have to end it. Tell her the truth.'

'Exactly.'

'I can't.'

'No, Gabriel. You can. But you're choosing not to. Let's be clear about that.'

'I know you don't believe me, Barbara, but being with her makes me want to be a better person. It's the truth. When I'm with her, I can actually see this . . . this possibility of being a better man.'

'I do believe you, Gabriel. That's what makes this so hard. Because it doesn't really matter what you *want*. It's your actions that matter, not your intentions.'

'My actions are changing too. All of me's changing.' Gabriel searched for an example, something he could present as concrete evidence to support this claim. 'I watched a film the other day,' he told her. 'It was *The Elephant Man*. Have you seen it?'

'Yes, Gabriel, I've seen it. A long time ago. Please tell me why it's relevant to the conversation we're having.'

He could have told her that the fact he'd watched a film was relevant in itself. That, previously, the only films he'd watched as an adult were . . . well, adult films. But he wasn't sure that raising this particular point would help him. Instead, he said: 'It made me cry. That's relevant for a start. And it stayed with me, too. It made me think about how I've lived my own life. It made me worry that I've always been . . . well, like a kind of *reverse* Elephant Man, I suppose.'

Barbara sighed, digging her fingers into her temples. 'Gabriel, you'll have to explain what you mean. It isn't obvious.'

'The Elephant Man was hideous on the outside but beautiful on the inside,' he told her. 'And that's like the opposite of me,

266

isn't it? Or it has been, for most of my life. Like I said, I genu-inely believe this is changing now. The tumour changed it. Meeting Caitlin changed it.'

Barbara shook her head wearily. 'As far as I can see, the basic facts haven't changed. You say you care for this woman, and yet you continue to abuse her trust. To put it bluntly, the way you're treating Caitlin is *still* hideous.'

Gabriel didn't reply. After just a few minutes of talking, he knew that they'd already reached an impasse. And Barbara knew it, too.

'I'm not sure what else we can say to each other,' she told him. 'I wish you the best, I really do. But I don't think I can help you any more. Not as things stand.'

So that was the end of Gabriel's psychotherapy. Officially.

He collected his coat from the back of her chair, then went home, to Lewisham, to wait for Caitlin.

Conscience

That evening, Gabriel watched Caitlin watching the news. It was a strange experience, seeing the day's events filtered through her eyes. Because Gabriel monitored the news pretty much continuously, from the moment he woke up until the moment he went to bed, he knew every item inside out. There were particular phrases and soundbites that he could have recited by heart, had he been asked to. So why did it feel so new and different, watching the tiny reflection of these same stories as they ghosted in her irises?

Caitlin's body language was very expressive when she watched the news – more so than Gabriel would have believed possible. She frowned and shook her head and tutted. At one point, during the item on the fire in a Bangladeshi factory, she actually put her hands to her mouth and gasped. Over fifty people had perished, so it was, Gabriel supposed, quite an emotive story. But still . . . people died all the time, many of them horribly. With seven billion people on the planet, it was a statistical inevitability. Caitlin must have understood this fact – as did the BBC.

They hadn't even led with the factory fire; it ran second, after the latest on the phone-hacking scandal.

It was then that Gabriel realised an obvious truth: despite viewing it a dozen times a day, he never *really* watched the news – not in the same sense that Caitlin did. He just sifted it for the relevant data.

When Gabriel saw a story about a factory fire, he never wondered about the victims; he wondered about which companies the factory supplied, which stock would start to fall.

And yet, at that exact moment, Gabriel, *was* able to feel something. He still couldn't have claimed to be affected by the story itself, but he was affected by Caitlin's reaction to it. His impulse was to reach out and put a hand on her shoulder, to tell her that everything was going to be OK. It wasn't of course; the death toll was fifty and rising, and people would continue to die in factory fires for as long as there were factories and people. But that was not the point. Gabriel was thinking about something more than the financial implications of the story, and for him this seemed a significant step. It was further proof of what he'd told Dr Barbara: that when he was with Caitlin, he really did have the potential to be someone else – someone different to the man he'd always been.

Unfortunately, he knew what Barbara's reply would have been. She would have told him that none of this was sufficient. She would have told him that he was still doing what he'd always done – he was focussing only on the information that was of benefit to him, that validated the things he wanted to believe.

And she would have been right.

As much as Gabriel needed to feel better about himself and his actions, deep down he knew he had no right to do so. He was still deceiving a woman he claimed to care for. There was still this vast gulf separating the man he was from the man he was pretending to be. If Caitlin could have peered into his head to see what was really going on – if she had caught a glimpse of the mind that viewed dead workers as nothing more than market data – how horrified would she have been?

In the past, he might have blamed Barbara for the sharp stab of guilt he felt in that moment. He would have said that she'd *made* him feel guilty, via some clever psychological manipulation. But it was not that easy any more. He could no longer think of guilt as something that could be imposed from the outside. If he felt guilty about his actions, if he felt like a fraud, it was not because Barbara had planted the idea in his head. She had merely located a hidden sore spot – located it, and prodded.

The truth, Gabriel guessed, was that he'd always been far too good at compartmentalising, at ignoring the consequences he did not wish to think about. But this was getting harder and harder to do.

A couple more stories had been and gone by the time Caitlin noticed him watching her.

'Gabriel, are you OK?'

'Yes. I was just watching you watch the news.'

'You say that like it's a normal thing to do.'

'You get very animated. Do you know that?'

'Well, there's plenty to be animated about.'

'Yes. Yes, there is.'

She looked at him for a few moments. 'Is something wrong?'

'No. Why would anything be wrong?'

'You don't seem very present. What's on your mind?'

'Oh, you know. Just the usual. Work stuff. Statistics.'

'Right.' She rolled her eyes, pointedly. 'So you've been staring at me and thinking about statistics?'

'Yes, among other things.'

'What other things?'

'You look very beautiful when you watch the news. You're very . . . you.'

Caitlin laughed at this. 'As opposed to what? *Not* me?'

'Yes.'

'OK. Well, I'm so glad we cleared that up.'

Gabriel didn't know what else he could say.

Nothing, that was the point.

A PR Disaster

It was early in December when Gabriel learned that the Occupy movement had been added to a list of known terrorists and extremists by the City of London Police. Mason showed him the official letter, which the police had sent out to 'trusted local business partners'. It was a short document, and Gabriel skimmed through it in less than a minute. Occupy London appeared halfway down the first of two pages, a couple of paragraphs after Al Qaeda.

'What are your thoughts?' Mason asked him.

Gabriel shrugged as he handed the letter back. 'It's absurd.'

He didn't know what else he could say. He'd been in the camp. He'd sampled their free tea and delicious moussaka. He'd heard their grandiose plans to power their water heaters with solar panels. But even without this insider knowledge, surely no sane human being could draw a parallel between these people and Osama bin Laden. Whatever else he was, Mason wasn't stupid. Could he really take a letter like this seriously?

Judging from his face – a mixture of surprise and irritation – he could.

'Explain.'

Gabriel reined in his impatience and tried to put this in terms the other man might understand. 'Listen, Mason. These people aren't terrorists. Terrorists blow up buildings and murder people. They don't make banners and strum guitars.'

Mason's eyes narrowed for a moment, then he barked a laugh. 'You're right, Vaughn. Terrorists actually get things done, don't they? They don't sit around smoking drugs and whining about the privatisation of the railways.'

'Yes.' Gabriel used what Caitlin would have identified as his deadpan voice. 'That's exactly what I'm saying.'

Mason scrunched up the letter and tossed it over his shoulder into the bin. 'Still, it's good to know the police are taking a hard line on this. The sooner those *people* are evicted the better, and if labelling them terrorists speeds up the process, I for one am all for it.'

'Right. Assuming, of course, it doesn't backfire.'

Mason frowned again. 'What do you mean?'

'I mean that the police better be sure they've only passed that bulletin on to people they *can* trust. If it found its way to the protesters, it would be a PR disaster.'

Mason nodded, his frown becoming a grimace. He went over to his desk and got out a bottle of whisky and two tumblers. 'Vaughn, this, *this* is why you're such an asset to this firm. You don't let your emotions cloud your judgement. You see the bigger picture. Cheers.'

The next day, the police's counterterrorism briefing did find its way to the protesters. It was a PR disaster.

A Conversation with Matt

It wasn't Gabriel who'd leaked the letter, but there was a worrying part of him that wished it had been. This was a thought that kept returning to him at inappropriate moments. He'd spent at least five minutes fantasising about it in the morning meeting, and several more in his office, while an underling was telling him something tedious about the commodities market. And he was still thinking about it when he left Stanton House that evening.

This was part of the reason he didn't do his usual checks before stepping out of the foyer – though, in truth, he knew he'd grown more and more careless with each passing day. Several weeks of getting in and out of the building without incident had bred complacency.

He'd made it about twenty metres down the street, past Starbucks, past Marks & Spencer, when he heard his name being called. Walking on was not the most sensible option, but at the time it was all he could think to do.

He managed a few more strides before someone placed a hand on his shoulder.

'Gabriel.'

He turned. 'Oh, hello, Matt.'

'You ignoring me, man?'

Matt flashed a toothy grin, which Gabriel attempted to return.

'Course not. Busy day, that's all. I was miles away.'

'Hey, that is one sharp suit, my friend. Fits you like a glove.'

As far as Gabriel could tell, this was a statement made without malice. 'Thank you,' he replied, then gestured back towards Stanton House. 'Important meeting.' He had no idea if Matt had seen him coming out of the building, but he had to assume he had. As for the details of his supposed meeting, these were best left vague.

'Dude, it's like seven o'clock. D'you usually have meetings this late?'

'No, not usually. Not *this* late, but it was the only time they could fit me in.' Gabriel feigned a laugh. 'Don't worry, I'll be taking the time back. I think I've earned a lie-in.'

'Definitely.'

There was a pause, slightly awkward.

Gabriel was eager to steer the conversation to safer ground, so moved to the only topic he could think of – the one he'd been obsessing over all day. 'So, I hear you're all terrorists now. Is that right? I read it in the *Guardian*.'

Matt held up his hands. 'It's official. You can no longer question the status quo. If you do, you're an extremist. Long live democracy, right?'

'Right. If it's any consolation, I think you'll come through this looking better than the police.'

'Well, we're obviously doing something right. You can measure the success of a protest by how hard the establishment tries to suppress it.'

'Yes I suppose so.'

'Anyway, terrorists aren't all bad. Look at Nelson Mandela.'

Gabriel nodded, shuffling his feet.

'Listen, man, you look knackered. Why don't you come and have a cup of tea? Take the weight off your feet.'

'Thanks. I would, but I have a stack of paperwork to get through tonight. The life of an office drone.'

'Ten minutes?'

'No, seriously. Once I sit down, I think I'll struggle to get up again. Thanks for the thought, though. I appreciate it.'

'Any time.' Matt put his hand back on Gabriel's shoulder. 'Don't be a stranger, Gabe. If you're ever in the vicinity, pop in and say hi.'

'You can count on it.'

'Take it easy, my friend.'

'You too. Keep sticking it to the Man, er . . . man.'

Matt winked at him before disappearing into the camp.

Gabriel waited for a count of five. Then he turned the corner and got into the Mercedes.

A Conversation with Nicola

Gabriel felt irritated with himself for the rest of the evening. He was almost certain that no harm had been done – not in this instance – but that was not the point. He couldn't allow himself any more slip-ups. Matt was very trusting – naïve, even – but he was no idiot. If he saw Gabriel entering or exiting Stanton House on anything like a regular basis, he'd soon figure out that something was awry.

But the more immediate dilemma was what to tell Caitlin, if anything. The most normal thing to do would be to mention that he'd bumped into Matt – drop it into their next conversation as casually as possible. But, at the same time, he was eager to keep things as simple as possible; quite obviously, he did not want to draw attention to the various lies he had to keep spinning.

Fortunately, he didn't have to make any decisions straight away. He wasn't seeing Caitlin that night, so he decided to sleep on things, hoping the best course of action would become apparent in the morning.

It did, a little after nine o'clock. Gabriel was sitting in the chair in his office with his eyes closed, listening to a recording of Bruch's Violin Concerto Number One that Caitlin had said he should hear. It occurred to him, then, that the Matt situation was only going to become an issue if he said nothing. It might be unnecessary, but if handled properly, it eliminated the risk of his behaviour looking suspicious. All he had to do was mention that they'd run into each other while he was passing St Paul's, and that would be enough. Caitlin wasn't going to grill him about the precise circumstances – that was just guilt and paranoia talking. More to the point, once he'd told her, it would no longer be hanging over him. One less mask to keep in place.

Having resolved the problem to his satisfaction, Gabriel felt noticeably lighter, which confirmed to him that he'd made the correct decision. He leaned back in his chair, his hands cupped at the back of his head, and continued to listen to the music, his mind very far from work.

He was still like this ten minutes later, when Nicola knocked and entered.

'Um, Gabriel?'

'Nicola.'

'We need to go through your schedule. Are you busy?'

'No, I'm not.'

'No . . . what are you listening to?'

'It's Bruch's Violin Concerto in G minor. Do you like it?'

'Classical music's not really my thing.'

'Nicola, classical music is everyone's thing. They just haven't realised it yet.'

'OK. I'll take your word for it.'

Gabriel opened his eyes and gestured for Nicola to take a seat. 'So how's it looking? My schedule.'

'Well, I hate to be the bearer of bad news, but your day *is* going to get busier.'

'Nicola, you look tired. Is everything all right?'

Gabriel could see she hadn't taken this as he intended it. She stiffened in her chair, eyeing him with some suspicion. He decided to change tack. 'How are things at home?'

'How are things . . . Really?'

'Yes, really. I'd like to know.'

Nicola shifted uncomfortably, her lips contorted in a tight pout. After a moment, she exhaled and placed her iPad down on her lap. 'Look, Gabriel. I've been up half the night with a poorly six-year-old. So, yes, I'm tired, and I don't think it's something I should have to apologise for.'

'No, of course not. That isn't what I meant. I'd imagine it's very hard, trying to work a full-time job and raise children.'

'Yes. It is.'

'How old are they now?'

'Lucy's eight, Tom's six – Gabriel, what's this about? Are you unhappy with my work?'

'No, not at all. I was just wondering. Does it have to be about anything?'

Nicola laughed, somewhat scornfully. 'Well, forgive me, Gabriel, but I'm struggling to recall a single instance when you've ever taken the smallest interest in my life outside work. I'm looking for the ulterior motive.'

'There isn't one, trust me. But I'd like to ask you another question, if that's OK?'

Nicola shrugged.

'Do you like working here?'

'Ha! Gabriel, it's what I live for.'

'Can I take that as a no?'

'If you're looking for voluntary redundancies, you can forget it. Sadly, I need this job.'

'Nicola, you know how much money we're making here. And I've already told you that I'm happy with your work. More than happy. Trust me, redundancies are not on the cards.'

She still looked sceptical, but perhaps slightly less so.

'Can I ask you one more question before we get on with the schedule? Last one, I promise.'

Nicola nodded for him to go on.

'OK . . . This one's more hypothetical. If you had to explain to someone in very basic terms what we do here – you know, at Mason Wallace – what would you tell them?'

'Gabriel, it's not hypothetical. It happens all the time. Normal people don't understand hedge funds.'

'Right. I suppose that's what I'm driving at. So how do you explain it?'

Nicola exhaled again, making it clear that she was humouring him. 'We make money from trading shares and other financial instruments. That's enough for most people to cope with. Anything beyond that and eyes start to glaze over.'

'OK. That's fine. That's it in a nutshell. But say you had to explain it to Lucy or Tim.'

'Tom.'

'Sorry. *Tom*. Lucy or Tom. If you were explaining to a six-year-old, someone who has no concept of a stock exchange, what would you say we do?'

Nicola laughed. 'I wouldn't. It's impossible.'

'Why?'

'Because we don't do *anything*. Not in any sense that a

six-year-old can understand. We take money from rich people and make it into more money, basically by moving it around. It's not much more than a virtual coin trick.'

Gabriel thought about this for several moments. 'Thank you, Nicola. That's possibly the best explanation of our industry that I've ever heard. As soon as your children are old enough, that's what you should tell them. We do virtual coin tricks. Now let's crack on with the schedule.'

Nicola was staring at him, clearly perplexed.

'Unless you'd like to get a coffee first? Recharge the cells.'

'Gabriel, I'm not usually one to pay much attention to the Mason Wallace rumour mill. Frankly, I prefer to spend as little of my personal time thinking about this place as possible. But the word around the water cooler is that you're in a new relationship. Something serious.'

Gabriel shrugged. 'Rumours are almost always wrong.'

'You should hold on to her. She's good for you.'

The Possibility of Being a
Better Man

Gabriel had never had any trouble buying a present for a woman before. He bought designer clothes and shoes, expensive perfumes and underwear. He bought earrings and necklaces. He bought diamonds set in gold or platinum.

But when it came to Caitlin's Christmas present, he found himself in alien territory. He couldn't even decide what his budget should be. What was a sensible price tag for a girl who found a forty-pound bottle of wine painfully extravagant?

It was a problem that took the best part of a week to resolve. He started by googling 'gifts for musicians', but this threw up nothing but cheap tat. Themed mugs and cushion covers, novelty T-shirts, measuring spoons shaped like various instruments, a build-your-own ukulele kit. He refined his search by adding the word 'classical', and was directed at once to a cheeseboard shaped like a violin. Gabriel didn't know precisely what he was looking for, but a cheeseboard it was not.

Of course, there were advantages and disadvantages in trying to buy a musical gift for a musician. If he got it right, the effort would certainly be appreciated; but Gabriel knew it would be much easier to get it wrong. He stopped looking at websites that promised 'unique' and 'personalised' gifts, and started trawling through classical music forums. Soon he was neck-deep in debates – surprisingly heated – about the relative merits of different types of violin bow. A trail of hyperlinks led him to eBay, where a woman in Virginia was trying to sell a nineteenth-century French bow for forty thousand dollars. Gabriel had read nothing to convince him that a violin bow could be as well engineered as, for example, a BMW 3 Series – which he knew commanded a similar price tag – but this was nevertheless a world in which he felt far more at ease. Had money been no object, had he been living within his normal means, he would have happily paid forty thousand dollars for an antique violin bow. He would have gone much further: there were violins on eBay that cost several hundred thousand pounds, and this was just the tip of the iceberg. A little more research revealed that there were instruments that had sold at auction for millions. There were instruments that even Gabriel would have struggled to afford.

Fantasising was not a productive use of his time, but he found it irresistible. Gabriel would have loved to buy Caitlin a multi-million-pound violin. He even went as far as finding the exact violin he would have purchased. It was an eighteenth-century Italian instrument that had belonged to Niccolò Paganini, and was valued at ten million dollars. It would have come close to bankrupting him, but given his situation, Gabriel could think of no better way to dispose of his money.

For a short time, it did not seem such a crazy idea. It was a plausible way of coming clean, while simultaneously proving that he no longer wanted the life he'd had. He was willing to give it all up in one ludicrous, romantic gesture . . . Except, Gabriel knew how it was likely to pan out in reality. It would look as if he were trying to buy her forgiveness, as if he were trying to buy *her*; and this was precisely what he was trying to avoid. It was what made this present different and difficult. For the first time in his life, Gabriel was not treating a gift as a form of currency.

Still, he was struck again by the inescapable thought, almost a certainty, that he could not continue as he was for ever. The longer the deception went on, the more he got away with, the worse he felt. It was like a creeping sickness in the pit of his stomach, almost impossible to ignore; yet, for now, this was the option Gabriel continued to pursue. It was the only option he could see. He suppressed his guilt and went back to the task at hand, first making a note of the key boxes the gift had to tick:

- [ ] Inexpensive (without being 'cheap')
- [ ] Personal (not in the sense that underwear is personal)
- [ ] Heartfelt

It was a daunting list, especially on the last point, so Gabriel knew he had to find some way of playing to his strengths. Finding a musical present no longer seemed a viable option; between the thirty-pound cheeseboard and the million-pound Stradivarius, he felt he'd exhausted most avenues. It would be far better to focus his energy on an area where he at least had some basic knowledge to begin with. For this reason, clothing was an obvious choice. Gabriel knew that he had a strong sense of style, and he felt confident that even on a tight budget he could find something that would look and feel amazing. Much more problematical were the second and third boxes. How did you go about buying clothing that was personal and heartfelt?

The answer came to him after a day's worth of deliberation, and when it did, it was perfect. He should buy her a dress she could perform in. The key, after all, was to get something that wasn't just beautiful in and of itself, but which also had some larger meaning behind it – that said something about who she was and how he saw her.

The dress he eventually found was royal purple. At one hundred and thirty pounds, it was leaning towards the more expensive end of high street fashion, but still comfortably within the means of a humble research analyst. It was full length and had elegant panelling on the bodice. Gabriel thought Caitlin would look beautiful in it. More importantly, he thought she would *feel* beautiful in it.

He bought a box to wrap it in and had both delivered to his apartment the Monday before Christmas. Caitlin had a late concert that evening, performing carols at a church in Spitalfields, and they had not arranged to see each other afterwards. Given that Gabriel was not used to wrapping presents – he invariably had someone else do it for him – he had set aside a cautious half hour to get it right.

It didn't take that long. He poured himself a glass of red wine, watched an instructional video on YouTube and, ten minutes later, he had a finished product he was more than happy with. On the gift tag, he wrote the short message he'd dreamed up when he first decided on the dress:

For when you get to play the solos. G x

Afterwards, he sprawled out on his sofa, feeling generally pleased with himself.

It had just gone nine when she called him on his mobile. Aside from a couple of text messages, they hadn't spoken since the previous night, and her voice sounded slightly strange.

'Are you home?' she asked. 'I've had a bit of a crap day and I thought I might pop over.'

Gabriel remembered just in time that he *wasn't* at home – not as far as Caitlin was concerned. So where was he? 'I'm in transit,' he told her. 'Went for a couple of post-work drinks and I'm heading home now.'

'Oh. I didn't realise you had plans.'

'I didn't. It was a spur of the moment thing. Where are you? Are you at the flat now?'

'No, I'm— Well, I was about to come over, but maybe I'll just head back to mine instead. Get some sleep.'

'You can still come over. I should be back in half an hour or so, barring any mishaps on the Tube. You know, terrorists or—'

'Gabriel, please. This isn't what I need right now.'

'Sorry. Just trying to . . . Like I said, I can be home in half an hour. Forty minutes tops. You shouldn't have to wait very long.'

There was a lengthy pause while she considered this. Gabriel could hear the street noise in the background, the rumble of a passing bus.

'Caitlin? Would you like me to come over to yours instead? It doesn't make much difference to me.'

'No, it's OK. I think maybe I just need to get some sleep.'

'You're sure?'

'Yes. I'll give you a call tomorrow.'

'You can call me tonight, if you change your mind.'

'OK. Thank you. Bye.'

'I love you. You know that, don't you?'

It was not a good moment to say this for the first time. The silence down the line told him that she'd already hung up, leaving the sentiment to float unreciprocated in the empty space of Gabriel's apartment.

It was the first time he'd ever told a woman he loved her and actually meant it, so it was a little dispiriting to discover that he'd been talking to himself. But more troubling was the rest of the conversation. Gabriel didn't think he'd made any major gaffes, but neither had he handled it as well as he could have done. He should have said that he was picking up her Christmas present. It would have been closer to the truth and wouldn't have raised the spectre of the workmates she'd never met. He probably should have asked what was wrong as well. Perhaps that was what she'd expected? But when it came to providing emotional support for another human being, Gabriel still felt quite out of his depth. It was not something he'd had many opportunities to practise.

He poured himself another glass of wine and settled back down on the sofa, CNN flickering in the background. Try as he might, he couldn't shake the vague sense that the evening had gone awry. He kept replaying their short conversation, attempting to locate the fault lines so that he could do better next time.

At some point, he must have fallen asleep, because the next thing he knew, he was waking to the sound of knocking at his door. His first groggy thought was that it might be Caitlin – that she'd decided to come round after all. This hope was quickly replaced with disappointment as he realised he was in the wrong flat for this to be possible. It had to be someone else, though Gabriel struggled to imagine who. It was too late for any more deliveries, and no one had buzzed the intercom.

Now wide awake, he got up, went through to the hallway and opened the door.

It was Caitlin.

Caitlin

There wasn't any time to think, and there was nothing he could say or do. She stood there, just a couple of feet from him, her face a mask. Then she turned and started to walk away.

'Caitlin, wait.' He managed to get a hand on her arm, and she spun to face him.

'No, Gabriel! I thought I could do this, but I can't. You should be glad. We'll spare your wife, your kids – whoever the hell you've got—'

'It's not what you think.'

'Gabriel, I don't know what I think. I don't know where to begin.' She had started crying, her voice cracked and her whole body shaking. 'There's no possible explanation for this. There's nothing that makes sense.'

'There is an explanation. It's not good, but it's not what you think, either. Please, if you just—'

'Let go! Let go of my arm before I scream this place down.'

'OK, OK.' Gabriel released her arm and held his hands up. 'I'm not touching you. But you came for the truth, obviously.

It's in that room. Give me five minutes, then if you want to leave, you can leave. Just hear me out first.'

'No. There's nothing, *nothing* you can say that I can believe.'

'I'm not going to lie to you.'

'You've been lying from the very beginning!'

'Yes, I have. Almost everything I've told you about my life has been a lie. But not how I feel about you – that isn't a lie. I love you. I've never been more certain of anything.'

'How dare you! You don't love me. You don't know what that word means.'

'Caitlin look at me, please.'

'No, Gabriel. No! I don't ever want to look at you again.'

'OK, I understand that. But you need to hear the truth. Give me five more minutes and I'll tell you everything. After that, you can leave. I won't follow you and I won't try to stop you. If you never want to see me again, then you won't.'

It was pretty much the only card Gabriel had left to play, and he could see that she was torn. He pushed the door to the apartment wide open.

'Please. For your own sake, you need to hear this.'

She was almost at the lift before she turned and walked back. 'Five minutes! You go in first and leave the door open. Leave every door open between me and this corridor. If you try to touch me – if you come within three steps of me – I'm gone. Do you understand?'

'Yes, I understand. I won't touch you. Thank you.'

Gabriel turned and walked back into his apartment before she could change her mind, leaving the door wide open behind him.

The Truth

He backed though the apartment with his hands raised, making sure he kept his distance while remaining in her line of sight. She wasn't crying any more, but her breathing was ragged, and her hands were still shaking. Gabriel could see her eyes darting back and forth as she took in some of the details of his real life: the luxury hardwood flooring, the immaculate furnishings, the floor-to-ceiling windows overlooking the marina, the lights of bridges and high-rises twinkling through the glass. He wanted to know how she'd found him – of course he did – but he knew he had no right to ask. He backed to the far end of the living area, his shoulders almost to the wall, and gestured for her to take a seat on the sofa. She shook her head.

'Will you let me get you a glass of water or something?' Gabriel asked. 'Please?' He pointed across to the kitchen area. 'I'll be just over there. You can see what I'm doing the whole time.'

He took her silence as permission, filled a tall glass with water from the fridge, then set it down on the coffee table before returning to his original position at the far wall. After a couple of moments, Caitlin took the glass and drained most of it in a couple of gulps. Then she sat on the sofa, placing her bag very carefully beside her.

'Well, you're not a research analyst. That much was obvious when I got out of the taxi.' She drank the rest of the water, leaving the glass on the floor afterwards. 'Nice place. You should spend more time here.'

Her voice wasn't trembling any more. It had a cold fury to it, like a hammer striking marble.

'Caitlin, I'm sorry. It's—'

'You can spare me the apologies, Gabriel. They don't mean anything. Just give me the facts so I can get out of here. You can start by telling me what it is you really do.'

'I manage a hedge fund. Co-manage it.' Her expression remained flat. 'Do you know what a hedge fund does?'

'Yes, Gabriel,' she snapped. 'I know what a hedge fund does. I'm not an idiot, whatever you may think.'

'I don't think you're an idiot. I've never thought that.'

'You make vast amounts of money fucking about on the stock exchange. Is that it?'

'Yes, basically.'

'Right. Well, that explains the luxury apartment, anyway. I'm guessing you need a six-figure salary to afford the mortgage on a place like this, minimum.'

'Seven figures. And this place isn't mortgaged. I own it outright.'

Caitlin laughed bitterly. 'Am I supposed to be impressed?'

'No, you're not. It's contemptible, I understand that. But I said I'd tell you the truth and I'm going to.'

'What about Lewisham? Do you own that place too?'

'No. I rent it. I started renting it just after we got together.'

She closed her eyes for a second, tracing a finger along the arm of the sofa. 'You know, I had a couple of moments this morning when I imagined all sorts of exotic explanations. I had you working for MI5 at one point. But the truth was always going to be something far more banal. I think I knew that. I mean, you'd make a pretty lousy spy, Gabriel. You realise that your address is on your driving licence? Your real address.'

'My driving licence?'

'Your driving licence, Gabriel. I saw it yesterday when we were in the pub. You keep it in your wallet, in plain view. It's surprising what you can overlook, isn't it? I suppose when you're trying to maintain this massive façade the smaller details can slip your mind.'

'Yes.'

Gabriel didn't know what else he could say. She was exactly right; he'd been juggling all these complicated deceptions and had overlooked something that should have been glaringly obvious.

'You know what's really humiliating? When I found out, I was desperate, just desperate, to pretend it hadn't happened. I've spent the last twenty-four hours trying to convince myself that it was a simple mistake, despite all the signs that it wasn't.' Caitlin put her hands to her face and shook her head. 'Gabriel, I do know people who might forget to keep their driving licence up to date, but you're not one of them. Then there was the address itself. St Katharine Docks. It doesn't exactly scream affordable housing.'

'No. I suppose it doesn't.'

Caitlin bent to pick up her empty glass, looked at it for a moment and put it down again.

'I'll get you another one,' Gabriel said.

'Don't bother. Just tell me the rest of it.'

'What do you want to know?'

Caitlin gave another humourless laugh. 'What do you *think* I want to know?'

'Why I did it?'

'Right. Because that's the part that really starts to fuck with my mind. You've been spinning this lie from pretty much the first moment we met. Why? Why would anyone do that to a complete stranger?'

'Because I wanted to get to know you. I didn't want you to instantly hate me because of what I do for a living.'

'OK. And that would make perfect sense to anyone who knew me already. But it makes no sense with you. Not unless you make a habit of trying to impress women by pretending to have no money.'

'No, I don't. It was a first. It might be a first in the history of mankind.'

It came as no surprise that she didn't smile at this; but Gabriel knew whatever he said next, he wasn't going to come out well.

Caitlin took a deep breath before looking at him again. 'OK, so what are we dealing with here? Amazing intuition or something far more sinister?'

'The second. I wasn't just passing by when that man – that boy – tried to mug you. I'd followed you from St Paul's. The Occupy camp. I saw you busking there. I'd seen you a couple of times.'

'Oh my fucking God.'

'It sounds bad, I realise that—'

'I think I'd better leave now.'

She grabbed her bag and started to rise to her feet.

'Caitlin, there's more. Not much, but it's all I can give you as an explanation.'

'No, Gabriel. There is no explanation, not this time.' She took a couple of steps towards the door before spinning back round to face him. 'You were following me? Why were you following me? *Why*?'

'It was a compulsion. I heard you play, and it . . . well, it got to me. It affected me on quite a profound—'

'Jesus Christ. What the hell do you want me to say to that, Gabriel? This is just insane. You saw me busking, you liked my music, so you decided to stalk me? What part of that makes sense in your head?'

'You're right. It doesn't make sense. I realise that more than anyone. Like I said, it wasn't rational. It was a compulsion. But there's actually more to it than—'

'Gabriel you need help. Serious help. I have nothing more to say to you.'

'Caitlin, don't go, not until you've heard this last thing.'

'I've heard enough.'

'No, you haven't. You need to hear this, too. Trust me.'

'Trust you?' Caitlin shook her head in disbelief.

'This is the last thing, I promise. Then you can go. Just give me thirty more seconds.'

'Gabriel, what can you possibly say to me in thirty seconds? We're done here. It's over.'

'Let me show you this one thing, please. I'm going to—'

She turned and walked out of the room.

Gabriel didn't know what else he could do. He'd promised he'd let her leave.

He went to the bathroom cabinet, got out his medication and took a photo of the packaging on his phone, making sure the writing was clearly visible. Then he sent it to Caitlin as a multi-media message.

Caitlin, this is a photo of my chemotherapy medication. It's called Temodal. Google it. I was diagnosed with a terminal brain tumour two months ago. I'm dying. I have about four months left to live. This isn't an excuse for anything I've done, but it's the start of an explanation. Please come back and hear the rest.

He waited.

Please. I've told you the truth tonight and I'm telling you the truth now. You have to believe me.

After a couple more minutes, he figured that she'd probably switched her phone off. Or seen his name and deleted the messages without reading them.

He went back into the living area and retrieved her empty glass from the floor. He had just dropped it into the kitchen bin when his message tone rang.

I do believe you. I'm glad you're dying. Don't ever contact me again.

PART 3

The End of the World
as We Know It

The Room of Selfish
Heartless Bastards

Gabriel dreamed he was in hell. Or maybe it was purgatory. It felt more like purgatory because it bore a strong resemblance to the A and E waiting room. That was the setting: row upon row of cheap plastic chairs, closed doors on every wall, an unmanned reception desk. Some of the details shifted now and then – having that hazy, undecided quality that dream details often have – but the basic geography stayed the same. A large cold square room with not much in it.

Caitlin wasn't there, of course. Mason sat across from Gabriel, his back straight and his expression meaningless. To his right was Shipman and, further along, the rest of the Mason Wallace managerial team, along with most of the people he had worked with as an investment banker. They were all wearing very nice suits, and all had identical stony stares. No one was talking, though Gabriel didn't know if this was because it was prohibited or because they didn't have anything to say to each other.

Glancing around the room, Gabriel didn't think there was

anyone there *he* wanted to talk to. But then his eyes alighted on Nicola. She was sitting a couple of rows away, her shoulders slightly hunched.

Nicola? You're here too? But you just filed the paperwork!

Unfortunately, there was no one present to complain to. The doors leading off the room remained closed. No one got called. No one moved.

Gabriel looked again at Nicola, then down at his highly polished shoes.

Accessory. That was the word that hissed in his head.

It made a certain amount of sense, he supposed. Some people were guilty, and others were guilty by association. In this version of hell, it didn't matter if you were Hitler or Hitler's secretary. There were plenty of seats to spare.

3.30 A.M.

The reality he awoke to was not much better. Gabriel didn't believe in hell. He didn't believe in any sort of afterlife; the thought was preposterous to him. He knew that when his brain died, his awareness would cease. He would no longer be conscious of his many sins. They would continue to exist and have an impact in the world, but there was no wise and just creator waiting to judge him, to mete out punishment or forgiveness for what he'd done.

Yet there were times, like this one, at 3.30 a.m. in the darkness of his room, when he could imagine what it might be like to stand before his maker – to hear His verdict and sentence. In the unlikely event of absolution, Gabriel knew exactly what he'd say to God. Thanks but no thanks. You have no right to grant forgiveness, not this time. You need to ask Caitlin; look into her heart, do whatever it is you do. Hers is the only forgiveness that matters.

She would forgive him eventually, when he was no longer around to answer for his sins. Gabriel knew that because he knew she was a genuinely good person. She was the sort of person who thought that the teenage junkie who'd mugged her needed social care rather than prison. Yes, she hated him right now. She was glad he was dying. She didn't want to see him for the rest of his pitiful life. But this was not the same as wanting someone to suffer for all eternity. If Caitlin had to choose a suitable punishment for him, she would most likely choose nothing.

Unfortunately, none of this was any consolation. As far as Gabriel was concerned, the knowledge that he would not see her again *was* eternal punishment, and the fact that she was deep-down good made his crimes feel all the more despicable.

Over the past few months, he had discovered many emotions that were new to him – feelings better and worse than any he'd experienced before. But now something else was entering the mix. In the past, Gabriel had never had much of an imagination. He knew that, and it didn't bother him. He had been a man who thought about probabilities, likely outcomes, efficient routes from A to B. He had always been a pragmatist, concerned only with things he could see or touch, not intangibles. But in those dark, dark nights after Caitlin had left him, Gabriel discovered an imaginative capacity that was wholly unfamiliar. It wasn't just the vivid dreams or the fantasies about meeting God. Far worse were the recurring flashes – thoughts and images – that burst into his mind's eye with the sudden uncontrolled intensity of a lightning bolt. Some were memories – the tears in the corridor, her eyes when she started to comprehend the depth of his deception – and others were the scenes he hadn't even witnessed, the events prior to her arriving at his door, which he found himself picturing in startling detail. He could see her face as she got out of the taxi and started to take in her surroundings: the plush restaurants and the yachts on the marina. Presumably, she would have had to wait around outside his building until she could follow someone into the foyer, not wanting to buzz the intercom, needing to see the full truth with her own eyes. Had she hesitated once inside? How many minutes had she spent at his door before she knocked, praying she was wrong and knowing she was not?

Once, Gabriel would have laughed at the idea that you could experience someone else's pain as if it were your own. But this was precisely what he was doing now, over and over again. The pain of others, not just imagined in the abstract but felt as repeated stabs to the stomach.

Gabriel didn't know if this was something normal people experienced – something that was accepted as just another part of life by those not working in finance. But he suspected this was the case. It was a good explanation for why lots of highly intelligent and talented people chose *not* to work in finance. Instead, they decided to be paediatricians or human rights lawyers, conservationists or social workers.

For the first time in his life, Gabriel could see why these were appealing professions to go into.

A Couple of Days before Christmas

'Please?'

'Gabriel, no. We've been through this.'

'I need to see you.'

'No, you don't. I'm sorry, but it's just not going to happen, not this time.'

'I'm going to be on my own, you realise that? I'm going to—'

'Gabriel, have you been drinking? I think you need to get some rest, sober up.'

'It's just a couple of days. I can pay you whatever you want. Seriously. Just name a price.'

There was a long silence down the line. Gabriel took this as a sign she was considering it.

'Please, Melissa? I can't be on my own right now.'

More silence. When she answered, there was something very different about her voice, something sadder. 'Gabriel, listen to me. I don't want to feel like a whore at Christmas. Can you understand that?'

'Yes, I can, of course I can, but—'

'There are no buts.' She sighed down the phone. It wasn't the sort of sigh he was used to hearing from her. 'Look, you're obviously in a very bad place at the moment, and you have my sympathy, you really do. But my mind's made up. I'm going to spend Christmas with my family. You should think about doing the same.'

She hung up.

Family

Of course, he'd never thought about Melissa having a family – even though most people did in some form or another. Given her age and her perfect body, children seemed unlikely. As did a husband or boyfriend, given her lifestyle. She was probably talking about her parents, maybe some siblings, too. That was the more obvious assumption. She'd be spending Christmas with her parents, who, he was sure, had no idea what she really did for a living. No woman was going to admit to her parents that she made her money as a high-end prostitute. She'd have concocted some very elaborate cover story. Gabriel couldn't begin to imagine the details, but it was a situation – a scale of deception – he could relate to. Obviously.

Had they ever talked about her background? Not really. Why would either of them have wanted to? Gabriel could recall the odd scrap here and there. He knew that she was educated – that was clear from the way she spoke, despite the occasional slip in her accent that suggested, to his mind, humbler beginnings. She'd started working as an escort while studying for a degree.

She'd continued because she loved the money and enjoyed the work. Or was it something else that she'd said? That she was addicted to the lifestyle? Either way, it had been something Gabriel had been happy to hear, which he now supposed may have been the point. It was part of her job, allowing men to believe whatever they wanted to believe.

But now he'd had a glimpse of something else – a more depressing reality. *I don't want to feel like a whore at Christmas.* Gabriel suspected the only reason he'd been given that glimpse was to get rid of him, the client who was struggling to take no for an answer.

When he'd sobered up, he could see what a terrible idea it had been, but that didn't mean he had any good alternative. In fact, the *only* alternative he could find was the one Melissa had suggested – that he spend Christmas with his 'family', his father and Susan. It was so absurd that he'd initially rejected it out of hand. Gabriel hadn't spent any serious time with his father since the last of those awful lunches. They ran out of things to talk about if they attempted more than ten minutes on the phone, so the idea of spending a day or more together was almost unthinkable.

But on the Saturday before Christmas Eve, Gabriel was awake several hours before dawn, and found himself facing an uncomfortable truth: in his current situation, a strained, awkward Christmas was the best he could hope for. Otherwise, he was on his own for the next three days, with nothing to distract him from his darkest thoughts.

By nine o'clock he was on the phone to his father, who was, of course, extremely surprised to hear from him.

'Is everything OK?' his father asked.

Gabriel supposed this was the obvious response. But he still had no intention of talking about the tumour.

He told his father that he was at a loose end and had been thinking about popping over on Christmas Day, as if this were a perfectly normal thought for him to have. 'Would that be all right?' he asked. 'I mean, I don't know if you already have plans, or anything. I realise it's late notice.'

'No. No plans. Are you . . . Is it just you, or will you be bringing someone?'

'No. Just me.'

'Oh. OK. You know you're always welcome here. You know that don't you?'

Gabriel didn't know that. He thought it was something people occasionally said, but never really meant.

'You're welcome to stay the night, if you want,' his father went on. 'I'll make up the bed in the spare room. Stay as long as you like.'

'Thank you. I'm not sure what . . . Well, I guess I'll bring an overnight bag. Then I can decide on the day.'

In all probability, this would be the last time he would see his father, which was another factor he had of course considered when planning this visit. Gabriel had never been sentimental, and he felt no need to draw a line under whatever flimsy relationship existed between them. But at the same time, he had no desire to bring any more pain into the world. He didn't know the exact nature of his father's feelings towards him – whether there was anything remaining beyond a dull sense of mutual obligation – but he hoped that this last Christmas visit might, retrospectively, bring some comfort. It was important to say goodbye, at the very least.

Harrods

The immediate benefit was clear. For the next couple of days, at least, Gabriel had a purpose. Go out. Buy gifts. Come home. Wrap gifts. Drive to father's house. Exchange pleasantries for undecided amount of time. Drive home again. It wasn't much of a purpose, but it would keep him occupied until he could go back to work. For now, that was enough.

He showered, dressed and drove to Knightsbridge. It was excruciatingly busy, but that was part of the point. It took him well over an hour to fight his way through the congestion into central London, and it would take him a similar amount of time to get out again. Harrods would be hell, but it was the kind of hell he could deal with right now. Just the normal hell of other people.

He'd bought and posted a Christmas card over a week ago, and had received one back from his father, and usually they'd have left it at that. Gabriel had been dissuading his father from buying him anything for nearly a decade, ever since his salary went from being high to being ridiculous. When you could afford anything, presents became redundant. He remembered telling his father that around his twenty-third birthday. He'd just been pointing out an obvious reality – trying to make life easier – but now he couldn't imagine it had sounded anything other than smug and ungrateful.

Although he was out of practice, Gabriel didn't think that buying a gift for his father would prove all that difficult. Wine was a failsafe choice. He could buy some extremely nice wine, some of which could be opened for Christmas lunch, and he could spend as much as he liked without making anyone feel awkward. His father wasn't going to google the label.

Susan was more of a challenge. Gabriel didn't know much about her. He didn't know what a good present for a 58-year-old woman might be. So he'd have to browse, maybe ask some sales assistants, or grab a coffee and spend some time on Yahoo! Answers. It would all kill time.

Harrods was as frenzied as he'd expected – the usual mix of affluent shoppers and gawking tourists blocking the aisles. Gabriel wondered what sort of person regarded Harrods on Christmas Eve as an enjoyable point on their holiday itinerary. It would be even worse a couple of days later, when it opened for the Boxing Day sales. It was the kind of thing that had started making the news in recent years: *Five Injured in Selfridges Stampede!* Gabriel had no problem with consumerism, obviously, but he had never seen the attraction of sales. If something was worth paying for, it was worth paying for. Where was the satisfaction in degrading yourself to save a few pounds?

He spent a lot of time browsing, and even more time observing the other shoppers, trying to decode their expressions of frustration and weariness and expectation and grim determination and even, occasionally, happiness. Trying to figure out what made them tick, what they were getting out of this experience. As he'd predicted, it wasn't as awful as it would have been in other circumstances. He thought he was perhaps the only person in the store who wasn't in a dreadful hurry to get things done. Quite the opposite: he actually welcomed the delays. He took his time to look around, walking at an abnormally slow pace – the pace people used when they visited St Paul's. He didn't ask advice from any of the sales assistants because they all looked too harried. This was obviously an abysmal environment to have to work in, and he didn't want to make it worse if he could avoid it.

Instead, he ended up buying presents for Susan that felt like fairly safe bets. He bought a pack of luxury chocolates from the food hall. He bought an expensive pack of scented candles. He spent a lot of time in the perfume section. Did 58-year-old women bother with perfume? Or was it too old to think about smelling attractive, as opposed to just clean? He settled, eventually, on a bottle of Chanel No. 5. Timeless, ageless, classy. It was an obvious choice.

Thetford

Christmas Day was the best day of the year for driving. At eight thirty in the morning, the roads were essentially empty. Once he was on the motorway, Gabriel stayed in the right-hand lane and kept his speedometer hovering somewhere around a hundred and ten miles per hour. He wasn't worried about being stopped by the police as he assumed they had better things to do; and even if he had been caught speeding, he wouldn't have cared in the slightest. He'd likely be dead by the time his licence was revoked.

He was there well before ten, pulling onto the drive of a nondescript semi-detached housed in suburbia. It was the kind of house – the kind of lifestyle – that sang of mediocrity, and which Gabriel had always despised. But now, for the first time since his father had moved there, Gabriel could see a different side to it. The quiet, the simplicity, the neat rectangular gardens. It was, he supposed, a perfectly adequate house for two people to live in as they approached retirement together.

Gabriel's father met him at the front door and immediately

offered to move his own car, a Volvo, out of the garage so that Gabriel didn't have to leave the Ferrari on the drive.

'What's the problem?' Gabriel asked. 'Are you ashamed of your son's car?'

It took his father a moment to smile. 'An old banger like that? I wouldn't want the neighbours to think I've fallen on hard times.'

It was a relief that his father was able to accept and run with the joke, but the hesitation suggested there might be an element of truth there. With a yellow Ferrari context mattered, and what was suitable for Knightsbridge was less so for Thetford. It didn't look ridiculous, exactly; just incongruous. Very incongruous.

Regardless, he wasn't going to make a big deal of it. He assured his father that he had excellent insurance, and the two men went inside.

As always, he had no idea how to greet Susan. In the end, after some awkward manoeuvring, he went for the standard air kiss on both cheeks. Implied intimacy with minimal contact.

'Susan. You look well.'

Not strictly true, of course. She looked as 58-year-old women tended to look – those who hadn't had Botox. Crow's feet, skin far too loose at the neck. Not *un*well, but hardly a picture of health.

'Gabriel. It's good to see you again. It's been quite a long time, hasn't it?'

'Yes, too long. But I'm a workaholic. You know that.'

'Well, it's good to see you taking some time off. Let me get you a coffee or something. You must have set off very early.'

'No. I just drove fast.'

Susan smiled politely.

'Empty roads,' Gabriel added.

'Well, let me get you that coffee. Black no sugar?'

'Yes. Thank you. I'm just going to grab a few things from the car.'

Back outside, Gabriel checked his reflection in the near-side wing mirror. Dark bags under bloodshot eyes, skin pale and dry. He didn't look ill, exactly, but he could see why Susan was so keen to get some coffee down him.

He took his bag of gifts from the boot, set it down in the hallway and went to the bathroom. He let the water from the cold tap run over his wrists for a minute, then splashed plenty on his face and neck. Afterwards, he spent some more time looking into the bathroom mirror, setting the right kind of smile on his face, like a sculptor chiselling at a block of alabaster. When he was satisfied with the result – as satisfied as he could be – he went back through to the living room to talk to his father.

Talking

It was OK at first. Compared to the serious traumas he'd suffered recently, the moderate strain of small silences and Christmas TV was nothing to be feared. The conversation, for the most part, skirted the inconsequential fringes of a few familiar topics: work, the economy, property prices, the problems with the coalition government (the Lib Dems, obviously – they were the problem); Europe, the Euro, the weather. They didn't talk about prostitution or brain cancer or causing horrific pain to someone you loved and how that pain could feel far worse than your own. Gabriel tried to keep things light. He was astute and self-assured with his father, and witty and charming with Susan. He complimented her on the roast lunch and offered to load the dishwasher afterwards.

But he'd underestimated the mounting stress of the façade, of having to be a version of himself he did not want to be. Deception – more deception – felt like such hard work.

His solution was to drink. Just a little at first, to take the edge off. But the wine he'd brought went down far too easily, and by the time he was on his third glass, he knew he was on a downward spiral. The sort of trajectory you see in advance but are powerless to stop.

By early evening, he was finding it difficult to remain upbeat – let alone astute or witty or charming. He was slurring his words, and the relatively fluent conversation of before was now punctuated with protracted gaps, filled only by the increased volume of the television.

Susan went to bed early – not long after nine – though Gabriel didn't know if this was normal for her or a response to the circumstances. Either way, it meant that he was left alone with his father, who had also been drinking for some time. Gabriel didn't doubt the reason; it was fundamentally the same as his – an attempt to paper over this . . . *thing*. The chasm that prevented them from having a normal conversation, or what Gabriel imagined a normal conversation between a father and his son might be. It didn't have to be deep or meaningful. Just something that didn't feel so painstakingly constructed.

But the minutes ticked by and nothing much was said. His father drank the rest of his wine and started talking about going to bed. It was at this point that Gabriel decided to ambush his father with a question that, to the other man's perspective, must have come from nowhere.

'Dad, are you proud of me?'

It was clumsy and embarrassing, even through the numbing gauze of alcohol, but Gabriel figured it was never going to be anything else. And he knew he wouldn't get another chance to ask.

His father paused halfway to the kitchen, where he'd presumably been heading with his empty wine glass. He turned back to

Gabriel and looked at him for a few moments. He seemed unsure about what to do – whether this was the sort of enquiry that could be dealt with on the way to the dishwasher or if he should return to his armchair. Overall, Gabriel was pleased when he opted for the latter.

'Of course I'm proud of you. I've always been proud of you. Don't you know that?'

Gabriel shrugged. 'Sometimes I think I could have been a better person than I am. I could have lived a better life.'

The look his father gave him was a mixture of concern and confusion. 'Gabriel, you're thirty-three.'

'Thirty-two.'

'OK, thirty-two. Thirty-three next month. The point is, you're far too young to be having thoughts like this. Anyway, what have you done that's so bad? You've made money – a *lot* of money – but that's only because you've worked for it. There aren't many people who could do what you do.'

'I don't *do* anything.'

'What do you mean? Of course you do, you—'

'Exactly that. I don't do anything. I don't make anything or add anything to the world. I make money but I don't even make that, not really. I just perform a series of transactions that skims money off the productive economy, the bit that actually creates wealth.'

His father frowned. 'I think you're being a little hard on yourself. I mean, I know the financial sector's got some bad press lately, but you didn't crash the economy. You're one of the people who help to stabilise it. You keep capital flowing. You invest. That leads to growth, innovation, jobs . . .'

Gabriel drained the rest of his wine and refilled his glass from the bottle on the coffee table. He had the distinct impression he was hearing his own words fed back to him. These were all arguments he had made at one time or another, and they'd never sounded hollower.

'Listen, Dad. Nothing I do is for the benefit of the wider economy. My job is to make money regardless. You can think of me as a . . . as a parasite sucking resources from its host. I don't want the host to die, obviously, but that doesn't mean our interests are the same. I care about share prices, not economic health.'

His father looked at him blankly.

'Put it this way. Imagine there are two companies. One is progressive and innovative, treats its workers well, pays its taxes, gives a percentage of its profits to charities and social enterprises. The other pays its workers poverty wages and is engaged in aggressive tax avoidance – doesn't give a penny back to society. Essentially, it does the opposite; it takes money away from the workforce and schools and hospitals, and it hands it over to the shareholders. Which company do I choose to invest in? Let me tell you, in real life it isn't even a choice. Nine times out of ten, the first company will have gone bust. It can't compete with the second sort.'

'Gabriel, we both know it's more complicated than that. You have a responsibility to your—'

'OK. Let me put it even more simply. Which of these activities do you think's more profitable: producing renewable energy or selling guns to human rights abusers? And which—'

'I think you've had a bit too much to drink.'

'Yes, I have. But that's not why I'm telling you this. I'm— it's the truth, that's what I'm trying to say. Honestly, Dad, there are times when I've watched the news, lots of times, and there'll be war in the Middle East or drought or famine and I've actually been pleased with these things. It's meant a spike in oil or wheat. That's all it's meant. Higher returns. Do you understand what I'm telling you here? Because if you do, then you shouldn't feel proud of me. You really shouldn't.'

'Gabriel, I – I understand but . . .' His father slumped in his chair, his fingers over his eyes. After a few moments, he got up and emptied the last of the wine into his glass. 'Gabriel, why are you telling me these things? I don't know what it is you want me to say.'

'I want you to stop pretending. I want you to acknowledge that I'm a bad person.'

'You're not a bad person. That's absurd.'

'No, it's reality. But I can understand that it might be hard for you to accept. If it's easier, you can just admit that I'm not a *good* person. That much should be obvious.'

'Gabriel, I don't know where these thoughts have come from. I honestly don't.' His father wasn't looking at him any more. He was staring at the floor, one hand supporting his head. 'Listen, this is my fault. I know I've made mistakes with you, but after your mother died . . . Well, I didn't know how I could raise you on my own. You had all this potential and I didn't want to ruin that. I wanted you to have the life you deserved.'

Gabriel laughed bitterly. 'Maybe that's what I got.'

'I'm sorry.'

'Well, at least your intentions were good. I don't even have that as a defence.'

'I had no idea you were this unhappy.'

'I wasn't. It's a recent thing. Besides, how would you have known? We don't talk, do we?'

'No. We don't.'

His father fell silent, still staring at the floor. He looked old and tired and guilt-stricken, which was the exact opposite of what Gabriel had intended.

'Listen, I'm not blaming you for any of this. I just wanted to . . . I don't know what I wanted. It's too late to change anything now.'

'No, it's not. I mean, if you don't feel like you're living a good life then you need to do something about it.'

'I don't know how to do anything else. This is all I've ever done.'

'You can do anything you put your mind to, Gabriel. I've always believed that. It's one of the reasons I *am* proud of you.'

Gabriel didn't say anything. He could have continued to butcher his own character, but what would be the point? His father already looked like a broken man, just from the little he'd heard. Gabriel didn't want to do any more damage.

'I'm sorry,' he said, after several more moments had passed. 'I shouldn't have dropped this on you now. It's late. We're both tired.'

'No, you needed to tell me. I wish you'd told me sooner.' His father looked up at him for a second, before shifting his gaze to the middle distance. 'Look, if you're serious about what you've said tonight, if that's really how you feel, then you need to get out, don't you? That's obvious.'

Gabriel shrugged again. 'Like I said, it's a bit late for that. There's nothing else I can do.'

'You don't have to do anything else, not right away. Just take some time out to think. God knows you can afford to.'

He didn't have any response to this. He nodded as if he were considering it.

'I mean, it's not as if you have to worry about paying the rent, is it?' his father went on.

'No. It's not like that. Not for the next two hundred years, anyway.'

His father gave a small smile of encouragement. He didn't realise how hollow the joke was.

'Look, Dad, I'm exhausted. I'm sorry for bringing this up, I really am. It was bad timing.'

His father looked like he wanted to say something more, but after a pause he sighed and shook his head. 'Can we talk about this again tomorrow?'

'Yes, maybe. I don't know. I can't really think right now. I just need to get some sleep.'

'Yes, of course. There's no point trying to sort this out when you're tired. Things might look different in the morning. We can talk then.'

Gabriel nodded without conviction. He wasn't sure there was anything else to say.

Ferrari

Whatever he'd hoped to achieve, he hadn't achieved it. He woke up at seven with another thumping hangover and an overwhelming desire to be back in his own bed. Unfortunately, when he went downstairs, Susan was already up; any thoughts of a note on the fridge and an early getaway were instantly shattered. Instead, he sat at the kitchen table, drank several cups of strong black coffee and made more difficult small talk. He didn't think his father would have had the opportunity to tell her about their talk, and she didn't say anything that contradicted this assumption. When she asked about his plans for the day, he told her that he needed to be back in London by lunchtime, claiming he had some work to finish before he went back to the office. She didn't try to persuade him to extend his visit.

His father was a different matter. He was adamant that Gabriel should stay at least another night. The only way Gabriel could get him to relent was by changing his story, and saying that in actual fact he was going back to London to consider his options. He would take the rest of the week as holiday and give himself the time and space to decide what to do next. This was met with lots of solemn nodding and reassurances that this was a far more sensible plan.

'Will you phone me in the next couple of days?' his father asked. 'Let me know that you're OK.'

'Yes, of course,' Gabriel said.

He already knew that he had no intention of taking the rest of the week off; just having to get through tomorrow's bank holiday was bad enough. When he did phone his father, he'd probably say that he'd decided to stick work out until the end of the tax year and then find something else. That would be the last he'd have to say on the matter. Hopefully, he'd be dead by April.

Shortly afterwards, he went outside to load his overnight bag into the Ferrari's tiny boot and found two boys gawking from the end of the drive. They were probably around eight or nine or ten; Gabriel found it difficult to estimate children's ages. Both were sitting on what looked to be brand-new BMX bikes, showing no sign that they intended to move. Gabriel tried to ignore them; presumably they'd get out of the way when he started reversing. He didn't want to have to ask them.

'That's the coolest car I've ever seen.'

'Thank you.' Gabriel didn't bother to look over.

'How much did it cost?'

'A quarter of a million pounds. But I'll sell it to you for half that.'

They both laughed over the sound of Gabriel slamming the boot.

'You must be rich.'

This was the second boy, Gabriel thought. They clearly weren't going to get out of the way until he'd indulged their curiosity. He turned to face them. 'Yes,' he said, 'I'm rich. Extremely rich.'

They exchanged a glance, appreciation tinged with awe.

'What do you do? Are you a footballer or something?'

'No, I'm not a footballer. I'm . . .' He glanced at the car, then back at their expectant faces. 'I'm a doctor. I help people with cancer get better. If you want a car like this, that's what you need to do.'

They looked less impressed now, but Gabriel didn't care. He got in the car and fired up the engine. The boys had moved, but only the few metres necessary to let him out. Gabriel could see them continuing to watch in his rear-view mirror, so he didn't hold back. Once he'd reversed past them, he turned sharply, jammed down the accelerator and sped off in a roar of petrol fumes.

Back on the motorway he made a resolution: as soon as possible, he was selling the Ferrari.

The Good News

December thirtieth. They were all there in the boardroom: seven sharp suits, no one talking. The scene reminded Gabriel of his vision of hell. The only real difference was that the décor was nicer, the chairs more comfortable.

Mason didn't keep them waiting long this time – just a couple of minutes to let the anticipation build. His entrance was characteristically no-nonsense: through the door at speed and straight to the head of the table without so much as glancing at anyone else in the room. He clicked open his briefcase and took out a single sheet of paper, his expression set to grim.

'Gentlemen. Let's start with an overview. Preliminary estimates suggest that the economy shrank by nought point two per cent in this last quarter, and the Chancellor is predicting zero growth for the first half of two thousand and twelve. But in all likelihood, this is a best-case scenario. Official figures tell us that unemployment hit a seventeen-year high this month, and the FTSE is down five and a half per cent from the start of the year. That equates to a devaluation of around eighty-five billion pounds.'

He paused for a moment, allowing these statistics to sink in. Then he grinned, flashing a full set of chemically whitened teeth. 'The good news is that we've done rather well this past year. The FTSE may be down, but Mason Wallace is up six point one per cent. That's around two hundred and forty million pounds' growth, taking the fund total to four point two billion.'

The whooping and mutual backslapping started almost at once. It was all a farce, of course; there wasn't a person in that room who didn't already know the year's financial results, down to the last penny. Mason's announcement and the reaction of the management team was just a piece of theatre, an annual excuse to let their egos run riot.

Mason raised his hands to signal silence, his face still split wide in a self-congratulatory grin. 'OK, settle down a second. I'm not going to bore you with too many details. The basic picture is that we've outperformed the market by a significant margin. Six point one per cent might not sound that spectacular, but given the economic climate, I suspect it will put us in the Bloomberg top one hundred for a second consecutive year. As for our slice of the pie – well, I'm sure you've all crunched the numbers by now. By my calculation, we're looking at a compensation pot of sixty-five million, or somewhere in that ballpark.'

Mason clapped his hands together and, on cue, his PA and one of the girls from HR appeared with champagne and glasses. Both had huge fake smiles plastered across their faces. Or Gabriel assumed they were fake. These women had no cause to celebrate. They were administrators, and would not be sharing in the sixty-five-million-pound compensation pot, or not beyond their basic salaries. As soon as they'd dispensed the champagne, they disappeared without a word, and Gabriel doubted that anyone else in the room had even noticed them go. His colleagues would all be estimating their bonuses, trying to figure out how much pie would be heading their way.

Based on his own performance over the past twelve months, Gabriel expected he'd be getting at least three million, possibly four. A century or two of salaries, as far as the admin girls were concerned.

Mason raised his glass and waited for everyone else to follow suit. 'Gentlemen, our very good health. If this is what a recession feels like, then all I can say is this: long live the recession!'

The toast echoed down the boardroom.

Gabriel was pinching the stem of his champagne flute so tightly that his fingertips had gone purple. He took one small sip, then set it back down on the table. For the past ten days, he'd felt nothing other than sadness and guilt, but now a new emotion was taking over, consuming everything in its path. As he glanced from face to face, he felt a coldly burning hatred – for himself and everyone else in that room.

Crude

Gabriel spent the New Year sober and immersed in statistics. For three days, he barely moved from the table in his living area. He kept his laptop on the whole time and printed off several hundred pages of data – reports and graphs and spreadsheets. He drank coffee by the gallon and ate nothing but pre-packed sandwiches and takeaway. At night, his dreams were still bad, but they were fewer and briefer. He found that working himself to the point of exhaustion was a more effective remedy than anything else he'd tried. It meant that by midnight he was able to sink into sleep like a stone falling into a deep, deep lake. By the time he started to resurface, the worst part of the night would be gone.

He was hunting for a new investment – something big – and at that point, it was the only thing he felt he could do. Thinking about Caitlin was unbearable. He needed something else to obsess over, and the markets provided a temporary haven. They offered a mental landscape that was familiar and comforting, but also complex enough to engage his full attention. On those few occasions when his mind did start to falter, he forced himself to picture Mason's face – the self-satisfaction with which he'd announced last year's results, that venomous mix of smugness and *Schadenfreude*. A glimpse was all it took to shock Gabriel out of his malaise, renewing his laser-like focus on the task in hand.

He looked at stocks and derivatives, commodities and currencies, and by Monday, he had a shortlist of five potential bets. Some basic maths told him that they were all likely to yield decent returns in the next couple of months, so the sensible course would be to spread his investment across all five. Then, if the market moved against his expectations on any one bet, he'd still be likely to succeed on the strength of the others. But Gabriel was in no mood to play safe. Instead, he picked the bet he had the most confidence in and decided to throw all his resources at it.

When it came to the markets, there were never any certainties. Gabriel knew that as well as anyone. But as far as he could determine, this was as close to being a sure thing as any bet he'd ever placed.

He got up from his chair and retrieved a knife from the kitchen drawer. Three days of ploughing through facts and figures had led him to a single-word conclusion, which he now scratched into the table in jagged capital letters.

CRUDE

Budget

Mason had his chair swivelled to the window when Gabriel walked in. His hands were locked behind his head and he was half-slouching in a pose that Gabriel recognised only too well. It was like looking at a not-too-distant reflection – the alternate version of himself from just a few months ago. Brash, privileged, complacent.

'Vaughn, pull up a pew.' Mason spun in his chair and clicked his fingers at the window. 'Just been keeping an eye on the Great Unwashed. Month three of the *occupation*. Can you believe that?'

Gabriel took a seat on the leather sofa. 'I remember you predicting it would all be over in a week.'

'Ha! Human Rights and due process – they've been holding this country back for years. Let me tell you, this would never have happened under Thatcher. She'd have dealt with this protest the same way she dealt with the miners. She had bigger balls than Cameron, Osborne and Johnson combined.'

'I'll take your word for it.'

'Fuck it. They'll be gone soon enough. The hearing's in a

fortnight and they don't stand a chance. It's just a formality. Most likely, the decision's already been made.'

Gabriel nodded. His suspicions were the same.

'You know what we should do when the eviction finally happens?' Mason's sneer transformed itself into a broad grin. 'We should come and watch. After all, we have the perfect ringside seats. We can get out the good Scotch, savour the experience. With any luck it'll all kick off.'

Gabriel shrugged. 'I doubt it. It's all stayed peaceful so far. I can't see that changing.'

'Christ, how pessimistic. Tear gas, that's what I want to see. Tear gas and tasers.'

Gabriel waited for him to shut up.

'Anyway, Vaughn. We've more important matters to discuss. Let's talk capital.' Mason glanced at his computer screen and clicked his mouse a couple of times. 'You're looking at a bonus of three point four million. How much of that are you going to reinvest? Shall I put you down for seventy-five per cent again?'

'Actually, Mason, I'm going minimum this year. Put me down for fifty.'

'Minimum? Vaughn, I don't want to question your financial good sense, but that's a lot of money you're planning to lose. Keep it offshore. Let it appreciate.'

Gabriel forced his face into a congenial smile. 'I'd love to, but I'm expanding my property portfolio. Something in Chelsea, I think.'

'Chelsea?' Mason gave a nod of approval. 'OK. Your judgement remains intact. Fifty per cent it is. I'll have the rest transferred to your account ASAP.' He clicked his mouse again, pulling up another file. 'That leads us on to this year's budget.

I'm assigning you another two hundred million. Think you can handle it?'

'Yes, I can handle it. I can handle as much money as you want to give me.'

'Good. That's the exact attitude I'm looking for. Because this year I want us back up to double-digit growth. I'm expecting results this quarter. Big results.'

Gabriel allowed his smile to widen. 'Trust me, Mason. The next few months are going to be spectacular.'

Futures

Gabriel spent the next couple of hours consolidating his research. As far as he could see, the picture hadn't changed much in the last few days. Brent Crude stood at $111 a barrel and was trending upwards, as it had been since late December. The movement was modest, but every sign indicated it would be accelerating soon. The markets were easily spooked, and increased instability in Syria and Yemen was certain to push up prices. Even more significant, potentially, was the ongoing situation with Iran. The EU and US had been threatening further sanctions for months, and the moment these were voted through, oil was going to soar.

He checked through his figures one more time, then got on the phone to UBS. Within twenty minutes he'd liquidated half a dozen stagnant positions, freeing up another hundred million with which to speculate.

Placing his new bet proved harder. Despite everything, there still seemed to be something inside him, something hard-wired, that recoiled at the thought of what he was about to attempt.

He stood for a long time at his window, as he had so many

times over the past few months. He looked at the Occupy banners: **WE ARE THE 99%; CAPITALISM IS CRISIS**. Just to the right of the Tea and Empathy tent, there was a woman of thirtyish carrying a baby in a sling. She was the sort of woman Gabriel couldn't *not* look at.

He felt a desperate urge to punch the glass until the view was obscured by his own blood.

He didn't.

Instead, he turned back to his desk and got back on the phone to his broker, cutting straight to the chase. 'I want you to short Brent Crude futures for April, fifty thousand contracts.'

There was a long pause down the line. 'You want to *sell* fifty thousand? Gabriel, do you know something I don't?'

'I expect so. I usually do.'

This was rewarded with a nervous laugh. 'Fifty thousand? That's huge. We're talking a significant slice of the market.'

'Thank you. I'm aware of that. Just get me a quote.'

'You're looking at five hundred and ten million dollars. Three two five sterling.'

'Perfect. Call me back when it's gone through.'

Gabriel hung up.

When he reached for his coffee, he saw that his hand was shaking.

The Annual Review

It was a week later when he got the text message. He was looking through Nicola's personal file at the time, trying to bring himself up to speed before her annual review the following week. Unfortunately, it was proving more difficult than anticipated. The urge to check the spot price of crude was more or less constant.

It had been down a dollar at the beginning of the week, but now it was starting to rise again, slowly, in a series of jagged peaks and troughs. Prices over the past couple of days looked like an alarming cardiograph. Not that this was at all unusual. Prices were always volatile, and crude would often fluctuate by a dollar or two per barrel within a single trading day. The only thing that had changed was the significance of those incremental movements: for every cent crude rose, Gabriel lost half a million dollars; for every dollar it went up, he lost fifty million. By any standard, the bet he'd placed was huge.

So, increasingly, he found himself looking for distractions, and Nicola's review had provided one. It was mostly a question of ticking boxes, of keeping the paperwork as minimally up to date as employment law required. She was due her yearly pay rise, too – inflation plus one per cent – which would take her salary to just over thirty-four thousand pounds. The disconnect between this and the numbers Gabriel was used to dealing with was like a sharp punch to the stomach. Even worse, he knew that, in some twisted sense, Nicola could count herself lucky. In the wider economy, pay was falling sharply against inflation. There were probably lots of people out there who would envy Nicola her extra twenty pounds a week, this insignificant crumb from the Mason Wallace pie.

When his phone beeped, it was a momentary relief to be able to abandon the file. He grabbed for it straight away, then spent the next several minutes staring at the screen, literally unable to move.

I haven't forgiven you, not even close, but there are still questions I need answering. Do NOT call me. If you're available to meet this weekend, then let me know. I'll send you a time and place. A simple yes or no – this isn't open to discussion.

He read it and reread it. There was no trace of warmth, obviously, but he knew he'd been offered more than he had any right to expect. For the last three weeks, this had been his only real wish: to see Caitlin one more time before he died.

Yes

Gabriel picked up his coat and left the office.

Damaged

The coffee shop she chose, another independent, was in south Hackney, a couple of minutes' walk from Victoria Park. Gabriel didn't know why she'd chosen that location in particular, but he guessed it was because it was neutral territory, more or less equidistant between them. It was quiet, too – at least compared with central London. The kind of place where you could talk without having to raise your voice. At 10 a.m., it was barely half full. The décor was what Gabriel believed was termed shabby-chic: lots of scratched, uneven wood and bare light bulbs. Along the counter were rows of home-baked pastries and artisanal breads and, in one empty corner, a couple of vintage bicycles were propped precariously against the bare wall. It struck Gabriel as the kind of place where most of the clientele would be cyclists. He had driven. His Ferrari was parked on a nearby residential street, looking every bit as incongruous as it had outside his father's house. Despite his resolution, he hadn't been able to bring himself to sell it. Not yet.

He was on his second cup of black coffee when she walked

in. He'd chosen a table for two where he could face the door, and had spent the last ten minutes staring at it, mentally bracing himself. But seeing her was still a wrench beyond anything he'd been expecting. She looked as if she'd lost a stone or more in the four weeks since he'd last seen her, and her face was pale and her eyes dark. She looked cold and sad and defiant, beautiful and damaged.

Her expression didn't change when she saw him. She barely even acknowledged his presence – just walked over and pulled out the chair opposite. She didn't remove her coat or put down her handbag.

'Let me get you a coffee,' Gabriel said. He was surprised at how normal – how clear and decisive – his voice sounded.

'I don't know how long I'm going to stay,' Caitlin told him.

'You're under no obligation to drink it,' Gabriel pointed out. 'You can still leave at any time.'

She nodded at the logic of this and started to remove her purse from her handbag.

'I'm paying,' Gabriel told her. 'Obviously.'

'No, I'd rather you didn't.'

'Caitlin, please. You do understand how ridiculous it is if I *don't* pay.'

'Well, it's always been ridiculous, hasn't it? But I don't recall it bothering you much before now.'

'No, that isn't true. It bothered me all the time.'

'If you say so.' She looked at him for a moment, then shrugged. 'Fine. Get me a flat white.'

When he returned from the counter she'd put her coat over the back of the chair and set her bag down at her feet. He put her coffee on the table along with an apple Danish.

'I'm not hungry,' she said.

'Perhaps not, but you look like you need to eat something.'

She stared at him across the table, her eyes flashing. 'Gabriel, you can keep any *concerns* you have to yourself. I don't want to hear them.'

There was a long silence. Gabriel took a small sip of his coffee and waited.

'You're really dying?'

'Yes.' He didn't think there was anything else he needed to say at this point. Probably better to keep things as simple as possible – let her decide on the relevant questions.

'How long do you have?'

'A few months. I can't give you a precise figure, just statistics.'

'OK. And what do the statistics say?'

'That I'll be dead by the summer. Anything beyond that would be a minor miracle.'

She didn't say anything to this, and her expression didn't alter.

'The good news is it's likely to be relatively clean and painless. I've been told that the size and location of the tumour increases the chance of me suffering a serious blood clot or haemorrhage. Hopefully, something like that will kill me while I'm still relatively fit and able. I won't have to go through the indignity of being in a hospice.'

Caitlin had closed her eyes and put her hand to her mouth. She was clearly upset by what he was telling her, but Gabriel wasn't going to read too much into this. It might have been the details that bothered her rather than the man to whom they pertained. Most people didn't like to think about haemorrhages, even as an abstract concept.

'I'm sorry,' she said eventually. 'No one deserves that.'

339

Gabriel forced a smile. 'Well, almost no one.'

'How long have you known?' she asked.

'Since the beginning of October. A month before I met you.'

She nodded a couple of times, then took a very small sip from her coffee cup. 'I suppose that makes some sense of this. As much sense as I can expect. You're having chemotherapy?'

'I had chemotherapy for six weeks, but it was only to buy me some extra time. I have steroids to relieve the worst of the symptoms, the seizures and the dizziness. Anti-emetics for the nausea, codeine for the headaches. It's allowed me to live a fairly normal life.'

'Right. Very normal.'

Gabriel shrugged. 'More normal than I'm used to, believe me.'

Caitlin closed her eyes again, exhaling deeply. 'Look, I think you'd better go back to the start. I need to come to terms with all of this, but I still feel like I'm missing half the pieces. Tell me what I need to know.'

So, for the next fifteen minutes, Gabriel retraced most of the major steps that had brought them to that coffee shop. He told her about the diagnosis and the radiosurgery. He told her about the symptoms he'd been suffering – emotional lability, crying on the Tube. She interrupted only when she wanted him to clarify a detail. Otherwise, she seemed content just to let him speak, her gaze not quite meeting his.

By the time he'd finished his account, he thought that her expression had softened fractionally. Or perhaps more accurately, it had lost its edge. There still wasn't much warmth there, and certainly no forgiveness, but the contempt, at least, was gone.

Strangely, Gabriel felt a little better too. Nothing much had changed, but there was nevertheless a sort of catharsis in being able to talk honestly at last. It was, he realised, the first time he'd spoken about his condition to anyone who wasn't a medical professional.

'You know what's really difficult here?' Caitlin asked. 'I find myself having to rethink all my memories of the past few months. All the things I thought I knew about you were wrong.'

'Not everything.'

'Near enough. The truth is I have absolutely no idea who you are any more.'

'Neither do I.' Gabriel could see she was irritated by this claim. 'It sounds like a cop-out, I know, but it's honestly how I feel. I don't think I'm the same person I was six months ago.'

She didn't say anything for a moment, then sighed and nodded. 'OK. So tell me about six months ago. Who were you then?'

'You might not want to hear it.'

'Maybe not, but I think I should. I think I have a right to.'

Gabriel held her gaze. 'I was arrogant. Selfish and self-obsessed. Vain. Callous . . . Well, you get the idea. Pick any negative trait you want and it would probably apply. The point is, that's who I was, but it's not who I want to be. Not any more.'

She laughed, very coldly. 'So these last few months have been your attempt at being a better person? Is that what you're telling me?'

'In some sense, yes. But I can understand why that might be hard to believe.'

Caitlin shook her head and looked away.

'Listen,' Gabriel said. 'I'm not trying to shirk any responsibility for the things I've done. But I'd like to think that I'm not just the sum of my worst parts.'

'Yes. I'd like to believe that too.'

It was clear from her tone that she didn't believe it. Gabriel frowned and tried to mentally regroup. Trying to explain the mess inside his head was a challenge that seemed utterly insurmountable. How could he articulate a concept that he himself barely understood? In desperation, he found himself grasping for something Dr Barbara had told him.

'You know, I was seeing this psychotherapist for a while,' he began. As opening gambits went, he knew it wasn't the best, but he couldn't see any choice but to plough on regardless. 'She was supposed to be helping me with my emotional problems, but . . . well, obviously she wasn't all that successful. My fault, not hers. Anyway, that's not really relevant right now. What I'm trying to say is this: she told me she didn't believe that most people are fundamentally good or bad. The majority are capable of being both, depending on the situation.'

Caitlin looked at him blankly.

'I'm sorry. I'm not explaining this well. I think what she was trying to get me to understand – one of the things – is that personalities aren't set in stone. A lot of it's to do with the choices we make. Can you believe that, at least?'

'I don't know. Maybe. But it hardly improves your position, does it?'

'No, I've made some awful choices. I realise that. But I also . . .' Gabriel trailed off. 'Well, I suppose it doesn't matter much any more. It's a bit late in the day to be thinking about changing my life.'

She looked at him for a long time without speaking.

'Caitlin, I'm so sorry. I hate myself for what I did to you. It was truly appalling.

'Yes. It was.'

She reached for her coffee cup, realised it was empty and set it back down again.

'Would you like me to get you another one?' Gabriel asked.

'No.'

She had risen to her feet and started to put her coat back on. Gabriel felt suddenly sick. He had the impression she was about to walk out without another word, and that would be the last he would see of her. Instead, she looked at him, then nodded towards the door.

'I don't want to be inside any more. Let's go for a walk.'

A Walk

Once they were outside, Caitlin lit a cigarette. Gabriel decided that he shouldn't comment on this, then found he couldn't help himself.

'I don't think you should start smoking again,' he said,

'Gabriel, you're too late by about a month. I *have* started again, and I don't think I'll be quitting any time soon.'

'Cancer's not much fun. Take it from me.'

'Well, unfortunately, thinking about the future is beyond me right now. I'm sure you can understand that, too.'

Gabriel looked over at her as they paused at some traffic lights. She put her head back and blew a small stream of smoke upwards. 'I hate to resort to emotional blackmail,' he said, 'but I'd be much happier if I could die knowing that you're going to be OK. I'd like to think you have a very long and healthy life ahead of you.'

Caitlin gave no sign that she'd heard him. It was only when the lights had changed and they were walking again that she replied. 'I will be OK. Eventually, I'll be OK. But for now, I'm just going to keep on smoking. You'll have to find a way to bear the unhappiness of it.'

They walked on in silence until they reached Victoria Park. Although it was January, it was mild and there wasn't much of a breeze. Beneath the leafless trees and at the edge of the lake, clumps of snowdrops were already in full bloom. Gabriel thought it had probably been a good idea to leave the coffee shop. They hadn't said a word to each other for going on five minutes, but somehow things felt better than they had. Open space had helped to relieve some of the tension. It struck him, then, that silence could mean so many different things depending on the context; it had room to hold a full spectrum of emotion.

Several more minutes passed before Caitlin spoke again. She stopped first to light another cigarette, flicking her hair back from her face.

'You know, Gabriel, I might regret telling you this, but I think I'm going to anyway. A month ago, I was probably the happiest I've ever been. It's ridiculous, I know – I mean, we'd known each other such a short time – but I actually thought we were going to have a life together.'

She wasn't looking at him as she said this. She was facing out towards the lake, where a dozen or so ducks were moving silently across the water. Gabriel waited; he felt hollow in the pit of his stomach, but suspected there was worse yet to come.

'I'm not a romantic,' Caitlin said eventually. 'When I was growing up, I was never the girl who dreamed about white weddings or fairy-tale endings. But that *is* what I imagined when I was with you. It feels so humiliating now, but . . . well, I suppose that should be the least of my worries. The truth is, it didn't matter how long we'd been together. I was already daydreaming about our future: marriage, kids, the works. And I hate myself for that, I really do. I can see how utterly absurd it was now. But that doesn't seem to make much difference. It's still been hard to let those ideas go.'

'It doesn't sound ridiculous,' Gabriel said. 'I would have loved to have had that life with you.'

'Right.' Caitlin blew a cloud of smoke in the general direction of the ducks, who paddled on, unperturbed. 'Except none of it was real, was it? It was all just this colossal fantasy.'

He was close to reaching out and putting his hand on her shoulder, but he wasn't sure the gesture would be appreciated. 'Listen, Caitlin. I know you must find it hard to believe anything I say any more, but I don't want you to think that everything was a lie. My feelings for you were genuine. They *are* genuine. That hasn't changed.'

Caitlin shrugged, then started walking again. 'You might believe that. I'm not sure if I do.'

'Do you really think I could have faked something like that?'

'I think it's easy enough to delude yourself. I think we both know that.'

'No. That's not true. I don't—'

'Gabriel, if I'm being honest, then what I think is this: I think you're scared of dying. I think you're scared and confused, and you've probably got all sorts of genuine regrets about how you've chosen to live your life. And I think, more than anything, I'm just a symptom of that. I'm part of this huge, fucked-up redemption narrative you've been writing for yourself. But I *can't* be a part of it, not any more. You understand that, don't you?'

Gabriel found that he could no longer look at her. He lowered his eyes and watched his feet crunching softly on the loose stones of the path. 'What I understand is that my life had some meaning with you in it. It doesn't any more.'

'I'm sorry. I can't help you with that.'

Gabriel nodded bleakly. He had no right to expect anything else.

After a minute or so they had come to a point where the path forked, with one branch continuing south towards Bethnal Green and the Tube, and the other looping back towards Hackney, where Gabriel had left his car. Caitlin stopped and turned to him. It was just about the only time she'd done so since they'd left the coffee shop.

'Look, Gabriel, I'm not glad that you're dying. It was an appalling thing to say. I'm sorry.'

Gabriel did his best to smile. 'It's OK. I can understand why you said it, obviously.'

'I don't hate you, not any more. But there's nowhere we can go from here. You can see that, can't you? It wouldn't do either of us any good.'

'It might do me some good.'

Caitlin looked away. 'Please. This is hard enough already.'

Gabriel nodded silently. After a moment, Caitlin turned back to him. She had started to cry.

'I don't hate you,' she repeated, 'but I'm going to leave now.'

It took all his willpower, but Gabriel stayed still and silent.

'Goodbye, Gabriel. Goodbye and good luck.'

'Goodbye, Caitlin.'

She turned and walked away. Gabriel watched her until she was out of sight. Then he took the other path and headed back to his car.

Scans

He had no right to feel better, but he did – if only by a fraction.

It wasn't immediate, of course. For the next twenty-four hours, he couldn't do much but play it over and over again, torturing himself with the details. He hadn't expected forgiveness, and certainly not reconciliation, but neither had he realised how painful it would be just seeing her – just meeting and parting one more time. He supposed it was the finality of it. A week ago, he would have traded whatever time he had left for the chance to say goodbye; but in the immediate aftermath of this fulfilled wish, with an unknown amount of time still left to him, he failed to see what had been achieved. Nothing had been set right. Wounds had been reopened rather than healed.

It was only when the detritus stopped swirling that he found things he could cling to. Caitlin didn't hate him. She didn't hate him and, eventually, she was going to be OK. It was the last fact more than the first that brought him comfort.

There was something else, too. Gabriel realised that he had lied when he said that his life no longer had any meaning. For the next few weeks, at least, it had a very clear meaning and purpose. He had his plan, and he was going to stick to it. Half the wheels were already in motion.

On Monday, he phoned his estate agent from work and told him to put the apartment on the market. He wanted a quick sale and was willing to drop the price by up to thirty per cent for a cash buyer. His estate agent seemed morally outraged at this proposal, and spent the next minute advising against it. In the end, Gabriel had to cut him off mid-sentence.

'Sell it in the next fortnight and I'll pay you a bonus of five K on top of the usual fees.'

That shut him up.

Gabriel's life may have been unravelling, but he was pleased to see that his money had not lost its power.

Afterwards, he called Armitage's secretary to ask for a digital copy of his brain scans. He could tell from her baffled silence that this was not a usual request, but having put him on hold for several minutes, she eventually told him that the doctor had given his approval.

They arrived by email before lunch, and Gabriel printed them off when he got home that evening, using high-quality A4 photographic paper. He then placed them in his briefcase, ready for the next day.

Proposition

He sat at a table in Starbucks waiting for Nicola to arrive. It was just coming up to eleven. The official reason they were meeting here was for her annual review; Gabriel had suggested it might be nice to discuss her progress over coffee. He had ordered two macchiatos and a selection of cakes, which he had arranged as a sort of buffet at one end of the large table he'd chosen. On the chair next to him was his briefcase, which contained none of the paperwork he supposedly needed. He'd not even bothered to print it out. The annual review was pointless, obviously.

Gabriel was on edge, but the upcoming meeting – what he had to say to Nicola – was only a small part of it. For the last five minutes he'd been on his phone, looking again at the price of oil. It had dropped by over two dollars at the end of last week, giving Gabriel an accidental profit of over one hundred million dollars; it was spectacular enough to warrant a call from his broker, who wanted to congratulate him on a stunning piece of fortune.

'Fortune has nothing to do with it,' Gabriel had told him, as smugly as he could manage; on the inside, he felt nauseated.

But now prices had started to rally once more. For the last two days, oil had been creeping back up, cent by cent. The important thing, Gabriel knew, was to stick with the long-term game plan. The fundamentals of his research were still sound; he just had to keep his nerve over the next few weeks.

Nicola walked in at eleven on the dot, bringing his mind instantly back to the task in hand. She looked, as always, more than a little harried. She'd probably spent the time since Gabriel left the office going over her notes, preparing responses to the questions he was supposed to be asking. All a completely wasted effort, of course, but never mind. Gabriel had set her dozens of pointless and thankless tasks over the past couple of years, and he hoped and believed that this would be the last.

She glanced warily at the elaborate display of cakes before taking the seat opposite.

'I wasn't sure what you fancied,' Gabriel explained, 'so I just got a selection.'

'What's the occasion?'

Gabriel shrugged, then took a small sip of his macchiato. 'Actually, it's my birthday, since you ask.'

'Oh . . . Many happy returns.' Nicola looked at the cakes again, frowning slightly. Gabriel supposed there was an element of tragedy to it from her perspective; no one at work knew about his birthday and he was celebrating it in Starbucks with his secretary. Of course, that wasn't the reason he'd wanted to hold this meeting out of the office, but she wasn't to know that.

She fumbled for a moment, before saying, 'You're not expecting me to sing, are you?'

'No. I'm not sure who'd find that the most embarrassing: you, me or the barista.'

'I think we'd all be equally mortified.' She smiled thinly. 'What number's this? Thirty-four?'

He didn't answer for a while – long enough for her to start fidgeting with her coffee spoon. 'Um, Gabriel?'

'Thirty-three, Nicola. I'll be thirty-three. The same age as Jesus when he died, reputedly.'

She stared at him in perplexed silence for several moments. 'Gabriel, no offence, but you're acting very oddly this morning. Also, I don't think you should make a habit of comparing yourself to Jesus. Perhaps we should just crack on with the review?'

Gabriel didn't respond to this suggestion. Instead, he took another sip of his macchiato, then said, 'Nicola, I want you to do something for me, and if it's OK, I'd like you to do it without asking any questions. It might sound strange, but please indulge me, just this once. Can you do that?'

She frowned at him for a while, then rolled her eyes and sighed. 'Yes, I can do that. I mean, it's pretty much the essence of my job, isn't it? What do you want me to do?'

'Can you check your bank account on your phone?'

'Yes, but why would—'

'No questions, Nicola. Just do it.'

She glared across the table before picking up her bag and removing her phone and debit card. It took about two minutes for the relevant information to come up. Gabriel watched as she stared at the screen in silence, the colour draining from her face.

'Gabriel . . . What is this?'

'It's fifty thousand pounds. It's what you earn in a couple of years, after tax. It's what I earn in a week. A slow week.'

'Cut the crap! What is this money doing in my account?'

'It's yours. I'm giving it to you.'

'Oh, God.' Nicola put her head in her hands. 'Gabriel, why do I get the feeling you're going to ask me to do something illegal?'

'I'm not. Don't worry.' He sipped his drink and waited for her to look at him again. 'I do have a proposition for you, you're right about that, but it's nothing illegal. And that money is yours regardless. Believe me, you've earned it.'

Nicola didn't look up. For a minute or more, Gabriel had to wait patiently as she slumped forward in her chair, raking her fingers through her hair and swearing intermittently. Then she took her phone from the table, very slowly, like someone handling a primed mousetrap, and returned it to her bag.

'I think you need to tell me what's going on here. Because honestly, Gabriel, I'm at a complete loss. What's this about?'

He didn't answer. Instead, he took the scans from his briefcase and laid them in front of her on the table. 'Those are images of my brain,' he told her. 'The coloured area is a tumour. I was diagnosed with it at the beginning of October and given six months to live. The outlook hasn't changed much since then.'

He'd rehearsed it, of course, and had decided to keep his statement of the facts dispassionate and to the point. But Nicola's gasp – almost a yelp – caught him off guard. Prior to the past month, their relationship had never been anything other than professional, with an undercurrent of mutual disdain. There was no real reason for her to react so viscerally to the news of his impending demise. But, in hindsight, Gabriel supposed he was piling one shock on top of another. It was also possible that his matter-of-factness made the revelation worse rather than better. In some sense, Nicola was having to emote for both of them.

After a moment, he reached out and placed an uncertain hand on top of hers. She immediately shifted and grasped his thumb in a tightly clenched fist. It wasn't awkward in the way he might have expected. It was the first time anyone had comforted him physically since he learned about the cancer – it was the first time anyone had comforted him physically since he was a young child – and he was surprised by the simple power of it.

'Gabriel, I'm so sorry. I don't know what to say.'

'You don't have to say anything. I think your sympathy is implicit.'

If possible, she looked even paler now than she had two minutes ago. She looked as if *she'd* been the one who'd been diagnosed.

'Listen, Nicola. I'm OK,' Gabriel told her, before immediately retracting this statement. 'Well, obviously, I'm not OK. I have a brain tumour and I'm dying. But what I mean is I've come to terms with these things. As much as one can.'

'Who else knows?'

'At work? No one, and I'd like to keep it that way, at least for now.'

'Gabriel, why are you still working? Shouldn't you be . . . God, I don't know, anywhere else but here. You have so little time.'

'It's complicated. It's . . . well, it's tied to the proposition I'd like to put to you. Are you still happy to hear it?'

'Yes, I'll hear it. Of course I'll hear it.'

'OK. But first, I need you to know why I'm telling you about my . . . situation. It's not to sway your decision in any way. It's just to explain the position I find myself in.'

She nodded for him to continue. Gabriel sipped his coffee, taking a moment to collect his thoughts.

'Nicola, to put it bluntly, I have a lot of money that I no longer have any use for. In all honesty, I'm not sure I ever had any use for it. I've never used it for anything worthwhile, that's for certain.'

Nicola averted her eyes, but didn't contradict him on this point.

'But I want to change that,' Gabriel continued. 'I want to die knowing that I finally put my money to good use.'

'OK.' Nicola looked at him again, nodding a couple of times. 'That's admirable, but I'm not sure where I come into this. If that's how you feel, why don't you just give it to charity?'

Gabriel smiled thinly. 'I think my first priority should be trying to undo some of the harm I've done. Starting with you.'

'Me?' Nicola almost laughed at this. 'Gabriel, you've been a terrible man to work for, I'd be the last person to dispute that. But let's not get carried away here. I've always had a choice. If I was that unhappy, I would have quit.'

'No, Nicola. *I* had a choice. You didn't. You had two young children to raise – in one of the most expensive cities in the world. You had bills to pay and food to put on the table. I expect your *choice* was between going to work or losing your house. Am I right?'

'Yes, in a sense, but—'

Gabriel cut her off. 'So let me give you a real choice. How much will it take for you to be able to quit without consequences? Give me a figure.'

Nicola looked at him blankly.

'OK. Let me make it easier,' Gabriel said. 'The figure I had in mind was half a million.'

'Half a million?' Nicola echoed. 'Gabriel, you can't be serious?'

355

'I am serious.'

'Let me get this straight. You want to give me half a million pounds so I can quit my job?'

'Yes. That's the crux of it.'

She stared at him in silence, then began swearing again, loudly. Gabriel thought he'd better interrupt sooner rather than later.

'Nicola, the money itself is unimportant. This isn't about money, not really. It's about second chances.' He waited until he had her full attention before continuing. 'It's too late for me, as we've established. I've wasted my life doing something I no longer believe in. But you don't have to be in that position. What I'm offering you is a way out.'

Nicola shook her head in disbelief. 'Gabriel, this is insane.'

'It's not insane. It's probably the sanest decision I've ever made.'

She put her face in her hands again; it might have been a misperception, but in the silence that followed, Gabriel thought he could detect the sound of her sobbing.

'Listen,' he said, very gently. 'This is what I think you should do with the money. Actually, no. Scrap that. This is what I think you *will* do with the money, regardless of what I say. I think you'll use it to buy some real security for you and your family. I think you'll use it to live a happier and more productive life. You'll spend more time with your kids. Maybe you'll even retrain – find a job that's actually worth doing.'

If she hadn't been crying, she was now. Gabriel handed her a napkin to dry her eyes.

'Do you still think I'm insane?' he asked. 'Because the way I see it, you'll use my money in a way that I never could. You'll do something meaningful with it. Something good.'

It took Nicola some time to calm down. Gabriel ate a slice of carrot cake while he waited. Then, finally, she reached across the table and took his hand again.

'OK, Gabriel. You can tell me the rest of it now. There's more, isn't there?'

'Yes, there's more, but only a little, and nothing too difficult, I promise.'

'Tell me what you want me to do.'

'Two things,' Gabriel said. 'First, I don't want you to quit immediately. I'm afraid I'm still going to need you for the next few weeks. But after that you're free, I promise.'

Nicola squeezed his hand and smiled. 'OK. I think I can live with that. What's the second thing?'

Gabriel allowed his shoulders to relax. He felt lighter than he had at any time in the past month. 'The second thing's very simple,' he told her. 'I need you to set up a meeting.'

Judgment

When Gabriel looked out of his window, it didn't seem as if anything had changed. The tents, the banners, the pallets and Portaloos – all were still there, encrusted with three months' worth of inner-city grime. Three months of unflagging condemnation. Given everything that had happened to him in that period, it was hard to believe that so little time had passed, just as it was hard to envisage how St Paul's Churchyard ought to look, with the camp not there. When Gabriel did envisage this, the truth was he saw no improvement. All he saw was absence: an absence of ideas and idealism, an absence of generosity and compassion, an absence of dialogue.

But the High Court disagreed. The previous day, it had ruled in favour of the City of London Corporation. There would be a month or so in which appeals could be launched, but in the medium term, the writing was on the wall. The demonstrators were to be evicted on the basis that they were obstructing a public highway.

There was a bitter sort of humour to this outcome, Gabriel

supposed. The protesters had argued that the current economic system was flawed, unfair and corrupt; that it enriched the few at the expense of the many; that it led to crisis after crisis; that it was wrecking the planet. The City of London had argued that the protesters were blocking the pavement.

Inevitably, it was the latter charge that had stuck.

Weapons of Mass Destruction

Although the outcome of the court case bothered Gabriel, he knew there was no point dwelling on it. Mason was right: the judge's verdict had never been in doubt, and any attempt at appeal was likewise doomed from the outset. Moreover, whatever Gabriel's feelings on the impending eviction, he could take some consolation in the thought that he would not be around to see it. One way or another, he expected the protesters' tenancy of the square to outlive his own.

In the meantime, he had more pressing matters to worry about – though worry was perhaps the wrong word. Somewhat perversely, Gabriel found that he was enjoying his job for the first time in months. In part, it must have been because the nature and purpose of his work had changed. But even more significant, he thought, was the transformation in his relationship with Nicola, and the fact that they were now truly pulling in the same direction. Of course, she'd always been adept at helping him to evade unwanted appointments, visitors and phone calls; but in the days that followed their conclave in Starbucks, she raised her game to the level of an art form. While Gabriel spent more and more time listening to classical music and napping in his chair, Nicola gave the impression that he was working at least twice as hard as anyone else in the company. Callers were put on hold, emails were politely stalled, requests for information were rerouted and, all the time, Gabriel felt quite certain that no one ever suspected they were being given the runaround; Nicola had created an impenetrable smokescreen of prior engagements and more-urgent commitments. To the outside observer, Gabriel was simply a man with no time to spare.

His own contribution to this façade was to affect a purposeful frown and walk at pace whenever he passed anyone in a corridor. It was basically the opposite of what he'd been doing for the previous three months, and far, far easier. Now, while pretending to be grimly determined, overworked and adrenaline-pumped, in reality he was as relaxed as he'd ever been, inside or outside of work. He was still having trouble sleeping at night, so the possibility of unhindered naps in the day was a tremendous boon. For the first time in weeks, Gabriel felt that he was not only taking care of himself, but also being cared for. It wasn't just the newfound ferocity with which Nicola guarded his private time; he also noticed a profound change in the way she spoke to him, the way she carried herself, the way she looked at him when she brought his coffee and pastries. Gabriel wouldn't have believed it three months ago, but it turned out that a muffin brought voluntarily was far more pleasant than a muffin brought under duress. He added this new information to the growing bank of things he wished he'd known much earlier.

Unfortunately, Gabriel couldn't spend the whole day napping

and taking coffee breaks. There were still plenty of demands on his time, but these demands were, in general, novel and interesting. He now spent a large portion of his day falsifying the accounts. After all, there was no getting out of the usual internal meetings. He still had to present data, report on his positions, justify his investments as part of the fund's wider strategy. In this respect, he had to keep track of twice as much information as before. There was his actual portfolio and his fake portfolio – the one he talked about at the managers' meetings – and both required his sustained attention.

It was fraud on a massive scale, but Gabriel was unsurprised to discover that it came naturally to him. Compared to deceiving Caitlin, deceiving the Mason Wallace managerial team was child's play, and it certainly felt more wholesome. However large the lie, whatever sabotage he was committing, Gabriel felt not the smallest qualm. When he delivered his sham reports, his voice never wavered. He looked his colleagues in the eyes, slapped their backs, massaged their egos and spoke with an air of absolute conviction and authority. Of course, the task was made far easier by the nature of the men he was dealing with; it would have been difficult in the extreme to find a more self-absorbed group of individuals. The prime concern of every man in that boardroom was his own opinions, his own achievements. They were all far better at talking than listening.

More broadly, Gabriel was aided by the pure insanity of what he was attempting to do. He planned to lose as much money as he could as quickly as he could. So far as he knew, he was the only trader in the history of the stock markets who'd ever implemented this as a deliberate strategy. But as things stood, it was not as simple as it should have been. After a fortnight of unhedged betting and falsified accounts, the only thing he was hiding was a substantial profit.

The problem was that the markets were behaving far more rationally than was usual. While the threats to the global oil supply remained, a serious disruption was yet to materialise. Slowed growth in China and the US meant that demand was down and prices were falling – not quickly, but given Gabriel's level of exposure, every tick mattered. Going into the fourth week of January, his profit had risen to 120 million dollars.

He was concerned, of course, but it was a muted kind of concern, and still subservient to his wider appraisal of the situation. His conviction, based on all the available data, was that he was two or three weeks ahead of the curve and that, when the picture began to change, it would change very swiftly. All that was needed was one piece of bad news to spook the markets.

It was only a matter of days before he was proven spectacularly correct. On 23 January, following another breakdown in negotiations over Iran's nuclear programme, the EU voted through an embargo on Iranian oil. It wasn't going to take effect until the following June, but as far as the markets were concerned, this was a secondary point. The price hike was instantaneous.

In London, a mild January became a bitterly cold February, and as Gabriel moved to the next phase of his plan, he had the satisfaction of seeing his profit annihilated.

Liquidation

He managed to sell his apartment not far below market value to a 'Russian property investor'. The too-casual tone with which his estate agent spoke these three words, not to mention the speed with which the sale went through, made Gabriel certain that something dodgy was going on here. Money laundering at the very least. But that was a hazard of selling property in London, and given how little time he had left, he knew he had to pick his moral battles carefully. Any misgivings he had over the provenance of the money were salved by the knowledge of what he was going to do with it. In a sense, he would be the one laundering that cash. Whatever its past, it was going to help him build a cleaner future.

He arranged for the apartment to be cleared out on a Friday in early February. Despite all his money, Gabriel did not own much. He'd always preferred to keep his décor stylishly minimal, and he never kept anything he no longer needed. The few items he was keeping – his coffee machine, his expensive towels and bedding – all fitted comfortably in the boot of a car that had not been designed with luggage in mind. The things he was getting rid of were going to charity shops, where they would presumably be sold for a song.

As for the Ferrari, it was weakness, he knew, but it turned out to be the one thing he could not bring himself to part with. The apartment block in Lewisham had limited underground parking, so Gabriel paid what most would have considered a ludicrous fee to rent a space that had just come up for auction.

He didn't know how he'd feel moving into the flat in Lewisham, since he associated it so strongly with Caitlin, and what he'd done to Caitlin, but after a couple of trial nights, he was satisfied that it was no worse than being at St Katharine Docks. In many ways it was an improvement; there was less empty space to fill.

The last working day before he was due to hand over his keys, Gabriel arranged for the cleaner to come over for a few hours to ensure the place was spotless for its new owner – the Russian property mogul who probably had no intention of ever setting foot on the premises. On the kitchen counter he left a note:

Dear cleaning lady

I'm sorry, I don't know your name, but I wanted to thank you for keeping my apartment so clean and tidy for the last two years. You've done a really excellent job, and that's something that deserves to be acknowledged. Please find enclosed your end-of-contract bonus. If I were you, I wouldn't declare it to the taxman, but it's your decision, obviously.

   Yours gratefully
      Gabriel Vaughn
P.S. Please leave your key on the counter.

Next to this, he stuffed an A4 envelope with ten thousand pounds in twenty-pound notes. Then he went downstairs, got in his Ferrari and drove to Lewisham.

He parked in his new space, between a Toyota Yaris and a Ford Focus.

Traitors' Gate

The space Gabriel had hired for the meeting was in a Victorian pub on the north bank of the Thames, half a kilometre west of the Tower of London. He'd been there the previous week to make sure it was suitable for his purposes, and discovered a twisting warren of corridors, staircases and snugs built into a vast railway arch. A hundred and fifty years ago, it had probably been an opium den, frequented by smugglers, brigands and pickpockets; but, according to the Polish woman he'd spoken to on the phone, its function rooms were now used mostly for corporate parties. It was called the Traitors' Gate.

The name was apt, of course, but this had only played a small part in Gabriel's choice of venue. More importantly, the space he'd been offered for his 'event' was as good as any he'd seen. It was on the mezzanine floor, just off the central bar, and could seat up to twenty. It was dim without being dingy, and secluded without being enclosed; the last thing Gabriel wanted was to make anyone feel trapped or anxious. At the same time, he did need privacy, and a place where he could talk to an audience of twelve without fear of his voice carrying. On a weekday evening, the cordoned-off mezzanine would be quiet enough so that he could speak without having to raise his voice, but it would not be *too* quiet. The bar below would generate enough background noise to render his words inaudible to anyone else on the premises.

On the evening of the meeting, he arrived just before half seven, having come straight from work, and found Nicola waiting for him out the front. She gave him a reassuring smile as he approached. 'They're all upstairs,' she said, tilting her head towards the entrance.

'Everybody?' Gabriel asked. 'They all came?'

Nicola nodded as if this wasn't a big deal, but Gabriel knew it must have taken some careful engineering to get everyone here, for reasons none of them understood; it was a testament to her competence, and to how much she was liked. It would make things far easier, too. While it wasn't essential that he got the entire team on board, his plan would work better with unanimous support. At the very least, he had to give every one of them the opportunity to say yes.

Nicola nudged him and gestured again at the doorway. 'Are you ready?'

He hesitated a moment, prompting her to roll her eyes and tut. 'Oh, Gabriel. You're not nervous?'

Gabriel shrugged sheepishly. 'What can I say? This feels big.'

'Seriously? You're used to having meetings with some of the richest men on the planet. You've had dinners with members of the Cabinet!'

'Yes, but I know how to act with those men. They respond well to arrogance and bullshit. This is different.'

Nicola sighed and took hold of his arm. 'Agreed. So leave the bullshit outside and just say what you came here to say.'

She didn't give him an opportunity to dither any longer. He was led like a child through the doorway, under the large chandelier that illuminated the bar and up the short staircase to the mezzanine, where he was greeted by a dozen bemused faces. Bemused and worried.

They were all there, as Nicola had promised – the entire Mason Wallace administrative staff. Sarah, the receptionist he'd rarely, if ever, bothered to say hello to. Karen, who spent most of her days collating tedious data for the investors' newsletter. Caroline, Mason's PA. She had been the person he'd been most worried about in the early planning stages. After all, she did work for Mason directly, so Gabriel hadn't been certain where her loyalties might lie. But Nicola had been quick to set his mind at ease: Mason treated Caroline with the same level of respect he afforded the photocopier or filing cabinet; she had more reasons to hate him than the rest of them combined. Next to her sat Bridget from HR, whose scowl was probably an accurate reflection of what every woman in that room was now thinking. It went without saying, but over the years Gabriel had done little to endear himself to the support staff. In his better moments, he'd treated them with indifference rather than contempt, and viewed their opinions of him as largely irrelevant. He'd always imagined that not caring what others thought of him was a measure of his strength of character.

A positive sign was that no one got up and walked away, though several accusatory glances were now being fired in Nicola's direction. She seemed completely unperturbed by this; judging from her expression, she found the situation amusing. She cleared her throat, still holding on to Gabriel's arm.

Gavin Extence

'OK, so I have a small confession. We're not here to socialise. Gabriel asked me to set up this meeting because he has a proposal to put to you. Yes, I know you all despise him' – Gabriel was not surprised when no one disputed this observation – 'but let's just set that to one side for now. You need to hear what he has to say.'

With that, she released his arm and took a seat at the nearest table, and whatever words Gabriel had rehearsed went straight out of his head. He stood stock-still, acutely conscious of the sweat that was starting to bead on his forehead.

'Hello, ladies. Thank you for coming.'

From the deepening frowns, he suspected he was off to a patronising start, but it was arguably better than standing in silence for another ten seconds. He looked to Nicola for support and she glared impatiently at him.

'Um, as Nicola told you, I have something I'd like to put to you, and I hope it's something that might make up for the fact of my being here, which obviously you'd rather I wasn't . . .'

Gabriel raked his hand through his hair. Most of the assembled women were refusing to meet his eye, either through disdain or general embarrassment at the way the evening was proceeding. Gabriel wondered if he was having a panic attack; he wondered if it was the tumour, sabotaging his capacity for coherent speech at the precise moment he need to be articulate. It seemed like the sort of sick joke the tumour was capable of.

After a moment, he closed his eyes and counted to five. Then he removed his tie and placed it in one of his trouser pockets. It was an extremely nice tie; it was a silk–cashmere knit and had cost him three hundred and fifty pounds.

'Let me start again,' Gabriel said. He took a deep breath and straightened his back. Then he turned and smiled at Bridget, who was still looking daggers at him. 'My name is Gabriel Vaughn,' he said. 'Most of you know me as the arrogant prick who earns several million a year and refuses to acknowledge you in the corridors. Some of you have had the great misfortune to work for me directly, for which I can only apologise.'

Obviously, no one knew how to respond to this, but Gabriel at least had their full attention now.

'This isn't a joke,' he clarified. 'I understand why you all hate me, and you have every right to. I've lived my whole life putting my interests ahead of every other person on the planet, and it's an attitude that has seen me very well rewarded. Last year, my compensation amounted to just under four million pounds.'

Gabriel paused to let this figure resonate; judging from the expressions that met him and the sharp intakes of breath, it was resonating furiously.

'As you probably know,' he continued, 'compensation is what we at the top call our earnings, as if *we're* the ones getting screwed over here. But the truth is I find it hard to imagine what anyone in the real world would have to suffer to be compensated to the tune of four million pounds. I guess it would probably involve losing limbs.'

At this moment, Nicola decided to intervene. 'Gabriel, I think you've made your point. You're an arrogant arse and you earn too much money. Perhaps we should move things along?'

'Yes, we should. Thank you, Nicola.' Gabriel nodded a couple of times, then cleared his throat. 'The compensation has been going to the wrong people. That's the point I wanted to make, and that's what I want to remedy. None of you has any reason to trust me, I understand that, but hopefully you still trust Nicola, and she can verify what I'm about to tell you.'

Gabriel glanced at Nicola again; she nodded for him to continue.

'Two weeks ago, I paid Nicola half a million pounds on the condition that she quit her job and find something worthwhile to do instead. This is the same proposal I'd like to put to everyone in this room. Half a million pounds, to be deposited in your accounts straight away, and the only condition is that you have to leave your jobs, on a date that I will specify. I can't tell you exactly when that date will be, not yet, but we're talking weeks rather than months or years.'

It wasn't quite as eloquent as he'd hoped, but, then, it didn't have to be.

A long, stunned silence followed.

Eventually, Bridget raised her hand.

'Yes, Bridget?'

'Um . . . I have no idea what sick game you're playing here, but it's—'

'No game, Bridget. The offer's one hundred per cent genuine. Half a million pounds, and all you have to do is say yes.'

Bridget stared at him. Everyone was staring at him.

'Like I said, you can think of it as compensation. Or profit-sharing – something like that . . . Oh, and I'm dying. I should have mentioned that earlier. It's also relevant context.'

Gabriel thought it might be better to give them some time and space to digest what he'd told them. He went to the bar and bought a large Scotch. A few minutes later, Nicola came over and placed her hand on his arm.

'I think they're ready to talk now.'

LOSS

In his final month at work, Gabriel managed to lose eight hundred and fifty million dollars. It wasn't the largest trading loss ever recorded – not by a long shot – but on the whole, he was satisfied that he'd performed as well as he could, given the circumstances. He didn't have access to the whole fund, just his portion of it, so he was never going to match the six billion lost by Amaranth in 2006; nor could he compete with the biggest losers of the financial crisis, whose balance sheets dwarfed that of Mason Wallace. The amount Gabriel had lost was more in the Nick Leeson ballpark, but still a very respectable sum, and more than sufficient for his purposes. Furthermore, he knew he could take a unique pride in his achievement. While his forebears had racked up their losses through a combination of incompetence, greed and spectacular misfortune, Gabriel's had taken genuine skill. He viewed it as the pinnacle of a fifteen-year career, and the perfect note on which to make his exit.

Everything had started to go right not long after the meeting in the Traitor's Gate. On an otherwise unremarkable Monday morning, Gabriel found himself punching the air as the latest bulletin came in from Bloomberg. Pre-empting the EU embargo by several months, the Iranian government had voted to stop all oil shipments to Europe, effective immediately. It was a move that saw the price of crude jump to its highest level in months, and within days it had risen by seven dollars a barrel. At this point, two-thirds of Gabriel's initial investment had been wiped out, and he received his first phone call from UBS, demanding that he either deposit additional capital in his trading account or cut and run. His broker's firm advice was that he choose the latter option.

The only way to deal with this very sane suggestion was to dismiss it out of hand. He liquidated most of his other positions, deposited another three hundred and fifty million dollars in his account and sent his broker a one-word email: **HOLD.** Gabriel figured that this would be enough to quell any further resistance. His outrageous display of hubris might provoke anger and resentment, or it might win him admiration; in the world of finance, both reactions were plausible. But in both scenarios, the final outcome was likely to be the same. His broker would do as instructed, either respecting Gabriel's superior judgement or waiting for him to fail.

After a tense ten-minute wait, Gabriel's reasoning was confirmed. He received a standard acknowledgement from UBS saying that his instructions had been carried out. Nothing else, no personal message, was included.

It was an exhilarating time for Gabriel – as exhilarating as any period he could remember in his career. Fifteen years of watching the markets move had numbed him to the thrill he'd felt as a nineteen-year-old, speculating for the first time. More than this, he'd trained himself not to feel the thrill, to avoid any emotional reaction to the continual rise and fall of the stock charts. But now he couldn't help it. With every dollar that oil went up, Gabriel was a step closer to achieving his ultimate goal. He was a step closer to his day of reckoning.

At the same time, something else was starting to happen to him – something novel and peculiar. He was aware, day by day, of a subtle shift in his perceptions, as if the sharper edges of reality were beginning to soften. For the first time in months, there were mornings when he awoke feeling something other than pain and remorse. It was nonsensical: he knew that. He was now living full-time in a drab one-bed in Lewisham. He was alone. His personal fortune had diminished to a shadow of its former glory. And yet – and yet there were times when he could have sworn he felt happy – a strange, deep-down happiness that seemed perversely undisturbed by the material facts. There were times when even dying seemed acceptable.

Medically nothing had changed. The tumour was still growing, and it was still going to kill him sooner rather than later. But this was not something that Gabriel needed to think about. His focus was on a different clock, its ticks marked by the falling millions in his trading account. What he was waiting for was the next margin call from UBS, which would be triggered automatically when the value of his contracts fell below a certain level. At that point, the game would be up. Gabriel had nothing left to invest, and when he failed to inject fresh capital into his account, his remaining assets would be liquidated.

But Gabriel had no intention of taking that call. He planned to walk out just before the game was up.

*

The moment finally came on February 23, a Thursday. On that day, oil prices leaped by over three dollars a barrel, wiping another hundred and fifty million from Gabriel's account. He didn't even know what had caused the spike, and he wasn't curious to find out. There was no longer any point. By the evening, he was essentially bankrupt.

All that was left was to phone Nicola.

'Tomorrow,' he told her. 'We quit tomorrow.'

94

Notes

It started as an almost normal day. Gabriel woke at five, break-fasted, showered and put on his Desmond Merrion suit. By six he was being chauffeured through the almost deserted streets of south London, and by ten past the Mercedes had come to a gentle stop at the edge of the Occupy camp. At this point, Gabriel touched his driver on the shoulder and passed over another of his A4 manila envelopes.

'This is for you,' he told him. 'I'm leaving my job, so I don't need you to pick me up any more. But thank you. You've made my life very easy.'

He didn't wait for his door to be opened for him. Gabriel hopped out and was already walking towards Stanton House when his chauffeur called to him. 'Um, sir?'

Gabriel spun to see that the window had been lowered. 'Yes?'

His chauffeur looked completely perplexed. He glanced at the envelope, which he held, opened, in his lap, then looked back at Gabriel, not quite smiling.

Gabriel gave a small nod. 'Have a good day.'

Upstairs, he folded his coat neatly over the back of his swivel chair, and then clicked open his briefcase, from which he removed a small screwdriver set. It had been many years since he'd had to get hands-on with a computer, so he'd spent some time last night refreshing his memory with an instructional video on YouTube. It took him less than five minutes to detach the casing and locate the hard drive, which he immediately removed and placed in his briefcase. He then reassembled the outer shell and returned the computer to its original enclave.

The next job was to deal with his phone. UBS would have marked Gabriel's futures contracts to market at six thirty the previous evening, which meant he could expect a call from his broker at any time. Usually, it would have been left to a slightly more sociable hour – between eight and nine, based on prior experience – but given the sums they were now dealing with, Gabriel knew he couldn't count on even this small reprieve. He disconnected his office phone from the wall and switched his mobile to silent.

Satisfied that he was now uncontactable, he took a pen from his desk drawer and scrawled swiftly on a Post-it, which he stuck to the screen of one of his dual monitors:

IOU: $850 million

Then he left his office and went to see Mason.

Mr Vaughn

With his classic good looks, Gabriel had always taken it for granted that he could have made it as a model; but more recently, he'd started to think that acting would have been an even better career choice. He was definitely leading-man material, and with the right breaks, he might even have ended up earning more than he had at a hedge fund.

For the next hour, his performance was faultless. He chatted nonchalantly with Mason until a couple of minutes before the morning meeting, at which point he mentioned, as if it had just occurred to him, that there were a few details from his portfolio that he'd like to discuss afterwards.

'We're talking ten minutes, tops,' Gabriel told him, 'but I think you'll find it highly illuminating.'

It didn't take much – just a certain look, a meaningful inflection of the voice. Mason snapped at the bait, a greedy smile spreading over his face. 'Vaughn, you sly bastard! What have you got for me? Something big?'

'Huge.'

'Ha!' Mason slapped him on the back; it would probably be the last time that happened, Gabriel decided. 'I take it this is something we're going to keep strictly off the record?'

Gabriel nodded, mirroring the other man's smile. He did have the full story worked out – a tip-off from an ex-colleague at Goldman who now worked at the Bank of England – but it was clear he wasn't going to need it, at least not yet. The vaguest hint of insider trading and Mason was on to it like a greyhound.

The morning meeting passed without great incident. Gabriel presented the last of his bogus reports with a smug smile curling his upper lip. When yesterday's oil spike was mentioned, he assured his colleagues that his positions were stronger than ever; his long-term strategy was panning out precisely as his analytics had predicted, naturally.

At a quarter to eight, he was heading back to Mason's office. On the desk outside, Caroline had just arrived, for what would be the shortest working day in the history of menial labour. She hadn't even bothered to remove her coat. Mason didn't pick up on this detail; he didn't even look at her. 'Caroline, coffee,' he barked. 'And no calls for the next fifteen minutes. Mr Vaughn and I aren't to be disturbed.'

Caroline smiled, then gave the finger to Mason's passing back. Gabriel winked at her and mouthed *two minutes*.

Inside, Gabriel sat on the sofa while Mason lounged indolently in his executive swivel chair. 'Is coffee good for you, Vaughn? Maybe we should be cracking open the Scotch?'

'Coffee's fine,' Gabriel told him.

'Right you are. I'm itching to hear what you have for me, obviously, but let's just wait until Caroline's been and gone.'

Mason cracked his knuckles before gesturing over his shoulder at the window. 'Eviction's happening next week. Did you hear that?'

Gabriel nodded curtly. 'I heard that the appeal had been rejected. I didn't know a date had been set for the great cleansing.'

'It hasn't, not officially. But I have it on very good authority that it's going to be Monday night. The City's giving them the weekend to leave voluntarily – another PR gesture.' Mason snorted. 'The last PR gesture. After that, the gloves come off.'

Gabriel didn't have to reply. At that point, Caroline came in without knocking, the coffee conspicuously absent. Mason's initial bemusement was replaced almost at once by irritation.

'Problem, Caroline?'

'Yes, there's a problem.'

Gabriel was in the interesting position of knowing what was about to happen but not knowing exactly *how* it was going to happen. He hadn't deemed it necessary, or appropriate, to dictate the specific manner in which anyone else should quit, not beyond setting the timescale. He figured that everyone had their personal reasons to tell Mason to go to hell, so there was no sense in trying to micromanage that part of the project. It was more satisfying just to sit back and watch.

'There's a problem.' Mason's voice was flat, but his bearing had become uneasy. He'd stiffened in his chair and was looking at Caroline with more than a hint of suspicion. Gabriel could understand why: there was nothing apologetic or deferential about the way she was holding herself. Her back was straight and she was coolly returning Mason's stare. 'Well, spit it out, woman. We haven't got all morning.'

He was probably expecting a reaction, but not the contemptuous smile that now spread across her face. 'Mason, the problem is that you're going to have to get your own coffee. As of now, I no longer work for you.'

Mason didn't move or say anything for several moments. Then he glanced quickly at Gabriel and gave a hollow laugh. 'Are you hearing this?' He turned back to Caroline. 'You, sweetheart, should have checked the terms of your contract. You can't just walk out any time you choose. You owe me a month's notice.'

Gabriel felt certain that the *sweetheart* was mostly for his benefit. It was possible that Mason might have handled the situation a bit more gracefully if there hadn't been another man present. But as things stood, there was no way he was going to soften his stance. He had already started ranting about legal obligations and suing her for breach of contract. Caroline never flinched. She just stood and waited until he'd run out of steam, then said:

'Mason, I *am* leaving. It doesn't matter what you threaten me with. I don't care.'

Mason was burgundy with rage. 'Caroline, these aren't *threats*, they're promises. You're never going to work in this industry again, you realise that?'

'Yes, I realise that. And you've no idea how good it feels.'

'You're a secretary, for God's sake! What are you going to get that's any better? With your CV you'll be lucky to get a job stacking shelves!'

'Goodbye, Mason.' Caroline turned her head to Gabriel and nodded politely. 'Mr Vaughn.'

'Goodbye, Caroline. Best of luck to you, whatever you end up doing.'

'What the hell just happened?' Mason spat, the moment she'd left the room.

'Your PA just quit,' Gabriel noted. 'No big deal. You can borrow mine if you like.'

'Cut the crap, Vaughn! You know what I'm talking about. Best of luck? Whose fucking side are you on here?'

Gabriel shrugged. 'Why rise to it? No point losing your cool just because some nobody has ideas above her station. Anyway, you know what women are like. They're hormonal. It's probably her time of the month.'

He could see that Mason was torn: on some level, he'd realised that something was seriously wrong, and at the same time, he was desperate to deny it. He was willing to grasp at any plausible explanation thrown his way, female hormones included. Gabriel got up and placed a supportive hand on Mason's stiff shoulder.

'Look, you said it yourself: she's just a secretary. They're ten a penny. Let me call Bridget and she'll get the position advertised straight away. In the meantime, I was serious about you borrowing Nicola. I'll level with you, her attitude's not always great, but she's at least competent.'

Mason nodded dumbly as Gabriel picked up the phone from the desk. Thirty seconds later Bridget was standing in front of them, a small sheaf of papers clasped to her chest.

'Bridget, small issue here,' Gabriel began; Mason was still somewhat dumbfounded, and seemed content to let his deputy do the talking. 'Caroline just quit without notice, so we're going to need a replacement ASAP. I can't stress how urgent this is. We don't even have anyone to bring us coffee.'

'Ah.' Bridget, too, seemed to have discovered a new enthusiasm for amateur dramatics. She inhaled sharply, glancing at the papers in her hands. 'I hate to be the bearer of bad news, but you might have a few more issues to deal with.'

'Issues?' Gabriel threw a puzzled glance at Mason before looking back to Bridget. 'What are you talking about?'

Bridget shuffled forward and offered him the stack of papers. 'What are these?'

'They're letters of resignation.'

At this point, Mason snapped out of his temporary paralysis. 'Letters? Plural?'

Bridget nodded. 'Eleven letters, I'm afraid. The entire admin team, minus yours truly.'

Understandably, Mason did not know how to react to this news. He spent some moments with his eyes scrunched closed, his fingers digging into his temples. Bridget allowed him the luxury of this respite before sinking the knife in deeper.

'Oh, and in case you hadn't guessed, none of them is giving notice. They're all clearing their desks as we speak.'

'What the hell is going on here?' Mason thundered. 'Why are they doing this to me?'

Bridget took the resignation letters back from Gabriel and made a show of leafing through them. 'Well, the consensus seems to be that you're a terrible man to work for. That you're a terrible man full stop.'

Mason watched in silence as she let the eleven letters fall to the floor. 'I quit too, Mason. You'll have to find some other schmuck to clean up this mess. Mr Vaughn.' Bridget gave Gabriel a small smile, then turned on her heel and left.

'Fuck! I can't run this firm without back-office support.' Mason uttered this truism as if it were astonishing new knowledge. 'Vaughn, what the hell are we going to do? How the fuck . . .'

Gabriel was watching his boss very closely, so he saw the exact moment when the penny started to drop. Mason turned his chair, the colour draining from his face. 'You! You did this.'

Gabriel shrugged.

'Why? What possible reason could—' Mason stopped and slapped his desk with a loud crack. 'You son of a bitch! You're setting out on your own, aren't you? You think you can poach my staff and get away it? You think—'

At this moment, Nicola came in, carrying Gabriel's coat and briefcase. She made a point of completely ignoring Mason and his histrionics, although she did have to raise her voice to speak over him. 'All done here?' she asked Gabriel.

'So it would seem, Nicola.'

Mason finally shut up. He slumped in his chair with his mouth wide open. Gabriel turned to him and said, 'Cheer up, Mason. It's not as if this day can get any worse, is it?'

'I'm going to have you killed, Vaughn. You understand that, don't you? As of now, your life is over.'

Gabriel shrugged again. 'My advice to you is don't hang about.' He walked to the door and held it open. 'After you, Nicola.'

Outside, the phones rang and rang.

96

Damage Limitation

Gabriel had managed to shrink the fund by just over twenty per cent in a matter of weeks. It was impressive going – no one would have disputed that – but as yet it wasn't necessarily a fatal blow. Other funds had suffered similar losses, especially during the financial crisis, and a reasonable proportion of them had lived to trade another day; some had bounced back stronger than ever.

Gabriel imagined that his Post-it would be found in a matter of minutes. Mason would then spend the rest of the morning trying to figure out what had happened, and the afternoon, evening and weekend trying to patch his sinking ship. It wasn't going to be easy, obviously. There would be crisis talks lasting long into the night, and with no secretaries available to bring the coffee or order the pizza. But Gabriel knew that not one of the managers would yet be thinking of throwing in the towel. They would be thinking in terms of damage limitation and, in the first instance, that meant a cover-up.

For this reason, Gabriel did not expect that the police would be knocking at his door – not for the next few days, at least. Of course, there was also the fact that Mason's threat was probably genuine, and he really did intend to have Gabriel killed rather than prosecuted. Gabriel couldn't imagine his ex-boss becoming any less rabid once the full extent of his sabotage was uncovered. But for now, this was a secondary issue. Both Gabriel and Mason knew that a loss of confidence could destroy a financial institution far quicker than a loss of capital, and this would be the disaster everyone at Mason Wallace was now trying to avert. As soon as the facts of what had happened became public, the firm's credibility would be in tatters.

So that afternoon, while Mason and his remaining team were presumably devising a ten-point strategy to staunch the flow of information, Gabriel was on the phone to the financial sections of all the major broadsheets. He called *The Times* and the *Financial Times*, the *Telegraph* and the *Independent*; he even called the *Guardian*. It was a little tedious, but Gabriel wanted to ensure that the story broke everywhere and, after the first couple of calls, he got more proficient at relaying the relevant details with minimum interruption. He still had to spend quite a lot of time persuading the various editors that it wasn't a hoax call. In the long and varied history of financial misconduct, few of the perpetrators had been as eager to confess as Gabriel Vaughn.

As hoped, it was all over the papers the next day, and it didn't stay confined to the broadsheets. By the afternoon, most of the online tabloids had also latched on to the story. In the present climate, there was obviously a mass market for financial sleaze, and the sums involved were large enough to make for a compelling headline. **IOU $850 Million!** was the half-page banner many of the papers plumped for.

On Saturday night, Gabriel packed a suitcase and checked in to a cheap hotel. He paid in cash and gave a false name. For obvious reasons, he wasn't particularly worried about the criminal investigation that would now come sooner rather than later; nevertheless, it seemed a hassle he could do without.

His one minor regret, as he settled down on his somewhat saggy mattress, was that the mass exodus of the administrators had now also made the news. He had no idea how; he'd not breathed a word of it, figuring that they had a right to their privacy. But he still felt secure in the knowledge that no one else would be facing criminal charges. No one else had known that he planned to wreck the company – not even Nicola. As far as Gabriel knew, there was no law against quitting your job when you got a better offer. Mason could rave about breach of contract all he liked, but he'd be the last person who'd want to have the inner workings of his firm brought under the close scrutiny of a court.

As for the half-million-pound pay-offs, Gabriel's lawyer had assured him that this money was now untouchable. Inheritance tax would have to be paid, but this could be provided for in Gabriel's remaining estate. After that, the administrators would be entitled to keep every penny.

Satisfied that every eventuality had been covered, Gabriel got on the phone to his father. It was the third time he'd called him in twenty-four hours, and he found that it was becoming easier and easier.

He repeated all the things that he hoped would bring his father some solace, if only in the short term: he was safe, he had no regrets about what he'd done. He felt lighter – and more content – than he had in a very long time.

But the hard part, he knew, was still to come.

Acceptance

His father looked ashen. He looked as if someone had punched him in the stomach.

'When did you find out?' he asked eventually, his voice barely audible over the background hum of the hotel's restaurant-bar.

Gabriel reached across the table and put his hand on his father's shoulder. 'I've known since the beginning of October. I'm so sorry. I should have told you then, but . . . well, there are no excuses. I've made a lot of bad decisions in my life, and that was one of them.'

His father nodded silently, looking as though none of this had registered. A couple of tables away, the waitress who'd brought their coffee was clearing away breakfast plates. Gabriel moment-arily caught her eye, and she smiled, so he smiled back. It was the kind of social interaction that he'd once have dismissed as meaningless, but now it seemed the opposite. It was a small source of warmth when he really, really needed it.

It might not have been ideal, but Gabriel felt reassured that coming down here, to the restaurant, had been the best option available to them. His hotel room would have been too claustro-phobic, too deathly quiet, for the conversation he and his father needed to have. It was far better to be among people. Life quietly continuing around them.

'I realise how hard this is for you,' Gabriel said, 'on top of everything else. But I couldn't tell you over the phone. I hope you understand. I needed to see you.'

His father closed his eyes for a few moments, then said: 'Where do we go from here? What treatment options do you have?'

He squeezed his father's shoulder, ever so gently. 'Dad, I've told you. There are no treatment options. Not any more.'

'No. Please, please don't think that. You *cannot* give up hope, Gabriel. You're a fighter. You always have been. You, you can beat this thing. *We* can beat—' He looked away sharply, his words becoming a strangled sob.

Gabriel waited a moment, determined to keep his own voice steady.

'Dad, this isn't giving up. It's acceptance. They're not the same thing.' He took another breath before he continued. 'I am going to die, and I've made peace with that – or as much as anyone ever can. I'm going to die knowing that my life finally had some meaning.'

His father started crying. It was quiet, but it still caught the attention of the people sitting at the next table. Gabriel could not have cared less. He wouldn't have cared if the whole restaurant had stopped to stare. He got up and put his arms round his father.

'It's OK,' he told him. 'It's OK.'

Afterwards, they went for a walk in Greenwich Park. Gabriel still felt nauseous and headachy – he had since he'd woken up – but the cold air helped. Walking did, too. The simple exertion of putting one foot in front of the other, feeling his heart pumping. It was ironic, he supposed, but Gabriel felt more vividly alive than he could ever remember feeling. He was aware of the smell of the grass and trees, the sound of birdsong and dogs barking and children playing, the breath of the breeze on his face. In the far distance, above the treeline, he could see the high-rises of Canary Wharf glinting like daggers in the sunlight. Barclays, where he'd started his career. HSBC and Citi. JP Morgan, who'd moved into the building vacated by Lehman Brothers, who'd moved in after Enron collapsed. Several million square feet of office space dedicated to the accumulation and management of wealth.

'I wish you'd come back with me,' his father said, for the third or fourth time since they'd left the hotel. 'You shouldn't be on your own at the moment.'

Gabriel looked at his father, who seemed to have aged by a decade in the last couple of hours. *He* was the one who shouldn't be alone; and he wouldn't be, not for very long. Once Gabriel had seen his father back to the station, he'd make sure he called Susan to tell her what had happened. It would be kinder to let her know himself – save his father the pain of having to repeat it all.

He held his father's eye and gave a reassuring smile. 'Dad, I *will* come back, I promise, but not today. I just have one more thing I have to do first. It's important to me.'

His father hesitated for a moment, then nodded.

Soon after, they turned round and headed back to the hotel.

98

Eviction

If Mason's sources in the City were correct – and they usually were – the eviction of the Occupy camp would be happening that Monday night. Gabriel had decided, as soon as he'd heard, that he needed to be there. He wasn't going to involve himself in any way; he just wanted to bear witness. It wasn't as if he had any other demands on his time any more.

He slept late that morning – as late as he'd ever slept in the past decade – then spent the rest of the day holed up in his hotel room. He had a headache that two doses of codeine failed to touch, but he couldn't decide if this was anything he needed to worry about. It was true that his symptoms had been more evident in the past twenty-four hours, and it wasn't just the headaches and nausea; there had been a couple of dizzy spells, too. Yet he couldn't be *certain* that these problems were getting worse. Perhaps it was just perspective. Before, he'd been too busy, too focussed, to pay full attention to the ongoing effects of the tumour, but now there wasn't much left to distract him. It made sense that he might notice his symptoms more under these circumstances; it didn't mean that his condition was actually deteriorating.

He ordered room service and spent most of the afternoon napping in front of the rolling news, finding that sleep continued to come easily. In the evening, he showered, dressed and got in a taxi to St Paul's Churchyard. He arrived a little after nine thirty and sat on the paving stones at the south side of the square, with his back against a bollard. From there he had a clear view across the cathedral steps and the main part of the camp. In the background was Stanton House. All the lights had been left on, including those in the Mason Wallace offices, but this was just a standard security measure. Gabriel doubted that anyone was in the office that evening. After the weekend's press, there was a good chance that no one had been in all day.

Nothing was happening yet, and Gabriel didn't think it would be for at least a couple of hours. Logic said the authorities would want to minimise the chance of this becoming a public spectacle, and that meant waiting until the surroundings were clear of passers-by. Nevertheless, Gabriel wasn't the only person who'd taken up position at the edge of the square. Small pockets of onlookers were starting to form in several places, with a number of people toting expensive-looking cameras. They were obviously professionals, but Gabriel had no idea if they were there because they, too, had received a tip-off. It was equally possible that many of them had been coming over to St Paul's every night since the appeal against the eviction was rejected. Either way, the atmosphere seemed to Gabriel heavy with expectation.

Within the camp, most of the protesters had already gathered on the cathedral steps. A democracy to the end, they seemed to be carrying out some sort of last-minute debate. There was a lot of gesticulating, culminating in hands being raised and counted, but Gabriel was too far away to hear what was being discussed. Whatever the fine details, the demonstrators had apparently voted for the status quo. People smoked and continued to talk, most of them now facing out onto the square, watching and waiting. Some went to the Portaloos or back to their tents, but few left the steps for any length of time. No one looked as if they were about to pack up and leave.

Gabriel settled back against his bollard and waited. It was another cold evening – too cold to be sitting out on bare paving slabs – but after a while, he hardly noticed the discomfort. He still had his ridiculously expensive coat, and as long as it didn't rain, he was content to stay put. In truth, he'd have stayed whatever the weather – even in a downpour.

Despite the light from the street lamps, the cathedral and offices, it was still difficult to make out faces at a distance. Gabriel had thought that he might see Matt or Lucinda or Cressida; he'd hoped, of course, that he might see Caitlin. But so far, he was out of luck. The cathedral clock marked the passing minutes, and the pavement started to fill with a growing number of observers, but that aside, nothing much changed. Gabriel waited, trying to ignore the throbbing in his skull.

The first sign that something was about to happen came just after half eleven, and it was subtle enough that he almost missed it. The small flow of road traffic around the square – the taxis and night buses – had stopped entirely. It was a sudden anomaly, like the moment before a tsunami when the sea rushes back from the coastline. It told him that somewhere the roads had been cordoned. Moments later, the square started to flood with riot police.

At this stage, the operation was swift and efficient. The police quickly established a perimeter around the camp, placing themselves between the protesters and the onlookers, and at the same time, a small number of official vehicles had pulled up around the square. There was a dump truck and at least half a dozen police vans, a couple of which had parked with their full-beams illuminating the camp and cathedral steps. Gabriel was only a few metres away from the nearest line of riot police, but no one told him to move back. For now, it seemed that the police had been instructed to do nothing more than impose themselves as a physical barrier around the protest site. No move was made to confront the occupiers; there had been no dialogue between the two sides.

Several minutes passed before two bailiffs in high-vis jackets walked into the camp. In lieu of any obvious leader to deal with, they simply approached the nearest group of protesters and started talking. Gabriel couldn't make out what was being said, but he assumed an official statement was being made: the demonstrators were to leave the site at once or face arrest for defying a court order. Whatever the specifics, it took less than a minute for the bailiffs to say what they had to say. Then they moved on to the next group of protesters to repeat the information.

What followed was a strange sort of stand-off. The bailiffs retreated back beyond the police lines, and for a good fifteen minutes not much happened. It looked as if the protesters were again debating their options, but afterwards, it was clear that no consensus had been reached. The majority did nothing at all. They stayed where they were, by their tents or on the cathedral steps. But a handful were gathering some belongings from the camp, having apparently decided to resist no further. Another faction had started to build some sort of barricade out of pallets and bins. Gabriel was surprised that the police didn't intervene, but they obviously had a well-rehearsed strategy that they were sticking to. Furthermore, he wasn't certain what practical function the barricade could serve; it was out in the open, not really blocking off any part of the camp. His answer came a few minutes later, when the structure had grown to the size of a large bonfire. At this stage, about a dozen people climbed on top of it, making clear that the only way *they* would be leaving would be through physical intervention. Gabriel could see that Lucinda was among their number. She had taken her position at the centre of the platform, and was glaring defiantly at the backs of the riot police. It took him a couple more minutes to locate Matt. He wasn't with the group at the barricade. He was sitting at the near end of the cathedral steps, now illuminated by the headlights of one of the police vans. It was difficult to be certain, but it looked as if he had his eyes closed. It looked like he might be meditating.

In the next half hour, the bailiffs moved back in. There were perhaps thirty or forty of them. Small teams started dismantling the larger tents, while others hauled poles and sleeping bags and inflatable mattresses over to the waiting dump truck. There wasn't much resistance at this point, not beyond the shouts that were erupting from the barricade. On the steps, groups of protesters had unfurled their banners, and the flashes of cameras increasingly cut the darkness to Gabriel's left and right. Some of the occupiers had managed to climb the trees that lined the pavement near Stanton House, and one of them was now waving a smoke bomb back and forth, sending thick white plumes over the roofs of the remaining tents.

And at some point amidst all this, Caitlin emerged from the crowd to Gabriel's right and sat down beside him.

Deep Clean

She didn't say anything for a while, and she wasn't looking at him. She just hugged her knees to her chest and sat there, with barely six inches between them.

'So, what have I missed?'

Gabriel looked at her face in profile. 'Nothing much. Lucinda's on the barricade. Matt's meditating on the cathedral steps.'

This drew a small smile, but no other reaction.

'What kept you?' Gabriel asked eventually. 'I was starting to think you weren't coming.'

'I was working late. I only heard this was happening on my way home. Someone tweeted it, asking people to come down as a sign of support.' She flicked a strand of hair back from her face, still not looking at him. 'Then I spent quite a lot of time procrastinating. The more sensible half of my brain told me I should stay away.'

'Why?'

'Because I thought you might be here.'

'Oh . . . Well, I suppose I shouldn't be too offended. You came, after all.'

'I managed to convince myself that you wouldn't have heard. Didn't think you'd be following Occupy on Twitter.'

Gabriel shrugged. 'I heard some rumours at the end of last week. I used to be quite well connected in the City.'

This provoked another flicker of a smile. 'Not so much any more?'

'No, not so much. Things can change very quickly in finance.'

'So I'd heard.' She took a cigarette from her bag and lit it. 'How does it feel, being unemployed?'

'Well, it's still early days. I suppose it's day one, technically. But so far, it feels pretty damn good.'

'Been to sign on yet?'

'I'm not sure the Job Centre's my scene. I think they'd struggle to find me work.'

'Yes. I suppose you're pretty much a hopeless case.'

On the far side of the square, the camp was rapidly disappearing, tent by tent. The bailiffs were moving back and forth to the dump truck like an army of ants, paying no heed to the non-stop chant of *shame on you* that was now coming from the cathedral steps. After a few moments, Gabriel caught Caitlin's eye and pointed towards the top floor of Stanton House.

'You see that window, third along from the corner? Until last Friday, that was my office. The one at the end is my boss's – my *ex*-boss's. He had this plan to come in tonight, the night of the eviction. He was going to sit with a glass of very expensive whisky and toast the final triumph of capitalism over the forces of anarchy. I like to think that was the one concrete thing I managed to change, even if I achieved nothing else.'

Caitlin shook her head. 'I think you may have achieved a little more than that. The way the papers reported it, you pretty much bankrupted your company.'

'Well, yes, in the sense that it's unlikely to still be in business this time next week. But that's not the same as bankrupting the individuals who ran the fund. They've taken a small hit to their personal fortunes, but they're still multimillionaires. They get to walk away from this relatively unscathed. In that sense, I'm not sure anything I did made a huge difference.'

Caitlin considered this for a few moments, before saying: 'I read that you gave all your money away to the admin team. Is that true?'

Gabriel shrugged again. 'Well, you can't take it with you. Right?'

She didn't reply to this. Instead, she shuffled across and leaned her head against his shoulder. After a few moments, Gabriel put his arm round her.

'Why did you do it?' she asked.

'Because it felt right. Because I thought it might be nice to see a financial collapse where the rich suffered rather than the poor.'

'I thought perhaps you were trying to impress me. Maybe I'm just being vain?'

'No, not entirely,' Gabriel told her. 'You're one of the few people I've ever wanted to impress.'

She leaned more of her weight into him, and though it might have been foolish to read too much into such a subtle gesture, Gabriel felt it was a response of sorts. Not forgiveness, not absolution, but a comfort all the same – one that he intended to savour.

'How are you doing?' she asked, after another moment of silence.

'My health, or in general?'

'Both.'

'Headaches, tiredness, nausea. Some dizzy spells. But I'm not reading too much into it. I've had a busy few weeks, so it could just be my body adjusting. I've probably got a year's worth of sleep to catch up on.' It seemed easier to downplay the situation, but Gabriel was aware even as he spoke that his words were striking a false note.

'Have you seen your doctor?' Caitlin asked, her voice not much more than a whisper.

'No. I don't think seeing a doctor's going to do me much good. Not any more. I still have medication to help with the symptoms, and in the longer term . . . well, there is no longer term. I might have a week or I might have a month, but knowing the specifics isn't going to help me. I think it's better to just accept each day as it comes.'

Gabriel thought that she might dispute this, tell him that he needed to see his doctor as soon as possible, but after a couple of moments, she nodded against his shoulder.

A minute or more must have passed before Gabriel said: 'You may find this hard to believe, but there are lots of things I wouldn't want to change any more. I mean, if someone could click their fingers and make the last few months disappear, if my life could go back to exactly how it was before – I think that's a deal I'd probably have to refuse. Does that make sense to you?'

Caitlin thought about this for a while. 'I think you're saying that you'd rather die good than live bad.'

He managed to smile at this. 'It sounds so unlikely when you put it like that. But yes. I guess that *is* what I'm saying.' Gabriel paused for a second, then asked: 'Do you think there's some alternate universe where things might have worked out differently between us?'

She reached up and placed her free hand on his. 'A week ago I would have said absolutely not, but now I'm not so sure.' She shrugged. 'It would be nice to think so, anyway.'

Neither of them said anything for a long time after that. They sat together in silence, watching the piecemeal removal of the Occupy camp. When the bailiffs had taken away the last of the tents, the police moved in to tackle the barricade. It took a while, but gradually the outer defences were dismantled and carted off to the dump truck. After that, a ladder was brought over and the authorities started to implement the only strategy they had left to them: grabbing at legs and manhandling the protesters from their precarious platform. Lucinda was one of the last to go; she managed to raise her fist in the air and scream 'Fuck the police!' before being hauled off to the back of the van. Over on the cathedral steps, Matt was offering a different form of resistance. He was now lying on his front as a team of police officers poked, prodded and otherwise cajoled him. Eventually, four of them managed each to get hold of a limb, and he was carried out of sight out of the far end of the square. Gabriel couldn't help but think that Gandhi would have approved.

By the time the cathedral clock struck two, the entire site had been cleared. Temporary fencing was being erected where the lines of riot police had stood, and teams of cleaners were moving into the vacated space in St Paul's Churchyard, armed with brooms and bin bags and hoses. The police had started to advise people that they should disperse, but as of yet, no one was being forced. Gabriel and Caitlin were still sitting in the exact same spot, her head now resting against his chest. He kissed her hair and she stirred a little.

'Caitlin?'

'Yes?'

He was surprised at how difficult it was to speak. It was like there was a delay or disconnect, a loose wire in the circuit between thought and words. But he was determined to struggle on regardless. 'I was . . . I was thinking that I might like to get out of London soon. I don't want to boast, but I'm not completely broke yet. I still have a few thousand left in the bank. Enough for plane tickets and a decent hotel.'

'What's your destination?'

'I've always thought the Cayman Islands look nice. Good climate, pretty scenery. Shall I count you in?'

She snorted softly. 'Are you serious?'

'It depends on your answer.'

'Well, I'd be lying if I said I wasn't tempted . . . OK, sell it to me. What exactly are we going to do in the Cayman Islands?'

Once, Gabriel might have had difficulty answering this question. But not any more. 'We'll listen to music,' he told her. 'We'll drink cocktails and watch the sunrise and swim in the sea. We'll enjoy being alive.' She'd started to shake a little; Gabriel didn't need to see her face to know that she was crying. He kissed her hair again. 'Which part sounds so terrible?'

'None of it. It all sounds perfect.' She took a deep breath, and he felt some of the tension leave her shoulders. 'OK. Absolutely. Let's leave tomorrow.'

Gabriel didn't say anything to this. Caitlin tucked her head up underneath his chin, and he wrapped his arm tighter round her.

It wasn't going to happen, of course. He knew that as well as she did. But that wasn't the point. Sometimes, you just needed to imagine a better world. Better than the one you had.

The dizziness was coming in waves now, but Gabriel found that it no longer frightened him. Caitlin was still there, and that was enough. Her warmth, the gentle weight of her. She was still there.

She was—

The last of it he saw through blurring vision. Camera crews packing away, pavements slowly starting to empty, the lines of police and temporary fencing.

And beyond this, in St Paul's Churchyard, a team of poorly paid workers begin to sweep the streets clean.

Author's Note

This novel draws on actual events, and, wherever possible, I've tried to keep the background details as accurate as I could. Quotes attributed to real people were sourced in contemporary newspaper accounts and broadcast media, as were the pension statistics given in chapter eighteen. However, there were also a couple of places where I used a bit of creative licence. The actual Canon Chancellor of St Paul's, Giles Fraser – a man for whom I have a huge amount of respect – really did resign in protest over the Church's handling of the Occupy demonstration. But he did not, to my knowledge, make the impromptu speech I have my Canon make in chapter ten. In addition, the staff of Starbucks, St Paul's Churchyard, did not forbid the protestors from using the Starbucks' toilet, as I imply in chapter thirty-six. By all accounts, they were extremely friendly and accommodating to their temporary neighbours. Unfortunately, I liked the scene I'd written too much to change it. So apologies for this.

Acknowledgements

I'd like to thank everyone at Occupy London Tours, and especially Paul, Dan, Angus, Christian, Beth and Jon. For any readers interested in alternative sightseeing, Occupy Tours run monthly walks around the City, Mayfair and Canary Wharf. They're free, they're fascinating, and they're a lot of fun. If you'd like to learn more about the financial crisis, hedge funds or the rise of modern capitalism, I can't recommend them highly enough.

For support past, present and future, huge thanks are also owed to: Nathaniel Alcaraz-Stapleton, Anna Alexander, Jason Bartholomew, Naomi Berwin, Sarah Christie, Jasper Fforde, Emily Kitchin, Jacqui Lewis, Sharan Matharu, Ruby Mitchell. (Sincere apologies to anyone I've missed out; three years of sleep deprivation has ruined my memory.)

Separate thanks to: Kate Howard/Fogg, for early encouragement and generally enabling my career; Stan, for ongoing support and some excellent editorial advice (in the face of unreasonable resistance); and Sara Kinsella, for so much, energy, hard work, enthusiasm, and for pushing me – and pushing me again – to write the best book I could.

Finally, thanks as always to my family, for keeping me afloat.